The *Indomitable* Mr. Temple

A NOVEL

LINDO FORBES

NAPART INC.

The Indomitable Mr. Temple

Copyright © 2024 by Lindo Forbes

All rights reserved.

No part of this publication may be reproduced, distributed, or transmitted in any form or by any means, including photocopying, recording, or other electronic or mechanical methods, without the prior written permission of the publisher except in the case of brief quotation embodied in critical articles and reviews.

The story, all names, characters, and incidents portrayed in this production are fictitious. No identification with actual persons (living or deceased), places, buildings, and products is intended or should be inferred.

EBOOK ISBN: 979-8-2279195-8-8

PAPERBACK ISBN: 978-1-7381463-1-4

Book Cover by Zandra Murray, Zandragon Designs.

First edition 2024

Also by Lindo Forbes

The Insufferable Mr. Fletcher – Junior and Davis
The Inscrutable Mr. Yang – Claudia and Ian

To those who bear the weight of familial responsibility, try a little
selfishness

Chapter 1

"FIX YOUR FACE." LEIGH pressed her thumb into the space between her sister's eyebrows as she scowled into a box of cookies.

"These aren't even on the menu. Why would anyone ask for such an abomination?"

"They're not bad," Junior Sano added through a mouthful of cookie, "I've definitely had worse things in my mouth."

"Better things, too," Desiree Walker winked.

"I need you to be serious right now. Oatmeal raisin cookies, you guys! *Raisins.*" Ava Bridger complained.

"Ava, you don't have to eat them, you just have to drive them to a house in Etobicoke so I can deliver this other order in Scarborough," Leigh explained with the soothing patience honed over the entirety of Ava's forty-two years. Though her sister was always willing to eat whatever was put in front of her, she only had to dislike it once to write it off forever.

Standing in the bakery area of her store, Peach's Books and Bakeshop, Leigh Bridger ran through the list to make sure she had everything ready. She was simultaneously preparing two orders for delivery on opposite sides of Toronto and closing down for the day, hence the additional presence of her two best friends and sister.

"Why do you even offer delivery anymore? It's so much extra bother." Junior put another cookie in her mouth.

"It's a personal touch," Leigh shrugged.

"Then you should at least charge more for the service. Like, three hundred bucks or something." Junior griped, still chewing.

"For three hundred dollars Dolly Parton better be on the other side of the door when I open it," Desiree snorted her derision.

"What is it with you and Dolly Parton?" Ava asked, laughing at Junior's answering pantomime of Ms. Parton's silhouette.

"She's a songwriter, musician, singer, actor, philanthropist, literacy advocate," Desiree counted off on her fingers, "She's a top tier white lady."

Junior's face scrunched at this revelation. "You have a list of white ladies?"

"There are usually three but never more than five," Leigh sighed, long used to her friends and their antics.

Ava was wide-eyed. "It caps at five?"

"If I can think of five. A white woman's tears will be the death of us all—I don't mess with 'em if I can avoid it."

"Who's on the current roster?"

"With Miss Betty White called home to Jesus—"

"Que dios la tenga en su gloria," Junior crossed herself.

"—it leaves Angelina Jolie and Kelly Clarkson." Desiree finished.

"What are the criteria for this list exactly?" Ava challenged, "Why Angelina and not, say, Dolly's homegirl Jane Fonda?" Off Desiree's blank look, Ava shook her head in disbelief. "How can you know Dolly Parton but not Jane Fonda?"

It never failed to amaze Leigh how little white media Desiree consumed in her youth. Though they both grew up in small towns, Desiree's hometown of North Preston outside of Halifax was predominately Black while Leigh grew up outside of Stratford. In the 80s. She couldn't immerse herself exclusively in Black media and hope to get by in the tiny town of St. Mary's, Ontario.

"Among other things, Dolly wrote Whitney's iconic hit *I Will Always Love You* and starred in *Joyful Noise* with Queen Latifah," Desiree said, as if it were obvious.

Leigh was surprised her sister wasn't already aware of Desiree's Unproblematic White Lady List. She'd been compiling it as long as Leigh has known Desiree, which was six months longer than Ava has known Desiree, so her current disbelief was as amusing as it was puzzling.

"Okay, so who are your top tier white men?"

Desiree reared as though Ava said something profoundly ridiculous. "There are none."

The corners of Junior's mouth turned down as she considered this proclamation before nodding her acceptance. "You know who else is an unproblematic white lady?"

Desiree's expression made it clear she was not open to discussion on the matter.

"Britney Jean Spears." Junior gleefully answered her own question.

At a volume that could only be called disruptive, the iconic 'it's Britney, bitch' started, the bass line rattling Leigh's speakers, as Junior held her phone aloft, announcing herself the playlist hijacker. Just like that, Ava, Desiree, and Junior were dancing and giggling and whooping their enthusiastic support of Ms. Spears.

Leigh shook her head. Asking her friends to help prep orders was equal parts fun and frustrating. When the work needed doing, Junior and Desiree were better and more efficient than any factory line. Once the work was done, however, getting them to focus was like herding cats.

Turning the volume down, Leigh reminded them "I have neighbors."

The three women looked at each other, moderately chastened, until Desiree made a whip sound from the side of her mouth, "Now get to work, bitch!"

All displays of contrition dissolved into raucous laughter that bounced off the walls of Leigh's tiny shop.

With a smile teasing the corners of her mouth, Leigh rolled her eyes. "Can't take you nowhere."

The four women returned to the last of the tasks required before they could head out.

"Good evening." The voice was deep and rumbly and did not quite match the face it came from. Well, that wasn't strictly true. The face was very handsome—devilishly so—belonging to a man who was probably very used to getting his own way. He was heavy built, average height, with dark brown skin, and a small, neat afro. He was wearing a brightly coloured short set that complemented his complexion beautifully and had the same brash, cocksure confidence as her son Langston. It made sense as they appeared to be about the same age. "How are y'all doing tonight?"

"Better now." Junior gave him a flirtatious once over.

"I know that's right." Desiree agreed almost to herself.

Say what you wanted about this man, he was handling Junior and Desiree's overt attentions like a pro. In Leigh's experience, only men used to being propositioned by bold and audacious women could withstand her friends' attentions—causation and correlation be damned—and those men were not for her.

"I'm here to pick up an order. Miles Temple."

"Books or bakery?" Ava asked, rising from behind the display case, getting her first look at the man.

Based on her sister's sudden speechlessness, Leigh had to step in if only to spare her establishment a sexual harassment charge. "Books."

Junior pounced on the opening. "Miles? You don't strike me as a Miles."

"No?"

"No. Unless…" Junior gave him an appraising glance. "Miles means soldier. Do you enjoy taking orders?"

Did he? Leigh couldn't imagine this man doing anything less than what he wanted. Or maybe he did enjoy being ordered around—what did she know about it?

"I don't know about all that but you're right," he moistened his lips before continuing, "I'm Quincy. Miles is my brother."

Leigh spoke up just as Junior was opening her mouth. "Well, Quincy, you're lucky you found us at all. We're closed."

"Oh, my bad." He gave Leigh his full attention and she felt warm all over. "I mixed up the address or I would've been here sooner."

Too much! This man's focus on her was too much to absorb and Leigh fought to keep from fidgeting. Which was only because she had things to do and not because of this stranger's studied attention.

Desiree leaned on the counter. "You're right on time."

Quincy took in his surroundings. With the main lights off, Leigh knew all he could see was the outline of the oak shelving lining four of the six walls, a features table, and the glass display case of cakes, pies, cookies, and tarts. The tiled section they were currently in had four small bistro tables.

"Are you a bakery that sells books or a bookstore that sells cake?"

"What would you prefer?" Junior practically sparkled at the man.

"It's both." Leigh spoke over her friend, putting an end to the interaction. Handing him the parcel that was behind the register, she told him, "It's an online order. Already paid."

Again, he focused on Leigh, "Do you need to see some ID or anything?"

Her skin flushed and she worried about this unstable fluctuation of her internal temperature. Was this the start of perimenopause? She'd have to make an appointment with her doctor.

"Yes, she does!" Desiree piped up.

Leigh ignored her friend and focused on maintaining Quincy's eye contact without squirming. He smelled like chocolate and his lips curved in a way that signalled trouble. The naked kind that ruined lives and broke hearts. "Thank you but it's not necessary."

"You're sure?" he offered, his voice low for Leigh's ears only.

Leigh shook off the flutter his deep, rumbly voice put in her belly. "I'm sure. Have a good night."

"Come back any time!" Desiree waived.

"Yes. Any time at all," Junior agreed. "Day or night."

Quincy looked at the four women with varying degrees of interest. "I most certainly will."

Ava followed him out and locked the door behind him. "That," she sighed, flipping the closed sign, "was an exceptionally good-looking man."

"One that seemed keenly interested in a certain book and bakeshop proprietress." Junior teased.

Leigh scoffed. "Who, that child?"

"That was a man, hermana. A whole lot of man." Junior countered.

"I like me a thickum," Desiree added agreeably.

"Did you notice how his Js perfectly matched the pink and orange floral of his short set?" Ava was always drawn to beautiful things.

"I did." Junior nodded, "I also noticed the PRX on his wrist."

"And what does his watch have to do with anything?" Leigh gave a small, exasperated sigh. If they insisted on discussing the details of that young man's appearance, surely they could do it while they packed up.

"Let's not pretend the world of watches is any different than other jewelry. His retails for about a thousand bucks. An Omega DeVille runs about two-hundred-and-fifty grand and that's not even the middle." Junior's smile was mischief and indulgence as she continued, "That Tisot is the perfect starter piece. It's a classic style from a solid brand. Added to the way he confidently rocked such colorful clothes and shoes? You've got yourself proof that he's willing to play."

It would be a lie to say Leigh didn't know about the kind of wealth Junior came from—she was basically a shipping heiress. It would be more accurate to say that Leigh couldn't fathom the scope and so routinely allowed it to slip her mind.

"That, or he has a generous benefactor." Desiree offered.

Junior made finger guns at Desiree in agreement.

Leigh knew exactly what came next. She could almost predict, to the letter, the varying and intersecting interests they were about to share like some ancient Greek chorus, whether Leigh wanted to hear about it or not.

Ava, who came out as asexual in her late 20s and experienced what she referred to as 'aesthetic attraction', pondered aloud, "He probably gives really good snuggles. They'd be like literal bear hugs."

"Mmm... just think of the power that much body could throw into a thrust." Junior, an Afro-Latina stunner and incorrigible flirt who chased her pleasure with reckless abandon, wrapped her arms around herself at the imagery.

Desiree, who started as a phone sex operator to subsidise her transition and now had an impressive portfolio built from her evolving sex work empire, added as if on cue, "Slamming into you while he pinned you down, whispering praise for taking it so well. Imagine all that mouth could do. Good Jesus Lord!"

Leigh had been trying very hard to not do that exact thing.

"If you don't mind taking your minds out of the gutter, we have to deliver these orders." Leigh reminded them of the task at hand.

Desiree laughed in her face. "Gutter? That grade A certified beast of a man was very interested in you."

"He wasn't," Leigh waved Desiree off.

"Uh... he barely looked at Junior and she was actively flirting with him," her sister countered.

It was a fair point. Most people couldn't resist Junior when she turned on her charm. Still, Leigh dismissed the very idea whole cloth. "A, Junior'll flirt with anybody—it means nothing, and B, why would he bother with that green mountain on her finger?"

"I don't mean to brag, but this ring hasn't exactly dimmed my shine," Junior bragged while holding her hand up to admire her ring.

Leigh rolled her eyes at her friend's familiar straddling of friendly flirt and femme fatale. "Davis must be thrilled."

Junior tilted her head in contemplation. "You know, I think he is."

"You two are sickening." Desiree teased. Junior gave an impish shrug in reply.

"Even if he was interested in me—which he was not—I'm not interested in him. Besides, I'm likely older than his mother." Leigh argued.

Ava snorted her laughter, "As if!"

"I could be!"

"Por favor, who cares? You're not *his* mother!" Junior cried.

"And anyway, he seems like he'd prefer being called Daddy." Desiree added to Junior's cackling delight.

Leigh huffed her irritation and started aggressively jamming things into bags.

"No one is saying you have to be interested," Ava looked to Junior and Desiree for support. At their nods, she continued, "But why is it so inconceivable that he'd be into you?"

"Because men like that are too slick—too full of themselves—and want a woman to be grateful for their attention. I have no time for that."

Leigh knew what it was like to be with a man at the centre of his own orbit. To know that she had his attention so long as she was willing to share him with everyone else—she'd spent her teens and twenties with one. Even when they were alone, she'd vied with school and practise and family obligations.

Leigh's focus had to be on her son and her business. A man who would only show up when he needed an ego boost wasn't someone she needed to know. "Can we please stop wasting time fantasizing instead of getting everything ready?"

"My car's already packed, patrona." Junior popped a piece of fudge in her mouth. "Estoy lista."

Ava pushed the final box along the counter, "I just need the serving kit."

Leigh was both unsurprised and a little bit irritated, if she were being completely honest, that they'd managed to stay on task despite all their goings on. Looking around she had to admit her scold was wasted. "Well... then... okay. Let's go."

Junior wrapped a cupcake in a napkin and pulled her keys out of her pocket. Desiree hauled her purse from under the counter as she also made her way to the door. Ava joined them once she'd got the tote bag and box balanced in her arms. They stood still while Leigh armed the security alarm and then briskly followed her out the front door. Giving the door a pull once all the locks were engaged, Leigh repeated the plan for the fourth, or was it the sixth, time. "Ava, you and Des just need to drop it off. They are going to handle the set up on their end. Junior and I will head to Rouge Hill to set up the anniversary party."

Ava leaned into her sister's side and whispered loud enough for people across the street to hear, "Okay, but before I go… will you at least admit that he's attractive?"

"I'm not disputing his looks, Ava."

"Then, admit you'd consider it if he asked you out." Ava amended.

Rubbing her nose against her sister's, an action she'd done since Ava was brought home from the hospital, Leigh said, "I'm never going to see him again, so it doesn't matter."

Walking to the passenger side of Junior's car, Desiree's teasing voice floated along the evening breeze, "That's not a no."

Chapter 2

LEIGH WAS ON HER stool where the book desk and bakery counter converged. It was the perfect spot to smell the mix of books and baked goods. She often puttered around the space moving between the shelves and her office, but it was a fairly quiet afternoon, so she took the opportunity to catch up on some celebrity gossip.

It was rare for Leigh to have this kind of downtime—she was mostly a one woman show which meant she handled everything from social media to special orders to the day-to-day running of the place.

Recently, after a great amount of pressure from Junior and Desiree, women who managed organizations more complex than hers, Leigh finally agreed to hire someone in the store. Lucien, a twenty-year-old queer kid who was managing a full college course load while unhoused turned out to be the perfect addition to her only other staff member, Maureen.

It galled her to admit what a difference it made. Asking for help wasn't how she was wired. In fact, Leigh spent so much of her life being responsible for others she was simply unequipped to share the load or delegate. Aside from the occasional request to cover a closing—an ask she'd only ever made of her son, sister, and two friends—Leigh was very used to handling everything on her own.

If she'd ever stopped to think about it, ever allowed herself a moment of self-reflection, she might admit that being the oldest of her parents combined seven children put her on this path, for better or worse.

She might also admit that her relationship with jock heart-throb Kingston "KC" Coffield was more of the same.

The one time she let herself get caught up in a moment and act without thinking about anything like consequences or fall-out she'd become a statistic: pregnant at seventeen; a mother and high school drop-out at eighteen. Well, she wasn't technically a drop-out. She finished the last semester and graduated with her class, she just did it all from her bedroom in her mother's home.

Leigh's innate ability to put her head down and work, make a plan and follow through, was her saving grace. It was her slow and steady approach that saw her through night school to her degree. It found playgroups and affordable art camps for her son and made budgets that were adhered to with military precision. It kept her in well-paying mind-numbing jobs until Langston was ready to leave the nest.

No, Leigh didn't often succumb to bouts of self reflection. She couldn't afford it. She had too much riding on her ability to stay the course, there was no room for the distraction of emotional toll. Her regrets were few—none of which included her son or the path her life took as a result of his existence—so she saw no reason to dwell.

The bell above the front door pulled her from her musings. She looked up to see the guy from a couple of weeks ago. Miles, wasn't it? No. Quincy.

Less flamboyantly but still impeccably dressed, he held the door open for the elderly woman who'd been browsing the military section.

Entering the shop he smiled, "I wondered if I'd see you again."

"I beg your pardon?"

"I was here the other day picking up an order for my brother."

Slick. Was she supposed to say 'oh, yes! I remember you!' Leigh chose to wait him out.

"It was late and you ladies were closing up so I didn't have a chance to look around." Quincy continued.

"You're welcome to do so now," she gestured to the almost empty store.

Quincy let out a chuckle that rumbled like boulders shifting in a canyon. "I have. I mean, I came back to check it out. The first time an Asian woman with a pink fade was here and the other times it was a young brother with platinum micro-braids and killer acrylics."

Maureen and Lucian.

Mo was her assistant baker and Luc covered the retail store. Except when Mo did, apparently.

"Were they unable to find what you needed?" She kept her tone pleasant but distant.

"No, but—"

"But?"

Quincy looked into Leigh's eyes hoping to see what? Recognition? Understanding?

When he didn't elaborate further, Leigh said "I'm sorry to disappoint you but those women don't work here so if that's who you're looking for you can save yourself future trips."

"But you're here."

Leigh tilted her head in confusion. "Yes, it's my shop."

"This is your place? You're the owner?"

Her mild confusion gave way to annoyance. "Can I help you with something?"

"I hope so," he gave her a smile she supposed got him out of many a scrape. Leigh had no intention of falling for it today. "Do you remember me from that night?"

"It might not seem like it at the moment but I have enough people in-and-out of here that one face wouldn't stand out in the crowd."

"Did mine?" His crooked smile suggested it should.

"No," she lied. "Not particularly."

"Then let me try again." Without missing a beat, he stuck out his hand. "Quincy."

Oh, he was smooth. Too smooth by half! "Hello, Quincy."

"And you must be Peaches." He lowered his hand without comment when it became clear she had no intention of taking it. "It suits you."

How often did this work for him, Leigh wondered. More to the point, why was he working his game on her? "I don't see how," she clasped her hands on the counter between them, "I named the place after a video game character."

His bravado faltered for a moment.

"For real?"

Leigh nodded.

"Princess Peach from Mario Brothers?"

"Correct."

Quincy looked around. He seemed to see the place with new eyes, taking in the light pink boxes and the crown decals on the tables and napkins. "Can I ask why?"

"You can." Leigh tilted her head in acknowledgment.

When she didn't elaborate, he asked "Will you tell me?"

"If you answer one question honestly."

"Of course," he put his palms up for her to see, "I'm an open book, ask me anything."

"Why did you come here?"

"I told you—I wanted to check it out."

"Except you've been here a couple times now. Surely, you've gotten a handle on it at this point."

Another rumbling chuckle came out forcing her to school her features. God, his voice!

"I told you that, too. I wanted to see you again."

"Me?" Leigh's guffaw almost unseated her.

"Why is that funny?"

"How old are you?" she shot back.

"Old enough for you to not worry about how old I am."

Leigh rolled her eyes at him which earned her another butterfly launching chuckle.

"You had a chance to see for yourself the other night. Now, I've answered your one question," the emphasis on *one* made her roll her eyes a little, "It's your turn."

Was she supposed to believe that he was looking for her specifically?

She wasn't being self deprecating—she was pretty. She'd always been pretty. A nice pleasantly inoffensive face on an average body. Leigh had the type of face babies smiled at. Turning heads and being the center of attention wasn't her domain. Still, she'd agreed to answer him.

"On your many visits to my store," she began, "did you notice anything about the books?"

Quincy looked around. Taking in the category labels atop the shelves, he read the ones he could see from where he stood. "Historical. Fantasy. Paranormal. Suspense. Thriller. Contemporary." Turning back to Leigh he asked, "This has something to do with Princess Peach?"

"To me, it does. I loved Super Mario Brothers. I played it all the time." A wistful smile played on her lips at the memory. "The game was built around saving the kidnapped Peach from Bowzer."

"You're really pressed about my age, huh? Talking like nobody knows about Mario beefing with Bowzer."

Leigh smirked a little before continuing, moving from behind the counter and leading him through the stacks of books making subtle motions towards the forward-facing covers. "To me, Peach was a major player. She had information. She was the guiding force of the game and kept Mario focused. But because she wasn't the one stomping on mushrooms and kicking turtles, her contributions weren't valued."

Stopping at a table featuring stories that take place at pools and beaches in celebration of the last month of summer vacation, Leigh tidied a pile. "I only sell romance books."

Quincy did a double take.

"I've always been an avid reader of all genres and styles. But when I imagined opening my own space, I always envisioned comfort. Curling up with a good book, a mug of tea, and a plate of cookies is my perfect day."

"I can see that," he said, taking her in. "How does that relate to Princess Peach?"

"Somehow, romance—genre romance, not love stories—has been stripped of its agency and devalued as smut for lonely housewives."

Quincy nodded along, keeping up with her explanation.

"I want to make it perfectly clear that people should read all the smut they want. The men who mock it don't understand the first thing about desire or fantasy. Which... of course."

Leigh always marveled at the complete lack of self-awareness men like that displayed. To boldly and loudly claim things about a woman's pleasure without ever once considering it was a direct result of their subpar efforts was baffling.

The sequence of events would have to take place in a man's brain for him to claim such fallacies as 'the female orgasm is a myth' while simultaneously protesting against a woman's sexual agency would always mystify her.

"If they were satisfying their partners they wouldn't need those books?"

Leigh made a buzzer sound. "Many sexually satisfied men and women read romance. Sex on page isn't the guarantee, happily ever after is. The joy is in the journey. No. My point is that men, largely straight cis men, tend to degrade what they cannot perceive of value. These stories run the gamut of style and substance but because they by-and-large center women and queer men, they are dismissed as frivolous.

Quincy snapped his finger in understanding. "Pink washing."

"Exactly!" Leigh beamed at him. "You can choose a pink hardhat because it's cute and fun but pretending it serves any different function or the wearer is any less skilled than the wearer of a yellow one is purely marketing. All fiction is literature. Pretending that the value of one is more serious or more substantial is just marketing."

"You're a secret subversive, Peaches!"

"Have I radicalized you?"

"I think you have."

She extended her hand, "Leigh. Nice to meet you, Quincy."

He took her hand in both of his. "A pleasure."

The soft glow from his compliment bloomed when he wrapped his large hands, warm and soft, around hers. She had to concentrate on keeping her hands from jerking spasmodically as he released her.

"Now that you've been indoctrinated, can I entice you with a book?"

"I'm embarrassed to admit I'm not a big reader. That is, I read a lot for work but not for pleasure."

"Nothing to be embarrassed about." She certainly wasn't embarrassed by the sound of the word 'pleasure' coming from his lips.

"If I did read for entertainment, what would you recommend?"

"What do you do for fun?" The question seemed too broad so she tried again, "What kinds of movies do you like? Big 'splody' blockbusters? Espionage? Comedy?"

"I like a lone wolf going against the establishment."

"Okay." Leigh led him to the section "Try this. There are 3 books in this series so far, but each one is functionally a stand-alone."

"Mercenary librarians?" He read the back summary with a bit of skepticism.

"Maybe you like it, maybe you don't. The key is to start as close to your interests as possible and branch out from there."

"Aight, let's do it."

"Yeah?"

"I trust you."

Leigh let the words sail over her head. She couldn't, *wouldn't*, allow herself to reckon with the implication of such a statement.

"Come back when you've read it, we'll talk then," she said instead, leading him back to the cash register.

"Bet."

She rang up his purchase and watched as he made his way out the door, thinking all the while about the man that didn't read for pleasure but called her a secret subversive. A man who wore his confidence like a coordinating pocket square to his handsome's bespoke suit and listened intently when she spoke about her love of books. Engaged enough to buy one and read it!

No, she was being fanciful. He had no choice but to get a book after all that, right?

If not for her bone deep certainty that women like her weren't the usual objects of interest to men like him, the knowledge that her simple brick-and-mortar lifestyle was at odds with his high-speed digital one, Leigh would have had more cause for alarm.

It was unlikely he'd come back. Even less likely he'd actually read the book. And when he didn't, when she swallowed the inevitable disappointment, she could douse the teeny flame of curiosity he'd stoked once and for all.

Chapter 3

"S'UP Q-BALL?" HIS BROTHER'S voice rang out through his Suburban's speakers.

"I'm in the neighborhood, need anything?"

"What are you doing in Leslieville?"

"Yo, you need anything or not? All up in my business. Damn!" Quincy grumped.

Miles chuckled at his brother's annoyance. "I'm good. The physiotherapist just left if you're passing through."

"Yeah. For a minute." Quincy disconnected the call just in time to pull up to the store and place his order.

His older brother was recovering from the aftermath of knee surgery which meant he was basically bedridden. Miles had been a distance runner since their youth, a thing most people scoffed at for his size. Six weeks ago during his routine run through Taylor Creek Park, his foot got caught in a gopher hole and snapped his knee almost in two.

Sharing one of their favorite childhood treats would do them both good. Squeezing his SUV in the last available spot on the street, Quincy grabbed his charger knowing Miles was obstinately an android user, and slipped down the narrow alley between the houses to where he knew the kitchen door was unlocked.

"Bighead, I'm here!" Quincy called out.

"You weren't joking, you must have been around the corner," Miles called from the living room.

Quincy searched the cabinets for bowls and a platter. Their mother's stringent housekeeping meant that every Temple kitchen was laid out almost identically, scaled to size.

"Do you need a drink?" Quincy asked.

"Nah, I'm good."

Entering the den that now served as the bedroom, Quincy laid the platter of mini samosas and sauces on the coffee table beside the chaise Miles was propped on.

"Oh, shit!"

"Who can say no to a classic?" Quincy chuckled.

"Mom would have something to say about using pinch bowls for sauces," he teased.

Mrs. Leona Temple raised her boys with an eye to style and decorum that rivaled Martha Stewart's. Water was served in the water glass; dinner was eaten off a plate; napkins were made of fabric; and never was anyone meant to put their lips directly on a can or bottle. Ever.

"She'll have more to say about this no-name paper towel you're using so I'd keep my trap shut were I you."

They shared a laugh. Their mother came from the generation that bought into the myth of respectability. She'd drilled it into her sons that impeccable manners and perfect diction could smooth the bumpiest surfaces, regardless of their skin color. As they got older, Miles quickly disavowed Quincy of that notion. The reality was stark and simple: they were big, dark-skinned Black men and all table manners in the world wouldn't help them against those who didn't need a reason to think the worst.

"You got me." His brother raised his hands in surrender.

Quincy gave him an exaggerated nod of victory before giving Miles a critical once over. "How was physio?"

"Slow. Hurts like a motherfucker."

"You like your therapist?"

"Yeah, he's cool. I just feel like an invalid."

Quincy dipped his samosa in the tamarind sauce. "You are an invalid."

Miles punched him in the arm. "Bastard."

"But for real—what's it looking like? Will you gain full mobility?"

"That's what everyone says."

They continued to eat in silence, dipping each samosa in increasingly erratic sauce combinations.

His synapses were still tingling from the wordplay exchanged with Leigh. She had been rapier sharp and endlessly intriguing and he was amped up from being on the receiving end of her attention. If there was one thing Quincy enjoyed, it was putting his skill as a wordsmith up against a worthy opponent.

"Why didn't you get that book delivered?"

"Huh?"

"You asked me to pick up a book for you but you could have had it delivered."

The sheer confluence of events required to even have crossed paths with Leigh didn't escape Quincy's notice. It wasn't an exaggeration to say he'd been set on this course, putting him in the path of a fascinating woman, by a gopher.

"Okay, random. Curbside is faster and I didn't want to wait. Not to mention delivery still requires me to walk to the door so..." Miles gestured to his crutches leaning on the chaise with a loud yet unspoken *obviously*. "That answer your weird, non sequitur question?"

"Have you been there before? Peach's Books and Bakeshop?"

"Nope. I figured I'd shop local instead of the 'zon and it was the only place listed with the book in stock."

Quincy leaned back in his seat. "The night I went there, I walked in on four of the most gorgeous women you've ever seen laughing and cutting it up."

"Word?" Miles wiped his fingers and tossed the soiled paper towel on his plate.

"I shit you not. It was a murderer's row of baddies. Melanin in all shapes and sizes—short, tall, slim, curvy—each one a straight stunner."

Quincy thought back to that night. He'd had a list of things to do before the August long weekend and nothing had gone right. Getting lost trying to find the weirdly named bookstore was the last straw. He wanted to get in and get out so he could finally head home. He'd heard them through the propped open door, calling out like siren song. Upon entering, Quincy was sure his exhaustion had conjured a mirage.

Quincy Temple was a lover of women. It was family lore that he had, from infancy, always responded well to a beautiful woman. From orderlies to nurses to doctors, if they were a man he fussed. If they were a woman, he calmed. If they were a beautiful woman, he cooed and gurgled.

He also knew he was a good-looking guy. He might not tick any of the physique boxes society insisted women found most desirable, but he was well spoken, had impeccable manners, a good job, and a stamina to rival most plug-and-play toys around. Quincy was objectively a good catch, which meant getting and keeping a woman's attention was an enjoyable endeavor.

In his experience a group of women acted like a house of mirrors reflecting and inflating the overall hotness of the individual members. When he'd walked into Peach's, the women were spread out in the space allowing him to experience them individually.

The first woman who spoke to him was mesmerizing. Her smile dazzled and, if not for the giant green rock on her ring finger, he might have taken her flirting seriously.

The woman behind the counter was short and chubby and had that flawless no makeup look Quincy had come to understand required a lot of makeup. Still, something told him cosmetics were an enhancement rather than a mask. Her eyes were an odd shade of brown—dark yet see-through like a beer bottle—that promised sin and temptation.

The woman that popped up to ask him if his order was books or bakery had a slim build and wore a stunning cap of indigo curls with a gap-toothed smile hidden behind full, pillow soft lips.

He hadn't gotten a clear look at Leigh until she handed him the book for Miles. In all his life up to that very moment he'd been misusing the word pretty. Leigh was pretty. Pretty face, pretty voice—a soothing gentleness that made him feel like a brute for daring to sully it.

And he was a brute because when her breath hitched and her eyes widened at his nearness, all Quincy wanted to do was make her gasp again and again with his hands and his dick and his mouth.

Her mocha brown skin was smooth and unblemished, and her eyes, even behind her glasses, were warm and inviting. She was average height but built like a brick shithouse—an expression he remembered his buddies' grandpa using back before he truly understood the implication. She wasn't even dressed to impress which made Quincy all the more certain of the figure she carried.

"And?" Miles prompted.

"I was having the worst day and was off my game, so I decided to go back a couple days later."

"But..." his brother was hooked. The surest sign this confinement had on his boredom.

"There was an Asian woman with a pink fade but none of those other queens from that first night. There'd been no sign of them until today."

"Wait. Are you telling me that you've been stalking four women at a bookstore for almost three weeks?"

"One woman. Leigh. I met her today." Quincy's sigh was a cross between contented and aspirational. His brother's censure couldn't dampen his good mood.

"Leigh. So what happened?"

"She sold me a book."

"At a bookstore? How groundbreaking!" Miles rolled his eyes with such intensity it would give Quincy a headache to replicate.

"At her Romance books only bookstore." He gave his brother a knowing look.

"Romance only. Is that sustainable?"

"That's what you want to discuss?"

Miles gave his brother a speaking glance before leaning back on the chaise. "Well, I know you're not trying to shame me for my reading choices, especially not after you said she sold you a book, so what else is there to discuss?"

How Miles managed to loom over Quincy while being almost horizontal was both infuriating and impressive.

"She told me all fiction is literature and everything else is just marketing."

"I don't disagree," Miles adjusted himself in the daybed before continuing, "A lot of what we were told was 'great art and literature' is really regular old art and literature made *by* a bunch of white guys *for* a bunch of white guys who collectively decided amongst themselves it was great."

Quincy cut his brother's meandering lecture off before it could gain any steam with a sharp, "Seriously, what book did you get from a Romance only bookstore, man?"

"I found a Buzzfeed listicle about Greek mythology retellings last year—"

"I should have known," Quincy rolled his eyes in a more manageable way.

"Most of the entries were Hades and Persephone but there were a couple that caught my eye: a Bronx set Orpheus and Eurydice in YA; a kids book about the muses helping a Cuban girl save the world; and an Aphrodite and Hephaestus adult romance. So I got them."

For as long as Quincy could remember Miles had been fascinated by mythology. He talked about the way the Romans and Greeks 'borrowed' from each other without ever once acknowledging the Egyptians. He enjoyed the parable and the allegory. But mostly, Miles loved how the all-powerful gods were depicted across cultures as vain, vengeful back-stabbers. Something about it gave him comfort in their very strict, very Christian household.

"Please, not another mythology lecture." Quincy put his hands up in surrender, having dodged one monologue only to land in the path of another.

"Okay." Miles clapped his hands, rubbing them together. "Let's unpack your stalking instead!"

Quincy had hoped to catch his big brother off guard with his revelation. Not to shame him, per se, but to—for once in their lives—be a step ahead. Even in this, trapped on a chaise, Miles was unflappable.

"I wasn't stalking! You don't understand—I thought I was tripping! The women had vanished, the place suddenly looked like a cafe... I had to figure it out!"

"How many tries?"

Quincy put the last samosa in his mouth and answered, "I've been there five times in total."

"And that isn't stalker behavior?"

"Not when I only saw the woman on visits one and five." Quincy said, around a mouthful of samosa.

Miles narrowed his eyes in skepticism but gestured for him to continue.

"She's smart and funny and so pretty. There's no other word for how pretty she is."

"Well if this Leigh got you to buy a book, I like her already."

"I'm gonna read it too."

Miles' laughter quickly devolved into a painful coughing fit. Catching his breath, he wheezed, "You what?"

Quincy knew why Miles was laughing. He was a solid student but Quincy would never be considered academic. Not in the same way his brother was. For Quincy, reading was a way of gathering information—the stats and trends and intel he needed to stay current at his job. If he had free time, if he wanted to escape, he preferred to do it literally.

"She said to come back when I finished reading to discuss it. I don't think I have a way in otherwise."

"What do you mean?"

"As much as it pains me to admit, my usual charms will not work here. She doesn't seem remotely impressed with—" he moved his hands across his body in an abstract shape "—any of this. So this—" he tapped his forehead "—might be my only shot."

"She's not impressed with all your accessories and embellishments? I like her even more."

Miles didn't understand his job in Premium Sales. Or, more accurately, he didn't relate to how Quincy had the energy to be *on* all the time. Miles found the constant gladhanding and upselling exhausting and artificial in a way Quincy didn't.

Quincy wore his success, the embellishments as Miles called them, to breed more success. It was part of the gig.

"Also, I think she's older. Maybe your age."

"Soon to be thirty-six? Three or four years is hardly worth mentioning."

"Yeah... maybe older, then. She asked me how old I was when I admitted to looking for her and she talked about Mario Bros like it was revolutionary."

"She's forty?"

"There's no good way to ask, is there?"

"Nope."

"What should I do, Milsy?" Reverting to his childhood nickname for his brother was exactly how far gone he felt. Leigh was so unlike the women he normally associated with it forced him to reconsider all his usual methods of pursuit.

"There's nothing to do, Wincey. You know her first name and where she works. Until she lets you know that she's interested, you're nothing more than a random customer."

"You're saying I should go back and become a regular. Someone she's familiar with."

"I am very concerned about your relationship to boundaries." Miles said in a dry deadpan.

Quincy's brow furrowed deep in thought. He had boundaries. He was a huge dude with dark skin and a deep voice. He knew all about making sure people—women—didn't misconstrue his intentions. He wasn't trying to force himself on Leigh. What he wanted was to explore this attraction, to understand if it was all in his head.

"Don't be. I have a plan."

"That's exactly what worries me."

Chapter 4

"**Y**OU'RE BACK!"

Quincy waited a week to return to Peach's which meant he'd spent four days resisting the urge to jump in his ride and head east to the little shop in Leslieville. Hearing her bright, cheerful welcome was like a reward for his patience.

"Did you miss me?"

"Hardly," she smiled teasingly. "You've finished the book already?"

Quincy rubbed the back of his neck with a sheepish smile, "No. I'm still working on it."

Something flickered in her gaze, but it was gone before he could pin it down. Resignation? Disappointment? Whatever it was, her demeanor cooled significantly. "Then how can I help you today?"

"Would you believe me if I said I just wanted to see your face?"

"Not even remotely."

"It's true." Quincy didn't lie to flatter women. His approach was a directness that proved more effective. In general, he found women had an excellent sense of their strengths and gave too much attention to their perceived flaws for baseless flattery to work any-way.

This woman, however, wasn't susceptible to any of that. Everything about her screamed 'forbearance' yet there was a vein of mischief just beneath her restrained surface. It was this conun-drum that had hooked him from the start.

"I'm going to stop you right there. Whatever game you're playing—"

"I'm not playing any games." He interrupted, bristling at her dismissive tone.

"—will only be a waste of time. You're entirely too young for me to take any of this seriously."

The way she'd lifted both eyebrows while still managing to keep one higher than the other was compelling. He couldn't think of anything to say except, "Wow!"

"Can I offer you a triple chocolate brownie or maybe a pine tart?"

A what?

She must have read the confusion on his face because she gestured to the bakery case with the same indifferent courtesy used when offering a piece of gum to those in your immediate vicinity. "A Guyanese confection. Stewed pineapple folded in pastry baked to triangle shaped perfection. A Peach's specialty."

"I'd like to come back to the age thing." How old could she possibly be to insist his age meant he wasn't a viable option for dating? "Are all Guyanese women so mistrusting?"

"I'd wager it's most women." There! The hint of a smirk as she leaned slightly toward him while drumming her fingers on her bicep, daring him to continue. The playful fire flared bright but burned out just a quickly. She returned to her blandly helpful tone to ask, "Do you prefer savory? There's some quiche left. Perhaps a cheese roll or spinach tart?"

She embodied the expression 'silk hiding steel' and Quincy couldn't get enough. Leaning on the pastry case, he held her gaze. "Why are you talking about food?"

"This is a bookstore and a bakery. Since you're here and not perusing the shelves, I have no idea what else you'd expect me to discuss with you."

"I think you have some idea." His voice deepened with his frustration. If he hadn't been looking at her so intently, he might have missed the small hitch in her breathing.

Was it possible she wasn't as unaffected as she claimed?

He was in sales. He knew when he was close to sealing a deal and knew, also, that sometimes you had to retreat and regroup. Even though it had a smarmy connotation, his job made him excellent at reading people and his instincts said the exuberant woman who'd teased and challenged him the other day would be willing to hear him out if she could get past the controlled and determined woman he faced now.

"Hey boss, do you have a sec?" A female voice called up from the stairwell Quincy hadn't noticed before.

"Be right there!" she gave Quincy a look that said place an order or leave and started towards the back corner.

He jammed his hands in his pockets to keep from reaching for her as she passed him. "Wait! Leigh—will you answer me one thing?"

She gave him a tight, patient smile as she waited for him to speak.

"Is my age the only thing preventing you from taking me seriously?" He couldn't help the peevish emphasis he gave 'taking me seriously'.

She obviously heard it because some of the irritation left her posture as she looked him in the eye and said, "No. But it's the biggest."

He struggled against the questions and rebuttals piling up in his throat, almost choking him with their affronted indignation, as she made her way to the back of her shop.

She didn't even know how old he really was—how could she be so certain he was too young? And what did that even mean, anyway? Because from where he was standing, they were both gainfully employed adults managing their assorted responsibilities. He'd accomplished all the things he was told he needed to be a 'success': a formal education, a good job, a couple of stamps on his passport, and an ambition for more.

What else was she looking for? Was she worried he lived with roommates or that he still lived at home? And even if he did, would it be so wrong in this economy? He didn't see how fiscal responsibility could be seen as anything other than a positive.

Okay, maybe that last was a stretch. He and Miles could have continued living at home with their parents full, enthusiastic blessing and yet both men had homes in the city a far enough drive away to discourage unannounced drop-ins but still close enough to make it back quickly in case of an emergency.

No, this was a feeling Quincy didn't have quite the right words for. She was smart and capable and made something inside of him sit up and take notice and she said he couldn't be taken seriously! If that wasn't some bullshit.

He was a lot of things but a joke wasn't one of them.

The sting of her rebuke landed with a familiar weight. Every day he had to weigh which slights to swallow and which to push back against and this one, regardless of his attraction to her, needed some push back.

Two days later, Quincy sat at a bistro table with the book Leigh had recommended.

"You don't take no for an answer, huh?" she commented when she'd noticed him.

"To be fair you didn't actually tell me no and anyway I'm here patronizing this fine establishment and not, as you can plainly see, playing games of any kind."

"I don't believe that for a minute." she scoffed.

"That's unfortunate," He gave her a pleasant smile—which she returned with an eye roll—before continuing his book. An hour later, he got up, threw some change in the tip jar, and left with nothing more than a wave in her direction.

Quincy continued this way for three weeks. Every couple days he'd show up with his book, choose a pastry, and sit down to read. He was man enough to admit that on that first day, he'd been motivated by his wounded pride. Leigh had essentially called him a frivolous child and he wanted to show her just how wrong she'd been.

The subsequent visits... Well, he didn't have a rational explanation for those other than to say he liked hanging around at Peach's—she didn't even need to be there for him to kick it! If that wasn't proof of Leigh's dream of providing comfort being realized, he didn't know what was.

The bakery seemed to have a steady stream of foot traffic and regulars getting things to go. Occasionally he was joined by someone else at the bistro tables.

The bookstore buzzed like a perfectly calibrated dinner party, with her patrons engaging in spirited discussions in hushed 'inside' voices and, as promised, the clientèle varied in age, gender, and class. Whether it was the woman asking about tentacles, the couple who wanted to fill the *Fringe* shaped hole in their lives, the skittish teen looking for queer stories, or the man who raged against tie-in covers, Leigh engaged each person with a judgment-free curiosity he admired.

He would be lying if he said his interest in Leigh had waned. In truth, he found her more fascinating.

He liked the way she caught the corner of her bottom lip in her teeth when she was deep in thought. The way she scrunched her nose to keep her glasses from falling. The fact she didn't seem to curse with anything stronger than 'darn it'.

But mostly Quincy liked being able to look up and see her pretty face.

He'd known beautiful women, gorgeous and sexy women, women who were cute and women who were adorable. If he thought about it, he probably also knew other pretty women now that he understood the difference.

Quincy couldn't explain the feeling Leigh provoked in him. He felt base and barbaric. She wasn't a delicate porcelain figurine to be collected and coddled yet he wanted to protect her. She wasn't some corruptible damsel, innocent of the desires of men, but he wanted to corrupt her. She wasn't a prize to be won yet all Quincy could think about was the 'mine' that echoed in his head when their eyes met.

Quincy had followed this instinct to great success many times in his life and was sure this would also prove fruitful.

"I give up." Quincy looked up into Leigh's expectant face. "You must have classes or work or something? How are you here all the time?"

He leaned back on the chair and gave her a haughty glance. "Do you need that information for me to frequent this establishment?"

"You must think you're slick."

"Can I ask you something?" She narrowed her eyes at him but didn't respond, so he continued, "It seems pretty obvious that the soldiers and librarians are going to pair off but I have a couple chapters left. When will it happen?"

"Often the payoff happens in a future book. Sometimes the couple become the main characters and sometimes they'll remain supporting characters for which the author provides occasional updates. Though I wouldn't count these couples out... you might still experience the pairing you anticipate."

"Really?" Quincy looked down at his book as though he could divine the answer through osmosis.

Leigh made a zipping motion across her lips and said, "No spoilers."

Quincy's phone buzzed with a familiar ringtone in his pocket. He watched as Leigh took in the silent phone on the tabletop beside his empty plate before pulling it out to answer, "What up, Bighead?" Watching Leigh return to the counter to give him privacy for his call, he cursed his brother's timing.

He listened as Miles relayed their mother's latest drama and how it translated to her son's riding in to save the day. This cycle was so typical, the brothers Temple were sure she created the problem so she could valiantly swoop in, offering up her sons as the solution.

"All of that to say, you're probably on the hook to donate a pair of tickets."

Grinning a little, because that was always how the story ended, he thanked his brother for the head's up and promised to swing by later.

"Oh. While I have you... if you haven't already been hit with a restraining order, can you pick up a book for me if they have it in stock?"

"You've got jokes, eh? That's how you ask for a favour?"

"You are my baby brother. You should be grateful I'm *asking* at all!"

Quincy laughed at this familiar refrain. "Yeah, Bighead. I'll pick up your book. Text me the deets."

"Thanks. Later."

When his phone chimed, he looked down at the image and scoffed to himself. Having a professor for an older brother was a blessing and a curse. On the one hand, he always had amazing insight and offered sound advice when asked. On the other, he treated everyone like one of his hapless first-year students. "I just needed the title, damn." He grumbled while he gathered his things and headed into the stacks.

Leigh's shelves were laid out like every other bookstore he'd ever been to so he didn't anticipate too much trouble finding what he needed. The Mythology shelf was on the back wall and the author's surname started with V. Crouching down to his haunches, he scanned the spines. Finding the one he needed, he'd started to stand.

"Need any help?" Leigh's voice came from behind him and when he shifted to answer her, his mind flooded with all the things he could do from this angle, starting at her feet and working his way up her body. The view of her standing over him was a good one. He liked it. A lot.

Clearing his throat, and the images flooding his mind, he rose to his full height and smiled, "Miles asked me to pick up a book."

"Athena and Dionysus."

"He's a huge mythology nerd. Which is weird because he majored in physics."

"And what did you major in?"

His answer was quick and automatic, "Sports Management."

"Sales?"

"Pardon?" He gave his head another shake. The lusty cobwebs hadn't completely cleared.

"You have two phones. Is it because you're in Sales?"

"I could have two phones for another reason."

"You could," she allowed while pushing her glasses further up her nose, "but announcing yourself as a player wouldn't help your misguided pursuit of me, would it?"

Quincy was in trouble and he knew it. Leigh was smart and perceptive and more than his mind was rising to the challenge.

"There could be other reasons, Leigh."

Her pretty brown eyes widened, "Yeah? Like what?"

Damn.

Leveling her with his most charming smile, he answered, "I'll let you know as soon as I figure it out."

The sound of her laughter, loud and boisterous and unexpected, was its own reward. He wanted to beat his chest and demand everyone take note of this wondrous achievement. He doubted anyone in the history of humanity had accomplished a worthier feat.

"Well, to answer your original question, yes—I'm the Interim Director, Premium Sales for our two-time world series champs."

Leigh's face lit up and Quincy prepared for what came next. He'd be lying if he said he wasn't hoping to impress her. Maybe parley this into a stadium tour before a game or something to show her what he was about. Most people reacted the same way when they found out what he did for a living, so it wasn't anything he'd judge her for or hold against her. He was proud to be part of the front office and hoped she would recognise the accomplishment he'd achieved.

"Is Clarence Stanford still the usher for section 124?"

That was... not what he expected her to say. "I beg your pardon?"

"Oh, it's been a while now. He's probably retired. I just can't imagine him anywhere else."

"Clarence?" Quincy had the sneaking suspicion that he was not going to come away from the conversation with the win he'd wanted.

"Right. You're front office. Maybe you don't know the hospitality team. He was always so kind to me. Gosh, he'd be in his what, late 60s by now? I don't know how he managed to keep working that section but it was always lovely to see him each game."

"Do you go to a lot of games?" He tried to pivot. Maybe working there wasn't enough but if he could get her to a game or two? Though now that the shock cleared, it occurred to him that section 124 used to be right over the home dugout before the renovation. They weren't 'anyone off the street' seats.

"Not as much as I used to. My Dad was super into baseball. So was my high school boyfriend. My whole town, really. When I moved to Toronto I went to as many games as I could." She gave herself a small shake and returned to business. "Do you mind if I make a suggestion?"

"Please do."

She reached behind him, leaving a lemon-y scent in her wake. Leigh handed him a paperback with a pink glass heart on it. "This is Eros and Psyche. It's a bit steamy but if he's moving forward in the Gods of Hunger series something tells me he won't mind the Dark Olympus series." He followed her back to the counter where she rang up his purchase. "Tell your brother that if he reads this and doesn't like it, he can bring it back for a full refund."

"I'll let him know."

Her smile was so warm and pleasant, it wasn't until he was in his car and turning into the flow of traffic that he realized how expertly he'd been managed. She'd maneuvered him right out the front door and he hadn't a clue.

Shaking his head, he made his way back to his office. Even if his colleagues were able to pry it from him, they'd never believe it.

Chapter 5

"WAS I RIGHT? I was right, wasn't I?" Leigh heard the telltale clacking of Luc's acrylics—the surest sign that he was in the midst of some wild gesturing—as he demanded accolades. "Didn't I tell you?"

She turned the corner from her office to see Luc and Quincy in an animated conversation. Though she wouldn't admit it, Leigh looked forward to Quincy's impromptu visits. Every couple of days, he'd show up and just... hang out. She'd been expecting him to say something suggestive when he'd reached the first sexy bit of his book but he'd kept a straight face while, hilariously, looking around as though he was about to get caught doing something illicit.

A couple of times she'd heard his deep, rumbling voice order something and chose to stay out of sight, just to see what happened. It turned out not only did he sit with his pastry and read but, to her horror, the flutter of butterflies in her stomach were more potent when she couldn't temper her attraction by seeing the young face that came with the voice.

She was never sure which day he'd arrive or what time it would be, but now that she knew he worked in Premium Sales, she knew enough to know he was very beholden to the team's schedule.

God, she still could not believe how much she'd told him. Why did she mention knowing the stadium usher at all? Besides the obvious—she'd adored Clarence Stanford and wanted to know that he was living a good and happy life. It was at the tip of her tongue to explain how she preferred to sit in section 136 above the bullpen but that Clarence always brought a small fruit tray for little, preschool Langston to munch on and made sure she was especially cared for.

The other ushers were kind and treated Langston like the adorably pudgy distraction he was but Clarence treated her like she was his own kin. Having that kind of care and attention in the place that had meant so much to her dad... If she hadn't distracted him with the book for his brother, who knows what else she might have divulged in her nostalgia weakened state!

She could imagine it now, 'You see, my dad loved baseball and when he died, my grief manifested in a rebellion. I fell for the star of my high school baseball team and, like a cliche, with only a semester left, was a pregnant dropout at 17. Plot twist—my jock boyfriend and I stayed together. He worked his ass off to make it to the majors and, miraculously, got signed to the home team so, yes, me and my young son spent a lot of time at the SkyDome where Clarence made me feel like I hadn't wasted everything my dad worked so hard to give me'.

No, he didn't need to know any of that. He wasn't more than a distraction trying to prove something to his ego by winning her over. Though, to be fair, more and more he felt like a friendly, quirky repeat customer whose disinclination towards drinking from the disposable paper cups would never not be funny to her.

Still, Leigh didn't completely trust his motivations. The other shoe would drop eventually.

"Yo, it did what it had to do for real, for real." Quincy held out his fist for Luc to bump.

Noticing Leigh, Luc swatted Quincy's arm with a smug cat-that-ate-the-canary grin "Go on, tell her."

"Hey, Leigh. I umm...I, uh, have a confession?" He started awkwardly, "I didn't want to tell you or—I didn't want you to get the wrong idea."

Oh, no. She'd spoken too soon. Here was the other shoe about to fall.

"The truth is I don't like cakes and such. The idea of hot fruit grosses me out. I didn't mind the oatmeal cookie or the marmalade scone but the rest just not my thing."

"I beg your pardon?" Leigh was flooded with a confusing mix of relief and horror.

"Wild, right? Who doesn't like a cinnamon bun?" Luc scoffed.

"No, I mean your confession is... that you don't like pastry? But... Why have you been eating them all this time?"

Quincy gave a half-hearted shrug.

Leigh looked between Luc and Quincy, waiting for either of them to elaborate. This whole thing was surreal.

"If it counts for anything, you're really good," Quincy offered. "I just don't want to eat any of it again."

Leigh's jaw dropped. It was one of the better back-handed compliments she'd received, all things being equal. She pinched her nose bridge under her glasses and silently counted to ten.

"You have an audacity I admire." Luc clicked his nails together for emphasis.

"This is why I didn't want to say shit," he complained to Luc through gritted teeth.

Luc inspected his nails, unbothered by Quincy's discomfort. "I told you to say the other part. You didn't have to say all that."

"What other part?" Leigh demanded. There was *more*?

"He doesn't like sweet things but he loves savory."

Quincy nodded. "That garden focaccia is fire."

"And?" Luc prompted.

"And I was gonna try the quiche but Luc insisted I take it home to have with a salad—"

"So some of the dressing could mix in with the crust." Luc said excitedly, his platinum braids swaying in time with his moments.

"—and it was amazing. I'd definitely do that again."

"My work here is done." Luc dipped into an elaborate curtsy and returned to his perch behind the register.

Leigh pushed her glasses onto her forehead and rubbed her eyes. Squeezing her eyes shut, she attempted calm but only managed to make herself feel woozy.

"I wasn't trying to upset you." Quincy offered quietly.

"I asked you if you liked sweet or savory. Obviously I know people have preferences. Why didn't you say something then?"

"If you recall, I wanted to talk about your concerning display of ageism."

Leigh's eyes widened in affront. Ageism? "Is that what this is? You've been sitting here choking back cakes and cookies to what, impress me?"

"No!"

"No?"

"Can you sit down for a sec, please? I have a crick in my neck." He winced a little, creasing his forehead. "Looking up is a lot right now."

She snorted her derision but lowered herself onto the opposite chair, staunchly refusing to wonder what he'd been doing to get a crick in his neck.

"I tried reading this at home but it wasn't working. I couldn't get into it—the first couple chapters were... a lot. It was an over-whelming amount of information."

Leigh took in the dog-eared pages motioning for him to continue.

"I admit I felt a way about you calling me trivial—"

"I did no such thing!"

"—and showing up to read in stoic silence was admittedly childish, thus proving your point." he gave a self-deprecating grin and continued "That day, sitting here in my stalwart maturity, reading this got easier."

"Some books are like that." Leigh ran her finger along the book's spine.

"The next time I came, I was thinking about what you said—about how a book, a mug of tea, and some cookies is com-fort? So I tried it." He lifted his hands in a gesture of helplessness "Having something to nibble on and a warm cup to hold helped. I don't know... I figured I'd try everything once. If I was going to find something I liked, odds are it would be here."

Leigh closed her eyes and took a deep breath. That was either the sweetest thing she'd ever heard or the most sociopathic. Exhal-ing slowly she opened her eyes to find Quincy studiously avoiding her gaze.

"Hey," Leigh pushed the book so it bumped his knuckles. "I'm glad you powered through but you should know there's no rule saying you have to finish a book once you start it."

"I'm into it now. Besides, I meant what I said. Just because I prefer the other stuff doesn't mean I can't tell if something is good or not. I promise you I wouldn't have had a second thing if the first was trash."

Leigh couldn't contain her laughter. "Thanks."

"You've created a really great space here, Peaches."

Pride straightened her spine and melted her heart. "Thanks."

His phone rang and whatever he saw on the screen made him grimace. "I gotta take this. Are we cool?"

Leigh gave his forearm a squeeze, "Yeah, we're cool."

The answering smile she received heated her entire being.

Even when he wasn't trying, she was fairly certain he was too contrite for the hard sell he normally blasted her with, he oozed devilish charm. His full lips and laughing eyes were a combination she fought against every time he visited.

"Quincy Temple." He packed up his few belongings and headed out with a wave while he listened intently on the line.

"Quincy Temple." Luc sounded the words out as he typed into his phone. "Here he is. LinkedIn, clock app, sky app, IG... Bird app? Really?"

"Lucien!"

"What? It's basic, level one recon. You'll thank me later."

Leigh wiped off the table and made her way to the counter. Placing the mug and plate in the bus tub, she gave Luc a stern, "I highly doubt it."

"Ooh, look at this!" He leaned over to show her Quincy's Instagram, ignoring her censure completely.

Image after image showed fancy, fast-lane people doing fancy, fast-lane stuff. She was actually surprised at how unsurprising it was to have proof of Quincy in fun places, eating at funky restaurants, and visiting fabulous sites. There wasn't room for disappointment. How could there be when it was exactly as she'd suspected.

This irrational attraction she felt was just that. They didn't make sense and this was one more reminder of the disparity between her analog life and his digital one. A reminder she'd keep repeating until the message stuck.

"Don't you have books to shelve?"

Luc seemed to have moved from casual scrolling to an in depth cross-platform exploration. They might be in the middle of a lull but surely there was something more productive he could be doing.

"Did it."

"And the—"

"Also done." He hauled himself off the stool with a long-suffering sigh and sauntered to the front door.

"Where are you going?"

"Next door. Since you refuse to live in reality, I'm betting Marcus will appreciate what I'm trying to accomplish here and probably will have some useful contributions."

Marcus ran the cheese shop in the neighboring building and always had time for gossip. Leigh's exasperation and disbelief collided to create an indelicate, garbled snort noise.

"Text if you need me," he waved his phone over his head and walked out.

She slipped her hands beneath her glasses to pinch the bridge of her nose. God save her from men who 'knew better'.

Chapter 6

Leigh's eyes flew open. She awoke out of breath and disoriented by the little fissures of pleasure flooding her system. It was a dream—a sex dream!—that ended in an orgasm. She tried to grab on to any remnant but couldn't remember the details.

Bringing her breathing under control, Leigh attempted to perform her usual morning ritual—five minutes of mindfulness recitations and visualizing her day's goals—but the rogue climax was too distracting. Forty-four was too old for acne and wet dreams yet here she was, plagued by both.

The obvious answer, the easy and lacking nuance answer, was that she should get laid.

Getting laid wasn't her problem. She was surrounded by available men and her friends were nothing if not joyously sex positive. No, what Leigh lacked was the time and energy required for even the most casual strings free arrangement. Ten years sounds like a long time, and occasionally it felt like a long time, but it also happened so gradually Leigh didn't even notice.

A young, working, single mother of a boy—of a *Black* boy—was an all-hands-on deck endeavour. His father had had an unconventional job and Leigh did everything she could to provide Langston with stability.

Her son was inquisitive and spirited and Leigh had done her best to keep him engaged. School and programs and homework and meal prep left her little downtime. In those early days, if Leigh was able to read one book in a year or eat a meal while it was still hot, she felt victorious.

As Langston got older and his needs changed, so did his awareness of his parents.

She and KC had fallen into a parenting style that mirrored their relationship: Leigh made the plans and KC showed up with the exciting deviations. There was little she could do about KC's need to be the fun one. He loved their son and never missed a visit or broke a promise. He was there for Langston in all the ways that he could manage, which left Leigh with the drudgery of dentist appointments and laundry.

After their split, when Langston spent a week a month during summer break and every weekend possible with his father, Leigh had the wherewithal to manage the odd hook up. She chose the men carefully—no fathers from school, camp, or lessons and no man who made overtures of blending or extending families—and prized discretion above all else. As he got older and the fluidity of custody moved at Langston's whim, his whereabouts on any given night became so unpredictable Leigh had no choice but to let her situationships wither on the vine.

Leigh focused on raising her child—preparing him to finish high school and go off to university—while she worked and scrimped to save every spare cent for business classes at night so she could upgrade her diploma to a degree. Studying the market for the perfect location, working and reworking business proposals for bank loans, making it through the first and second years in the volatile and cut throat market, and finally—*finally*—in year four feeling like she'd arrived? Ten years could go by very quickly.

Leigh didn't hate men or hate sex. She wasn't licking her wounds or healing from a great trauma. She wasn't skittish from a devastating heartbreak. She didn't have any biases or hangups. She wasn't even concerned about the judgment of having had her child when she was a child herself. Not anymore.

No, what Leigh had was a bone deep weariness that she couldn't shake. The kind of tired that numbed everything from her libido to her willingness to put herself out there. She'd carved out a space for her son, her family (and not even all of them), and her business—she simply didn't have the energy for more.

Stumbling to the shower Leigh tried to put the stopper back in the bottle. Yes, she found Quincy attractive—she had from day one. It didn't change the fact that she was too old for someone who so obviously lived in the proverbial fast lane. The deep base of his voice might cause her stomach to drop and her insides to clench but the reality was she was starting her day at 4 AM and he was likely just finishing his.

Leigh pinned her hair back and wrapped it in her now signature pink leopard print scarf and headed downstairs.

In her small but functional kitchen, Leigh pulled eggs and butter out to get to room temperature and got started on melting chocolate and stewing fruit.

"Morning, Boss" Maureen had stowed her things in the locker and washed up at the sink "Any changes?"

"Morning, Mo—no changes but it's early yet."

They started each day that way both as an attempt to ward off any calamities and as a gentle mocking of Leigh's notoriously intractable planning.

Leigh's mind was suited to schedules. Since she had to order books so far in advance, holding the bakery to a similar standard helped her keep organized and had the added benefit of reducing waste. There was a small amount of freedom in the routine which she much rather preferred to the alternative.

"I need to work on October's menu. Any thoughts?"

"For the Foodland feature?"

Leigh's bakery menu was fairly static. She focused on crowd pleasing standards with the odd anomaly thrown in to gauge interests. Since it wasn't a traditional bakery, she was able to build herself a bit of wiggle room. The one variable was the Foodland Friday item featuring Ontario grown produce.

"Yeah, what says October besides pumpkin?"

Mo thought about it. "Hmmm...Pear? It's late in the season for fruit. Lots of good veggies, though." Mo floured the table and began rolling out the pastry for the assorted tarts.

"Good point."

They worked in a companionable silence—a small miracle considering both of them had Caribbean ancestry, a culture world famous for its raucousness. The whirring of mixers and clatter of baking trays was their only proof the other was in the room.

Taking advantage of the small window of things going in the oven, setting up to cool, and prepped to go upstairs, Leigh stood in front of the whiteboard. Picking up the blue marker, Leigh tapped it on her chin while she gnawed on her bottom lip and filled in the four October Fridays.

"They're all savory." Mo stood behind her taking in the potential menu.

"You said it yourself, it's late in the season for fruit."

"I also suggested pear," Mo glanced at Leigh and then back at the whiteboard, "I don't suppose the thick slab of man who's been hanging around lately has anything to do with this?"

Leigh felt her face flush and sent up a quick prayer in hopes her complexion would conceal it. "What, who?"

"You really tek people fi eediot," Mo let out a long, censorious steups, "Quincy, that's who!"

Luc had obviously been filling her in so Leigh had no choice but to brazen it out. "Oh, please. What does the blue marker mean?"

"A possible idea," Mo cut her eye at Leigh.

"Correct. An evolving plan that can change many times before it's finalized, which is then?"

"Written in black," Mo droned.

"Exactly." Leigh gave a decisive nod, as if the case was closed, and strode back to her station.

A wry smile curved Mo's lips as she stared at the menu items in blue marker. Leigh ignored her when Mo chuckled to herself as Leigh tested recipes and ordered the supplies. Two weeks later when those same words were written in black marker, Leigh didn't fail to notice how loudly Mo had held her tongue.

Chapter 7

"LET ME TRY THE fontina again."

"I don't know what you're after, Lovey, but the fontina and the comté are obviously not it."

Leigh had popped in to visit Marcus. They were business neighbors turned friends. Where Leigh lived in the apartment above the shop, Marcus and Rafferty used theirs as an office with a small living space they used like a pied-à-terre.

They also ran four separate book clubs in the back room of their store and had come to a mutually beneficial agreement with Leigh: she would provide the baked goods and sell her books when possible and Flynn's Fine Foods would get a feature pastry for the cheese they provided. Leigh nibbled on the sliver of French cheese.

"I want something smooth like this but with a surprise kick at the end." Leigh's face furrowed in concentration as she explained.

"Honestly, darling, why you don't tell me these things first," his Irish accent made it sound like 'deeze tings furst', "We'd save so much time."

"But then who would you gossip with?"

"Lucian." Marcus winked.

Leigh swatted his words away, not wanting to hear his and Luc's thoughts about Quincy. "Hush. Now, what happened with the great swingers debate?"

Marcus had been convinced the president of their BIA was a member of the oft rumoured swingers club and had been trying to discreetly invite him to join.

"C'mere to me till I tell you!" Marcus was such a fabulous storyteller Leigh's sides ached and tears streamed down her face. There was talk of pineapple home décor as secret signals and coded language, she could barely keep up.

"Now tell me about your man. He was in here the other day."

"I'm sure I have no idea what you're talking about." Leigh gave a missish sniff, irked her deflection didn't work.

"No? About ye high, voice deep as the Marianas trench, skin dark like velvet with a body made to hold on to—ringing any bells?"

"Do you profile all my customers or only this one in particular?"

"Customer, is he? I wouldn't mind him frequenting my establishment, if you get my meaning." Marcus waggled his eyebrows because he'd yet to find use for subtlety.

"Yes, Marcus. You're usually so circumspect yet somehow manage to make yourself understood."

He threw his hands up in resignation. "All right, all right, save that awful puss. I thought you had some news to share."

"While you were busy cataloging his features, did you happen to notice how very young he is?"

"What's that to do with the price of tea?"

Leigh sighed. How could she make him understand? His age was a huge factor but it wasn't the only factor. Quincy was obviously used to getting his way with women. Even the most generous read allowed for a certain amount of drama. Leigh simply had no time for that.

"Fine," she conceded. "He's not too young but I most certainly am too old."

"Maybe you should read next month's book club selection. It might inspire you."

"This cheese is all the inspiration I need."

"How depressing! Please, you're bringing me down—I can't bear it!"

She waved the small package and pressed a quick kiss to his lips "Thanks for this!"

"I'll come by later for tomorrow's books, yeah?"

"I'm around!"

It had been a long day. A backorder of books finally arrived hours before an unexpected early delivery which meant Leigh was a sweaty mess from unpacking, hauling, and carting books. She wanted nothing more than to lay in a bath but she still hadn't heard from Marcus so a hot shower would have to do.

Her phone dinged on the bathroom counter. Squinting through the rising steam, she made out the words 'stop by' and 'pick up'.

Marcus.

She quickly replied using the speech-to-text feature 'package on the table—side door is unlocked' and hopped in the shower.

Leigh let the hot water pound her sore back and shoulder muscles, twisting and bending under the spray for good measure.

She'd planned to experiment a bit in the kitchen but decided against it. As soon as Marcus left, she would shut it down and crawl into bed.

All her oils, salves, and ointments applied, Leigh pulled on her favorite sleep shirt—a long Racer back tank top—when she heard voices, one of them Langston's, coming up from the store.

A pleasant surprise, Langston often stopped by for a quick visit to update his mother on his goings-on and to forage for food.

Leigh threw on her favorite kaftan-turned-housecoat. It was a soft bamboo rayon in a bold floral pattern on a bright azure background with a dramatic batwing and ruching that gathered on a small ring that sat beneath her cleavage elevating the dress from a standard muumuu by adding a bit of shape. It always made her feel glamorous to have the smooth fabric swishing around her legs as she moved.

Leigh made her way down the back steps. As she approached the cafe section of the store, she noticed Langston and a similarly dressed man gesturing to each other. Looking at her son was like stepping through a time machine. Without her glasses, she could easily believe a young KC was standing in her shop right now. Her son managed to be the spitting image of his father with nary a trace of her genetics to be found anywhere on his person.

This wouldn't be the first time he'd brought someone over after hours. Usually he was trying to impress them by rooting through any of the leftover pastries as they headed on to other destinations. They were probably just friends, based on what she could make out of their body language but, when Langston had leaned in to deliver some secret or punchline or the other, Leigh considered that her baby could be laying the groundwork. She decided to be Cool Mom and show this friend-possibly-more how great Langston's family was. She was mere steps away when she heard, felt, the familiar boulder rumbling chuckle.

"Quincy!" Leigh gasped. "What are you doing here?"

His smiling, jovial expression was replaced with a brow furrowing frown. "I asked if I could stop by to pick up the book for Miles. You said," he pulled up his phone to read "package on the table, side door is unlocked."

"I thought I was texting Marcus. He said he'd come over later."

Quincy turned his screen towards her as evidence that she had, in fact, texted him.

Langston, the traitor, let out an uproarious cackle. "Mom!" He gasped for breath through his full body laughter, "Mom, where are your glasses?"

"Oh, for crying out—excuse me." Leigh fussed as she stomped to the cash register, one of the many 'spare glasses hiding spots' in the building.

"Classic Dottie. Texting without her glasses." Langston could barely get the words out; he was laughing so hard.

Leigh returned to them with her glasses and her phone and reread the text: '**if you're still at the shop can I stop by to pick up the book for Miles?**'

Good Lord, he'd had no idea she lived here. "I'm sorry, Quincy. With the steam and my glasses…"

"Were you in the shower?" Langston howled, "This is too good!"

"Who are you texting?" Leigh demanded. Keeping her focus on her son's shenanigans helped her from thinking about texting Quincy while she had been naked.

"Dad! The other day KC put the cheese in the cupboard and the crackers in the fridge. I don't know which is worse."

"Never you mind." She reached for his shoulders and physically turned his body toward the door. "Go make yourself useful and take that box next door. Give it to either Marcus or Rafferty."

Giggling his way out the door, she heard his delighted "Only you, Mom."

Quincy cleared his throat and Leigh realized her tactical error. She was now alone and half dressed with the man. The man, her brain unhelpfully reminded her, she'd communicated with whilst in the nude.

"If you give me a sec I'll–"

"Leigh." Quincy's voice cracked on her name, "I didn't know... I never would have come at this hour if I'd known this was your spot. I'll come back another day during business hours. Miles will survive."

"No, no—it's okay." Leigh took a fortifying breath and added "I'm sorry for all the confusion. I'll be right back."

In the privacy of her bedroom, Leigh let the full horror of events wash over her. Quincy was in her home. He'd basically seen her in her underwear while her son laughed his head off. If there was an upside to this mortification at least this would put an end to Quincy's ill-advised interest in her.

Now clad in Langston's OCAD University hoodie and a pair of sweatpants, Leigh found Quincy exactly where she'd left him, holding his phone leaning on the counter.

"So now you know where I live," Leigh was attempting gentle humor but it came out sounding more like nervous embarrassment. Which, she had to admit, was more accurate.

"I feel terrible. I can't have you scared or worried about me. The way you're looking at me right now cuts." He gave a glum shake of his head.

"What do you want from me?"

"I think I've been pretty clear about what I want."

"And I've been clear about why it can't happen." Leigh said. His blank look told her she was going to have to spell it out for him. "You just met my son."

"He seems dope."

"He is. And you're the same age which makes you, this, off limits. It's a complete nonstarter. Can not be clearer."

Quincy's frown seemed equal parts disbelief and confusion. "How old is he?"

"Langston turned twenty-seven in the spring."

God, even saying it in this context floored her. How on earth had she managed all these years? How had she brought that colicky baby through to adulthood? Thinking about her happy, healthy, thriving child was like looking directly at the sun—appreciating the full scope of its wonder was too impossible to contemplate and left her feeling woozy and headache-y.

"Him and me are not the same age. I'm thirty-two. And unless he," Quincy pointed to the door Langston went through, "is super smart, which is possible, or I," he pointed to himself, "was mad dumb, which I was not, we weren't even in high school at the same time." His shoulders were tense but his voice sounded mildly amused.

Good Christ almighty, he was a solid twelve years younger! "You're being obtuse."

"I'm really not. You're not saying you're not feeling me or you don't find me interesting or easy to talk to, you're not saying you've got someone and you're off the market. And honestly I know you don't have to give me a reason." He sighed, dragging his hands down his face in a defeated gesture. "I just hate that I know what it is."

She crossed her arms and stood at her full height. "I like you Quincy, I do. But this can't happen."

"I get that it wasn't supposed to happen now but—"

"Not ever." She cut him off.

He reared back in genuine alarm. "Are you banning me from Peaches?"

"No, of course not." She rushed to reassure him. "I'm sorry. I didn't mean it like that. Can we just continue the way things were? Can we be friends?"

Quincy searched the ceiling for a long tortuous moment before meeting her gaze. "Good night, Leigh. I'll see you around."

"Good night," she whispered and hoped it was true.

Chapter 8

IT HAD TAKEN A week for Quincy to return to Peach's. His ego demanded he make an appearance. He wouldn't prove her right no matter how badly his pride was stung. There was no reason for him to avoid the bakery turned bookstore (or was it a bookstore turned bakery?) so he convinced himself that a tomato asparagus tart and some tea while tackling a few more chapters of the second mercenary librarians book was just the thing his Thursday afternoon needed.

Except when he pulled up, the parking lot was packed and there seemed to be a backlog to get in. As he drove along the side street looking for a parking spot, he tried to imagine what was happening in Leigh's shop.

Making his way through the cars, Quincy joined the line, craning his head to get a sense of the commotion. Two young hijabis hurried out, arm-in-arm, giggling their delight. The burly white guy in front of him called out, "Is she actually in there?"

The taller girl answered, "The Mother herself, in the flesh!"

"No more sugar cakes, though." The other added with no small amount of disappointment.

Quincy couldn't stand it any longer. "Excuse me, my man, what's happening?"

The man whose general aesthetic could be summed up as 'LARPing is Life' let his eyes bug out in naked disbelief. "The Elemental Sorceress? Mia Robyn?"

The line started to move as a few more people exited. Turning back to Quincy he continued, "The entire cast was at Fan Expo except her—she couldn't get away from the feature she was shooting."

Quincy kept nodding, hoping that a penny would drop and any of this dude's words would start to make sense. When it didn't, he pulled out his phone. A quick search told him Fan Expo had happened a month ago. Now, at the end of September, whoever Mia Robyn was, was taking the opportunity to make it right.

"I brought a poster, a head shot, and the unlicensed graphic novel. You think she'll sign them all?"

"It won't hurt to ask," he allowed with hopeful encouragement.

Nodding with what Quincy could only imagine was a bolstering of nerves, LARP Guy straightened his spine and strode into Peach's Books & Bakeshop with Quincy on his heels.

Even seeing the parking lot and knowing he'd waited in line—a line!—he still wasn't prepared for the pandemonium of the small space. There were people milling around, chatting, waiting to pay. And in the center of it all was a tall, slim woman of ambiguous ethnicity, sitting at his favorite table, posing for selfies, signing things thrust at her, and generally encouraging the melee.

"Perfect timing," Luc foisted a heavy box in his hands and pointed to the woman in his chair, "Put this on the table beside hers. I need to get on cash."

"What?"

"The books. Take them over there."

Realizing more explanation would not be forthcoming, Quincy did as he was asked, maneuvering through patrons on his way to the table. Setting the box down as instructed, he came face-to-face with Leigh, who was bringing the woman a mug of something hot.

They stared at each other for one charged, awkward moment.

"Hi." She was tentative. Wary.

"Luc gave me this box?" Ugh. How lame. Clearing his throat he tried again, "Is this where you want it?"

"Oh. Here's fine, thanks." Leigh flipped the tabs open and began setting the books in neat stacks.

"You've got a lot going on today."

"I'm afraid that's my fault." The woman extended her hand, "Hilary Welland."

"Quincy Temple."

"Hilary is the star of *Elysian*. She asked if she could do a small meet and greet which turned into..." Leigh gestured to her possible fire-code violation.

"We have the best fans in the world!" Hilary called out. Her accent sounded British by way of West Africa. Her happy assertion was met with cheers and applause.

A young Black girl, probably six or seven, was ushered to the table by an older man. She was wearing a high collared dark-green cape with intricate gold embroidery at the cuffs and hem.

"Look at you!" Hilary gushed with palpable delight. The young girl was wide eyed with awe.

The man spoke up, "We just started watching the show as a family. She's obsessed. I pulled her out of school so she wouldn't miss the chance to meet you. My husband is going to be beside himself."

Hilary's voice pitched in register, "You honor me, Sorceress."

As she engaged the child, Quincy turned to Leigh, "How can I help?"

"You don't' have to—"

"We're friends, right?"

Leigh looked up at him, a small smile curling her lips. "Right."

"So? Put me to work."

For the next hour Quincy hauled boxes of books, trays of baked goods, dabbled in some light photography, and even engaged in a bit of crowd control. Hilary made sure she stayed until every one of her fans went through the line and ended her IG Live with the promise to do it again sometime soon.

As Leigh escorted Hilary and the security detail Quincy hadn't noticed out the back door, he and Luc collapsed on the chairs in front of them.

"Real talk? I hope she don't never come back." Luc groused.

They sat, silently recovering from the frenzy, for a few moments before Luc pushed himself up with a bit more verve than he'd had moments before. "I'd better start closing up." With a roll of his shoulders and a languid stretch he was off through the shelves and down the back stairs.

Quincy turned at the sound of Leigh coming through the front door and locking it behind her. She'd pulled the blinds and flipped over the open sign before noticing him.

"You're still here." It was an observation more than a question.

"I swung by to get one of those asparagus tarts and walked into a war zone. What happened?"

The stunned, beleaguered note in his voice brought an answering smile to her face. "Short answer? Junior happened. Thirty-four years ago."

She went to the coffee station, picking up random bits of trash on the way.

"And the long answer?" He asked, after the noise of the coffee machine died down.

Making her way over to where he sat, Leigh set a London Fog and a small plate of pastries in front of him, then lowered herself into a chair with a soft groan. She pulled her glasses off and cleaned them with the small square of fabric stashed in her pocket.

Placing them back on her face, she explained "When I finally got up the nerve to pursue this—once I'd jumped through the myriad hoops and got the shelves stocked and was ready to open the doors—Junior hosted a soft launch. She commissioned loot bags with business cards, custom sampler boxes, and a bunch of other swag and invited her friends, family, and colleagues. It wasn't long before I was filling custom orders and being added to welcome baskets for film sets all over the city." She broke a piece of shortbread and nibbled delicately before continuing "That woman, Hilary, is the star of the show Junior works on. One of the sampler boxes was in her suite when she arrived and she's been hooked ever since. She comes in every now and again. Sometimes she places special orders or buys some platters to take when she flies home. Today she asked if I minded her posting her location so she could mingle with a few people since she missed Fan Expo. And, well, you saw the result."

Taking a moment to savor the spicy bite of the cheese roll, he voiced the obvious, "...but how is it Junior's fault?"

"In my experience, it saves a lot of time and energy if you start with Junior as the culprit."

"We puttin' this on Junior?" Somehow Luc managed to make the act of hauling a mop and bucket seem mischievous.

Leigh picked up the empty plate and headed back behind the counter. "Sure, why not?"

"So she's the troublemaker in your crew?" Quincy asked. He'd bet she was the one with the green rock on her finger.

"Would we say Junior is more trouble than Desiree?" Luc wondered aloud, as he tapped a glitter tipped acrylic nail on his chin. He glanced at Quincy for his verdict.

Was Desiree the one with the gap in her teeth? Were any of the women from that night the ones they were talking about? "I'll have to take your word for it, man. I haven't had the pleasure."

"But he knows who they are," Leigh added as she sprayed the tabletops.

"I do?"

Rolling her eyes at his ignorance, her delivery was a dry, simple, "You do."

Luc set the mop handle against the wall and proceeded to clarify. With his hand just above his head, he gave a smoldering, heavy-lidded pout, "Junior." He lowered his hand to his eyeline and batted his eyes demurely, "Ava." Then he lowered his hand to his chin, gave a swing of his hips and a glamorous toss of his head, "Desiree."

"After everything my cousin Desiree has done for you!" a new voice entered the room. Quincy turned to see the Asian woman with the fuchsia fade. Mo, wasn't it? "You see how di yute dem stay?"

"Ooh, you're in trouble now!" Leigh teased, flipping the wiped down chairs onto the tables. "And in front of all these witnesses!"

"Cousins by marriage!" Luc brazened it out. "And where is the lie?"

As he and Mo devolved into their bickering, a pattern that sounded familiar to him for its probable frequency, he brought his empty mug to where Leigh stood. "Where should I put this?"

Extending her hand, she took the mug and added it to the small dishwasher he hadn't noticed before.

Seeing his surprise she asked, "Did you think I would be stooped over a sink of soapy water every night?"

His imagination needed no further prompting to take that image and run with it. Leigh with her back to him, her clothing wet and clinging, outlining her body, his hands coming around to cage her against the sink as he pressed himself along to soft curves of her... He was so lost in musings, he almost didn't hear Luc and Mo bid him goodnight. Clearing his throat but, unfortunately, not the image, he waved at them. "I didn't think about it."

"We don't have that many dishes to wash. This little guy is plenty for the cafe's needs."

"What has to happen next?"

"Next?"

Quincy gestured to the space that was empty save for them and her squabbling staff.

"Oh," she looked surprised to need to explain. "Um, well, Lucien brings up the mop on his way out the door so all that's left is to wash the floors and engage the alarm."

"Okay, so let's get started."

"Wait! You—you don't have to do that. I mean, I really appreciate all your help today but you don't have to stay here and clean up."

"I know. But you'll be done and off your feet faster if I help, right?"

She nodded slowly.

"Then let's go."

Quietly, they worked together stacking the bags of garbage at the side door and wiping down the counters. He found a small broom and started to sweep while Leigh did some tinkering with her register. Finally, he'd rolled the giant bucket to the center of the room before she stopped him. "If you start at that door, you can work your way through the entire shop and end at that door," she indicated the side where the garbage bags were piled, "without having to double back."

Nodding, he got to work. At some point Leigh must have taken the trash out to the bins because she was walking back inside just as he was finished mopping. "Well, boss, what do you think?"

She smiled, giving him an exaggerated once over. "Very impressive."

"My mom made sure we knew our way around a broom handle."

"And not just because you were wild and lawless and in need of discipline?" she teased

His mock affront made his voice even deeper. "I was, and remain, an angel."

"Well Mr. Perfect Angel, you want to come up for a bite? I'm so hungry I might not bother with cutlery."

He would love nothing more. But he'd got what he came for—proof that he and Leigh had come through the other side and could work towards a friendship—and like The Gambler said, you had to know when to hold 'em. It was best for him to quit while he was ahead.

"I should probably deal with what I'm sure has become an unruly inbox. I felt my phone buzzing a while ago. Another time?"

Leigh smiled and nodded. "Another time."

He walked out to his car feeling exhausted and still somehow more energized than he had in a while.

Chapter 9

"**H**AVE YOU EATEN? **I'M leaving my brother's and thought I'd take you up on that rain check.**"

Leigh almost ignored the distinctive text notification to concentrate on clearing the board she'd be struggling with when a rogue sniper took her out. Smiling at her phone, she answered "**I don't recall extending you a rain check.**"

"**Don't be like that. I'm in the neighbourhood and offering to bring food.**"

"**I guess I could eat.**"

"**Keep playing with me and I'll eat my food while you watch with nothing.**"

Leigh laughed at that. "**Some friend you are!**"

"**Be there in 30.**"

Chuckling to herself, Leigh took a moment to double check her appearance. Sure, they were going to remain platonic but that didn't mean he had to see her looking disheveled. A quick tidying of her hair and switching to a pair of less tragic pants and Leigh was back on the couch trying to stop the mercenaries from killing her. Again.

She was so engrossed in gameplay, the loud knock at her door was startling. With her heart already racing in her chest, the sight of Quincy added an extra spike of adrenaline. Trying for calm but only achieving slightly bored, Leigh opened the door wider. "Come on up."

Quincy stood on the landing and took an interested look around before heading up the stairs. "Oh, shit."

"What?"

"This is exactly how I pictured your spot."

She scoffed but understood what he meant. Three bookcases stuffed to overflowing lined one wall. Her TV was mounted on the wall opposite a large chartreuse coloured sofa with navy blue throw pillows and twin teal arm chairs facing each other. Her faux bearskin rug lay under a cluttered circular coffee table.

"The kitchen is this way, smartypants."

Resting the bag on the counter, Quincy continued to marvel at her space.

"Quick tour?" she offered. At his nod, she led him further down the hall. Pictures and photographs lined the walls on both sides while a royal blue oriental rug cushioned their steps as they went.

"This is Langston's room. I don't know why I bother, he'd moved in with his dad shortly after I got this place." Her delivery was droll, not malicious.

The room was a time capsule to a student who went to university in the new millennium. His art, posters, pictures were placed in a collage style reminiscent of a high school yearbook over his bed, his knickknacks and tchotchkes covered his desk and dressers.

"This technically is the guest room but it's my dressing room, also known as my overflow closet." She opened the door to a small-ish room across the hall painted robin's egg blue with a large armchair that folded out to a bed, a chest of drawers and full-length mirror in the corner. There was one large painting of six Black women in profile with colourful headwraps.

"Here's the washroom," she indicated the closed door beside the guest room, "The linen closet." She pointed to a door on the same wall as Langston's room. "And there, at the end of the hall, is my room."

Leigh's insides clenched. It wasn't that her room was messy or that there were scandalous things laying around. She knew it was tidy and all the laundry folded and put away. It was the reality of him even being in her home—where she lived—increasingly closing in on her. She had no idea what she thought would happen once she started opening doors and letting him see the bits and pieces of her personal life, but the further down the hall they went, the more panicked she became.

Quincy gave her an assessing look but didn't say anything. Likely he understood that she wasn't eager to have him in her more intimate space just yet. "It's dope. I wouldn't have guessed it was so spacious up here."

In light of how much time she spent working on the shop, it had been more practical to clean this area up for habitation instead of maintaining two mortgages. Pleased by his compliment but not knowing where else to take the conversation, Leigh demurred "Shall we eat?"

"This is from the best Indian joint ever." Quincy gamely seized on the change of topic.

"That's a big claim to make to someone who lives blocks away from Little India." Leigh strode back to the kitchen to lean over the bag so she could inhale the fragrant steam rising from the takeout dishes. "Let's see what you got!"

Once they'd fixed their plates, Leigh returned to her spot on the couch while Quincy settled into the armchair closest to her.

Her first bite made her moan her pleasure, "Mmm... so good. Thanks for feeding me!"

"Thanks for honouring the raincheck."

Leigh chuckled around the forkful of food with a small head shake. "You're welcome."

His gaze held hers for a beat. Then another. She returned her concentration to her plate and they fell into an easy silence while they finished their meal. Leigh collected their plates and took them to the kitchen. She settled herself back on the couch, a little closer to where Quincy sat.

"Should we talk about it?" Quincy asked with a bit of wariness.

"It?"

"The elephant in the room."

Leigh worried this was coming. She'd said all she planned to on the matter but figured it was likely Quincy wasn't finished making his case. Pushing her glasses higher on her nose, she nodded for him to proceed.

"He doesn't deserve Elena. He's lucky she went after his ass or he'd be dead on that island."

Leigh blinked her confusion before the penny dropped. He was talking about the game!

"Nathan is always dating out of his league. That's what scoundrels do."

"It is definitely that."

Laughing, something inside Leigh settled. Having Quincy in her home was going to take some getting used to, sure, but it didn't have to be awkward.

"I guess I shouldn't be surprised. You named your spot after a video game character."

"*Seminal* video game character."

"Settle down." He matched her playful, haughty tone while waving away her words. "She's a Pollyanna at best; a Mary-Sue at worst."

Leigh's gasp was loud and sharp. "Out! Right now!"

"The truth hurts, don't it?"

"How dare you?" She shrieked, barely holding back her outraged laughter. "You need to leave!"

"Yo, I'm trying to keep you grounded in reality. I'm doing you a favour. You should be thanking me!"

Leigh picked up a pillow and swatted him, "Don't even stop for your shoes, you beast!"

He dodged the blow and it landed with an unsatisfying plonk beside his shoulder. She tried again. It connected this time though he brought his arms up to block. Emboldened, she continued her assault while he dodged and ducked the blows. Picking up his own pillow, Quincy put his hand out to stay her motion.

"I don't want to hurt you, but I will not be bullied by your Mushroom Princess Propaganda. I will defend myself by any means necessary."

"Her name," Leigh drew her arm back, "is Princess Toadstool!" and launched the throw pillow at his head. Too late, she realized she'd left herself unarmed. Glancing quickly to her left, she lunged for the pillow on the armchair. Quincy, recovered from her attack and seeing her intention, flattened her to the couch with a blow from his pillow. Launching himself over the coffee table Quincy and Leigh reached for the blue velvet cushion at the same time.

"Let go, you brute!" Leigh tugged with all her might to no avail.

"So you can throw more furniture at me? No ma'am!"

"Furniture! It was a tiny pillow you baby." Stubbornly refusing to let go, Leigh's chest heaved with exertion.

With barely a tug, Quincy pulled it to his chest, bringing Leigh to her feet along with it. "And risk this face?"

No. No, that face should never be put at risk under any circumstances.

With a start, Leigh was suddenly very aware of her proximity to Quincy. They weren't touching, though it was only by the strictest definition—his breath blew the stray tendrils of hair on her face and neck and her middle school teacher would have strained to find the requisite space for Jesus between their bodies.

This close, she noted that he wasn't that much taller than she was. He might not even be a full six feet, for all it mattered. He was a mountain of a man that exuded strength and dominance and Leigh couldn't decide if she should be alarmed or aroused. She didn't think she was in any danger. Quincy didn't set any warning bells ringing, though that wasn't enough to completely discount any potential threat. Not that type of threat, anyway.

It was more the fact—the truth, really, even though she'd deny it to anyone who asked—that if he wanted to, Quincy could haul her up off her feet and against his body, stalk down the hall, and toss her on the bed and... and maybe... she wouldn't say no. Which was the most dangerous thing about him.

"I've certainly seen worse faces," her voice was thin and reedy, "it would be a shame to ruin a perfectly acceptable one."

He leaned closer and her stomach dropped. The dark smoke of his voice pebbled her skin. "Perfectly acceptable?"

"Assuming we're grading on a curve." Why couldn't she get her voice under control? Her voice, her heart rate, her hormones—all three were working in tandem to overrule the logic and safety of her brain. "You wouldn't want to bring down the average."

"Leigh." Quincy licked his lips.

Leigh did the same, like some type of addled Pavlovian response. It would be so easy to press her body on his. Barely any muscles at all were required. A simple sway, a subtle tilt, and they'd be touching. She felt the flush crawl along her skin and knew it wasn't from the pillow fight. Trying to get herself back under control, Leigh let go of the pillow, cleared her throat, "Yes?"

He looked down at her mouth and back up to her eyes. Swallowing, he did it again. It seemed she wasn't the only one who needed to wrangle their self-control. "Who are Dottie's Darlings?"

What?

"What?" Following his gaze, she found the large silver picture frame on her bookshelf. "Oh!"

Stepping away from him helped bring some much-needed sanity back. Taking a breath that wasn't filled with his rich chocolatey scent cleared the last of the fog. With her back to him, she tried to quickly straighten her clothes and hair before picking up the frame and handing it to him.

"I'm Dottie and those are my Darlings."

"Oh, so... that time when your son called you Dottie he literally meant—"

"My first name is Dorothy but I hated it." Taking the frame from him, she returned to the couch and gestured for him to sit. Placing the frame on the cushion between them, she continued, "I grew up in a really small town. Of the few minority families, three were Black. Of those three, ours was the only one that sent their kids to the Catholic school. I got tired of explaining I was named after Dorothy Dandridge and had nothing to do with tornadoes in Kansas."

Leigh considered explaining the distinction she was making between minority families and minority children adopted into white families but decided against it. It was already so weird to think about her small, small life outside of Stratford now that she'd lived in Toronto for so long. She knew there were hundreds—thousands—of racialized kids who grew up the way she did. She knew she wasn't special because she was the Only One in her class until she got to grade four. What she didn't understand, what she never would, was how some of those people managed to shed their identity like snakeskin.

How could you deny or denounce such an integral part of yourself when you are constantly reminded every day in ways big and small that you were Other? How could giving such a crucial part of yourself away be worth conditional acceptance?

She'd learned early on about the power of code-switching. It was a valuable coping device. But it was a device all the same. Leigh promptly turned it off as soon as she walked through the door of her home. Truth be told, it wasn't like she'd had a choice. Her parents would never allow for any "North American foolishness" in their Caribbean household.

Quincy was studying the image she could see with her eyes closed. It was her entire family, sans parental units, all in blue with matching sashes indicating their relationship to her in celebration of her fortieth birthday. Leigh was pretty sure she knew what came next.

"There are seven of you?"

His barely concealed horror was adorable. She grabbed a pen from the coffee table to do the introductions. "We have the same mother," she pointed out her three siblings. Pointing to her other three, she said. "We have the same father. You with me so far?"

He nodded.

Taking a deep breath, she launched into the nitty gritty. "Anita's children are me, Ava and Sidney," she tapped their faces, "who have the same father, and Otis," she tapped on his face, "who has a different father."

"Okay, okay."

"Trevor's children are me, Catherine and Rhonda," she circled their bodies, conveniently beside each other in the photo, "who have the same mother, and Julian," she indicated her youngest sibling, "who has a different mother."

The complexities of her family unit hardly fazed her anymore. The painful adjustment happened some thirty years ago and she found that pressing the bruise, looking the pain right in the eye, centered her in a way little else did. Waiting for Quincy to put it together, she took in the faces of her family. Each one of them a link in the chain that anchored her for better or worse. Whether it was Cat's refusal to accept her daughter had a developmental problem, Julian's crumbling under the pressure of their father's expectations, or Otis' general... uselessness, Leigh had—for as long as she'd known each of them—been the shoulder they cried on and the bringer of solutions.

"Then technically you are—"

"An only child, yes. But in practice, I am—"

"The oldest of seven." He finished, putting the puzzle together quicker than she'd anticipated.

"Sometimes I feel overwhelmed by the pressure of being the Big Sister, but mostly it is what it is. I'm so used to it now; I can't imagine my life any other way."

"That's wild. I have so many questions."

"You can ask two. Choose wisely."

Quincy did a double take. "For real?"

"That's one. You have one left." She intoned gravely before breaking into giggles.

Quincy rolled his eyes. "Who's this white girl? She looks familiar."

"Hyacinth Perry. She's an influencer. Or is it brand ambassador? Trend architect? I can't remember what she's calling it now.

She's Hi, Hy on all platforms—which is how you probably know her. Her dad is married to my mom."

"On top of everything else, you have a step-sister?" He shook his head in pure scandalized incredulity.

"Allan has three kids—Dahlia, Hyacinth, and Rowan. We only see each other at holidays and special occasions but I'm close to her." Off his look she agreed, "I know, the flower names are too much. Their mom apparently is a raw food vegan who started an ashram in Guatemala. So. You know."

"Your girl comes by her bullshit honestly."

"Poor, Hy. She's a lot, trust me I'm aware, but she's really sweet. And she's been super supportive of the shop. She promotes it at least once a quarter, not that she eats or reads anything I sell." Leigh laughed mostly to herself but then a little louder when Quincy joined in. "It's true. She takes these super complicated pictures with a cookie or muffin and then leaves it behind in a cloud of air kisses and verbena."

They descended into the kind of punch-drunk laughter that fed on itself. The original joke stopped being funny yet they both snorted through the tears streaming down their faces. Leigh pulled a tissue from her pocket and dabbed her eyes. Once they regained their composure, she nudged him, "Enough about my and my chaotic family. It's your turn. Tell me about your brother... Are there more of you roaming the streets of Toronto?"

Quincy lay his head back on the couch, looking at nothing in particular. "Nah, it was just me and Miles running wild in the streets of Markham. Our parents had us when they were in their forties so I feel a lot of pressure to get settled and start a family even though I'm nowhere close to wanting that."

"Not yet or not ever?"

"I still have so much I want to do!"

She waited for him to continue, enjoying his company more than she thought she would.

His hands twitched as though he planned to lift them before changing his mind. "I don't have a set-in-stone plan, if that's what you're waiting for. It's more... I want to be able to take advantage of opportunities and I don't know if a family—roots—is conducive to that."

"You don't think you'll have opportunities once you have kids?" The idea that a man's life had to change in any real way was so counter to societal mores, she couldn't help the mocking judgment in her voice.

"Let's say I get a chance to help build an NFL expansion in the UK—it's never going to happen, but like, as an example—if I have a family, moving to England becomes less likely. The project would be for a year or two, max, and then I'd be on to something else. I'm supposed to pull my kid out of school and throw their whole shit into chaos? I love how transient my life is but it isn't exactly family friendly."

"Two words: Military. Brat."

"You were a military kid?"

"No, not me. People. Lots and lots of people grew up that way." She said, patiently. "You aren't forging some uncharted path. If you want to have a family and your fly by night career, you can."

"And my spouse just drops everything with no concern for their career goals to follow me around? You don't think that will be a problem eventually?"

She was curious about his gender-neutral language. Was he queer? It didn't matter, really, and it certainly was none of her business. More pressing was his very salient point. "Point taken."

"If I get a call tomorrow to pack a bag and head to Jakarta, I want to be able to do it."

"How likely is a Director of Premium Sales for a Major League franchise getting a call to go to Indonesia?"

"As the Interim Director? Highly unlikely. But I'm in the position until Erika comes back from mat leave. The promotion looks stellar on my resume which might open me to other prospects which makes such a call very likely."

Leigh was quiet while she let the impact of his words land. She'd always known he lived a life faster than hers. Everything about him screamed Scene but this was beyond even her wildest imaginings.

Her musings were broken by the sound of his phone.

"It's Game Day. I gotta get going." He silenced the alarm and started to gather his belongings from the coffee table.

She looked at the time as it bounced around on her TVs screensaver. "Already? But it's a night game."

"There's only one October, as they say. It's all hands on deck."

"Right. Of course." She stood, a little embarrassed by her outburst. "Well... thanks again for lunch."

"Thanks again for having me. Maybe we can do it again sometime."

Leigh stared up at him, lips parted, as though caught in a snare. "Yeah," her voice was barely a whisper. She cleared her throat and tried again, "Yeah, I'd like that."

She felt the weight of his attention, neither of them moving to break the spell, "Okay."

Finally, with a rallying grasp at her common sense, Leigh took a deep breath and stepped back. "Okay."

It wasn't until she heard the door click shut at the bottom of the stairs that she dared to exhale.

Chapter 10

LISTENING TO LEIGH YELL at the TV with a forkful of food halfway to her mouth was fast becoming one of Quincy's favorite things. Trash talk was always a good time, but it was especially entertaining hearing Leigh disparage the refs, coaching staff, front office, and certain players' Little League teams all without dropping a single f-bomb. It was a thing of beauty. Poetry in motion. Inspirational quotes meant to be cross-stitched and hung in living rooms everywhere.

"Want to come with me to a kickback?" The question surprised them both.

"A what?"

"It's a casual hang at my boy Travis' place. We all bring a little something for the table and catch up. We do it every year."

Leigh put her plate down. They were having souvlaki dinners. It was impressive how she'd systematically gone though her plate, maintaining the same ratio of potato to rice to salad to pita to pork cubes as when she'd started. "Like a Friendsgiving?"

"The weekend after. It started as a way to commemorate or commiserate the Turkey Dump as applicable."

Quincy explained how he and Travis had been friends since middle school but hadn't gone to the same university. When they'd linked up with each other over the Thanksgiving holiday, they swapped stories of all the people they knew who were going home to break up with their high school sweethearts. Travis had talked himself into throwing a small hang for the folks coming back to campus with brand new relationship statuses. By the end of the night, Travis had convinced his entire friend group to participate on their own campuses. "And thus, the Turkey Dump Debrief was born. Travis has kept it going every year since."

Leigh was looking at him with amused confusion. "Turkey Dump?"

"It's a right of passage! Realizing your unbreakable bond didn't even last the first seven weeks of school? Most of them were probably on shaky ground after Frosh Week, if we're being really real."

Quincy couldn't help but laugh at Leigh's crestfallen expression. "Oh, those poor babies—what an awful thing to call it!"

"This can't be the first time you've heard that."

"It is!" Her words came out part laughter, part incredulous disbelief. "I didn't go University, as you know, and Langston went to OCAD mere stops away on the subway from my old place. He also didn't have a high school sweetheart he pledged to go the distance with."

"I assure you, we didn't make it up. The Turkey Dump has been happening for generations."

"But the name, Quincy! Surely there's something better than 'Tukey Dump!"

"Like what? 'My entire world view has been irrevocably changed and I need to release myself from commitments I made before my eyes were opened at the soonest opportunity!' doesn't exactly roll off the tongue."

She was laughing in earnest now. The sound burnishing his ego and swelling his chest.

"No, I guess it doesn't."

Leigh's smile made Quincy want things he'd agreed to not want anymore. "So, you interested in a casual hang with a questionable origin story?"

"Can I confirm later? It'll depend on what's going on with my granny when I'm home at Thanksgiving."

Nothing in her tone suggested cause for alarm but Quincy still felt its cold grip on his insides. He'd already been to a couple grandparent funerals this year and didn't want that for Leigh, regardless of its inevitability. "Going on? Is your grandmother alright?"

"Oh! Yes, she's fine. I mean, she's getting up there in age but so far she's still going strong. I like to spend as many holidays with her as I can. It's much harder to get back now that I have the store. I used to bring her to Toronto to spend time with me before one of us, usually Langston, drove her home. But this place and the stairs...it's not as easy."

Quincy hadn't met any of his four grandparents. Neither had Miles. He'd romanticized the idea of a soft, kindly grandmother who would make his favorite meals and plan special visits with all his favorite activities. As he got older, he'd learned that grandparents, like the taste of barbecue flavored chips, varied wildly.

"Langston's lack of seniority gets him the grunt work?"

Leigh giggled at his obvious joke. "No. Well, maybe? More that his three grandparents still live in St. Mary's so he can clear a lot of boxes with one chore. Plus, his Memere, KC's mom, spoils him rotten so he takes every opportunity to bask in her attention."

"Sounds like your son knows what's up."

"He seems to. His father was the same way so I don't know what I expected." She gave her head a fond shake and then resumed eating.

"Well let me know if you think you can roll through. No pressure. It's super casual, like I said. No one will be keeping track at the door."

She smiled around a mouthful of food and Quincy had to look away before his face betrayed him. He hadn't intended to invite Leigh to the kickback, but now that he had, he really wanted her to show up.

He'd always trusted his gut when swinging for the fences. His adult life had been ruled by the concept that closed mouths don't get fed. Saying what you wanted made things infinitely more possible. And what he wanted was to be out, in public, with Leigh.

***

"I can dress myself, Ava!" Leigh watched as her sister swiped hangers from one side of her closet to the other.

"We took a vote on who would supervise specifically because you cannot be trusted with the responsibility." Ava paused on a sundress but kept swiping.

Leigh gestured at the bed now buried under discarded items of clothing. "His boys are having a kickback. We're going for ice cream after passing through. I don't need to be doing all this."

"It's an evening out." Ava caught Leigh's eyes over her shoulder and stressed, "Where you'll meet Quincy's friends."

"Where a bunch of friends will be gathered." She corrected sternly.

Ava pulled her phone out of her pocket and menaced Leigh, "I thought you'd appreciate my gentle approach but if you require something a bit more...."

Leigh collapsed on her bed in a huff, message received. Ava had always had an enviable style. Probably because her aesthetic choices weren't motivated by courting a sexual gaze. She'd hoped Ava's effortless cool would strike the better balance for tonight. Unfortunately, she forgot that in order to achieve Ava's look, one needed to have access to Ava's closet. What Leigh had was a serviceable closet full of comfortable elastic waisted pieces in similar shades of black and charcoal.

Nodding her victory, Ava asked "What do you know about the venue?"

"Umm... it's at Travis's apartment in The Village."

"Wait," Ava paused her hanger swiping, "One of his boys is named Travis?"

"Yeah. So?"

"Nothing, I guess." Ava's wrists moved as though she were weighing something. "'Travis'. It's, like, the Jeremy of Chads."

Leigh nudged her from in front of the closet. "Be that as it may, this is a casual hang."

"Is he picking you up?"

"We're meeting at Wellesley station."

Ava tapped her chin and hummed. "Here. Try this on."

"Were you listening? It's a hangout, Ava. This is too much."

"Sorry to burst your bubble, Dot, but threadbare black leggings aren't the universal option you think they are. Now move."

Leigh could not make herself treat this as anything more than Quincy said: a small hang. She knew little bits about them and their goings-on but she and Quincy were separate from that and tonight changed nothing on that score. They were 'food on the couch while the game was on' friends.

"Don't make me say it," Ava's smug smile confirmed what Leigh saw in the mirror.

The pink paisley cigarette pants and soft grey, lightweight boatneck sweater were the perfect balance of comfy and stylish. She looked put together without a whiff of effort.

Leigh stuck her tongue out. "That's why your head is so big."

Ava returned the gesture while snapping a picture.

While she fastened the clasp on her earring, her phone buzzed on the dresser. Shooting her sister an annoyed glance, she answered with a beleaguered "What?"

"My sister in Christ, what would it take to convince you to put some color on your face?"

"I'm wearing mascara!"

Leigh's complaining fell on deaf ears as Desiree didn't so much as go to the grocery store without highlighter and gloss.

"What about a nice lip stain? You won't have to reapply it, I promise."

Makeup was the first thing to go when Langston was born, followed closely by underwire and non-elastic waistbands. Even her brief foray into corporate life was marked by loose fitting shift dresses and cardigans. Any items remaining were akin to a vestigial tail or a phantom limb—she knew it existed at one point but was no longer a functioning part of her life.

"Heels or lipstick" Leigh bartered.

"Lipstick!" Desiree declared without missing a beat. "Those pants require a nice brogue."

Ava snickered in the background "Sucker!"

Leigh gave a resigned sigh. "Which one?"

To Desiree's horror, Leigh owned exactly four lipsticks if you counted her tinted lip balm—which Desiree unequivocally did not!—two tubes, one gloss, and one lipstick pencil.

"The pencil. The pinkish lavender will give a bit of clash while still complementing your sadly bare face."

"I am wearing mascara!" Leigh repeated

"Do me a favor and run a quick swish of eyeliner on your lids for funsies."

"Is that all?" There was no use fighting.

"At this juncture? Yes."

Leigh opened her mouth but hesitated, torn between the sudden desire to make a good impression and truly not giving a damn, before asking "I don't have brogues. What shoe should I wear?"

"I'm on it!" Ava called out as she hurried out the room and down the hall. She returned brandishing a shoe box. "These."

Leigh took the box. "Really?"

Ava raised her voice so Desiree could hear "Low rise Chelsea boots."

"Perfect!" she agreed, now on speaker.

"Okay, let me finish getting ready."

"Text me when you get home!" She added in a scolding schoolmarm-ish voice, "And don't get on the back of any motorcycles!"

Leigh and Ava laughed as the call disconnected. Their mother's constant vigilance against the ever-present threat of daughter thieving bikers was a running joke that hadn't lost its appeal these thirty years later. They had no idea where it came from—they didn't even know anyone who *had* a motorcycle much less a desire to ride one.

Ava gave Leigh a quick once over. "My work here is done. You ready?"

Leigh inhaled and let it out slowly. Was she ready? She had been when she'd texted Quincy that she'd join him for The Great Debrief. And when he discovered she also didn't limit ice-cream consumption to summertime, she'd felt good about the addition to their itinerary. Now, feeling a bit trussed up and out of her element, the first stirrings of unease were starting to take hold.

Sensing her inner turmoil, Ava gave her a tight hug. When she stepped back, she looked Leigh in the eye and said, "You're just going out for a drink with a friend. You'd wear jeans but you're excited for an opportunity to finally wear these impulse buy pants. It's an unseasonably warm October night—perfect for a bit of ice-cream. You'll be home, cleaned up and in bed, way before bedtime and when you finally lay your head down, you'll think to yourself, 'that was fun. I might do it again some time'."

Leigh closed her eyes and let her sister's words wash over her. It was one night. She and Quincy had hung out a bunch of times already. All they were doing was taking their show on the road. She could manage that.

Opening her eyes, she gave Ava a decisive nod. "Can I get a ride to the subway?"

Chapter 11

Q UINCY WAS WAITING BY the collector booth when he saw Leigh come up the stairs.

She was so pretty.

Leigh was usually in work mode or chill mode; he'd never seen her in street wear, nevermind makeup. It made her usual approachable demeanor a little more daring. Her lipstick, specifically, was daring him to kiss it right off her mouth.

"Evenin', Peaches."

"Slick." Leigh nodded in greeting.

"Look at you, you clean up nice!"

Leigh looked down at her outfit and back up at him. "Is this too much? I know you said it was a hang..."

"It's perfect. You look perfect." He extended his arm with a smile, "Shall we?"

It was a short walk to Church Street. Travis's apartment was one of the newly converted buildings switched to condo in recent years.

The neighbourhood itself, widely known as The Village, was that peculiar Toronto blend of old and new, trendy and dodgy.

The myriad rainbow flags and other identifying markers of expression and acceptance in no way precluded the steady rise of strollers and minivans.

As they approached the intercom, Leigh's hand flew to her mouth "Shoot! I forgot to ask if there are any allergies! I'm good with the majors but it never hurts to ask. Darnit."

Quincy looked at her with amusement—she really didn't swear!—and confusion.

"I brought salara," she indicated her ever present tote, "but maybe it will be a problem? Not everybody likes coconut."

"Who doesn't like coconut?"

"You'd be surprised," Leigh insisted. "There was a woman in my night school class, a beautiful blonde from Montreal. She hated coconut. She liked Thai Coconut Curry, though, so... I guess there's that."

"Peaches, these animals will eat whatever you put in front of them. Don't trip."

"Okay," she let out a calming breath. "I don't know why I'm suddenly so nervous."

He watched as she smoothed the furrow in her brow, perturbed by this turn of events.

"I've known most of these people for years. You have nothing to worry about."

They rode the elevator in comfortable silence, floors chiming as they ascended. The sounds of merriment reached them even before the elevator doors fully opened.

She arched a brow at Quincy, "A small hang?"

"You know how it goes."

He led her to the end of the hall where the door was propped open with a six-inch Bulbasaur figurine.

"I'll explain later," Quincy leaned in to whisper. If he happened to inhale her fresh herb-y lemon-y scent, well—it was a happy coincidence.

He led her to the kitchen to get a drink and set out her contribution to the evening's nibbles. He took a quick look around and gestured widely to indicate, regardless of what she heard from the elevator, there were maybe only a dozen or so people milling about.

They took in the space together. The large balcony door was propped open, giving the smokers space and a stellar view while the island in the open kitchen kept the flow of people from getting too blocked up. The dining room, with its furniture momentarily relocated, was now the main gathering area. The three-bedroom unit was an impressive get in the city's cut-throat real estate market.

With a tilt of his head, he continued toward where the majority of the noise originated—the obscenely massive TV where Leigh took in Travis, a white guy, and Carter, an obviously mixed Black guy, hurling insults at a soccer game. Since Carter was a full time all the time Gunner, Quincy guessed Arsenal was losing to a team they should be dragging across the pitch.

"Somebody has the ref's mama gagged in a panel van. Got to be," Cater lamented, "No other explanation for that call!"

"Other than your team is shit?" Travis asked with faux earnestness.

"Man, fuck you!"

"Yo!" Quincy broke in, before things devolved.

The men looked over, noticing them, and gave Leigh matching smiles. Travis extended his hand "You must be Peaches. Welcome to Casa Me."

Carter gave Travis a speaking glance. "Carter. And that jackass is Travis. Welcome, Peaches."

"It's Leigh," she shook each of their hands in turn.

Travis's face twisted in confusion as he looked to Quincy for clarity, "I thought you were bringing the bookstore lady."

Carter huffed an impatient noise. "Bakery lady, dumbass."

"Oh!" Leigh gasped with delight. "You're brothers!"

They smiled their identical smiles again.

Travis launched into the explanation unprompted, "Bio Mom split almost immediately. Pops remarried and had this fool before I was one and our sisters when I was three."

With all the snark and jostling and posturing, Quincy was sure the subtle change in Carter's body language, as though he were standing sentinel for his brother's story, didn't escape Leigh's notice. They'd been on the receiving end of insensitive and ignorant comments over the years and, though Travis tried to hide it with blasé indifference, it isn't easy to explain again and again that your biological parent bailed before the ink dried on your birth certificate.

Quincy wasn't worried. Even if her own family tree wasn't as gnarled and twisted, Leigh was the kindest person he'd ever met. She wouldn't ever intentionally make someone feel unwelcome or uncomfortable. He watched her take it all in with her keen, knowing gaze.

Leigh kept any questions she may have had to herself and admitted, "My first guess was cousins. You have the same face but different shaped heads."

"See? Even Peaches can see how weird your head is!" Carter crowed.

"I got your weird head right here!" Travis grabbed his crotch in response.

Quincy's bark of laughter only highlighted Travis' massive self-own. "That doesn't even make sense!"

"Those who know, know." Travis straightened his imaginary tie.

"You don't know shit!" Carter laughed

"Or maybe you're one of the ones who don't know?" Leigh asked with a gentle tease.

"Exactly!" With a comically exaggerated bow, Travis said "I'll see you at the Cookout."

Leigh's laugh was warm and genuine, "Is that right?"

"That's what he likes to think," Carter's eye roll was impressive for its scope and duration.

"My mom is Black. That's guaranteed, all-access entry."

"I'd think being able to answer 'Who was in Paris?' would be your all-access entry." Paviter said, joining the scene with his usual dry, deadpan delivery.

Carter and Quincy both folded over with laughter. Yvette Grant loved Travis fiercely and yet all four men knew she'd feed him his teeth if she ever heard him use the slur from the popular song title Paviter mentioned.

Leigh turned at the sound of the new voice entering the space while Quincy and Carter cracked up.

"Whatever," Travis scowled, "You can't say it either."

He smirked, "My tiny Punjabi parents are from Jaitu. I don't need to say it."

"Pav, this is Leigh. Leigh, meet Paviter."

Leigh lifted her hand to his, still speechless from the initial sight of him. Paviter was, unquestionably, one of the most beautiful men alive which was saying something because between his friend group alone they had their fair share of fine men. Paviter gave a slight bow over their clasped hands. "A pleasure."

"Yes, a pleasure."

Travis' indelicate snort snapped her out of her trance-like state. With a shake of her head she added, "For me. Also. It is my pleasure to meet you, too." Clamping her mouth shut, she clasped her hands together in front of her.

"Aw, Q—looks like Pav's gonna steal your girl!" Travis's outburst had the friends breaking into jokes and insults and reckless laughter.

"We're not together." Leigh's reflexive answer made Paviter's brow arch. She must have realized it sounded as though she was interested in *him*, so she quickly added. "I'm older than your mothers, for chrissakes."

Quincy's voice was tight with irritation, "She's not."

"Nothing wrong with a spin through Cougartown." Travis benevolently granted permission no one asked him for.

"Please excuse Travis. He's barely housebroken." Paviter smiled into Leigh's flushed face. "We keep him around because we worry that he won't be able to fend for himself in the wild."

"And because you like free haircuts."

"How you ever get laid remains God's own private mystery." Carter sighed with a despairing shake of his head.

"Offside." Leigh muttered under her breath and Quincy's head snapped to her, to ease any insult or discomfort his friends caused.

Carter also looked over at Leigh, then followed her line of sight. Turning to the screen in time to catch the sideline ref raise the flag, he countered, "No way."

Quincy hated Leigh's shrug, conceding to Carter's decision, as though she was long used to her knowledge being underestimated.

On the screen, the official blew the whistle and jogged over to confer with the sideline ref. Just as the replay started, Quincy said, "I'll put a bill on it."

"Are you high?" Carter demanded.

Paviter lunged for the remote and paused the game. "Me too."

"You want to put two bills on whether or not that call comes in as fair?" Travis was flummoxed.

"I want to put two bills on whether or not Carter has to admit Leigh was right." Quincy winked at her.

Carter sputtered his disbelief, "Be serious."

"He's right," Leigh added, "It's not that big of a deal."

"If it's not that big of a deal, then take the bet C Money." Paviter taunted.

"Please don't. I'm just saying sports words." She pleaded with them to stand down.

Quincy leaned close and said in a low voice, "What are you doing?"

"I…"

Holding her gaze, he waited for her answer. He had no idea how many times she put on this farce, chose to make herself small and downplay her accomplishments, but he'd be damned if she did it here with these knuckleheads. Leigh knew more about baseball than anyone he'd ever met. They'd eaten all manner of takeout in front of almost every major sport, a fun scheduling quirk of October, and she was knowledgeable about other sports, too. Quincy dared her to look away.

He called out to the room, "Double or nothing."

"Quincy!" She hissed her scold but did not blink.

"I'm willing to bet on you, Peaches. Why aren't you?"

He stared down into her dark eyes and watched as she gnawed on her lip, grappling with her various responses. He waited, unconcerned with the commotion his friends were making, for Leigh to decide how this would go. Quincy was rewarded with the smallest quirk of her lips.

Still looking at him, Leigh announced, "Number 7 leaned out from behind the defender before his striker passed the ball."

Paviter restarted the game and, just as Leigh said, Number 7 was called offside.

If they were noisy before, Quincy's three friends broke into an all-out fracas. Leigh stood in stunned amazement at how physical they got with each other. The pushing and shoving and name calling must have seemed completely out of line with their surroundings and attire.

Carter broke free of their hold and straightened himself. Facing Leigh with a forced dignity, considering she just watched him get jumped by his friends, he said, "I'm not paying these assholes shit. You, however, are welcome to kick it any time. Anyone who knows the offside rule enough to call it in real time is aces in my book."

Leigh gave a small, gracious bow and stepped aside so Carter could pass.

While Paviter and Travis got momentarily sucked into the game, Quincy checked in with Leigh, "You good?"

"Are you always this unruly?"

Quincy's answering chuckle was soft and light, "Boys will be boys. You have brothers, you know how it goes."

"Sidney is ten years older than Otis and neither of them are related to Julian. I do not know 'how it goes'." She laughed with a small shake of her head.

People started to spill in from all sides.

"Come on," Quincy nudged her with his shoulder, "Let's do a lap."

At the bar cart, Quincy fixed himself a rye and ginger and poured Leigh a glass of rose. He caught her sly look at his use of glassware when everyone else was using plastic.

They took advantage of the empty balcony and enjoyed the night air. The breeze managed to be cool and refreshing and the familiar sound of traffic was a pleasant bit of white noise at this distance. There were a few stars visible but with the amount of light pollution they didn't put too much effort in the task. Mostly, they took in the city's bustle. This close to Hallowe'en, the city's historically queer neighborhood was already showing out which made for excellent people watching.

Quincy looked over at Leigh's soft laughter. He hoped she was having a good time. This was their first outing together—taking their friendship to the streets, so to speak—and he wanted it to go well. And while he understood that presenting his friends together in one large group might be overwhelming, and might also, frankly, vindicate her belief that their age was an obstacle preventing them from being more than friends, nothing would make him happier than being able to bring her into the fold.

For one, hanging with Leigh was fun and he legitimately enjoyed himself when they were together. Moreover, his limited free time would be vastly improved if he could spend the occasional evening with both groups. The idea of Leigh and Carter vibing on the couch with a six-pack and some takeout made him smile.

"What are you smiling about?"

"I was thinking about you kicking Carter's ass at Madden."

Leigh's brows knit together in confusion. "I don't know how to play that game."

"Then we better start practicing."

She gave him a playful swat and tsked at him on her way back inside.

Quincy made his way through, introducing Leigh to people and stopping to catch up every few steps. As he expected, she was a curious, inviting, and keen conversationalist. Most of the people here were people he knew in one way or the other because of his decades long friendship with Carter and Travis. He'd be surprised if there was someone here from whom he had more than two degrees of separation.

"Bridge?"

Leigh's head spun, searching for the voice.

"Oh my god, Bridge! It is you."

A man scooped Leigh into his arms and spun her around. He was tall, east Asian, well built with dark, shiny, chin-length shampoo commercial hair, and a large dimple on his right cheek. He was very handsome, if you liked that sort of thing.

Quincy decidedly did not.

He was all but forgotten as the two caught up.

"Kyle!" Leigh giggled her delight as *Kyle* continued to hold her aloft.

"I just knew it was you. I've never had that coconut roll any-where else."

"Salara." She corrected in an absent way that made Quincy think they'd had this conversation numerous times before. Finally, Kyle set her down.

"Yes, salara," he snapped his finger with the reminder. "I live in the building!"

"You live in Toronto? Since when?"

"A while now. Travis and I are in the same pickup ball game at the gym. We figured out that we're also neighbors and..." He let the sentence finish itself. He looked around the room, searching, "Is Ava here?"

"No, I'm here with a friend. Do you know Quincy Temple?" Leigh used her upturned hand to indicate where he was standing. "Quincy, this is Kyle Kim. We grew up together."

Quincy wasn't proud of the added grip he used when he shook Kyle's hand.

"Bridge and Case were the only reason I made it through high school."

"Oh, I forgot that he tried to be Case because of Ma$e." Leigh groaned into her hands, "The 90s were not kind."

"They weren't. But you guys? You literally saved my life." Kyle added, taking Leigh's hand in his.

"Stop." Leigh demurred, leaning into his side, "We didn't do anything."

"Bridge and Case?" Quincy asked, trying his best to sound like he wasn't gritting his teeth.

"Leigh Bridger and Kingston "KC" Coffield. She was the quiet brainiac, he was the popular jock, and they ruled our school." Kyle explained to Quincy before turning to Leigh to confess, "It was surreal seeing KC at his locker that final semester without you. I mean, obviously you did what you had to."

"Yeah, it was pretty surreal for me too." Her small, dazed head shake told Quincy she was caught in a memory. Snapping out of it, Leigh asked "How's your mom? She still at the store corrupting the youth one Choco pie at a time?"

Once again, Quincy was shut out of their reminiscing and Kyle's single dimple was back on the scene.

"No, they sold a couple of years ago. She's retired which means I hear from her more than ever. Do you know she tuned in for every one of KC's games? Every single one. She bragged and bragged about her son and his friend, the pro athlete. That team photo from our yearbook has probably circulated throughout all of Korea."

Leigh threw her head back and laughed. For reasons that could only be chalked up to 'insidious ways to torment Quincy', Kyle was still holding Leigh's hand.

"Hey!" Kyle tugged on her arm in a scold that had no heat, "Where's your hometown pride?"

Leigh made a grand show of lowering her head in contrition, "You're right, my apologies."

Then they both collapsed on each other giggling.

Quincy could not see the humor. In any of it.

"You don't mind if I steal Bridge for a sec?" Kyle asked. Looking down at Leigh he explained, "There are some people I want you to meet."

This was his homeboy's place. Who on Earth could Kyle know that Quincy didn't? If there was someone here that Leigh needed to meet, it sure wasn't Kyle's job to do it. She was here with him, damnit.

Before the cloud of irrational thought enveloped him completely, Quincy rattled the ice in his glass, "I need a refill, anyway. I'll see you around."

"Don't go too far. You still owe me ice cream!" Leigh smiled at him over her shoulder as Kyle towed her through the party. He maintained eye contact until they were swallowed up by the crowd and Quincy was left alone with his empty glass.

He tried everything. Watching the game, catching up with friends, a puff or two on a spliff that was being passed around—he even checked his work emails. Nothing helped.

He couldn't stop watching them together.

Quincy wanted his better nature to prevail. He was an evolved man of the 21st Century. Goddamnit, he was a feminist! He knew Leigh didn't need to give him a reason as to why she wasn't interested, and he also knew the expression 'friend zone' was sexist bullshit. He didn't view his friendship with Leigh as a demotion in any way.

He knew all of this and yet he was trapped in a miserable spiral.

Reminding his lizard brain it was perfectly within Leigh's right to hold Kyle's hand if she wanted only worked long enough for Quincy to notice Kyle's hands on her waist and it'd start all over again. Reason had lost control of the ship and nothing he did got it back. By the end of the hour, he was convinced she and Kyle would date, get married, and have a slew of beautiful, bespectacled Blasian babies.

The final straw was watching Leigh raise on her tiptoes to whisper something in Kyle's ear. The way his hand splayed along the small of her back, protective and possessive, sent a hot, primitive spike of jealousy through Quincy he actually felt his lip curl into a snarl.

"Unclench, dude."

"It's not a good look." Paviter added to Carter's directive.

Quincy took a deep breath and held it for a count of three, then exhaled slowly.

Carter rolled his shoulders. "If shit's gonna kick off, then cool. Let's throw these hands, bro. I gotchu. I just think we need to be real clear about why we're planning to beat that guy's ass."

"At the very least you should be prepared for Travis to have an epic fit about it." Quincy wondered what it would be like for Paviter to just once have his heart rate raised by something other than film making.

Inasmuch as he knew his friends were teasing him, he also understood that they were ready to ride. The familiarity of their banter and unwavering support brought the layer of calm he'd failed to achieve on his own.

"I don't want to beat his ass," Quincy admitted on an exhale. Off Carter's look he amended, "Not really."

"Then why are in the corner grinding your molars to dust?" Paviter poked the side of Quincy's jaw for emphasis.

"Did I tell you I asked her out?" Their raised eyebrows said he'd forgot to share that particular tidbit. "Yo, honestly, I didn't even get around to asking her out. She shot me down before I even laced up. Said I was too young or she was too old. Whatever it was, she said she liked me but we could never happen."

Carter whistled long and low, "So she's out of your league on multiple levels."

"The fuck you mean 'multiple levels'?" Quincy glared at his friend.

"Were you really so pressed you didn't hear a word that Kyle guy said?" Carter asked, looking at his phone. "Her boyfriend, KC Coffield, was a top tier fielding catcher and might have reached HOF levels if he didn't blow out his knee in a highlight-reel level save. He also has a kid our age. I'm guessing she's the mama."

"What? How do you know that?" Quincy frowned his confusion before adding hotly, "Her son isn't our age."

Why did everyone keep insisting he and Langston were the same age? He was five years older than her son. It was practically a generational difference nowadays.

"Google is free, my man." Paviter was also looking at his phone. "Plus, dude basically spelled it out. Where's your head at?"

"Fuck, I don't know. He scooped her up and all I could see was every place his body touched hers. It's messing me up. She's not mine. I have no claim on her."

"But?" Paviter asked, encouraging him to finish his thought.

"But I want to go over there, rip his arms off, and beat him with them!"

Carter nodded thoughtfully. "An excellent way to highlight your maturity."

"Look at them." Quincy ignored the jibe and focused on his immediate problem. "That is Leigh with a man her own age. Would I really look so different?"

They stood together, watching.

"Does it matter?" Paviter asked, his hand clapped on Quincy's shoulder. "You're not together."

Chapter 12

A T THE EXACT TWO-HOUR mark, fifteen minutes after Paviter and Carter left him stewing in the corner, Quincy made his way to Leigh so they could leave. She readily said her goodbyes and followed him out into the cool night air. There was an itch in his brain and staying at the party only made it worse. He had to get his evening with Leigh back on track and get his head back in the game.

Quincy eased Leigh to his side as they wandered down Church Street. It was still early by nightlife standards and there were plenty of people milling about, lined up in front of bars, leaning on walls smoking, or generally making merriment in small clumps. Paviter's words rattled around in his head. You're not together.

You're not together.

They weren't together. It was a simple statement of fact.

If he needed to put a sticky note on every surface so he could be reminded of it, he would.

"Do you have a go to flavor?" Leigh asked, smoothly stepping around a group of rowdy college kids while discreetly slipping a toonie to a young panhandler.

"I mean, there are always the faithful standards; mint chocolate chip, cookies n cream, butterscotch ripple—"

"I hardly think those are standard."

Quincy almost recoiled at her interruption. "Of course they are!"

"The Neapolitan three are standard."

Quincy balked, "How do you figure?"

"Because chocolate, strawberry, and vanilla make the foundation for all the other flavors. Obviously."

He gave her a look of bald disbelief and continued as though she hadn't spoken. "They have a Flavor of the Day that's always interesting... it's what I normally get."

"Care to make it interesting?" She stuck her hand out and he took it, not caring what he was agreeing to when the opportunity to touch her freely had presented itself. "Just watch. I'll make you eat your words!"

Quincy enjoyed this playful, competitive side of Leigh. She was always ready to rise to a challenge. Whether it was concocting unlikely flavor combinations, putting the right book in a reader's hands, or beating a difficult level on a game, quiet and unassuming Leigh was a fierce competitor. Hell, Carter was four bills lighter because of it. Somehow, it didn't apply to the way she viewed herself but Quincy would take what he could for the moment.

"Did you have a good time? You handled the Grant brothers well."

"There was nothing to handle. Families are complicated—I know that better than anybody."

"Most people ask them a lot of bullshit questions. I've known Carter since we were in guardian swim classes together so I always knew he had a white dad. Having a white brother wasn't a huge leap from there, y'know?"

Leigh's voice held a hint of amusement. "People spend years at school studying philosophy to master theories like Occam's Razor when little kids have it already mastered."

"If you think that's a thought experiment, then wait until you meet William. He's half Chinese Chinese and half Chinese Guyanese and there's no way to know which parent is which until they open their mouths."

"Wait, so you know actual Guyanese people and still brought that food to my home?"

Quincy groaned his laughter. "How did I know you'd say that?"

"Because what else would I say?"

"Man," he heaved the word on a hard done by sigh. He played up his despair at the sound of Leigh's delighted laughter, stooping his shoulders and dragging his feet for a couple steps. He straightened himself as they crossed at the traffic light. The ice cream place was on the next block and it seemed to have a crowd out front. Strange.

"So it was you, Carter, Travis, Paviter, and William terrorizing the denizens of Markham?"

He smiled down into her bright eyes. He missed her glasses and the adorable way she wrinkled her nose to stop them from falling. "And Yemi. Together we're like the Olympic rings, representing four of the five habitable continents. We were in the streets from sunup to sundown. You know how it is to grow up in a small town."

"There is no way you're comparing our two situations, Quincy! There were about five thousand people in St. Mary's when I lived there, I don't even know if it qualified as a town back then! You only had to drive 10 minutes south to cross Steeles and be in Toronto. When I was growing up, people had serious apprehension about driving the 401! Almost *no one* travelled to Toronto unless they were seeing a game or going to the airport or something intentional like that."

Quincy pulled himself up to his full height, "I will not stand for this erasure. Do not diminish my idyllic, small town—"

"Suburban." Leigh interjected, haughtily.

"*Small town* upbringing just because we didn't hang out at a swimming hole."

"Shows how much you know. It's called The Quarry and the Thames River runs right passed it!"

It took Quincy a moment to realize she wasn't joking before his laughter erupted, loud and uncontrolled. He worked at calming himself but Leigh's nose, tipped dramatically in the air, made the task difficult.

They stepped up to the brightly lit shop and formed the line. While they waited, he told her about his life growing up with the mandem, bonding over the shared experience of being different in a way they each related with intrinsically. He explained how each household became its own base of operations. The Grant house, for example, had the most up-to-date technology. Paviter's house, with Mom and Pop Dhillon's large family always around, was the easiest to disappear in. William's house had the highest concentration of snacks and, when they were older, the most extensive bar from which to skim a little from the top. Yemi's African parents were both engineers so there were always puzzles and games and half-built automatons laying around.

"And your house?"

Quincy blanched a little. He could look back on it now with the distance of wisdom and see that his strict, borderline sterile, home wasn't all doom and gloom and Leona Temple added as much value to those boys' lives as Yvette Grant or Folasade Aluko had. But the residual embarrassment of not having a house conducive to fun, being the place where manners and propriety ruled above all else, still made him cringe.

"We didn't hang out at my place as much. Leona Temple believes children should be seen and not heard. A passel of ten-year-old boys make a lot of noise." He took a fortifying breath and continued, "In the end, the mandem liked coming over because, even with all the rules, they enjoyed being treated like grown ups—drinking out of crystal water glasses and using cloth napkins and such. When it came time to date, we were leagues ahead of our peers."

Quincy laughed to himself remembering how impressed his friends' parents had been with the changes in their ruffians. The difference being, they could put the comportment lessons away whenever they wanted. He and Miles lived that way all the time.

"A cadre of little gentlemen. You must have been adorable."

"We did alright."

"I hope all those fancy table manners will make eating your words easier." She nudged his side with her elbow, gesturing to the placard announcing the flavor of the day: Strawberry Cheesecake. Quincy groaned and hung his head. Driving her point home, Leigh added, "A vanilla base for a strawberry flavored confection. An unheard of .667 batting average!"

Quincy already knew Leigh was as graceless a winner as she was a loser. He stepped up to place his order and prepared for the inevitable gloating.

It was worse than he expected and he'd been ready for the worst. Leigh ordered a double scoop in a cup and then sweetly asked if it was possible to make Neapolitan for her. The young south-Asian woman eagerly agreed and presented Leigh with a perfect trio of chocolate, strawberry, and vanilla. Quincy barely suppressed his eye-roll when she silently but dramatically held her cup aloft, admiring it from different angles.

Choosing a table in the empty seating area, Leigh picked up their conversation where they'd left off. "I only have two friends to keep up with and it exhausts me. I don't know how you do it."

"Only two?"

"Yeah. I met Desiree in night school over twenty years ago and Junior on a fan forum message board about ten years ago."

"More mushroom propaganda?" He teased.

"No!" She screwed up her face in what he assumed was menace but was too adorable to take as any real threat. "For your information, it was a Starfleet Captain post. We both were very vocal about Captain Benjamin Sisko. Junior, because she is pro-Black, pro-Latine at all times, and me because he legitimately is an excellent Captain." He gave her a knowing look and she admitted, "And because he's Black."

"And Ava?"

"My sister, but fine. Three, technically."

He thought about her son's father cheesing in his Day One sash in the Dottie's Darlings photo. "What about KC? And dude from the spot next door?"

"Alright, five. I have five friends."

"And so do I! See? Another thing we have in common." Before he could stop himself, he added, "Our people even overlap, so you can keep all that noise about not fitting in."

"You mean Kyle? That was a huge surprise but I'd hardly consider him 'my people' anymore. It was good to see him, though. I'm so happy he's happy."

"What's the story there?" In an attempt at seeming merely casually interested, Quincy put a scoop of ice-cream in his mouth and waited for her to continue.

"The Kims were one of the minority families I mentioned. They owned the convenience store. Yes, I know." She said, staving off any commentary he might've made about the popular television show. "He and KC were buds because they were on a lot of the same teams—the two non-white jocks in a sea of Billys and Tommys—which meant Kyle and I were buds, too. Kyle was handsome and stylish in a way that didn't quite fit in 1990s small town Ontario."

"How can you be 'problematically stylish'?"

"Back then we used 'metrosexual' as a benign insult. I don't know what to tell you."

He couldn't help but laugh. Those weird generational memes always seemed to leave hers out of the equation. Some said it's because the Gen X kids were too feral to lob critique back and forth without drawing proverbial blood, that they had no concept of scale when challenged. He'd never really believed all the boogeyman whispers surrounding them but then something like this would happen, he'd be told that stylishness was grounds for insult, and he'd be forced to reconsider.

Leigh put her cup on the table and took a sip of water. "Kyle also didn't have a girlfriend, though it wasn't for lack of options. His athleticism made him an acceptable choice when he would have otherwise been seen as 'foreign' and 'weird'. But 'athlete' could only do so much and it wasn't long before 'gay' started being whispered behind his back. Even with being a star baseball player in a town where baseball is life, Kyle started to feel the slights. KC used his social capital to shield him as best he could but you know how it goes."

Tale as old as time, Quincy thought. He was willing to bet excellent money Kyle's foray into popularity via sport meant he was supposed to be grateful the Ashleys and Amandas were willing to date him. By refusing them, they'd been insulted. Yet had he attempted to approach one of those girls without the cover of popularity, as entomology club president or a cellist, they would have been equally insulted. The goalposts were always moving for marginalized people.

"At the same time, Ava—skinny, gap-toothed, nerdy—also didn't show any interest in dating. She was safe from any overt mistreatment by virtue of being my sister but Kyle's thing showed me it was only a matter of time. Since she was always with us when we hung out, it made sense for them to be a couple. So KC and I nudged them together. They genuinely liked each other, had lots of comic book stuff in common, and Mrs. Kim was only too happy to have the rapt attention of fourteen-year-old Ava who has always been willing to eat whatever was put in front of her." Leigh picked her ice-cream back up and put a spoonful in her mouth. Quincy did everything he could to prevent the sight from affecting him while still giving Leigh his full attention. She continued, "Anyway, long story short: turns out Kyle really was gay, even though we didn't know it back then, and my sister, who is also queer, though we didn't know it back then, was his beard."

"Your sister is queer?" Quincy wasn't sure why he asked the question. It didn't matter and it wasn't any of his business. It just surprised him to hear Leigh use 'queer', specifically.

"Pretty much everyone in my life is. I'm the token hetero. I'm the token everything, really."

"You're the token…" Quincy realized how his question might land so he chose to pivot mid-sentence. "You drive a Subaru."

Leigh's laughter rang out through the brightly lit space. "My 2008 Impreza was the smallest all-wheel drive on the market at the time. Do you know it's cheaper to insure vehicles with symmetrical full-time AWD? Still. Reliable, well made motor vehicles aside, I'm very much the only straight person in my immediate circle."

Quincy's face easily telegraphed his confusion, prompting Leigh to continue, "Yes, even KC. He always said that if he ever met a guy that made his thing jump," she stumbled adorably around the word *thing*, clearly a euphemism for 'dick', and Quincy suppressed a laugh, "he'd be a fool to not see where it led. To my knowledge, he's yet to meet said man but his openness to the possibility was a constant source of my teenaged anxiety."

His mouth tipped downward, telegraphing the censure in his tone. "You're not telling me you think bisexual people are more promiscuous, because..."

"No! No, I don't. I'm talking about a painfully average girl dating the star athlete already having to compete for his time with school, home, and the team worrying about adding the other fifty percent of the population as possible objects of his desire. That girl wanted to go to the Fair at the Flats with her boyfriend. She wasn't concerned with the greater LGBT community, only keeping the guy she never thought would like her back in that way."

"Painfully average?" Quincy wasn't sure how to respectfully articulate 'unless pregnancy gave you that tight little body and those kissable lips I'd happily put to good use, you were anything but average back then' but he was going to give it a try. She must have seen it on his face because she immediately held up her hands.

"I promise I'm not fishing for compliments. I've always been average and it's okay. Junior and Desiree balance me. Like, I'm not tall, I'm not short. I'm not sleek curves or built like a fertility goddess but I'm not skinny, either. I didn't grow up wealthy but we weren't impoverished. My hair isn't long but it isn't short nor is it wildly curly or bone straight. My complexion isn't dark, it isn't light. My voice isn't deep and raspy but it isn't soft and girly. I don't have a single distinguishing feature outside of my glasses. I'm just... average." Her explanation was punctuated with a little shrug.

"That is a staggeringly small sample size and a gross oversimplification."

Quincy was almost speechless. The bit upstairs with Carter and the offside call wasn't for show. Leigh had clearly spent years making herself small. He didn't know how she managed it. To him, she was the focal point in any room.

Quincy was literally and figuratively incapable of making himself small. So he leaned into it. *Look at me*, his whole persona said, *I'm so conspicuous, what could I possibly have to hide?* What he focused on instead was making his size palatable. Approachable. His goals were made attainable by sheer force of his will, powered by his charm and impeccable manners.

He opened his mouth to say as much, to rail against her tragic self-perception but she cut him off.

"Be that as it may," her eyes glinted with a mischief he'd come to recognize, "doesn't change the fact you owe this average St. Mary's girl a boon."

"A what?" He asked, laughing at her word choice.

His shoulders continued to shake as she explained herself, then his eyes teared up at her indignation when he explained that he'd eaten his words, i.e. the ice cream, thereby fulfilling the terms of the wager. The snorting guffaw couldn't be helped—it was all he could do to keep from falling out of his seat—at her taunt that he "didn't strike her as a man who welched" and insisted he owed her an unnamed favor, appropriate to the win.

They'd continued arguing and haggling this way, Leigh using ever more archaic words as he failed to keep his composure, while they gathered their things, put their trash in the bin, exited the shop, and stood at the curb waiting for her rideshare.

When the Corolla pulled up, she gave his arm a quick squeeze. "Thanks for inviting me tonight. It was fun."

"Glad to hear it. And, don't forget, you need to start your Madden training. I'll bring it by for you to start practicing."

She gave him a playful eye roll and got in the car, waving at him until the driver turned onto Yonge Street and drove her out of sight.

He flexed his bicep where she'd hugged him, committing the heat and pressure of her touch to memory. If nothing else came from this friendship, Quincy vowed to himself that he was going to get Leigh to stop making herself small.

Like a protostar in need of a bit of fusion to keep from collapsing under the weight of its own gravity, Leigh needed help realizing she was the brightest star in a constellation of stars. He'd be that for her. It was the very least he could do.

Chapter 13

L EIGH HAD BARELY SNAPPED her seatbelt on before a call came ringing through Quincy's car speakers. The display screen read Alice Vargas.

They were leaving Carter's place. He and Yemi, who Quincy explained was back in town after being away on assignment for three months, thus making him the perfect roommate, were beta testing his newest video game and invited Quincy to come through. He'd asked Leigh if she was interested and three hours and a long exit survey later, they were finally leaving.

She wasn't sure she'd be able to maintain these outings in her regular routine. And with the clocks turned back an hour, the sky was midnight dark at 5pm. It was wreaking havoc on her sleep cycle though she'd be the first to admit she was having fun.

"Wha gwan?" Quincy's rumbly voice filled his ride.

"No one answered my text. Carter said you were there gaming. I need to find an event space, like, yesterday." The light feminine voice started to rise at the end of each sentence until Leigh guessed she was on the verge of hysteria. "My cranky A-list client is ruining my life."

"I don't have access to event spaces, Vargas. What did Pav say? Isn't his sister in events?"

"Do you honestly think I haven't already reached out to Gurveer?"

"Yo!" Quincy scolded. Leigh had never heard Quincy use that tone before though she did think it was warranted. The woman was rather sharp for someone asking for help.

She let out a deep, weary sigh. "Sorry, Q. I'm spun out. The publicist he normally works with, the one who knew how to manage him, retired forever ago and somehow I'm supposed to figure it out. He's said no to literally everything and my deadline is immovable. If he goes back to his secret cabin in the Bruce Peninsula before I pull this off, who knows if he'll ever come back to Toronto. I cannot afford to blow it."

"Hang on."

Quincy pulled his phone out his pocket and tilted the screen for Leigh to read along.

I need a space for an author to sign some books in two weeks. Any ideas? Desperate.

He looked at Leigh with a quirked brow. He was clearly remembering the pandemonium of her shop when Hilary did her Live. Since he hadn't indicated that she was in the car with him, she mouthed *I guess* with wide eyes. She'd done some events for local authors over the years and could certainly accommodate a simple signing.

"I might have a solution. It's a bookstore in Leslieville. Small, neighbourhood spot. I'll send you the deets."

"Ohmygodthankyou!" The woman's voice came out in a rush of breath. "At this rate, he'll be signing in a food court. I'm willing to consider anything."

"I'll link you with the owner once you send over the particulars."

"Sent!"

She meant it literally because Quincy's phone lit up with the email notification.

"Aight, lemme check it out and I'll holler back."

He disconnected the call and turned to face her fully. "My homie is in a bind but you don't have to go through with this if you don't want to. Vargas will figure it out, she always does."

"It's signing some books, right? How complicated can it be?"

Quincy scrolled through his phone to open the email. "We're about to find out."

LEIGH CHECKED HER WATCH FOR what felt like the fiftieth time. Quincy was supposed to be here so that when Alice and Franklin Thorne arrived, he could do the introductions. She wasn't particularly worried about managing this meeting on her own, per se. It was only that she wasn't exactly sure what to expect, overall.

Everyone with even a cursory relationship to publishing knew the story of Franklin Thorne. He was a prolific writer of the Skip Whelan series—the kind of brooding, action heroes that got turned into summer blockbusters. If he hadn't famously refused every offer to release the rights of those books, Leigh was sure people would be lining up to see Skip Whelan 7: More Explodier come Labor Day.

What people didn't know was if he would ever write again. After the death of his wife and son, the man all but disappeared. It was rumoured that he'd adopted his wife's country of birth and had hidden away in the lakeside village of Pine Harbour, though no one could prove it. Until this year, when he'd allegedly sent a full manuscript to his unsuspecting publishers, he'd basically been written off as a lost cause.

She really wished she'd known it was him before she'd agreed to do this.

When had she become so foot-loose and fancy-free? It wasn't too long ago that such a request would have required a fully out-lined proposal and two weeks for Leigh to fret about it. Now? A text message and a vague date and she'd committed to this lunacy.

Well, not really committed. This was a walk through to see if Franklin would even condescend to having his signing at her establishment. According to Quincy, the publisher wanted to do a full press launch of this book. Franklin had refused any press at all. They'd haggled back and forth until he'd agreed to a one time, no interviews, still photography only signing of the promotional, pre-order copies. Alice's problem was Franklin had turned his nose up at every venue suggested.

Taking another look at her neat, tidy space, Leigh released a slow exhale. There were a few people milling through the shelves and a couple in the cafe section. It was otherwise quiet and inviting. She hoped.

She looked over at the sound of the door's tinkling bell and saw Quincy holding it open to a young woman of medium height and build, followed by none other than Franklin Thorne. He was a tall, thin white man, with a craggy, sun-kissed face that suggested days on end spent wandering outside. All three wore drastically different takes on 'winter outerwear' with Quincy in a fur lined leather bomber, Alice in a fancy looking knee length puffer, and Franklin in an olive-green wool pea coat.

"Hello, welcome to Peach's Books and Bakeshop." Leigh smiled her brightest customer service smile.

Quincy extended a hand, directing them towards her, "This is Leigh Bridger, owner and operator."

"Hi. Alice." She pronounced it Ah-LEE-see. She was polished in a way that suggested effort and had the generic 'tanned' complexion that could either be from her parents or a monthly visit to a salon. Her long, dark hair was thick and hinted at a natural curl she militantly controlled. Her wide smile did not reach her eyes nor did she extend her hand. "This is best-selling author, Franklin Thorne."

He smiled politely, "Frank. Nice to meet you."

Leigh watched as he took a slow spin, cataloging the space. "As you can see, there's an area that can be made as open or sectioned off as you choose and we can customize it with any posters et cetera if you wish."

He wordlessly stepped into the stacks, clearly taking note of their labels. Making his way to Action/Adventure, Franklin ran a lazy finger over the spines as he noted the authors in stock. "You only carry one of my books." It came out as a sentence but Leigh could hear the underlying *'why would I sign somewhere that doesn't carry my titles?'*

She made her way over to where he stood. "This is a romance only bookstore, Mr. Thorne."

"Frank." He interrupted Leigh, who now had his full attention.

"Frank," she amended, "As much as I enjoy your series—I like to live vicariously as a beleaguered soldier of fortune as much as anyone—men's fiction doesn't fit my theme."

"Men's fiction." He said it slowly, rolled it around his mouth like a full-bodied Malbec, as though it had only now occurred to him his books might warrant such a designation.

"You know, your Jacks Reacher and Ryan, Alex Crosses, Skip Whelans and other similar Lone Rebels with A Cause."

"Touche." He allowed.

"Genre fiction endures because it sticks to their conventions. Readers know that a Murder Mystery will be solved, a Fantasy heroine will forge ahead against all odds with the help of a ragtag group of found family, and they know that the hero in Men's Fiction will ride off in the sunset, alone, after saving the day. Romance's genre conventions are no different. Here, Happily Ever After is the promise delivered—in all its permutations. Book Twelve is the only one of your books that meets the requirement."

Franklin Thorne might have cut a fearsome figure in board-rooms, but at this moment Leigh couldn't help but think he was pleasantly surprised by this turn through the stacks.

"That requirement being Happily Ever After."

"Or Happy for Now. The infinitely patient and stalwart nurse patches him up and sends him back into the fray again and again. At the end of book 12, Skip stays. He chooses her and he stays. So, even though I've read every single one of them, twelve is the only one I can sell."

Franklin considered her words and nodded to himself as he roamed further into the store. Turning to see Quincy and Alice still at the counter where she left them, Leigh followed him.

"If I'm understanding correctly," he was taking in the labels, "You're presupposing that Romance can be anything so long as it satisfies the convention."

From someone else, she might have taken his words as disdain. Somehow, she wasn't getting a disagreement but an earnest wish to engage. It didn't surprise her that he'd been a titan of publishing without ever once having considered Romance as a genre. Most people didn't pay attention to things that didn't directly affect them and the characteristics of Romance absolutely did not need to factor in Franklin Thorne's day. Watching him absorb this in-formation, poking at the edges as though testing its boundaries, tickled her.

"Not presupposing. Asserting." They'd stopped in front of the mythology section. "There are hundreds of myth retellings. Any-one with even a passing understanding knows few of any culture's gods were a sane group of beings. Even at their most benevolent, gods are petty and cruel and jealous. Yet, we have turned those tales into sweeping tales of love and devotion—Hades and Persephone, Osiris and Isis—that keep the essence of the tale while modernizing it." Pulling a title from the shelf, she offered it to Franklin with a hint of challenge on her face. "Here is a book of short stories. Each a retelling of various ancient myths and folklores. Give it a try."

"I think I will." The smile he gave as he tucked the book under his arm must have been a relic from his wild bachelor days as even he seemed surprised to find it there on his face.

"If you don't mind my asking, Frank—why put yourself through any of this? You're obviously not interested in just doing the circuit and smiling for the cameras—why not write a couple of articles for promo, schedule a few social media posts, before signing the books and going back to your sanctuary?"

They'd been slowly making their way back to the front of the shop where Alice and Quincy waited. In the short time they'd spent together, Leigh formed a depth of emotion for this reclusive man based on nothing more than his willingness to accept that books can serve many masters simultaneously.

"No one has ever called it that. In all these years." His voice was thick. "I know what they say about me. I do my best to block it out, but I know. This book is the first thing that felt remotely close to stepping back into my old life and I don't know if I'm ready for normal. I don't know if I want it."

She knew exactly what he meant. If there was a Before, where he was an author who also was a husband and father, then the After—where the hole existed, would always exist—could not be normalised by behaviours of Before. He'd quit writing to maintain the distinction and now he worried the barrier would crumble.

Leigh couldn't help herself, she put her hand on his bicep hoping to provide a small measure of comfort, "It will never be normal again, Frank. That's just the truth."

He took a deep, ragged breath and nodded.

"Another truth?" She waited for him to nod before she continued, "You completed this new manuscript, yes, but you didn't have to submit it. You could have chalked it up to an exercise or a bit of indulgent folly. You can be whatever version of The Author Franklin Thorne you need. It's Frank who gets to decide."

His gaze held hers, a wordless conversation bouncing between his hazel eyes and her chocolate ones. Leigh's loss, over thirty years gone, changed the entire trajectory of her life. She hoped he found the understanding and compassion she felt, as well as the misery of a shared membership to unequaled tragedy.

"I'm so very pleased to have met you, Leigh Bridger."

"Likewise, Frank Thorne."

***

"How did you even find this place?" Alice pitched her voice so only Quincy could hear.

Something in her tone led him to believe this wasn't the first time she'd spoken to him. Dragging his attention away from Leigh, he looked down into Alice's keen gaze. "Miles ordered a book from here—maybe three months ago?—and he asked me to pick it up."

He could still remember walking into the shop that long ago night, seeing Leigh for the first time, the way she literally stole focus from everything happening around them. It was hard to believe sometimes, but it was still one of the happiest accidents of his life.

"And that was enough for you to ask this woman to host an event here? Is she that hard up for business?"

Quincy was used to Alice's sharp edges. She could be sweet and gentle when she wanted. Alice's problem was that she so rarely wanted to display softness, when it did emerge it was even more frightening than her brutality.

"Show me a business that isn't open to diversifying."

Alice scoffed and took another calculating glance at the space. "Is it a bakery that sells books or a bookstore that sells cake?"

"It's both," Quincy chuckled softly as he gave the answer he'd received when he'd asked the same question.

"Franklin seems satisfied, which is all that matters to me. I needed to have all the particulars nailed down last week. This whole thing is going to be a scramble and you know how I hate that."

"Don't worry. Leigh knows what's up."

"She can dial it back a bit. Franklin hasn't gone on so much as a date since his wife and son died eight years ago."

Quincy looked over to see Leigh and Franklin, heads together, in an intense conversation. She put her hand on his bicep and gave an encouraging squeeze and received a circular back rub in return. It looked reasonably platonic from where he was standing. Even so, he couldn't help but notice how good they looked together—mature, dignified, and literary.

"There probably aren't that many eligible men in her age bracket, so I can see why she thought she'd shoot her shot."

He laughed at that. Franklin was a handsome enough man but had lived a notoriously hard life before finding love and settling down only to lose her and his tween son to a drunk driver's recklessness. He carried every one of his fifty-eight years for all to see whereas Leigh looked only slightly older than Alice. "You're a trip."

"Whatever." Alice rolled her eyes then turned to face him more fully, her entire demeanor warmer and more inviting. "What are you up to later? Wanna come over for a bit? It's been a while."

He knew exactly what she was inviting him over for. There was no need to ask who else would be there. They'd danced to this tune for years.

"Nah," he said. Pulling his attention away from Leigh he looked down into her now shrewd gaze, he answered in the code they'd developed, "I'm busy."

Alice's eyes widened with a mix of surprise and disappointment, then narrowed dangerously. Quincy took in her slight sneer as she threw a dismissive glance at Leigh over her shoulder. "You can't be serious. Her?"

Alice might've made a comment here or there but she knew better than to openly criticize any woman Quincy had been involved with over the years. This edict was especially true for Leigh, a woman he respected and admired and didn't want to expose to any of Alice's scorn.

"Watch it." Quincy's voice was no less severe for its quiet. "She's a friend. A fact you'd do well to remember since she's here saving your ass."

Before Alice could respond, Franklin called over to her without breaking eye contact with Leigh "This will do nicely, Ms. Vargas."

Quincy smiled at her with all his teeth and gloated, "What did I tell you?"

Ignoring him, she went over to her client. He followed a couple steps behind.

"I'm glad to hear it," Alice cooed at Franklin. Turning to Leigh, she announced with a noticeable frostiness, "We'll have someone contact you with the specs and particulars."

"No need. Ms. Bridger and I have it sorted out. All you need to do is make sure the books arrive."

Leigh demurred, "I'm sure the publisher's guidelines are needed."

"Nonsense! It's a table and some pens." Franklin balked. He gave Leigh a warm smile and winked, "We can leave that in your capable hands."

It was only because Quincy knew her so well that he recognized Alice's astonishment. It wasn't often that she was caught out that way. A swell of pride surged in his chest for Leigh. He knew that she was special. Seeing the notoriously curmudgeonly author eating out of her hands only cemented his already high opinion of Leigh.

"We'll be in touch," Alice said to Leigh, barely concealing the disdain in her voice. "Until next week."

Chapter 14

QUINCY WAS SURE IT was a mistake to bring Travis to the shop, but he wanted to see Leigh for a minute before heading to his brother's. Stopping by for some snacks was the perfect excuse.

When they entered, neither Leigh nor Luc were around. Instead, he found two of the sirens from the very first night behind the counter. He took a look around the space to be sure. A middle-aged Asian woman was browsing the shelves and a dark-haired man about his age was reading something intently on his tablet with a coffee at the table closest to the door. Quincy couldn't help but notice the man's impressive bone structure.

"Shit, Q. I see why you do so much 'remote work' from a bakery in Leslieville." Travis had never shown any regard for the concept of the inside voice and the two women looked up at his proclamation. "I can't believe Vargas agreed to have her work thing here."

Travis' meaning was clear. No matter how many times she'd been proven wrong, Alice treated unknown women with *Highlander* rules—there could be only one. Whether it was warranted or not, Alice felt threatened by anyone with the capacity to pull focus from her.

These two women were exceptionally 'threatening'.

He hadn't the patience to explain to Travis that neither woman worked here and this was the first time he'd seen them in months, not that his friend would have listened. Travis was just as taken with them as he'd been that long ago night. All he could do now was hope his friend wouldn't embarrass himself.

"Well, well," the tall siren smiled, "look who it is."

The full-figured siren gave him a thorough perusal, "Mr. Dark and Lovely. Welcome back."

"It's very inconsiderate of you to show up just as I'm about to leave. I don't know how I feel about it." The flirty pout the tall one leveled almost had him promising any manner of ways to make it up to her.

The full-figured siren gave her a playful shove, "Don't worry, I'll take good care of him while you're gone."

Thinking back to Luc's description, Quincy took a chance. "Junior and Desiree, right? How's things?"

Junior brightened, "I see you've done your homework. I like it when a man is prepared."

"Yes, I find it very pleasing." Desiree added.

"What a coincidence as I too like to keep women pleased." Travis leaned on the counter between them. "Forgive my friend's appalling manners. I'm Travis."

Desiree and Junior shared a look.

Quincy jumped in before Travis made things worse. "Pay him no mind. We're only passing through to pick up some snacks before heading to my brother's."

"The soldier." Junior's recall of their exchange made him wonder if he hadn't made a bigger impression than Leigh had let on.

The woman approached the counter with three books. Junior smiled at her and gestured to the cash register "I can help you over here."

"You said you were picking up some snacks? What can I get you?" Desiree looked to Quincy for an answer.

"Is there maybe a secret menu I can order from? Maybe something... sweet but salty?" The look Travis gave her wasn't quite a leer but they were in the same family. Second cousins, perhaps. He was playing with fire and Quincy wanted nothing more than to haul his friend out of there. Would it add fuel to the fire? Quincy had often left Travis to crash and burn as he so chose but these were Leigh's ride or dies. Where did his responsibility for their relationship begin and his to Travis end?

"There is no menu. What you see here," Desiree indicated the display case, "is exactly what we have available."

"Three quiches, the assorted cookie sampler, and uhh," Quincy looked at the case thinking of what Miles would most enjoy, "the plain jelly donut."

Travis leaned on the counter and added in a laughable attempt at suave, "And maybe throw them digits in. We can discuss our tastes and other delights."

"What'chu know about it?" Desiree laughed as though Travis were a toddler trying to grasp quantum mechanics.

Undeterred, Travis insisted, "I know a gorgeous woman when I see one. And I know I'd like to see her again."

The bell over the door signaled that the woman had left with her purchases leaving only the dark-haired man sitting at the table. He had earbuds in and didn't seem to pay them any attention.

"You ever been with a fat girl?" Desiree asked with narrowed eyes. "This is a lot of body to handle. It'll change your life." Desiree winked at Quincy, conscripting him in a tacit declaration of how good fat people fucked.

He could only tilt his head in acceptance. He'd been bigger than most adults since grade seven and it didn't effect his game in any way.

Junior made her way back to them and put a hand on Desiree's hip, giving her a playful jiggle. "Mmm… look at how all of that *moves*."

"I've got big hands for you to fill any way you want." Travis placed his hands palms up, fingers spread wide, on the counter. "Go ahead and ruin me."

"It's always the muscle-y ones." Junior shook her head with mild amusement.

"Girl, I can't keep those gym rats off me. There was this one—wore me out holding my stomach like a lifeguard buoy."

Junior's brow furrowed as she tried to make sense of Desiree's words. Stepping in front of her, putting her back to Junior's front, Desiree said "Instead of like this or like this," she leaned forward and placed Junior's hands both on her hips and then on her lower back, "he held me like this." Desiree pulled Junior's hands around her side so that Junior was gripping the roll of her belly.

Simulating the motion, Junior commented, "Seems like it would leave bruises."

"You'd think," Desiree agreed, launching into the particulars.

Quincy and Travis were spellbound as they watched the two sirens have a sterile conversation about sexual positions and proclivities. Desiree, at one point, had spread her hands around Junior's ribcage and asked if it was one of hers. Junior promptly unbuttoned her sweater so Desiree could see whatever she was wearing underneath. Desiree proceeded to run her hands under Junior's clothes while asking her about fit and coverage and comfort.

"No," Junior mused, "this one is definitely better."

There was nothing remotely sexual about their interaction. They could have been discussing stretches to improve their posture for all the difference it made to the casual way they touched each other. They certainly weren't trying to be provocative—Junior's back had been to them, mostly blocking Desiree from view the entire time. It was simply the level of closeness, the intimacy, they shared.

One thing was for certain, these women kept nothing from each other. If there was one small upside to his relationship with Leigh remaining platonic, this was it. Quincy was willing to lay good money on the very real possibility either of these women would be able to pick his dick out of a lineup if he and Leigh ever took it there.

"Ladies, if the floor is open to suggestions..." Travis straightened, "I'd be more than happy to contribute."

Junior turned to face them and Desiree blinked as though she'd forgot he and Travis were there. Or, more likely, she hadn't considered that they'd involve themselves in her conversation. "Is that right?"

"I welcome the opportunity to assist with any and all problems you may have." Travis gave a magnanimous tilt of his head.

Quincy could hardly remember a time when the Grant boys weren't in his life. He'd been friends with them since they were in grade five. Travis was loyal, kind, and always up for an adventure. What he wasn't, what Travis had never been, was subtle. And while many women found his earnest try-hard ways endearing, Quincy worried these women would not.

Desiree and Junior communicated silently through a series of facial ticks until they'd reached their consensus. With Desiree's gesture to proceed, Junior smiled at them.

Junior's behavior to this point could best be described as impish. A bit of harmless flirting from a beautiful woman who knew she was beautiful. The sort of benign mischief his mother would attribute to a 'scamp'. Watching her entire demeanor transform—her posture, the curve of her smile, the tilt of her head—was alarming. She was suddenly oozing seduction and had turned all her attention on Travis.

She came around the counter in a gait that could only be described as a prowl. Walking her fingers along the counter as she approached, she asked, "Are you sure?"

"Sure?" Travis stammered.

"That you're up for it." She kept inching her way closer, never taking her eyes off Travis until she was directly in front of him.

"I'm sure." His voice lacked the conviction of his words as a splotchy blush crawled up his neck.

Quincy stole a quick glance around. Desiree looked mildly amused while the man at the table remained indifferent to all of them.

Junior leaned closer to Travis, invading his body boundary without touching him. "How sure?"

"Very." Travis held her gaze, continuing this weird, sexually charged staring contest.

"Enough to accept a base level of sluttiness?"

Travis straightened, narrowing his eyes at the blatant trap. "I don't believe in that. Women shouldn't be shamed for their sexual appetites."

"Ay, not her, chacho. You." Junior tossed a wink over his shoulder at Desiree. "She likes her men slutty."

Travis looked between the two women with a growing sense of urgency. He had definitely jumped into the ring unprepared for this opponent.

Junior continued in a husky drawl that curled through the air and landed on their skin like a caress, "Hot pants, crop tops, lace thongs, big cleavage—all of it."

"It's true," Desiree agreed with a casualness at odds with Junior's level of sultry.

Junior practically purred, "Can you keep high and tight?"

Quincy wasn't sure if he actually heard Travis swallow or if it was the aggressive way his Adam's apple bobbed, supplying his brain with the sound.

"Cheeks clappin', titties tittyin'—just a good old-fashioned, first class, grade-A hussy." Junior was so close to Travis, Quincy was impressed Travis continued to withstand this onslaught.

"Mhmm, that's hows I likes 'em," Desiree agreed

"So?" Junior ran her tongue over her top teeth. "You in?"

Quincy watched as they stayed that way, Junior holding his gaze, her lips parting, until Travis blinked. He leaned back and twisted away from her.

"You don't want no problems." Junior tsked, looking Travis up and down. Her frown was the genuine yet harmless disappointment of one who'd backed the wrong horse. She concluded with a sulky pout, "You just talk like you do."

"What on Earth?" Leigh cried from the front door.

Junior and Desiree turned to the front door and smiled. Desiree checked her watch, "You're back early."

"Did you get everything sorted?" Junior returned to her previous friendly disposition and made her way toward Leigh.

"Do I even want to know why you're tormenting Travis?" She'd taken one look at the tableau—Travis cornered and wide-eyed flanked by Desiree and Junior's bodies looming over his—and seemed to know exactly what was happening. That she wasn't surprised by this scene was a conversation he'd bring up with her later.

"I do. I want to know," Luc, who'd entered with Leigh, said with uncontained glee. "Tell me everything!"

Leigh swatted the man at the table, "Honestly, Davis. I at least expected you to be the adult in the room!"

"It didn't seem like my involvement was required." He defended his non-action while putting his earbuds in their case.

"Besides," Junior settled herself in his lap and leaned in to kiss him, "you do want these problems."

With his hands cradling her face, he said against her lips, "I most certainly do."

Ah. So he was the bestower of giant green gemstones.

"Ugh. Sickening." Desiree threw her hands up in a gesture that was part affection and part genuine revulsion at the now kissing couple. Quincy wasn't sure of the ratio. "Well, I guess I'm off the hook. Call me later?"

Desiree went behind the counter to gather her things.

"Let's go, Problems," Davis announced, standing and pulling Junior up with him. He gathered his tablet, phone, and keys. Tugging her with his free hand he said, "Or we're gonna be late."

Travis, finally returned to his senses, collapsed into the chair closest to him and hung his head in his hands. "I think I'm in love!"

As Leigh hugged and kissed her friends good-bye, Luc leaned over and said in a voice that wouldn't carry, "Don't let the jokes and good times fool you, bruh—them two right there are dangerous. I watched Desiree make a grown man cry all because he gave Leigh the creeps whenever he came in. Ava told me Junior unraveled a woman's entire life because she was rude to Leigh when she first started out. They have the will and the resources and they don't play behind their friend." Luc gave him a pointed look. "Whatever's going on between you, I hope you know what you're doing."

"Is this the 'If you hurt her' talk?" Quincy wasn't unprepared to receive those types of threats but he did find it funny coming from her 21-year-old employee.

"You're not listening, are you? They aren't going to give you any warnings. The Find Out portion of Fucking Around ends with you in some Panamanian cartel's shipping container or buried in the Nova Scotian outback. Don't say I didn't warn you." He flipped his braids over his shoulder and sauntered to his spot behind the counter where he proceeded to stuff his coat and backpack behind the desk and immediately got to work.

With her gloves in her hand and her coat unbuttoned, Leigh made her way over with a pleased smile on her face. "Hey, Travis. Welcome to Peach's Books and Bakeshop."

"I just met the woman of my dreams. At a bookstore in Leslieville."

Leigh gave Quincy a questioning look to which he mouthed, *Desiree.*

"He's still processing." Quincy explained. "Apparently she likes her men slutty?"

Leigh tilted her head in contemplation. "I've always said 'Eurotrash' but I guess slutty works, too."

"I don't think he was prepared for any of what just happened."

"No, most people aren't," she gave Travis a consoling back rub. She turned to face him "This is a nice surprise. Are you just passing through?"

A nice surprise. Quincy was embarrassed by how much he liked hearing her say those words. Any reservations he may have had about stopping by like this, outside of their new established normal, simply so he could see her for a moment, vanished.

"We're headed to see Miles so Travis can give him a lineup and I thought I'd check in, see if you were ready for the Thorne signing tomorrow when we ran into your girls." Quincy hoped she'd pick up on the unspoken question.

"They were tag teaming coverage for me. Luc can only close on Wednesdays and Fridays because of his class schedule and I had to run out to pick up my niece. Rhonda was supposed to do it but she got called about a last-minute availability at the specialist she's been waiting almost a year to see and Cat was freaking out because she's up against a deadline and will be at work until late. Thank goodness Junior and Des were available."

Leigh started pulling off her coat as she made her way to her office. Following her, Quincy's mind reeled.

Had she... Was she saying... Did Leigh leave her job in the middle of the business day to babysit? Quincy looked around. Travis was at the counter paying for whatever he'd had Luc box up for them, and there were three people milling around in the shelves. There was no indication at all a special event would be taking place in the morning. This signing seemed to be a big deal and she'd ducked out for that?

"You also have a deadline. How could you leave in the middle of the day like that?"

"Cat needed help." Her easy delivery lacked any acknowledgement of his concern in this matter.

"Because her sister prioritized her own needs and bailed! You should try it once in a while." Is this what she meant when she said being the older sister could be a lot at times? Because from where he was standing, she was taking the pressure on unnecessarily.

"My sister. They are my sisters." Her voice was low and had a hint of irritation.

His voice had no such ambiguity. "Who aren't remotely concerned that you have a business to run and can't be called on for last minute errands. Do they even know about the opportunity you're being given?"

"Excuse you? If I recall, I'm doing you a favor! This isn't some proving grounds—I know what I agreed to, Quincy. I don't need you to weigh in with your thoughts and opinions on my life!"

Their voices were raising and Quincy was sure they could be heard out in the store.

"You're about to make a huge connection in your industry and I vouched for you because I thought you'd be responsible enough to handle it!"

As soon as he said it, he knew it was the wrong thing to say. He didn't even mean it like that. Not really. He was simply stunned that she'd put her family's needs over her own even in the face of her business. Her face was a raging inferno of emotion for one searing moment. Then, like a switch was flipped, her expression was locked tighter than the Royal Canadian Mint.

"Thanks for stopping by, Quincy. As you helpfully pointed out, I have a lot on my plate so I'd better get to it."

He almost shivered, her voice was so cold and distant. "Leigh, I—"

"Please make sure Travis understands Junior and Desiree don't work here." She cut him off as though he hadn't spoken. "I don't want anyone else hanging around for the wrong reasons."

Ouch. When was the last time Quincy'd been so summarily dismissed? Maybe never. She wasn't even looking at him anymore, her attention fully on whatever was on her monitor. He'd insulted her, impact coming for intent off the top rope, and there was nothing for him to do but leave.

He made his way back to the front of the store where Travis was waiting with Luc. He didn't need to see their faces to know he'd fucked up. Travis's uncharacteristic quiet only underscored how bad it was.

"I'll see you tomorrow, man."

Luc's eyebrows shot to his hairline, "You sure about that?"

"Come on, Q." Travis clapped a hand on his shoulder and gave it a squeeze. "Let's get you out of here before you say anything else."

He heaved a weary sigh and let Travis lead him out to his car.

It took seven minutes. Seven minutes from the time Leigh walked in, greeting him with a warm, pleased smile to her all but snubbing him with the coldest of shoulders. And he didn't really have anyone to blame but himself.

Chapter 15

Leigh was in her office looking through titles for the up-coming season. It was called an office but in reality, it was little more than a storage room in which she'd managed to fit an L-shaped desk in one corner, a filing cabinet in the other, and three rolling caddies groaning under the weight of their books whose position changed every time she looked at them. She'd tried to address the abysmal lighting in the space. There was only the opening into the store, she lacked both a door and windows, and she didn't have space for floor lamps. Replacing the noisy, droning overhead fluorescents with bulbs that emitted cool, white light was the best she could do.

'I've got intel. Meet in an hour?'

Junior's text came in with a video conference link, no preamble or context, and Leigh wasn't in the least bit surprised. She put her phone back down to do her ordering. The gods knew Junior didn't actually require a reply to proceed with hijinks.

'Hot goss?'

'The hottest.' Leigh did a double take at the exchange be-tween Marcus and Junior. She hadn't noticed it was a group text.

This couldn't be anything but trouble. Tapping her screen, she saw the invite link had been sent to everyone. Granted, Leigh's everyone was only five people but it still made her wary.

She looked at the time to confirm what she already knew. The store would be closed in an hour and Leigh would only have her closing rituals, activities that could be delayed indefinitely, to keep her from attending this impromptu 'meeting' which was undoubtedly her friend's intention. Leigh tried anyway.

'I'm drowning in paperwork and I have the signing in the morning.' Even texting the words reminded her of Quincy's high-handed judgement, something she'd been trying and failing to put out of her mind all day. Hearing the word 'irresponsible' applied to her actions unlocked a violence in her akin to those sleeper agents in the spy books she'd read as a kid. It was hot and molten and she wanted to spew it all over his stupid, handsome face!

Did Cat call her first? Sure. Would she have figured something out if Leigh was unavailable? Without question. But she didn't have to. Which was the whole point—Leigh was able to help *because* Junior and Desiree were there to cover. Leigh made the decision based on what she was willing and able to sacrifice and it was nobody's business to weigh in on how she chose to use her resources.

Quincy didn't know how close her niece's school was to the shop. He had no idea how anxious the child would be with an unexplained change in plans, how she'd need the soothing reassurance Leigh knew to provide. He didn't understand how important it was for Rhonda to finally get to see the specialist.

He didn't ask. He simply presumed she was being weak willed and manipulated and worried about having his name attached, no matter how tangentially, to her inevitable failure. The very nerve!

'I'll fill you in later, Lovey' Marcus' text bubble appeared almost instantly.

'There. Problem solved.'

Junior's easy acceptance gave her pause. Out of all the members of this little posse she'd put together, Junior Sano was the least biddable. That woman was the physical embodiment of single-minded determination. If Junior wanted something—anything—rare was the no that stopped her from having it.

Deciding to focus on other things, Leigh put her phone down and went back to her ledgers and purchase orders. The bell over the door chimed and Luc's pleasant "Thank you!" followed the customers out the door.

Leigh wondered if she had enough books to make a feature table using exclusively Holiday titles. She grumbled to herself as she logged back into the software she used for ordering that kept timing her out. She wanted to finish this one publisher's catalog tonight. A quick look at the clock told her they were closer to closing time than she'd realized so she put all other thoughts out of her head and got to work.

It wasn't until she heard Desiree's husky laugh from the other room that Leigh noticed the hour had flown by.

"Of course I'm here," Luc sniffed, "I'm the one who gathered the source material. If there's tea, I want it!"

Leigh logged on in time to hear Junior say, "This is our mark," Junior's screen showed an enlarged Quincy, "and this is our source, Ian Yang." While Quincy's enlarged image continued to shake like an impatient video game avatar, another Black man's image proceeded to grow into the same animation. "I think he has a soft spot for Claudia. I can't think of another explanation for the sheer volume of detail, even with her proficiency for snooping."

"Claudia brought the goods? Then I know it's about to be mess." Desiree cackled.

Junior's cousin Claudia, affectionately referred to as La Chismosa among their family, was a tiny dynamo. Most people didn't realize her bubbly, sunshine-y personality was a front for her anxiety fueled misanthropy. It was very likely this Ian Yang confused her pumping him for information as interest and he was about to be walloped with a sad, harsh truth.

"This whole group are a bunch of incestuous overachievers," Junior clicked over to the next slide and the rest of the group were blacked out as though they were in witness protection, leaving Quincy and five other men visible. "But we're starting with them. This is the original six. They met at a fancy pants boys' school in Markham as kids and have been friends every day since."

The original image of about twenty-ish people around a bonfire was a recurring one. Since Luc first started scanning Quincy's social media pages, they'd noticed there was a version of this shot—sometimes a couple more people, sometimes a couple less—of a group of friends at a cottage type property for Canada Day, with the clothes and hairstyles the only nod to the passage of time. Leigh had a total of four friends plus her sister and she struggled to keep up with the ins and outs of their lives—the thought of being part of such a large friend group made her head spin.

"Ma'am! You went to 'fancypants private school'. What's with the mockery?" Desiree joked.

"When you're running the slide show, you can mock what you want." Junior's haughty reply made Luc and Ava snort their laughter.

"I really appreciate the production value, by the way." Ava added on the end of a giggle.

Junior winked at Ava, "I'll send your regards to the graphics department."

Leigh looked at the altered photo. She'd met Paviter, Carter, and Travis at the kickback and based on the stories she'd heard, the Asian man was William. The other Black man on screen was Yemi, who she met the other night at Carter's. It was mere moments before Junior confirmed as much for the rest of the group by naming each man with her digital pointer.

"This part is important," Junior continued, "Quincy, Carter, and Paviter went to Carleton. William, Yemi, and Travis went to Queens."

"Really? He didn't go to Western?" Ava's dubious look was followed with, "Someone named Travis would have thrived in that douche pit."

"Ava!" Leigh scolded while Junior and Luc—whose university experience was separated by over ten years—nodded their acceptance of Ava's decree.

Junior flipped to the next slide and two new faces were uncovered. "This is Domenic, who was Carter's roommate and this is Morgan who was Travis'." She pointed to a Black man and a white man in turn.

"Ruby," Junior continued after flipping a slide to uncover two women, pointed to a tanned woman who could be any combination of races, "is Morgan's childhood best friend. Their families are super tight, they've been together since the cradle. And Alice," Junior pointed to the woman who'd stood in her shop mere days ago, "was Ruby's roommate at Carleton."

Leigh looked at the screen and saw that, for the most part, everyone was keeping up. Luc was taking notes while Marcus looked close to bursting with devilish glee.

Junior flipped the slide to show the ten friends. "They have each been featured in some type of '30 under 30/Ones to Watch' list and are up and coming players in their respective fields. All of them managed to pursue high stress, fast paced careers: pilot, photojournalist, artist, architect, trader—this little posse, apparently known as The Byrons, have their hands in everything."

Leigh added the details she knew for herself. Paviter was an award-winning documentary filmmaker. Carter was a successful video game developer. Travis had a hair salon in midtown that had a months-long waitlist. Alice was a publicist at a big five publisher. And Quincy... Quincy wanted to conquer the world with a swing in his step and a song in his heart.

Leigh was determined to ignore the confusing disappointment that pooled in her stomach. This wasn't anything she didn't already know. She should be feeling vindicated! This was his world. These were his friends. They clearly embodied every single live fast, wild and free, higher, further cliche and were unapologetic about it.

And why should they apologize? This was the life they chose.

And if it made her wonder who she could've been if she were braver, flouted the rules more, dreamt bigger? Well, that wasn't their fault either.

"Enough with their CVs, Lovey, get to the incest!" Marcus demanded.

Junior flipped the slide back to the original photo of the twenty-ish people. "Every single person in this photo is connected to the original six one way or the other and, according to our source, they have all swapped fluids either directly or indirectly. The only exceptions to the direct fluid swap are Travis and Carter, who are brothers, and William and Domenic who are both Ian's cousins."

"But... not cousins to each other, right?" Luc clarified. "Those swords would be free to cross?"

"Oh," Junior's face scrunched in thought, "Yeah, you're right—I guess they are."

"I wish I knew about this horny tangle of limbs when them two were there earlier." Desiree made a sound low in her throat, then added, "If we're crossing swords, then I wouldn't mind seeing Yemi with that one in the green trunks."

"I just bet!" Junior laughed, "For your information, the one in the green was with Morgan—pre and post op—Ruby, Carter, and the one in the sunflower bikini. Travis and post transition Morgan both hooked up with her," Junior's cursor circled a woman in a 50s style polka dot one-piece, "who's been known to let Alice feel her up to make Yemi jealous."

Ava raised her hand out of habit before lowering it and asking, "Which one is trying to make Yemi jealous?"

"Polka Dots. Alice's been in a no-strings-whenever-you're-lonely situationship with Quincy since university."

"Junior!" Desiree almost choked on her laughter, "Why would you say it like that?"

Junior was genuinely confused. "Like what? They're consenting adults who fuck sometimes. What's the problem?"

Leigh felt like everyone was looking at her even though it was statistically impossible she was in the same place on all their screens.

"She's said she's not interested a hundred million times," Junior rolled her eyes, confirming Leigh's suspicion, "and besides, if something *were* to happen between them, then at least Leigh knows he's capable of maintaining friendships with casual hookups. It shows great strength of character."

"It's amazing that you haven't shared fluids with any of them, Junior. You're the same age and lead a similar fast paced 'dick forward' lifestyle," Ava mused.

Leigh thought 'fast paced dick forward' lifestyle was a funny way to describe the wealthy and beautiful pansexual hedonist. Would that make hers a 'cautious risk averse worker bee' lifestyle?

"There are three million people in the city, Ava. I can hardly be expected to know them all."

"True. But…" Luc trailed off in an obvious manner. When no one replied he gave a dramatic clearing of his throat and repeated himself *"But."*

"Oh, hush, you!" Marcus grumped. *"But* I know him. And him. Biblically."

Leigh had stopped paying attention and didn't see who Marcus had pointed to so the resulting reactions were little more than a bit of white noise she followed on her periphery.

"Aye, que sucio!" Junior gasped playfully while clutching her imaginary pearls.

"We've been scrolling his socials for weeks and you didn't say anything?" Ava sounded truly hurt by this omission.

Desiree gave him a knowing smirk, "Swimming in the kiddie pool will do that, eh Marcus?"

"Ten years in either direction is hardly worth mentioning at my age. Which I pointed out to this one," he thumbed toward where Leigh presumably floated on his screen, "all for naught!"

While her friends devolved into a rousing debate about how much was too much age gap, Leigh struggled to order her thoughts. Junior was right. She had no intention of pursuing anything with Quincy so who he chose to share his bed, in whatever way he chose to share it, was none of her business. And, the Quincy of it aside, judging a person's sexual history was gross. She'd always hated it.

Leigh was so completely clear on those two facts yet couldn't explain the childish jealousy rising in her like mist off wintery lake.

She liked hanging out with Quincy. Liked the laughing and joking and teasing. She was grateful that he'd accepted her offer of friendship without complaint, never making sly comments or inappropriate overtures and innuendo. The truth was, until today when she'd been faced with his judgmental superiority, she liked how it felt to have someone as exceptional as Quincy want to be around someone as unexceptional as she was.

Oh, God—did that make her some sort of creep? Was she a... what did Langston call it? A clout chaser?

"What's happening over there?" Desiree demanded. "Why is your face all screwed up?"

Leigh immediately tuned back in and fixed her features to smooth placidity. "Nothing's going on."

Desiree's pursed lips said she didn't believe her, but Junior continued pointing out all the overlapping love connections which was more interesting to the group at large.

"See? Domenic and William have shared fluids indirectly!" Luc's chest puffed with pride.

"Thank you for this very involved presentation—Claudia has once again proved to be more effective than a CSIS agent when it comes to information gathering," Leigh wanted this to be over. She hadn't wanted it to begin in the first place, not that anyone took her thoughts into consideration. "But none of this is any of our business."

"Tell me you're joking!" Marcus guffawed. "You can't be serious, Lovey."

Leigh pushed her glasses up and pinched the bridge of her nose. "Serious about what, Marcus?"

"Dottie, even if you're only friends with Quincy don't you want to know things about him? Granny always warned us to judge people by the company they keep." Ava's gentle voice made Leigh feel like she'd walked into a spiderweb. The tiny gossamer threads of her concern made Leigh's skin crawl.

"Yeah?" She asked a bit testily, "Then what do you heathens say about me?"

"Which is exactly what I tried to tell Quincy but he wasn't listening." Luc gave an airy 'what are you gonna do?' shrug.

Junior feigned outrage by covering her mouth with one hand and bringing her other to her throat. "En el nombre del espíritu santo, who are you calling heathens?"

Leigh rolled her eyes, thoroughly over this entire exercise. "I have work to do. Quincy and I are friends and I will learn things about him the normal way—when he shares them with me."

"Okay, okay," Desiree raised a placating hand. "In the future, when you bring someone new around, we'll keep our findings to ourselves, deal?"

"I would prefer," Leigh spoke slowly to make sure her point was made, "you not do any investigating at all!"

"Oh, no. I can't agree to that." Desiree said immediately. Luc's disapproving frown and Marcus and Junior's chorus of "Me either" followed close behind.

Ava had the decency to give a shame-faced grimace, but it didn't read as willingness to do Leigh's bidding any more than the others' outright refusal had.

Leigh inhaled on a count of five, held it, then exhaled on a count of five. "I have to go. I love you. Good night."

She didn't wait for any responses before closing out of the chat and letting her head fall back on her chair. She needed to take a minute to process how she felt about the information currently piquing the curiosity she didn't want to have. Especially not after the way things were left between them. And knowing she had to face Alice tomorrow with all this crashing around her skull was also not helping.

Her feelings about Quincy were even more tangled than ever. She was annoyed with him for what he said even if there was a small part of her willing to give him the benefit of the doubt. She still couldn't see how they could be anything more than friends—they both had demanding schedules, they both had familial obligations, and they both were fiercely loyal to their friend groups. When would she even have the time for a relationship?

She could still hear their spirited antics on the call. Luc was insisting women feeling each other up was not an indicator of queerness the way it was for men while Ava countered athletes hugged and kissed each other all the time.

Tuning them out, Leigh pulled out her notebook and went over her checklist. She was actually much further ahead than she'd initially thought, which was always a pleasant surprise.

Her phone's familiar text notification rang out. Cat sent a quick update and her profuse thanks for Leigh's help today. Leigh sent a picture of a field of sunflowers, Cat's favorite, in reply.

Closing out of Cat's message brought her attention back to the apology text Quincy sent earlier. When his name had initially flashed across the screen she'd debated whether or not to read the message. Deciding against churlishness, she'd unlocked her phone to see:

'I'm sorry about earlier. I didn't mean it the way it came out. It was inappropriate and disrespectful and I should've kept my opinions to myself. I wanna be there tomorrow for no other reason than to support you. I know it's going to be amazing because you're amazing. If there's anything I can do, just say the word.'

Leigh had read the words over and over again. She read them again now. She pulled her glasses off and rubbed her stinging eyes. She didn't know what to do with his apology. She understood his concern, misplaced though it was, and accepted he'd managed to hit a particularly sensitive topic for her. He was out of line and apologized—fully and completely. She didn't want to hold a grudge but she also didn't want to sail past the affront.

"Do you need anything before I take off?" Luc's voice broke her from her spiraling thoughts.

She put her glasses back on and looked at the time. "Oh, Luc—it's so late. Are you going to be okay to get home?"

He gave her an indulgent laugh and reminded her, "It's only 9 o'clock, Leigh. I'll be fine."

"Still. I worry. Just lock the front door and turn off the main lights so you can get going."

"Alright. I'll see you tomorrow."

"Have a good night, Lucien." She looked up to see he was lingering in the doorway, wrestling with something he wanted to say. "Luc?"

He continued to struggle with his thoughts until he finally came to a decision. "You've done so much to help me and my family. More than I can ever repay."

Leigh felt a flood of emotion thinking about meeting Lucien for the first time earlier this year. Desiree was one of his instructors at George Brown College and she'd recognised the signs of hidden homelessness. He and his younger sibling had been crashing with an older cousin who'd fallen on hard times and they were all three staying in one room at a seedy motel on Kingston Road. It took one meeting to fall completely under the spell of Lucien's considerable charm. He was smart, ambitious, a hard worker, and didn't deserve to have his whole future derailed.

"I'd say Desiree is owed the lion's share of your thanks," she demurred.

"Taking her class changed my life in so many ways. But you didn't have to hire me. You didn't have to fit in so many hours around my schedule the way you do. You didn't have to help me get into that apartment complex. You're a truly good person, Leigh. And I know it's probably out of line and might get me fired," she raised her brow and he rushed to add, "please don't fire me!"

She wondered how he would react to knowing Junior was his landlord. Leigh's reply came on a rise of laughter, "I'm not going to fire you, Luc."

"I heard you and Quincy arguing. You've been hiding out back here all afternoon. He shouldn't have said it that way, no question. But is it any different from all the times Junior's called Otis a moron or Desiree's begged you to stay out of Cat's parenting drama? We don't want to see you hurt, that's all. You make people feel protective, make it so they want the best for you. Not because you're weak but because you're good. Too good."

Luc stopped speaking abruptly, as though he'd used all his energy getting the words out. His hands were wrung together and his eyes were downcast.

"Thank you, Luc. I feel very loved and protected. It's unreal how safe a group of godless heathens can make a person feel." She poured all the genuine adoration she felt for the young man into her words.

She watched as the words landed the way she intended. His nervous fidgeting stopped and his posture regained its usual confidence. He tossed his hair over his shoulder dramatically, "Well, so long as you're aware."

"Get out of here. I'll see you in the morning."

When she heard him exit out the side door, Leigh picked up her phone and re-read Quincy's text. With Luc's courage bolstering her she finally wrote back, **'I'll take all the support I can get. Have a good night, Quincy—I'll see you tomorrow'**.

Chapter 16

S HE'D DONE IT!

Quincy looked around the shop and marvelled at how effortlessly Leigh pulled the signing off. Franklin Thorne was mingling with the few people who'd shown up—obviously prepared for their arrival—while his team packed the signed books up. He still wasn't clear on why this couldn't have happened at the publisher but everything he understood about Alice's job could fit on the head of a nail.

The photographer moved throughout the small crowd taking pictures of Franklin as he laughed and posed for selfies. Quincy even spied her snapping a couple of shots of Leigh's store which could only be a good thing.

He'd walked in to see Franklin greeting Leigh warmly and something about it made him swell with pride. This is why the signing was happening here—she was why. It had nothing to do with deadlines or last chances or the author's quirky obstinance. It was Leigh. The same thing that had him returning to the shop again and again. The thing he'd almost ruined with his outburst.

It wasn't that he thought she couldn't manage it. He'd witnessed her navigate the chaos of Hillary Welland's impromptu signing with grace and professionalism. Even Franklin had said it was a table and some pens—nothing to raise anyone's heart rate over. Leigh knew exactly what was needed for a signing. She would know what she needed to do to put this one together.

Yet he still couldn't put his behavior into words. He'd shown up to see her and offer his assistance only to find out she'd called her girls in to watch the shop while she rushed out to help her sister with something that, as far as he could see, didn't require Leigh's specific involvement. The one-sidedness of it galled him. Sure, he didn't have sisters, but was it really so different? Wouldn't siblings have enough awareness of each other's lives to know when big things were happening? He'd tried to convey that to her—to let her know she had a responsibility to herself first—but it had come out all wrong. Hell, it shouldn't have been vocalized at all if he were calling a spade a spade.

It frustrated Quincy to see the way Leigh never seemed to think what she wanted mattered. To hear the way she constantly dismissed all the ways in which she was remarkable. He'd built his career on casting for bigger and bigger fish, for speaking his goals out loud until they'd gone from aspiration to inevitability. There was nothing he couldn't achieve simply because there was nothing he thought out of his reach. Quincy hustled and schmoozed and worked his ass off, then luxuriated in his success without regret or apology. That Leigh didn't, wouldn't, put herself first had him sticking his entire foot in it.

He'd upset her, shown his whole ass, and for what? Leigh hadn't seemed to need him or anyone else. Everything at Peach's Books and Bakeshop was so pitch perfect, you'd never know the event was planned mere days ago. Leigh had rearranged the cafe seating to accommodate one sturdy six-foot table with the new book artfully piled on one end. She'd had a tray of beignets topped with a concerning amount of powdered sugar and a small pan of bread pudding with caramel sauce in honor of both Franklin and Skip Whelan's NOLA roots. When one of the guests commented on the coffee, Leigh stage whispered they were dipping into 'Fletcher's' special stash as a nod to Skip's repeated demand for 'coffee you can stand your spoon in'.

It was all one joyous celebration of this author and his new release while being exactly the low-key event he'd demanded; Quincy could only let the wonderment of Leigh's indomitable nature wash over him.

"She's amazing, isn't she?"

Quincy looked into the face of Kingston Coffield, former pro-athlete, hometown hero, and all around well spring of charisma. He'd been regaling the room with stories from his time in the Major League with such self-deprecating charm, the entire room was laughing and clamoring for more never once realizing how he'd kept the stories from being too personal or revealing. It was a skill not many could wield so effectively.

"She is."

"People tend to underestimate her because she doesn't seek the spotlight. They end up eating her dust every time." He said, conversationally.

Quincy wasn't entirely sure why KC was telling him this. He and Leigh were friends and Quincy knew he knew that. "Yeah, still waters as they say."

"Exactly." KC's jovial chuckle seemed to put an end to his covert messaging. He looked over at Ava and hollered, "ADB! Put the caramel sauce in your coffee, trust me."

Quincy looked over to see her give a 'sure, why not' shrug and proceed with the concoction as suggested. He supposed she never grew out of her willingness to eat whatever was put in front of her.

Quincy was generally very good at conversation. He had a natural gift for gab that translated well in his career, but this room wasn't big enough for him to simply walk away from KC and he didn't want to stand there awkwardly while KC continued to ooze charisma, so he asked, "Are you here for moral support or are you a fan of the series."

"Both. Me, Dottie, and Ava read those books in school. My Dad was a long-haul trucker and he used to look for the paperbacks in truck stops along his routes. We gobbled them up whenever we got our hands on one. It's the only real book overlap we had, you know? Dot's always loved romance but it wasn't for me."

"You don't like love stories?"

KC gave him an appraising look. "Nah, man. I like 'em just fine. The raunchier the better. But life isn't like that, you know? It doesn't always end happily. I can't afford to get caught up... it's not good for my mental. I need balance." He ended by tapping his forehead.

Quincy was sure he was talking around his career ending injury. "I'm not a big reader but I can see how immersing yourself in too much of one thing could make the rest a bit harder."

"Not a big reader, eh? So then you're here for Dottie?"

He phrased it as a question but they both knew it wasn't. "Moral support."

The topic of their conversation came over holding a copy of the newest Skip Whelan adventure. "I think that went well. It did, right?" Leigh looked at KC who was staring down at her with such fondness, Quincy felt like he was intruding.

"Yeah, Dottie, it did."

Quincy, not wanting to be left out of the Tell Leigh She Is Awesome chorus, cleared his throat and added, "I bet this is everything he didn't know he wanted. There'll be no topping it."

"Thanks for coming today, Quincy."

He felt KCs keen eyes on him but couldn't prevent his voice from lowering, brimming with emotion, "I wouldn't have missed it."

Leigh's pleased smile and gentle flush were all the reward he needed.

"My dear Ms. Bridger," the man of the hour approached. He put a familiar hand on Leigh's lower back which she answered with an arm on his shoulder, "thank you for today. Your beignets would make my Maman proud."

"It was my pleasure! I'm so excited to see what Skip gets up to." She hugged the book to her chest.

"And Mr. Coffield, if you'll follow me." Franklin turned to KC and gripped his shoulder. "We can get the particulars to Ms. Vargas who will take care of the details."

"Details?" Leigh asked with a small amount of alarm. "What details?"

KC held her face in both hands and stared into her eyes. "These are not the droids you are looking for."

He managed to jump out of the way of Leigh's incoming slap and laughed uproariously as he followed Franklin to the front door. She was shaking her head with exasperated affection when she turned to look at Quincy.

The exasperation morphed into something closer to apprehension before it settled into expectation.

"Leigh. About yesterday..." Quincy knew this wasn't the time or place but they hadn't had a chance to speak since he arrived some hours ago and he was, like everyone else, on his way out the door. "I—I'm... "

Leigh turned at the sound of her name being called from the door. It was the older couple who'd managed to incite the kind of low stakes argument that caused people to dig their heels in with righteous pettiness.

The Georgian Bay Wars, as Quincy had dubbed them, fell exactly as expected. Franklin remained firmly on Team Bruce Peninsula while they advocated loudly for Team Muskoka with both being thankful they weren't from Collingwood. Since the sum total of Quincy's 'lakefront Ontario' experience was his annual Canada Day weekend at Travis and Carter's cottage in Keswick, which was really their dad's renovated childhood home, he'd wisely remained out of the fray.

She turned back to him and smiled. It was sincere and reassuring and it went a long way to settling the turmoil he'd stirred with his high handedness. "We'll talk later. Okay?"

"I really am sorry."

"I know, Quincy. It's okay."

All he could do was nod. There were too many words racing each other to be the first out of his mouth and the logjam of conflicting emotions threatened to spew forth, making a mess of himself and everyone in his immediate vicinity.

Leigh went to see her guests off, her sister Ava making wild gestures of her delight while her regular customers thanked her for the invite. KC pressed his cheek to hers on his way out the door and Franklin enveloped her in another hug while Alice held the door for him with studied patience.

He'd have to find a way to order his thoughts so he could make his apology in person, but knowing he would have the chance—that Leigh had accepted last night's hastily sent text—helped.

Chapter 17

"WHAT ARE YOU DOING up here, Casey? You're supposed to be getting those ridiculous boxes out of my office." Leigh pronounced KC as one word the way her mother did when she found Kingston putting a dish in the microwave.

"You want me to do manual labour on an empty stomach?"

"I don't even want to know. Just, please, do not leave here without collecting your belongings from my office."

KC pulled the dish out of the microwave before it dinged—a habit maintained from childhood. "I like that guy. He's good people."

The signing was an unqualified success. Leigh worried she'd overstepped by getting Franklin Thorne to agree to a small fan presence but the eight people she invited, including Ava and KC, were excited and respectful and added a small amount of festivity to the drudgery of signing hundreds of books.

They'd made chit chat and even helped with the moving and organizing of the assembly line. She still didn't get a straight answer on why such pomp was necessary but she'd seen a few images from the uncorrected contact sheet and thought the sunny space was the perfect contrast to Franklin's stark image.

The fact that he'd stuck around to mingle with the small group was another sign of his comfort and enjoyment. She'd only spent a small amount of time with the man, but Leigh had no doubt Franklin Thorne would have strode right out the front door if he felt even a moment's discontent. Seeing him gamely pose for pictures with Mike and Martha, a retired couple who were avid readers and members of five separate books clubs, would go down as one of Leigh's favorite memories.

Whatever scheme KC and Franklin Thorne cooked up during the signing last week resulted in the publisher shipping something to Kington care of her bookstore. Leigh's unwillingness to get involved overrode the kernel of curiosity. Besides, either or both Kingston and Langston would fill her in soon enough. Both men were fundamentally incapable of keeping a secret from her.

"All that money on renovating the kitchen in your mid-life crisis of a condo yet still you're rooting around my fridge?" Leigh gently shooed Kingston out of her way.

Shoveling a mouthful of cook-up rice into his face, he hummed his enjoyment as he chewed. "Why isn't this ever on the menu at Guyanese spots?"

"Isn't it?"

The highly customizable one-pot meal of peas, rice, meat, and coconut milk was a hearty staple. But since Leigh was too much of a snob to eat at many Guyanese places, she couldn't say for sure. For all Anita's faults, her mother was an excellent cook as was her Granny. Leigh enjoyed Jamaican food and the odd ambiguously designated 'Caribbean' restaurant could do in a pinch but she preferred to eat at places distinctly different from the cuisine on which she'd grown up.

"Believe me, I've looked." He leaned against the counter with the dish held at his chest.

"For someone who's sworn off pork, you're really digging into those leftovers."

"With a gun to my head, I'll deny it," he admitted with ease, pushing another forkful into his mouth.

"And the candied bacon from Langston's birthday breakfast?"

"Car battery hooked to my balls, it didn't happen."

Shaking her head, Leigh's laugh tinkled in the small space. Like his athletic build and toothpaste commercial smile, KC's bravado hadn't changed in the last three decades. His constance in her life, the friendship they'd formed still solid after all these years.

"Now I know you're lyin'. You wouldn't put your precious jewels at risk for anything—especially not when I hear your latest fling was our son's TA in his Animation Theory course at Queens."

"Says Trevor's daughter."

"I beg your pardon?"

There was no mistaking the implication. Leigh's biological father was currently married to someone who sat in the front row of his son's kindergarten class photo. The only question was whether her infant sibling would arrive before or after Langston turned thirty.

"Don't think I didn't notice the vibes in the air."

"You are impossible. Franklin Thorne and I have exchanged polite, civil conversation. He wasn't sending me vibes." She drawled the last word to indicate exactly how ridiculous she found it.

"Real talk? Him too but I meant that youngster and the way he was looking at you."

Leigh kissed her teeth and waved KC's words away. "Your brain is like a calabash."

"Big and impressive?" He grinned.

"Smooth and empty," Leigh retorted. "It's not like that between us. Stop embarrassing yourself."

"If I'm wrong then explain why that l'il publicist girl was throwing so much shade?"

She might have been able to deny any vibes coming from Quincy. Alice, on the other hand, had been dismissive, cutting, and borderline rude. Leigh had written it off as work stress. She knew how much Alice had riding on the signing going smoothly and she'd, for all intents and purposes, gone behind the woman's back to curate the event directly with Franklin.

Even knowing what she knew about Alice and Quincy's decades-long friends-with-benefits situation, Leigh and Quincy were regular platonic friends. There were no benefits for Alice to be jealous of or threatened by.

"You're reaching."

KC audibly scoffed without choking or spraying rice everywhere. Pointing his fork at her for emphasis, he added, "Fact of the matter is: she wants him, he wants you, and you're out of your mind if you think you can't have him."

"That's just it, KC. I don't want him." It sounded truer than it felt.

Leigh opened the fridge to see what she could throw together for her supper now that KC had eaten her leftovers. Maybe a salad and a roasted chicken leg? Pulling the components from their various drawers and shelves, she continued, "Besides, I am entirely too old for him."

"Dottie," his chiding tone made her bristle, "Don't act like guys care about age when it comes to hooking up with a beautiful woman. We don't."

Leigh pushed her glasses onto her forehead and rubbed her eyes in exasperation. "Now you're just being ridiculous."

"You know what we care about?" KC started to dance on Leigh as he sang. "Good lovin', body rockin' all night long—"

The performance could be considered sexy by somebody who wasn't thoroughly mortified. She pushed his thrusting hips away from her body. "Kingston Cofield!"

"—Somebody rockin' knockin' da boots."

Leigh hissed, swatting him with a tea towel, "Quincy probably wasn't even born when that song came out, which is entirely the problem!"

The body rolls now finished, KC put his dish on the counter and searched for the scrubber he knew lived under the sink. "There's no need to get uptight. He's not that young, is he? You could hit that if you wanted. You not wanting to is not the same as you not being able to."

"Let's say I entertained this madness—which I am not—when would I have the time? I'm plenty occupied with my business and cleaning up after my family, which includes you and whatever fallout comes from the madness you got downstairs that will, eventually, become my problem."

Doing an admirable job of erasing all signs of his food thievery, KC dried the bowl and put it back in the cupboard. "It's only your problem because you let it be your problem."

"What's that supposed to mean?"

Something in his face let Leigh know he maybe said something he shouldn't.

"What, KC?"

"Nothing! I just meant that you like making shit your problem or you'd have put a stop to it forever ago."

Leigh reared back. How could he say such a thing to her? He'd been there when her dad passed and was suddenly introduced to a father she'd never known and new siblings she didn't want. He was there when her extracurriculars started to be curtailed as both sets of parents started relinquishing responsibility of their children to her care. Hell, KC started dating her, in part, because she was so good at keeping his life organised. The very idea that he would suggest she chose this role was galling.

"You think I don't want to put a stop to it?" Her voice rose in frustration. "You think I like it?"

"Maybe like is too strong a word. But it's, like, your love language or whatever. Acts of service, right? So...win-win."

The careless shrug that punctuated his statement was the proverbial back-breaking straw.

Leigh had never put much stock in astrology. All that focus on sun and moon signs and star placements seemed too circumstantial. But birth order was something she bought into wholesale and here was KC proving it right now. The consummate youngest child completely disregarding the burden of responsibility heaped on the first born simply because they did not have to deal with it themselves.

In their thirty-one years of friendship, Leigh and KC had had their share of arguments and fallings out. Their rows ranged from the incorrect use of highlighters to whether their son should be 'encouraged' to play sport and everything in between. What they had never disagreed on was the twisted relationships she had with her family and the obstacle to her life they represented. Hearing him call her response to trauma a love language was more than she could deal with.

"I'm going to hop in the shower." She stepped away from the counter, her voice tight with barely contained anger. "Lock up when you leave."

Ignoring his calls for her to come back as they followed her down the hall, Leigh closed herself in her room and tried to keep her frustrated tears from falling. It was too much, too close to what Quincy had said, for Leigh to take it as anything other than a criticism of her life, her choices, and the very nature of her person.

What hurt worse was the realization their long history gave him zero insight into why what he said was unfair and thoughtless.

"Dottie?" She jumped when she heard his insistent knock on the door. He tried again when she didn't answer. "Bridge?"

Leigh stared at the door, stared through it, waiting for KC to give up and leave. He would eventually. It was the rhythm of all their arguments. He advanced. She retreated, regrouped, and returned with a level head and a reasonable solution.

"Dorothy Leigh," he said it all together, like it's hyphenated cousin Anna-May, with a generic Caribbean inflection that paid homage to, without accurately depicting, her Granny's accent. "I'm sorry I pissed you off. Can we please try to talk about it now instead of waiting five days of you stewing in your own head?"

Well that was a new and mature addition to their familiar routine. His therapist was clearly earning every dollar of their fee.

"I can't talk now," she explained through the door, "I've changed my mind about the shower and am gonna have a bath instead." It wasn't a lie if speaking it made it true, was it? She felt rather in the mood for a bath come to think of it.

KC let out a loud, exasperated breath. "I hate it when you're not talking to me!"

She couldn't help but smile at his whingeing proclamation. They often went days, weeks occasionally, without speaking to each other with nary an issue. It was the thought of her actively not speaking to him that he couldn't bear. He never could.

Taking a page from his book, she went with unvarnished honesty. "Really, Case. I can't manage it now. Tomorrow. I promise."

"Pinky swear?"

The familiarity of the demand almost choked her. Leigh leaned her forehead on the door and waited for the swell of emotion to pass. She loved this man. He was her first friend, her first love, her first... *first*, the father of her child—which is probably why she found his words so difficult to hear. Taking a deep breath she promised, "Pinky swear."

"Tomorrow, then."

Leigh nodded even though she knew he couldn't see her. When she heard him down the hall, she turned on unsteady legs and went to the ensuite to start her bath. She'd work through it and talk to him tomorrow.

Later that night, after the restorative effects of a bath and a mug of hot tea, Leigh was sitting on the couch when her phone dinged with the chime of her group chat.

'Any fallout from the signing? What was in the box?'

Leigh gave a small chuckle. Leave it to her sister to follow up.

'What box?'

'You were up north with Davis' came Desiree's reply to Junior **'KC had a box of something from that dude's publisher delivered to Leigh.'**

'So?' Ava's text bubble almost vibrated with her curiosity **'What was it?'**

Leigh responded without thinking **'I have no idea because we got into a fight.'**

The replies poured in, short quick bursts of outrage on her behalf, before she had a chance to clarify her statement **'Not a fight. He just pissed me off.'**

'What'd he say?' Desiree's question was punctuated with a suspicion emoji.

She might not have intended on hashing all of this out but now that it was here, telling her friends would give her the validation and vindication she needed to process the insensitive remarks KC had made.

Even trying to sort the words to tell them tinged the corner of her vision red. After everything she'd been through—they'd been through—suggesting that she was a control freak that needed to manage everyone around her was a slap in the face.

As if he didn't know about the weight of expectation she carried. As if he hadn't seen with his own eyes how her family dropped their burdens at her feet and left without a backward glance. As if her whole entire life hadn't been one long series of rising above and doing what was right regardless of whether it was what she wanted.

'He basically said that I can't stand the idea of not being in control and everyone lets me because I would fall apart otherwise.'

There. Let them get a load of that!

Leigh waited for the indignation to come pouring through but her phone was oddly quiet. She looked at the window and saw the telltale blue checkmarks. The message had been delivered and read.

'He basically said that or he literally said that?' Desiree wanted to know.

What difference did that make? Leigh stared at her phone with a low-level thrum of dread.

'That was the gist,' Leigh admitted.

'Why did he say it?' Junior asked.

Again, Leigh failed to see how that mattered. **'We were talking about Quincy. I said that I didn't need another person to take care of then he said what he said.'**

Her phone remained devoid of supportive calls for KC's castration. The vein of dread opened and Leigh realized that her group chat wasn't quiet because they didn't know what to say, but rather because they had a lot to say and were debating how to do it.

'What aren't you telling me?' she demanded. It had been so quiet for what seemed like an age that when her phone vibrated with an incoming video chat, she jumped, bobbling her phone a little.

"I don't want you reading these words and putting weird meaning to what I say," Junior started, "I need you to hear my voice and see my face: the message isn't entirely wrong, if delivered poorly."

"It's not even the whole message," Ava jumped in to mollify. "It's message adjacent."

"Message adjacent." Leigh repeated flatly.

Desiree frowned. "Yeah, I don't know what that means either. What we're trying to say is taking the lead does seem to matter more to you. And we want you to be happy."

"Want me to be happy." The buzzing in Leigh's ears was the only thing tethering her at the moment. The only thing preventing her from raging or crying or lashing out. The effect of her calming bath and tea were immediately undone as her teeth clenched and her shoulders tensed.

"You're allowed to be happy," Ava nodded her agreement, "And if being in charge all the time doesn't do it for you anymore, then stop doing it."

"If I don't do it, who will?" Leigh snapped at her sister, one of the prime beneficiaries of Leigh's supposed overbearing control.

"Ay, mijita, it's not like that. We just want you to think about what KC said and why he said it."

Leigh looked at the quadrants of her phone screen as if seeing her friends for the first time. "He said it," her words were low and deliberate, "because he wouldn't recognise responsibility if it kneed him in the groin."

"Dottie." Ava chided.

"What?"

"KC is perennially childish and totally high off his own sup-ply," Ava explained with a patience normally used for the truly unhinged, "but he has all kinds of responsibilities that don't involve you. He has managed without you for years."

The truth of it didn't mitigate the sting. It hurt to hear she wasn't needed for reasons she suspected her friends were asking her to investigate.

"I can't speak for the rest of your siblings, especially your tonto brother Otis, but we understand your love language is acts of service. And so we let you love us with your suffocating mothering."

Leigh absorbed the backhanded compliment with a hunching of her shoulders. That was the second time she'd been told what her love language was and she wasn't sure she liked it. Yes, she did things for people but based on the little she knew of the five options, Leigh couldn't say she wasn't more inclined toward quality time or words of affirmation.

"So close, Junior." Desiree deadpanned. "How do you say 'quit while you're ahead' in Spanish?"

Junior's narrowed eyes, scrunched nose, and curled lip each answered Desiree individually.

Leigh struggled to put all the pieces together. She understood, empirically, what they were saying, but she couldn't apply it in practice. All these years she'd held all the pieces together and now she was supposed to accept that it was all for show? All her effort and sacrifice were for nothing? She didn't have to drag the weight of her family's expectations everywhere she went? It wasn't necessary to factor in their needs and wants when making a decision? Who was she supposed to be without it?

She'd put her own needs in front of everyone else's exactly one time in her life. The result of which was keeping her baby at the cost of even more responsibility. She'd happily paid the price, but she wouldn't pretend it hadn't taken its toll.

"So, you're saying... what? I don't pick up the phone when my mother calls? Don't reply to texts from Rhonda or Julian?"

She knew she was being a little bit obstinate but she couldn't help herself.

"What we're saying," Desiree answered, "is that you could try listening to them without personally taking action each time."

Not take action? Leigh was a doer, plain and simple. If there was something that needed doing, she figured out how to get it done and moved on to the next thing. Standing around talking about it wasn't her speed. She simply didn't see the point. You need a thing, let's get you the thing! Why lament about the needing when that energy could be put toward the getting?

She tried to see where they were coming from but she was too agitated. If she was suddenly supposed to 'step back' and not be so 'controlling', when exactly were they going to step up and not rely so heavily on her?

Instead of prolonging this conversation, Leigh deflected. "This is a lot to think about. I need to go lay down so I can process."

"You don't have to sugar coat it, hermana. You can just tell us to fuck off because you're tired of talking about this bullshit." Junior teased.

That brought the first genuine smile to her face since KC stepped in it earlier. Junior wasn't wrong even though she knew Leigh would never say those words. Her brash comment acknowledged and validated Leigh's feelings, giving her the freedom to remain as annoyed as she wanted. It was why even after everything her heart was full of love for these women.

"I'm tired of talking about it but I will be giving it serious consideration later." Leigh amended. "I love you. Bye."

Exiting the chat, she dropped her phone on the couch and rubbed her face.

"That's enough," she said to her empty house. "This drama will keep until tomorrow."

Chapter 18

DAYS LATER, LEIGH STILL hadn't shaken off her mood. She thought hashing it out with KC would make her feel better but the opposite had been true. In fact, the more she sat with it, the more she stewed.

KC's stupid voice coming out of his stupid face saying his stupid words wound her tighter and tighter until she was sure she'd crack a tooth from the pressure. And for her sister—her *sisters*—to agree with him, even tangentially, was beyond the pale.

While it was technically true that no one had ever asked her to do anything, they certainly didn't step in or take initiative at any point, either.

The doorbell broke through her spiraling thoughts. "Shoot," she muttered, hurrying down the stairs, "is it that time already?"

A gust of cold November air blew in and Leigh tried to use the door as a barrier to the frigid breeze.

Quincy quickly stepped in and hoisted the bag of takeout. "You like spicy, right? How do you feel about Hakka?"

"Unless you got it from the same place as that terrible pholourie—"

"You still on that?"

"—then I'm good." At his exaggerated eye roll, Leigh felt some of the irritation seep out of her pores. Quincy was good for lightening her mood—even if he lacked all knowledge of Guyanese food. "Come on, I have a bottle of Syrah that should pair perfectly."

Quincy followed her up the stairs, grumbling "How long can you hold me on that? Doesn't the thought count at all?"

"Sir. You brought a Guyanese woman sub par Guyanese food. I wouldn't be surprised to learn the people who sold it to you had never stepped foot in the country, much less be able to find it on a map. How long do you think I should 'hold you'?"

Heaving a dramatic sigh, Quincy lamented "A brother can't win for trying. Damn."

"Yes, yes—so very hard done by." Leigh pulled cutlery out while Quincy washed his hands. Without prompting, he grabbed two plates. It amused Leigh that he was so incapable of eating out of a container. She understood, of course. Her mother raised holy hell if you cross contaminated condiments or left crumbs in the butter which meant Leigh was evangelical about the avoidance of both. Still, something about seeing this large man pour his beverages into a glass before drinking tickled her.

Leigh twisted the aerator on the bottle and motioned for Quincy to pull a wine glass down. When he'd place two on the counter, she raised a questioning brow.

"I'm attempting to diversify my palate."

Once they'd plated their meal—house special noodles, chili mixed vegetables, and seafood chop suey—Leigh grabbed the bottle, Quincy carried the glasses, and they settled on to the couch to watch more of the glass blowing show.

Things between them had settled into an easy rhythm. With his occasional reading breaks at her shop or them grabbing dinner and zoning out in front of some low stakes TV or some type of sport, they'd seen each other a half dozen times in the month since they'd come to their understanding.

He'd not made any suggestive jokes or gestures, nor had he attempted extending their physical connection beyond the occasional high five or other equally platonic encounter. Even now, they sat together on the couch—a mere hand's width separating them—and he seemed completely at ease, commenting on the competition unfolding in front of them while he ate.

Unfortunately for Leigh, as it was wont to do, her unsettled mind started to wander with no regard for the fine food, entertainment, or company surrounding her. Leaning her head back, she tried pushing away the implication of KC's words. Again.

"Long day?" Quincy asked, scooping the last of his noodles into his mouth before placing his plate on the coffee table in front of him.

Leigh's smile barely made it to her eyes as she did the same. "Long week."

"I hear that. Do you want to vent, plot revenge, or have some distraction?"

What did she want? She hardly stopped long enough to consider it. Her adult life had been a series of 'what needs to happen next' regardless of her 'wants'. That he even understood the difference between the options was enough to silence her rambling mind. When was the last time she truly considered what she wanted?

Quincy took a sip of his wine and said, "Travis always says after two glasses of wine, he's ready to risk it all. I don't usually pay him much mind seeing how he's such an innovator in the field of not getting laid." It would appear Quincy decided on distraction until Leigh said otherwise. "But I'm feeling myself off this one glass. I might owe that fool an apology—it makes me want to kiss."

Leigh took in his hooded eyes and relaxed posture, the lazy curl of the right side of his mouth, the gentle way he cradled the globe of the wine glass to his chest, and impulsively—without thought or concern for consequence—leaned across the short distance to place her lips on his.

His lips were soft but firm. Very firm. She was surprised by how firm his lips were until she felt his solid grip on her shoulder. *Ohhh, he's one of* those! *I don't think I mind it.* Leigh was so caught up in her reverie, it took her a beat too long to realize Quincy had pulled away. Another moment cleared the fuzz from her brain to notice he had not kissed her back and, in fact, seemed rather annoyed with her altogether.

Oh.

Oh, no.

How utterly embarrassing!

Quincy's whole face shuttered, "That wasn't an invitation."

"No, I know."

"You said we could only be friends, nothing else was on the table. That's what *you* said."

"Because it would be irresponsible!" The words were out before she could soften them, give this moment context.

If his face was frosty before, it was positively glacial now. "Yes, you've mentioned."

"Sorry! I didn't... I—"

"You what, Leigh?" He interrupted. "Did our ages suddenly change? You forget how math works?"

"I didn't forget how math works," Leigh cut her eye at him while moving herself to the other side of the couch. She couldn't outrun her mortification but she could put some distance between herself and the warm cocoa scent of him. "It was wrong. I shouldn't have done it. I'm sorry."

He leaned over to place the glass on the coffee table and then rested his forearms on his thighs.

Leigh could hear his deep inhales and slow exhales. "It won't happen again," she assured him.

"Until it does." His bitter laugh came on a shallow gust of breath.

"Quincy..." she started, but bit back the words when he looked at her.

"The parameters of this thing between us have been established by you. I've complied willingly and without hesitation. So how come you get to cross the boundary? If you've changed your mind—if we're going to be the kinds of friends who kiss—then there's a conversation to be had about expectations."

"It wasn't fair for me to do that. I was in my own head and I'd gotten into it with my family and I'm so damn tired of being the responsible one. None of this is an excuse, I know. It makes it all so much worse, actually. But it's the truth. I wanted to just... do what I felt like."

"And kissing me is what you felt like?"

"No!" Off his hurt expression, she quickly amended "Yes!" She took a deep breath and tried again, "More like throwing caution to the wind..."

"So, I'm a means to an end?" Quincy went from pained to affronted which was infinitely worse.

How could she make him understand? She'd felt burdened by responsibility her entire life. To know that all of that pressure and restraint she'd lived with might have been unnecessary, cracked something in her entire sense of self. Getting involved with this beautiful man twelve years her junior was the height of irrationality and yet all she wanted was to kiss him. To feel a fraction of his fire and know, after everything, it burned for her.

Before she could come up with something to say, Quincy spoke.

"This isn't a game for me—I'm here because I like *you*, Leigh. I like being around you. If all I wanted was sex, I wouldn't still be here. I have options."

"Like Alice?" She shouldn't have said that and the narrow-eyed look he gave her only confirmed it. How would she explain having that information? How would she make it clear that it wasn't a judgment? Leigh held his gaze, hoping he understood.

After a long, scrutinising moment, he nodded, "Yeah, like Alice."

"You're my friend, Quincy. I don't have many of them and it's been such a long time since I've made one without it being tied to work or school or my son."

"Respectfully, I don't need another friend I can kiss."

Respectfully or not, the gut punch landed. "Okay, so..."

"So, I already know what I want and what I'm willing to bear. You're the one who needs to figure out their shit. And until you do, I don't think this is going to work." He stood, picking up his keys and phone, and made his way to the stairway without bothering to shrug on his jacket.

"What does that mean?" Leigh hoped she didn't sound as panicked as she felt.

"It means you have to decide whether you never kiss me again or you kiss me exclusively for the foreseeable future."

"I decide?"

"You've decided everything else so far." His shrug was equal parts judgemental and sarcastic. "Why stop now?"

Leigh wouldn't pretend she didn't understand his anger. He deserved better than for her to play dumb about the line she'd crossed and the insult she added in the balance. Still, this felt too... final. Mulishly, she asked, "What about a third option?"

"The third option?" He moved his hands out from his sides in a helpless gesture. "We cut our losses and call it a day."

A small gasp escaped her throat. She'd never been good at playing chicken. She had no idea why she was attempting it now but in for a penny, "You're leaving it entirely up to me to decide if we stay strictly platonic friends, embark on an ill-advised relationship, or never see each other again after you walk out tonight?"

Accusation radiated from him as he nodded slowly and turned to leave.

"Quincy, wait!" She didn't have anything to say, she only knew she didn't want it to end this way... for this to be their last night together. When she didn't say more, he shook his head forlornly.

"Good night, Leigh."

Chapter 19

Leigh tried her best to not let her relationship status distract her. She'd clouded too many pools lately and was reeling from the chaos of it all. Between her spat with KC, the sting of discovering he wasn't totally off base, and her mortifying blunder with Quincy she was rattled.

The worst part, she was becoming painfully aware, was that a large part of this turmoil was entirely her doing. Talk about a harsh dose of reality!

Giving her head a small shake, Leigh returned her attention to the inventory screen she was updating. Choosing which books to stock and in which quantities was a delicate balance. Insomuch as anyone could predict what would sell, Leigh had the added difficulty of trying to cater to as many fringe and marginalised markets as possible in one very specific genre. Paying attention to the kinds of requests her customers made was just as important as noting what sold and how fast.

"What's with you?"

She looked up to see Ava eyeing her critically. She hadn't heard her sister come in, which she suspected was the reason for the stern appraisal.

"Inventory." Leigh tried to inject nonchalance in her reply.

"Inventory of what?"

Pushing her glasses onto her forehead, Leigh rubbed her face. "The books, Ava. I'm inventorying the books in my bookstore."

"I didn't realize inventory could be so engrossing." Off her blank look, Ava added, "You didn't even notice me come in."

Leigh knew this for the indictment it was. She went out of her way to greet every single person that walked through the doors, a simple 'Hi' or 'Good morning', no matter what she was doing. She wasn't sure if she'd initiated a single conversation today.

It was one thing to be on auto-pilot in the kitchen, something Mo noticed and loudly did not comment on, but she couldn't allow her distraction to affect the retail aspect.

"I've fallen a little behind and need to get this done."

Ava's snort openly mocked her.

Straightening, Leigh plastered on an award winning 'service face' and smiled "I've been remiss. How can I help you?"

"The shoot at Eastbound Brewing finished early. I thought I'd swing by to visit my only sister and pick up some cheese rolls I plan to have for breakfast tomorrow before my six o'clock up at Downsview." Ava said, nodding meaningfully at the display case.

Ava was a commercial photographer that occasionally sold licenses of her work to stock image companies. Leigh didn't have the stomach for freelance work but her sister was thriving. Leigh busied herself packing the order.

"Should we keep pretending you're not distracted because of Quincy or...?" Ava asked.

Leigh didn't want to rehash this again. She couldn't. She'd barely slept that night with his words playing on a loop in her mind. She'd lobbed the whole sordid encounter into the group chat with no preamble, desperate for analysis. Fat lot of good it did her since she was met with variations of 'why not?' and 'do it, if you want'. Hadn't anyone realised not knowing what she wanted was entirely the problem?

No. She knew exactly what she wanted. She just knew it wasn't wise to want it.

And now here stood Ava, frosted lip-gloss and winged eyeliner, scrutinising her.

"It's that obvious?" Leigh cringed.

"Ehh." Ava made the so-so gesture with her hand. "So? What will you do now?"

"That's just it. I have no idea!" Leigh looked for the two customers. It wasn't so a large space, she needed to keep her voice down and her tangled drama to herself. "I like him. We have fun together and he's easy to be around."

"Intolerable!"

Leigh gave her arm an admonishing swat. "I am twelve years older than he is, Ava. Twelve!"

Her sister didn't answer right away and Leigh let the muffled sounds of the street mix with the soft instrumental playlist floating from the speakers. The woman with the stroller made her way to the door. Leigh gave her a bright smile and a cheery "Thank you!" to make up for her earlier distraction.

"I tried to invite him to Junior's holiday potluck–"

"Oh my god, remember that one year when her boss openly propositioned her cousin, Diego?" Ava's gasped interruption momentarily derailed Leigh's train of thought.

"I think she did more than proposition him." Leigh said, tilting her head a little as though trying to coax the memory forth.

"No way! Really? What happened?"

"Ava!"

She shook her head quickly while waving her hands in front of her, "Sorry, sorry—go ahead. What did he say?"

"He said William had him on stand-by for a flight to Hong Kong. That's the life he lives—jet-setting off to random places on a whim." Leigh still remembered the recoil she'd felt when he explained the flight wasn't full at the moment and William thought he could get a couple seats so Quincy figured he'd take advantage since it was off season and he had more 'free time'.

Ava looked at her as though she'd spouted horns. "So?"

"So? So that's not my life, Ava! The young and wild and free thing isn't for me."

"D'you want to know what I think?"

Leigh gave her a flat stare. They both knew she wasn't truly looking for an answer to that question.

"I think," she continued, proving them both right, "the age thing is an excellent problem when you're after an excuse." She continued speaking as though she hadn't heard Leigh's outraged gasp. "It's a date, Dottie. He's looking for a little tongue after dessert if all goes right, that's all. Stop borrowing trouble."

Leigh opened her mouth to protest then closed it again. Wasn't borrowing trouble just another way of saying 'proactive'? When did preparedness become a flaw? Waiting for a problem to arrive before working out how to deal with it seemed very inefficient, if anyone wanted Leigh's opinion.

A white woman with the greenest eyes Leigh had ever seen made her way to the counter with two books in the crook of her arm. She was chic in a black poncho-style coat and her auburn hair was swept up in an elegant twist. Her smile dripped with a knowing discretion Leigh felt like a flush in her cheeks. Had the woman been listening to their conversation? How mortifying. She rallied her professionalism and took the books for scanning.

Huh. The third in the Georgia Arcana series and the first of the Fire on the Horizon series. It would appear the stylish woman had a thing for sexy werewolves.

Leigh returned her smile.

Tucking her books away, the woman turned to Leigh and said with a wink, "Might as well, dear. Life's too short." and made her way out the door.

"Was that about you or about the books? Please tell me they are exactly what I think they are."

"I don't know, Ava. Do you think they are werewolf shifter romances?"

Ava's eyes were wide with shocked disbelief.

Leigh giggled despite herself. Resting her head on Ava's shoulder, she took a moment to enjoy her sister's presence before reminding her, "Traffic will be a nightmare if you don't head out soon."

"I know I can't stop you, but try not to wear yourself out from over-thinking, okay?" Ava twisted, wrapping her arms around Leigh in a comforting hug.

It took her a few days, but in the end, Leigh knew that she was avoiding the truth: she liked Quincy. A lot. And if the age thing didn't bother him, why was she letting herself get hung up on it. Ava was right—it was a date. Maybe a little light petting when the night was over. She was a grown woman who was allowed to have casual, care-free encounters.

But first she needed to apologize.

Then she needed to explain.

Knowing how well Langston responded to her random phone calls, she decided to text Quincy first. She might not want to focus on their age difference but she definitely knew there were some divides and phone calls were one of them.

Is now a good time to call?

Gnawing at her bottom lip, she waited for him to reply. She watched her phone for three solid minutes before chiding herself for being ridiculous. She was almost done going over her supply order when she heard the familiar text notification.

Maybe in an hour. Finishing a work thing.

Leigh looked at the time. An hour still put her well before bedtime. She'd enjoy her dinner while zoned out in front of the competitive glass blowing show until it was time to call him. In fact, she decided to complete her skincare routine now so that no matter how the call ended all she had to do was slide into bed when it was over.

With all her salves and oils going to battle against the ravages of time, Leigh settled down with her plate and ice-cold strawberry Bubly when her phone rang. Weird.

"Hey JuJube, what's up?" Julian, her youngest sibling and her father's only son, must be trapped in a ditch and about to be mauled by a bear if he was picking up the phone. Something was very wrong.

"Do you know what he just said to me? He said I need to start behaving like a man."

With no preamble or greeting, Julian talked like he texted. 'He' could only be their father, Trevor.

"You can't keep letting him get to you."

"He laid into me because I disrespected his wife by calling her Katie." Julian spit the word out with all the derision he felt. "She was Katie when she got lost at the zoo in grade one. She was Katie when she peed her pants at the haunted house in grade three. She was Katie when she got her own tongue stuck in her braces in grade five. The first time I've seen her since we left elementary school was last year when they announced their engagement! How can he be mad that I didn't call her Katherine?"

"I still cannot believe they're married. He has a daughter named Catherine. Isn't that reason enough to just... not?"

"We were in kindergarten. *Together.*" Julian stressed the last word through what sounded like gritted teeth. "Cat doesn't win this one, Dottie!"

Listening as her brother's misery poured through the phone's speaker, Leigh reflected on the mechanics at play for Julian and Cat to even know each other. Diane, Julian's mother and Trevor's third wife, wanted nothing to do with his daughters. She basically pretended that Leigh and her sisters were a fever dream to be ignored and Trevor allowed it.

It wasn't until Diane and Trevor divorced that the three girls met Julian, though they were vaguely aware of his existence. Of course, the fact Trevor tried scheduling the weekends so that his older daughters could babysit his young son while he tripped the light fantastic came as a surprise to no one. Why change a winning formula? Unfortunately, Trevor didn't consider Catherine and Rhonda were old enough to refuse him and Leigh had already had Langston.

This was a familiar call and response between the pair. Julian lamented trying to please their father while Leigh soothed his frayed nerves and tried her best to get him to cut Trevor loose. All three of his daughters had and none of them seemed to be too worse for wear as a result.

Rhonda flat out didn't speak to him. Leigh wasn't even sure Trevor had her current contact information. Because she and Cat had kids, they both kept the lines open so they could know their Pop-Pop. The only difference was Leigh insisted Langston understand that his grandpa died when his mother was a girl, giving him three grandfathers to his cousin's two. Trevor was a terrible father and the poster child for what Desiree called an Ain't-Shit Man, there was no way she would replace her dad for Trevor when it came to Langston honoring his elders.

They'd reached the part of the conversation where Julian listed all of his grievances. Knowing that this could take anywhere from five to forty minutes, Leigh grabbed her notebook from the coffee table and made a list of things she wanted to get settled for next quarter. She also needed to see if it made sense to outsource her bookkeeping—the major stuff, she would never relinquish it completely—or if she should keep slogging through it.

Her mind wandered further to her mortgage renewal. She was pretty sure she'd signed a five-year fixed and wondered if she could lock that rate in for another five years. Everything in her gut told her interest rates were about to climb again.

"Dottie." Julian sounded like he'd been trying to get her attention for some time. Whoops.

"I'm here. You asked if I thought trying to be a realtor was a mistake." Her phone lit up with a text. Otis. Her other brother. Her useless brother. She would (or would not) deal with that later.

"And? Do you?"

"It doesn't have to be a mistake. What does Jade think?"

"Basically the same thing. I have nothing to lose to try and that I can always return to HVAC even if it's not with Dad." His girlfriend was a civil engineer who also occasionally worked at her best friend's catering company for fun.

"Thirty isn't too late to start something new, JuJube. I was forty when I started the shop. You'll be okay."

Julian sighed and Leigh felt his pain. He was burdened by Trevor's unfathomable expectations. If she could be a refuge for him to calm his riotous feelings, she would.

Rising to put her dishes in the sink, Leigh gave a stretch while Julian started to wrap the call up.

"You don't have to pick up the phone when he calls, you know that, right?" Leigh said for the hundredth time. "Promise me you'll try to ignore it the next time he calls."

"He gets so bent when I don't answer or, if I'm legit busy, I take too long to call back."

"Yes. But my sweet darling, he's bent when you answer right away. So what's the difference?"

Huh. That advice was oddly applicable to her situation. Was this really the first time such a thought occurred to her? Had she really never considered applying such boundaries to her own life? She was willing to admit the topic was at the forefront of her mind recently, what with her conversation with KC and her girls and the fallout with Quincy still rattling around her head.

"You're right. I know you're right." He agreed. "I'll try. I promise."

Her phone lit up with another text.

Mom, is there something in the day-olds you can send? Dad will be in the neighborhood tomorrow.

"Thanks for listening, Dottie. Jade's an only child with normal parents. She doesn't quite get it sometimes."

"I love you, JuJube. Take care."

Ending the call with her brother she answered her son **What exactly are you looking for?**

I'm having a strategy session for festival season.

Got it. Tell your dad he can pass on his way home.

You're the best Mom ever!

She typed back with a wry smile, **I bet you say that to all the moms.**

Leigh rushed back to her notebook on the couch and made a quick note to put a package together for Langston. She did a quick inventory of what was available which led her down an imagination hole: red velvet cinnamon rolls? Chocolate chip cookie mini bundts? Lemon lavender cake? Satisfied with her list of experiments, Leigh returned to the sink, washed up the dishes and finally, exhausted by the events of the day, dragged herself to bed.

She'd just turned off the bedside lamp and lay her head down when she sprang up with a gasp.

"Quincy!"

Chapter 20

Q UINCY WORRIED A LITTLE when his meeting ran late. He didn't usually like to keep his team behind after a concert. It made the already long day intolerable. But as the meeting dragged and his phone didn't ring, he got increasingly annoyed.

Leigh had taken a week to get back to him and he was very much in his feelings about the matter. What was she thinking about so hard that she couldn't get back to him to let him know one way or the other? How difficult could it be to make a choice?

By the time he got home he was heated.

She'd texted asking if they could talk then she didn't call to talk!

He'd cracked open a beer and plopped himself down on the couch, stewing.

He didn't regret giving her the ultimatum. Feeling her lips pressed against his was everything he'd wanted and learning that it was a whim still roiled in his guts. If she'd said anything—anything!—remotely related to liking him, wanting him, he might have spent the rest of the night holding her close. Instead, she'd told him he was an afterthought. A convenient outlet for her frustration.

As he finished his beer, he questioned his unwillingness to call her. In the car he'd convinced himself the ball was in her court and she had to make the first move. Now, hours later, twisted with apprehension, he wondered why he didn't put himself out of his misery.

He checked his watch. Again.

When her name popped up on the screen he knew it wasn't because he'd summoned her or her call would have come through any of the dozen other times he'd picked up his phone to check. For a hot, petulant moment he considered not answering.

Taking a deep breath, he accepted the call.

"Sorry, is it too late?" Her soft voice was a little hoarse at the edge. She sounded exhausted. "I lost track of time."

She must have been busy in the kitchen. He didn't want to know if it was anything other than that. His nerves were already too frayed.

"Nah, it's alright."

"You were at work late. Is everything okay?"

Even with all this uncertainty, Leigh was still Leigh. "It was an unavoidable scheduling thing. Nothing to worry about."

"Listen, Quincy, I wanted to apologize for kissing you the other night. It wasn't fair and I was out of line." Her words came out in a gust of breath, like there was a countdown before she'd be cut off from further speech.

"I appreciate the apology Leigh, but—"

"Please. Let me finish." Her interruption was equal parts soft and assertive.

Quincy didn't want to let her finish if the rest of the conversation was going along this remorseful path. Yes, she'd been disrespectful but he wanted her to apologize for using him, not kissing him. For kissing him for the wrong reason instead of for kissing him at all. Forcing her hand was blowing up in his face and he wasn't sure how to course correct.

"Sure, go ahead." He relented.

"My Dad died when I was twelve. When I was thirteen, a man I vaguely remembered from the funeral was introduced to me as my biological father. Until that moment, I'd had no idea I wasn't my dad's natural child. I mean, I wasn't the same height or complexion as Ava and Sidney but I never felt different or less than for a solitary moment of my life. I was a Daddy's Girl through and through. I didn't even question why they were tested for the genetic heart defect that took our dad but I wasn't. And then, out of nowhere, Trevor is standing in our den talking about me getting to know my sisters."

Quincy only had a surface understanding of her complicated family. But finding out that your whole life was a lie? That would have been devastating.

"I was so angry and hurt and confused the only retaliation my young, rule-following mind could conjure was to transfer to Arthur Meighen from Holy Name of Mary and reinvent myself as Leigh. Dorothy was the quiet, dutiful daughter who never stepped a toe out of line. Leigh would be bold and daring. But becoming Leigh was harder than I thought. Turns out I'm hard wired to rule-following bookishness."

"Peaches," Quincy's voice cracked with heartbreak for her.

She carried on as though she hadn't heard him. "When I finally did it, truly made a choice that was selfishly, recklessly, out of character I ended up pregnant at seventeen and a mom at eighteen. I didn't even regret it. Not really. No one had ever been in love the way KC and I were in love and our baby might have been unplanned but he was chosen." Her rueful chuckle said she recognized her youthful bravado for what it was.

Quincy wasn't sure where she was going with this. It was nice to have the backstory but it wasn't necessary. It didn't change anything. He already knew she was a young mother; he'd seen Langston around and met KC at the book thing. None of this was really a revelation and it didn't change how he felt about her.

As if she'd heard him, Leigh said, "I'm telling you this because I need you to understand. My acts of rebellion are quantifiable. I have always, always been the responsible one. When Junior organized the Rail Fest weekend of debauchery in Miami to celebrate her best friend's divorce being finalized—"

"I thought you were Junior's best friend." Quincy interrupted.

"Best Friend is a tier designation, like Chef or Olympian, not a title." There was a hint of condescension in her tone but she continued before he could call it out. "Anyway, four days in Miami with indiscriminate hook-ups and you know what I was doing? Holding purses and discarding unsupervised drinks."

"Sounds like you were being a good friend."

"Sure. But also I was *making* it my responsibility. No one asked me to. No one expected me to. These were grown women, many who'd been actively partying, dating, and hooking up for years—they knew how to handle themselves. And yet, I righteously remained out of the fray ignoring men who flirted with me. I couldn't loosen up, even then."

"Do you regret not having a random hookup in Miami?" Quincy didn't need any explicit details about Rail Fest—Christ, even the name made him blush—but he was Leigh's friend first and foremost and he wanted to make sure she felt heard and understood.

"Maybe? Not really. Sometimes?" She worked through her feelings out loud. "It's not really the point, though, is it? The point is irresponsibility doesn't come easily to me."

"And being with me isn't responsible."

"It isn't." Quincy's stomach dropped hearing those words. He knew it was where the conversation was headed, but it still felt like a blow. She took a deep breath and he braced himself for impact. "But I want to anyway."

Wait, what?

"You want to anyway."

"If you still want to, that is."

What was he going to do with this woman? How could she think he didn't want to, didn't want her? Waiting for her verdict had kept him on edge all week.

"Leigh, I told you where I stand."

"Together or not at all."

"Yes. So the question is, are you in?" He wasn't sure why he was pressing the matter. She'd already said as much, hadn't she? But he'd spent the last week in his own head, convincing himself she was going to walk away from him entirely—no friendship, no relationship—with each passing day. He needed to convince himself the threat had passed.

"Yeah," she answered on an exhale, "I'm in."

Quincy's smile took over his whole face. He smiled so wide it was almost painful. If his boys could see him, cheesing in his apartment, alone, because a woman agreed to go on a date with him, they'd never let him live it down. He didn't care. Nothing could dampen his mood.

"So, I guess the only thing left to decide is when you're free for me to take you on a date?"

QUINCY HAD BEEN WAITING FOR this evening all week. After their fraught conversation, he was very much looking forward to taking these next steps in their relationship. Even the word thrilled him: relationship.

Sure, a friendship was a relationship and Quincy had enjoyed Leigh's friendship. Hanging around with her was fun and freeing and he knew without any doubt that if things never progressed further, he would have been happy with that place in her life. He'd spent too many years of Miles drilling 'no means no' into him that he would never pretend the long game to worm his way into a woman's favor.

Leigh had said no.

But now she said yes and it was going to be even better than before because now they could laugh and joke and tease each other, they could bounce ideas off each other, they could sit in companionable silence together—all like they had before—with the added bonus of kissing!

He checked the time on his dashboard to assure himself he was on time to pick Leigh up and make their reservation. Knowing that Leigh started her days before the sun, he'd asked his brother for a neighborhood recommendation and Miles had insisted he checkout a spot on the Danforth. When Quincy had looked it up online, he added another notch to the Miles Always Knows Best column he'd been tallying since they were boys.

The restaurant was a modest size with warm, wood floors, wrought iron accents, colourful textiles, and ornate chandeliers that gave the feel of decadence in an intimate setting. It was the perfect place for their first official date. He wanted to show her that things were different, that he took this seriously, without straying too far afield from their norm.

Quincy picked Leigh up exactly at 7:30. He texted her from the car and was waiting for her when she stepped under the awning to lock the door behind her.

She was wearing a wool dress coat with a soft looking scarf looped around her neck. Her feet were in stylish but practical boots and her legs were covered in shimmery black tights. He'd never seen her in a dress before. Or was it a skirt? Not that it mattered, really. It was more the surprise of it—the additional facet to her personality. The layers of Leigh Bridger kept surprising him. Kept intriguing him.

Pushing the code into her door, she smiled up at him "Ready?"

"Almost." Quincy stepped closer to her on the small cement block, "Would you mind terribly if I kissed you now?"

Her eyes widened behind her glasses but she nodded her assent.

Quincy leaned down and pressed his lips to hers in a quiet greeting then, before he could stop himself, he'd wrapped his arm around her waist and pulled her flush against him and deepened the kiss. Her lips were as soft as he remembered and they tasted like the watermelon lip balm she always had on hand. She let out a small sigh and Quincy took the invitation to let his tongue explore hers. Feeling her hands slide tentatively from his shoulder to a more assured clasp around his neck made him giddy with sensation.

Breaking for breaths that puffed in the night air like little clouds, fogging up her glasses, he rested his forehead on hers and whispered "I've been wanting to do that for so long. I didn't think I could wait any longer."

Leigh looked both pleased and overwhelmed.

He held out his arm to her "Shall we?"

Quincy led her to his truck and helped her in. When she was settled in her seat, he leaned in and pressed a quick kiss on her lips, giddy with the freedom of it, before closing the door and hustling to the driver's side.

"Now will you tell me where we're going?"

She'd asked once and had easily accepted his explanation that he'd had all the arrangements made and all she had to do was show up. Her only follow-up question was about dress code. "You'll see when we get there," Quincy answered cryptically.

"Fine." She gave a teasing eye-roll, "Then tell me about your day. How did the meeting go?"

Was it really going to be this easy to move from their friendship to this? All their firmly established routines and multiple conversational threads simply picked up and carried over? He wasn't a starry-eyed romantic. He'd had sex with friends before—he knew how to thread that needle.

This was different.

He'd always wanted to get to this place with Leigh. When she shut him down all those weeks ago, Quincy had also closed the door. In fact, he was so committed to the platonic friendship she'd offered, he'd closed the door, locked it, and parged it over with a layer of cement.

Now, chiseling through the drywall to walk through the other side, he wasn't sure what—if anything—would change. Leigh's usual care and curiosity settled something in him that he didn't realize had shifted.

"It was good. We have a couple last minute things to iron out but I think it's a done deal"

"Oh, congratulations Quincy! I know how hard you worked to secure that account. When will you know for sure?"

"It's after hours in the UK, so hopefully first thing in the morning?"

He'd pulled onto the Danforth which was always busy but tonight had increased foot traffic. Looking ahead to find the source of the congestion and noticed the tell-tale line of white trailers indicating a unit was filming in the area. Slowly, they made their way through the intersection and to their destination.

"What?" She caught him looking over at her feet.

"I was checking to see if your footwear needed me to let you out here while I find parking." The day had been sunny but the cold night air meant the possibility of black ice. He didn't want her slipping on the pavement.

"You haven't played in a Snow Pitch tourney, and it shows." She teased.

"I'm sorry, what?"

"Town wide baseball tournament in the winter. You start drinking in the morning then play through the day."

Quincy's eyes bugged out of his head. "Wait... for real?"

"That's life in a small town, Slick!"

He couldn't stop the raucous laughter from spilling out even if he tried. He'd balked when she'd told him their "Toronto transplant" experiences were not the same because he was from Markham. He might have to rethink his umbrage.

She caught him looking at her feet again and smiled, "I'm good for a bit of winter walking."

Pulling into the lot, Quincy entered the spot in the app to pay for parking before hopping out and opening the door for Leigh. "How do you feel about Ethiopian food?"

"I guess we're about to find out!"

***

Leigh was full. She was the kind of full that meant tonight's sleep would be uncomfortable, if it ever came. And still, she had no trouble admitting that she'd do it all over again if given the chance. Her dinner, a shared meat platter and vegetable platter, was so flavorful and the injera had a delicious tang she hadn't expected. She knew better than to think all African food would be the same.

Sure, there'd be similar ingredients and flavour profiles, much the way it was with Caribbean cuisine but her previous exposure to various African cuisines had not prepared her.

"That was incredible." The non sequitur was less embarrassing than giving herself a soothing belly rub while Quincy pulled up to her door. "I'd definitely go there again."

Quincy threw his car in gear and turned to her with a satisfied grin, "I'm glad to hear it."

The short drive to her place from the restaurant was spent in companionable silence. She enjoyed being the passenger, noticing things in ways she couldn't when she was the driver or even the simple luxury of leaning back with her eyes closed. Leigh almost giggled at the absurdity. It was definitely her dinner talking. A good meal produced endorphins, didn't it?

"Can I walk you to your door?"

Leigh opened her eyes to see that they'd pulled into the parking lot in the alley behind the storefront. Her goofy grin spread wider, "Yes, you may."

He leaned over and unclicked her seatbelt before getting out of the car and walking around to her door. She was, as always, taken by the way he moved with the surety that this world was his for the taking. Snapping herself to attention at the last moment, Leigh gathered her purse and took a cursory glance around even though she wasn't in the car long enough to misplace any belongings. She hadn't even bothered doing up her coat and scarf properly since Quincy ended up finding a parking spot fairly close to the restaurant.

"Peaches," Quincy offered his elbow and a solicitous tilt of his head.

The car door swung closed with a satisfying thunk and before she knew it, she was back on the step under her awning entering the code on the keypad. She stepped inside and turned to face Quincy, noting the unintended but unavoidable imagery of them standing on opposite sides of her threshold.

"I had a good time tonight."

"Yeah?" Quincy stepped through the doorway, forcing Leigh to step back.

This landing was larger than typical as it was the common exit from the back of the store, the stairs to the basement and the stairs to her living space. She hadn't decorated or personalized it in any way other than the piece of slate grey outdoor carpet on the floor. She probably could get away with a coat rack or an umbrella stand in the one corner, maybe some art on the walls? She still felt it was better to keep this space clear of obstructions...

"Where you at Peaches?" Quincy's voice broke her out of her spiral. She'd somehow been backed against a wall and he was standing dangerously close to her. His smile was one part fond exasperation for her wandering brain. The rest of his smile telegraphed a very keen intention.

As though a switch were flipped, Leigh's skin was flushed and her throat was dry. Her chest heaved as she tried to gather her wits, "In the vestibule. With you."

"That's right."

How had his voice gone even deeper? Weren't there limits to the range of frequency a human ear could detect?

"And when you're with me," he continued, his mouth grazing hers as he spoke, "I'd like you to be *with* me."

Leigh could only nod as her gaze flit between his eyes and his mouth.

"So, are you? With me?"

"Yes." Her answer was more air than sound.

"Good."

Hail Mary, full of grace, she wasn't ready. She was uniquely unprepared for the sound of that *good* from his lips. She'd missed the opportunity to part her lips and feel it—taste it—as it landed. She didn't lock her knees, straighten her spine, engage her core, or any of the things you're supposed to do to keep your balance when bracing for impact. Instead, it reverberated through her and made her second guess her ability to rise to this particular occasion. She was willing to admit that she, Dorothy Leigh Bridger, was completely unqualified to meet this moment.

Before she could explain this to him, before she could let Quincy know she'd made a grave error in judgement and beg his forgiveness, his lips were on hers.

His kiss was an unhurried exploration. Her top lip and bottom lip both received repeated, individual attention. When his kiss lingered on her bottom lip, a gentle suction into his mouth, Leigh's tongue gave his mouth an exploratory swipe of her own. Wasting no time, Quincy opened to her fully, letting the kiss grow more heated with each pass of her tongue.

She was sinking. Or was she floating? She lost all sense of herself while Quincy allowed her to kiss him because that's exactly what was happening. He was happily following her lead and it was making her dizzy with sensation.

Gasping for breath she tried to speak, but Quincy placed his hands on her neck, her scarf acting more like a harness than a barrier, tilted her head toward his mouth, and returned to their kiss. This time he was in the driver's seat and the difference was stark. Quincy used his whole body to kiss her. His thumbs running along her jaw, his body pressing against hers, his rumbling sounds of pleasure vibrating through her—all she could do was hold on and hope there was something left of her frazzled senses when he was done.

This wasn't a first date kiss. It was thrilling and expansive and all encompassing and everything about it felt right.

But this was their first date, wasn't it? Or did all their other evenings count towards the tally? Did people still do that? What was the correct number of dates before a person had to have condoms at the ready—three? Six? They'd spent months together as friends—did that mean he got to skip the proverbial queue?

"Leigh," Quincy groaned in her mouth.

Shoot! She'd let her mind wander.

"Do you," she gasped for air in large heaving lungfuls, and pushed through the uncertainty. "Do you want to come upstairs?"

That was the right call, wasn't it? She might not be ready to sleep with him just yet but surely you didn't rub yourself on a man's thigh in your front hall without even offering... what? More kissing? Some tea and biscuits? A hand job?

Quincy's smile was full of affection. He placed a soft, lingering kiss on her forehead. "Not tonight, Peaches."

Wait, what?

He'd kissed her like that and now spurned her offer of... she still wasn't sure what she was offering but it was very clearly an offer.

He must have read her confusion because he held her face tenderly and explained "There's no rush. We can take things slow until you're ready for the next step."

"But —"

"You're not ready, Peaches. When I 'come upstairs', it'll be because we both want it."

Shows how much he knew! She was feeling rather out of her mind with want right now.

Leigh took a deep breath and tried to find some semblance of clarity. Looking into his dark eyes, taking in the way the crinkled at the edges, she nodded her understanding.

"I had a great time. That was the best first date I've had... maybe ever."

He placed a soft kiss on her lips, "Me too."

"Goodnight, Quincy."

"Sweet dreams, Peaches."

And with that, he walked back to his car and drove away leaving Leigh to figure out how exactly she was supposed to regain control of her limbs enough to get up the stairs.

Chapter 21

THE MAIN DIFFERENCE BETWEEN dating and friending, it turned out, was intention. Gone were the quick 'I'm in the neighborhood' texts whenever he happened to be anywhere on the east side of the city, replaced by a synchronization of calendars that required thought and planning.

He wasn't simply showing up on her doorstep with shawarma and a smile. Now Quincy made sure their time together was purposeful and that she felt it. Making the transition wasn't difficult. Adding some heated make-outs to their repertoire certainly wasn't a hardship, though he'd be lying if he said he wasn't eager to take things to another level. They were doing their best to fit each other in whenever possible, but between their jobs, families, and other commitments, they had limited time together.

Once, when he'd started to undo the buttons on Leigh's blouse, her son Langston burst in the door hollering about grabbing something for NoNo that Teva wanted Granny to have. By time he'd tromped up the stairs, Leigh was in the kitchen and Quincy was throwing up a blessing that his dark wash jeans kept his appearance decent for company.

When Langston left, after something to eat and a quick catch up with his mom, Quincy'd figured out Teva was baby Langston for Auntie Ava, Granny was *her* grandmother but Langston had never called her anything else, and NoNo was Leigh's mother who'd apparently started every sentence of his childhood with 'No, no'.

"She doesn't have any other grandchildren, so she's kinda stuck with it." Leigh explained. She also went on to say it was a minor miracle her brother Otis didn't have kids since, "it wouldn't be a complete surprise if you told me he thought 'wear a rubber' meant 'put on rain gear'."

Another time, Leigh was at his place and things were moving along nicely when his personal and work phones went off at the same time. He'd thought his brother accidentally pocket dialed his work phone until he heard his mother in the background complaining that he wasn't answering his phone. When he told Leigh that Miles was running interference for him with their mom, she laughed and complimented their system.

He'd, unfortunately, forgot the most important part of their signal and didn't put his phone on silent. His mother's incessant calling forced him to answer the phone and, worst of all, killed the mood.

Could he have, over the course of these past few weeks, invited her over and immediately slipped her panties to the side so he could get to getting? Sure. He'd most seriously considered it after returning home from the League's winter meeting, when he'd spent four productive but exhausting days in Nashville. But he really did enjoy her company and talking to her always led to somewhere interesting and unforeseen. It was the only explanation he had for the words that had tumbled out of his mouth.

"How did you know about me and Vargas?"

He immediately regretted bringing it up. Especially when Leigh gave a pointed look to her position on his lap.

"Is that really what you want to talk about right now?"

He laughed, agreeing with her very excellent point. At her corresponding laughter, he brought her face to his and gave her mouth a loud, smacking kiss before explaining, "I was thinking about how much better this is because we're friends. Then I remembered telling you I had friends I could kiss but this isn't anything like that and I wanted to make it clear. This isn't casual for me even though you know I've done casual. But then I never figured out how you knew about it and so now here we are."

Quincy'd never had much occasion to notice if or how he blushed. He'd always figured with his complexion it was a non-issue. Now, as the heat crawled along his face caused by his word vomit, he was giving it a lot of consideration.

"Oh ho ho! Not so easy to stop your mind from wandering, is it?" The challenging quirk of her brow matched her haughty tone.

"No," he chuckled while shaking his head in resignation, "I guess it isn't."

"We'll see how long this contrition lasts. You were pretty bossy about it before."

"Real talk? I'll probably be bossy about it again." Leigh swatted him in response but then squirmed in his lap when he pressed feather light kisses on her collarbone. "Are you gonna answer my poorly timed question?"

"Short answer: somebody's cousin works with Junior's cousin Claudia and gave her the scoop which she brought to me. We're not sure if it's a bid to get closer to Claudia but may the heavens watch over them if that's the case."

"'Somebody's cousin works with Junior's cousin Claudia'?" He had to repeat it if only so she could hear how nonsensical the explanation sounded.

She side stepped his question and continued, "For the record, I did not ask for nor do I condone the act of social media scanning but it's apparently a perfectly acceptable thing you youths do—even expected, so I'm told—in this day and age."

Quincy narrowed his eyes at the backhanded slight and worked on putting it together. It was fairly straight forward. Someone went through his socials and found a contact in one of his posts to pump for information. Fine. But why wouldn't she tell him who it was? He'd only met Junior twice and based on what Leigh's told him, they didn't have any immediate people in common.

"And the reason you won't tell me their name?"

Leigh fidgeted in his lap a little, a delicious torment, before meeting his eyes. "I don't want them to get in trouble. If they did it to impress Claudia, they're already in for a rough ride. And it wasn't anything I didn't already know, really. I mean... I didn't know about you and Alice but it isn't any of my business anyway. Besides, Junior said it was an excellent sign of your character so rest assured no one was judging."

Well, if that didn't require a hefty amount of unpacking. He didn't even know where to begin. For starters, was she using they/them to be vague or because it was this person's stated pronouns? Might as well tackle it chronologically. "What's wrong with trying to impress Claudia?"

"She's... a beautiful, sparkling, misanthrope."

"A what?"

"She doesn't like people. Strangers specifically, though she seems to have issues with select members of their family, too." Leigh said, tilting her head in contemplation.

"So you're worried this person is gonna end up eating asphalt behind her?"

"She and Junior both have these gorgeous, magnetic outsides even though they both would rather be home alone with the lights turned low. The difference is that Junior's is like a mask while Claudia's is like one of those immunodeficiency bubbles—she can't exist in the world without it. I worry your friend might have fallen for the facade and will be dealt a hard blow when reality comes crashing down." She sighed heavily. "And if that's the case, they don't need you giving them a hard time about it on top of everything else."

Leave it to Leigh to have such consideration for a stranger's feelings. She truly was one of a kind. Her instinct to think of others, to be mindful of their circumstances, was probably how she ended up bearing the brunt of her family's problems. He guessed it was true what they say, people who were instinctively empathetic tended to take on the weight of the world.

"I probably wouldn't have said shit but there's no way William and Travis let it lie. They lean all the way into their Caribbean-ness when it comes to clowning bitches."

"Travis is the Caribbean one? Not Carter, who seems particularly sharp tongued?"

"Nah, between them two if there's an opportunity for clownery Travis will always be first to find it."

Their conversation flowed freely, like it always did, and—like that—another night ended with Quincy hard as a brick and Leigh fully clothed. He wasn't complaining. Not really. It was becoming increasingly obvious to him that he was unapologetically collared and Leigh held the leash.

Quincy's excitement for the gift exchange brunch he was having with Leigh vibrated through him. She was heading home to St. Mary's for the holiday and this was one the last opportunities he'd have to see her before the New Year.

Even though she hadn't said anything, and even though they weren't dating at the time, he knew she'd been disappointed when he wasn't able to commit to going with her to Junior's holiday function. So, to make it up to her, he'd insisted on recreating the experience to some degree for them to have together. Meaning it was to be brunch—he hoped lunch at a nice restaurant sufficed—with a Secret Santa where gifts were to cost no more than twenty dollars but no less than fifteen dollars purchased from the drugstore holiday section, with a forfeit should they be caught outside the budget parameters, per the official rules.

Apparently, the forfeit at Junior's was a shot of an unholy amalgamation of liquors and liqueurs called The Swamp. Since they were dining at The Hazelton's One Restaurant and wouldn't have access to a decades-in-the-making brew, they'd agreed the forfeit would be something of their choosing before the unwrapping began. Leigh had pointed out that the gift giver wouldn't be a secret but Quincy balked, exclaiming the spirit of the thing should still be honored.

He'd wanted to pick her up, as he did for most of their dates, but he'd had to make a quick stop at the office which would've made keeping their reservation difficult. Leigh promised she was fine to meet him there, insisting it made more sense since it was in the geographic middle of their homes.

When Quincy hustled into the hotel, he spotted her at the lobby bar with the remains of a Caesar. She was wearing a fuzzy cream-colored sweater that begged to be touched with a copper-colored skirt made of a slinky material and a sexy pair of matching heeled boots. Her hair was in an elegant updo and her face had the barest makeup. She was perfection.

She threw her head back and laughed her exuberant laugh, calling Quincy's attention to the man beside her at the bar. He was older than Quincy, maybe in his late forties or early fifties if the distinguished smattering of grey at his hairline was any indication, and his handsome, tanned face spoke of a Hispanic heritage. The way he was leaning into her space, laughing at the joke and flashing his straight, white teeth made Quincy's stomach lurch. If he didn't know any better, he'd say they were visiting from out of town, still hot for each other after a decades long marriage.

But he did know better.

Making his way over, he schooled his features. "Sorry I'm late."

Leigh looked up at the sound of his voice and the smile that broke over her face was slow and sweet like honey. "Not late at all. Quincy, this is Tomás. We were reminiscing about the '93 game."

"A pleasure." Tomás extended his hand and Quincy shook it. "I was helping Leigh pass the time while she waited. We got to talking and realized we were both at that game."

Tomás might not have said it, he might not have even meant it, but Quincy heard the unspoken taunt all the same—*we're old enough to have been there. Are you?* Quincy barely refrained from rolling his eyes. The World Series championship game was like Woodstock for the sheer number of people who claimed to be in attendance. Hell, Carter liked to say he was named because of Joe's history making play and it always amazed Quincy when he wasn't called out on the lie. Math, apparently, wasn't for everyone.

In a primitive show of possession he wasn't entirely ashamed of, Quincy let his hand rest on Leigh's waist.

Leigh sighed with her hand on her chest. "I still get teary when I hear Tom Cheek say 'Touch 'em all, Joe!'"

"You'll never hit a bigger home run in your life!" Tomás finished.

Quincy knew that part of Leigh's emotion came from the loss of her dad, still fresh, getting to experience something he never would. This Rico Suave motherfucker making a move on Leigh didn't.

"It's a bittersweet moment for you, isn't it?"

Her stunned expression mellowed into one of grateful relief. She'd never expressly told him about the tangled feelings she had surrounding the back-to-back championship win but it didn't take a rocket scientist to put those pieces together. Her dad hadn't lived to see his favorite team in his favorite sport's unexpected repeat world series championship win. From one ring to the next, her whole life had changed.

Leigh's eyes were glassy but she'd composed herself enough that her voice was strong and clear. "Yeah, it is." She pulled in a deep breath and the familiar glint of competition sparked in her eyes. "If it wasn't for the players' strike, we might have had a three-peat!"

"I always thought so too," Tomás agreed. He was sitting more squarely in his seat, obviously sensing his moment had passed but unwilling to be left out completely.

"Right?" Leigh gave him a bright smile that Quincy did not care for at all.

"Be that as it may," Quincy gave her waist a gentle tug, "we have a reservation."

Leigh gracefully slid off the barstool and bent to unhook her purse and tote bag from under the bar top. When she straightened, he bent to her ear to confirm that she'd checked her coat and was ready to go. At her nod, he gave Tomás a magnanimous tilt of his head, "Thanks for keeping her company while I was otherwise detained. She's always happy to find another baseball fanatic in the wild."

She gave him a playful, scolding swat but her voice was all tinkling laughter, "It's true. I can talk baseball all day."

"It was my sincere pleasure." Accepting his defeat, Tomás raised his glass to them both. "Until we meet again."

Not if he had anything to do with it, Quincy grumbled to himself. With his arm around her, the cool silky feel of her skirt under his palm, he led Leigh to the hostess who took them to their waiting seat. He pulled Leigh's chair close and gave her a lingering but socially acceptable kiss.

"Hi." She smiled her slow, sweet smile.

"You weren't waiting too long, were you?"

Straightening, she picked up the menu. "Not at all. You got everything sorted?"

"I did." Quincy had managed an epic amount of gladhanding at the League's Winter Meeting. It was a singular opportunity for him to network with the type of people he didn't usually have access to, but it meant these weeks required the fine art of the follow up. He needed to touch base to secure the connections without coming on too strong but also not seeming indifferent. It was a delicate balance. "Paviter knows one of the reps from the thing in Nashville, so we might try to make something happen over the holiday."

"That's fantastic!" She beamed. "Let me know if I can help... if they're into baked treats, maybe I can customize a sampler box or something?"

He was so touched by her thoughtfulness, her willingness to help him pursue his goals, he almost missed when the server arrived to introduce himself and take their drink order. A ginger beer for him and another Caesar for her.

"Are you driving?" Leigh asked once the server left, with a teasing, "There's usually rye with your ginger."

"Yeah, when we're done I'm gonna pick up Miles on my way to my parents. My mom is organizing something for the church which means we're automatically conscripted in her efforts."

It had been a long time since Quincy was an active member of his parents' church. As soon as Miles had stopped attending, his moving away for university the perfect, inarguable reason, Quincy lost all will to keep up the pretences. These little enlistments of his mother's were a small price to pay to keep the peace. Besides, there were few rivals to the ego boost derived from the fussy preening of church ladies.

Looking around the quiet restaurant, Quincy let himself soak up the ambiance. He was in a beautiful room with his perfect date about to enjoy a delicious meal. There was only one thing they needed to tackle.

"I think we should establish the forfeit now."

She raised a challenging brow, "Why, are you worried?"

"No. I just know how you like to twist the rules and I'd prefer to have it all clearly defined."

"Sounds like the words of a sore loser."

Just then, their server returned with their drinks. Taking a small sip after their ceremonial cheers-ing, Quincy put his glass down and returned to the subject at hand, refusing to rise to her bait. "Name the forfeit, Peaches."

"If you insist." She leaned over to rummage through her tote. Placing a small mason jar on the table with a small flourish, Leigh intoned, "The Swamp. Junior sent two shots when I told her about your plans for today."

"It is universally understood that a shot is an ounce. That," Quincy gave the mason jar a dubious look, "Is more than two ounces of liquid."

"This has been the forfeit at her holiday brunch since The Swamp was established. You wanted to recreate the experience, here you go!" Leigh said with a small amount of challenge in her voice.

"I think it's moving."

"Don't look directly at it," she counselled, rubbing soothing circles on his shoulder.

"No, for real—what is it?"

He listened with rapt attention as she explained the origin of the Swamp. She and Junior had been friends for a couple of years by that point and Leigh, tipsy and mentally exhausted from another week at her dead-end job, suggested the random bottles of liqueurs Junior had been dragging around since university might be more than the sum of their parts.

Junior, already well past drunk, had easily accepted the ever-practical and ten years her senior Leigh's edict as the smartest, most logical thing she'd ever heard. The next thing Leigh knew, Junior emptied all eight of the bottles into a crystal decanter and was pouring them shots.

"The next morning Junior woke up on the bathroom floor, dried puke in her hair and her mouth fuzzy and coated in regret. Her words." The nostalgic benefit of distance warmed her voice. "She decided under the hot spray of the shower that she would keep the demon's brew as both a trophy and a cautionary tale of the one drink that felled her."

Quincy was entertained by her antics but also thrilled to know other people knew her lighter side—the silly, playful, competitive side that he'd come to adore.

"Since you're driving, there is absolutely no way you can partake in the Swamp—"

"You're so sure I'm gonna forfeit, eh?" he interrupted.

"—so, I suggest a picture holding the bottle, should the forfeit become necessary." She finished as though he hadn't spoken. "Agreed?"

"Only a picture? We don't have to drink it?" Quincy asked, casting another wary glance at the small mason jar of opaque liquid.

"Oh, no. You'll have to drink it. The picture is to commemorate the moment for those of us who might forget their debts over the merriment of the holiday season." She pulled her phone out of her purse and lay it on the table beside her cutlery. "Ready?"

A small thrill stole up his spine when he noticed she'd placed a print of the stamp he'd had made in Hong Kong's Chop Alley in her cellphone case. William helped him with the translation, as different characters made the sound Leigh. He'd settled on the one for 'pear' as it was an orchard fruit and could reasonably be substituted for peach. When he'd explained it to her, she'd playfully argued he might as well call her Apple if all orchard fruits were interchangeable. For all her fruit-based ire, her genuine delight in the hand carved piece of jade made all the razzing he took from William and Domenic worth it.

"I'm ready. Ladies first?"

She pulled a small gift bag from her tote and placed it in front of him, which he reciprocated by pulling a small wrapped parcel from the inner pocket of his sport coat. "We open them at the same time."

Nodding his agreement, he peered the bag and tried his best not to burst out laughing in the middle of the fine establishment. Quincy hugged the pink mushroom plushie to his chest. It looked too much like Toadette from Mario Kart for Quincy to think it was a coincidence. "You wrong for this, Peaches."

"Not everyone was built for the Rainbow Road, Slick. As a wise woman once said, rookies should think twice before they get behind the wheel to race a thirty-year veteran."

"You said that. You're the one who keeps saying it."

She tilted her head and gave a solicitous spread of her hands as if to say, 'this wisdom is a burden'. Straightening with a cocky grin teasing the edges of her mouth, she neatly peeled the wrapping on Quincy's gift revealing the cranberry-colored box with glittery gold accents.

"I bet I know why you chose this one," Leigh singsonged, holding the box up to her face with a wide smile.

She was right, of course. He'd felt like he'd struck gold when he'd realized one of the 'Squeezy Trio' holiday gift set of lip balms was sweet peach. He had no idea if they were the sticky glossy kind, or how much tint constituted a 'hint of natural color', but the opportunity to gift her—a woman who seemed to be in possession of a dozen chapsticks at any given time—one in a peach flavour was too good to pass up.

"I know how much you like watermelon," he teased.

Giving him a devious grin she said, "I do, I do. But I think I'll start with the berry sorbet."

He was crazy about this woman. He enjoyed all the many facets of her personality but this playful side was his favorite for the ninja-like way it stealthily came and went. Luckily for him, his second favorite facet was her competitive side and it was about to be brought to the fore.

"I'm not even gonna waste time arguing with you." Quincy pulled out his phone and scanned the barcode with his camera. Turning the screen to face her, he said, "I have spent my fair share of time in the toy department. I know these stuffies aren't no twenty damn dollars."

"How did you do that?" She gasped, no doubt shocked at being caught out so easily.

"Can't do that with a Bic and a moleskine, can you? Technology up one hundred!" He crowed.

"You'll be singing a different tune when the machines rise up and a pen and paper are the only way to safely communicate."

He rolled his eyes at the familiar critique of his reliance on his phone's apps. "A half cup of water can erase your whole shit. Please be serious. Stop stalling and accept the forfeit, Peaches."

He liked the thought of Leigh being so driven by competitive pettiness she forgot all about her precious practicality and broke the rules. He liked it very much.

"Wait, wait... let me get the right angle. Okay. Go." Hitting record on his phone just as she picked up the mason jar, Quincy maintained eye contact with Leigh as she tipped the questionable brew back and drank a healthy three mouthfuls. It might not have been exactly half but it was plenty. "Holy shit, you actually did it!"

Gasping for breath, her whole face curdled. "Oh my god, it's worse than I remembered!"

He leaned over and pressed a firm kiss on her mouth. While Quincy was sure he never wanted to try the Swamp himself, he was willing to admit there wasn't much he wouldn't willingly drink directly from Leigh's lips as he gave her a softer, more lingering kiss before righting himself.

"Salmon?" A young woman asked, looking between them with proverbial hearts in her eyes from their tender display.

Quincy gestured to himself and waited for Leigh's pasta dish to be placed in front of her. Their server arrived with the pepper mill and once he was done grinding, Quincy asked for some sparkling water and a plate of sliced citrus. At Leigh's curious look he simply said, "Trust me."

They tucked into their meal and lapsed into companionable silence as they enjoyed their food. They'd devolved into the familiar pattern of bickering he so enjoyed when it came to choosing dessert. Leigh had insisted Christmas meant warm and spicy while Quincy pointed out dessert should be an indulgence, regardless of the season. In the end, they agreed to share the panna cotta because neither of them believed "white chocolate" should be consumed willingly.

It wasn't until they were ready to leave that he noticed how close to drunk Leigh actually was. She'd stood to go use the facilities and wobbled somewhat unsteadily. Quincy wrapped his hand around her waist and held her close until she reclaimed her footing.

"You good?"

She nodded on an inhale.

"Okay," he kissed her temple, "I'll get your coat and meet you at the valet."

He watched her make her way through the restaurant and wondered, not for the first time, what exactly was in the Swamp. She'd had a full meal, dessert, and the water he'd insisted she drink. A couple of mouthfuls of liquor, even with the two Caesars, shouldn't have had that effect.

When Leigh met him at the valet, she seemed surer on her feet but she still was slightly uncoordinated as he helped her into her coat.

As he pulled in to what he'd come to think of as his spot behind her store, Quincy walked Leigh to the door and stumbled when she flung her arms around his neck and planted a whopper of a kiss on him upon crossing the threshold. Her body molded to his, and the soft, touchable textures of her clothes made her curves feel lush in his hands as he ran them up her sides and around her back underneath her coat.

He was delighted to discover that the silky skirt was, in fact, a dress and wanted desperately to see her draped in the luxurious fabric and spread out before him. She started to writhe against his thigh as he pressed small kisses along the column of her throat and he wondered why they'd bothered to go out.

"It was your idea," she panted close to his ear. Taking a small nibble, she added, "Besides, I like being on your arm, Mr. Temple."

Had he said those words aloud? Realizing he was losing control of himself while stone cold sober, he pulled his mouth away from her body and tried to steady them both on their own two feet. When she swayed a bit, it only cemented his instinct to halt their progress. Leigh was the specific kind of drunk where she was both lucid yet muddled. Quincy would wait until they had time and sobriety on their side.

He helped her out of her boots and up the stairs to her apartment. She collapsed in an adorable heap on the couch, insisting she'd be good after a quick nap. Quincy got a glass of water and placed it on the side table closest to her.

She gave him a dopey grin and said, "Merry Christmas, Quincy. I'll see you next year!"

Kissing her again, because how could he resist, he smiled against her lips, "I'll call you later, Peaches."

And with that, he headed to pick up his brother so they could do their mother's bidding.

Chapter 22

"Hey, guys?" Leigh wanted to open this can of worms like she wanted an enema. "I think I'm ready."

"Finally!" Desiree dropped her cutlery and took a sip of her mimosa. "I think turquoise or even fuchsia. One chunky strip from the crown to start."

"What? No," Leigh shook her head and whispered "Sex. With Quincy."

"What did I tell you?" Junior gestured with her glass. "They haven't left first base."

They were at Leigh's enjoying the last day of Peach's holiday closure she had off by celebrating the new year with a boozy breakfast.

Leigh appreciated how her friends made her feel like a priority in their busy lives. Between their jobs and other friend groups—Desiree's dolls, a sisterhood she'd found when she moved to Toronto and who'd been by each other's sides through every transition, medical setback, heartbreak, and joyous achievement, were never far from her thoughts while Junior's curated group, who Leigh admittedly had become closer to since she spent a long weekend in Nassau with them for Junior's thirtieth birthday, were the exact mix of laidback and exuberant she'd come to expect from her loyal friend—she never questioned her place, what they meant to each other.

Nursing her Caesar, Leigh wrestled with saying anything at all. The truth was she was nervous—she hadn't had sex of any kind in over ten years and while she felt ready to take the next step with Quincy, Leigh needed to know just how out of date her information was.

What good was having a sex worker and a hedonist as best friends if not for moments like this?

"I thought you were joking!" Desiree swatted Junior, before pushing her plate away and turning her attention to Leigh, "There's really been no holiday hijinks or Naughty/Nice role play? He hasn't woken up with a handful of your titties?"

"What is that about? I barely have anything yet men treat it like a stress ball!" Junior cupped her modest breasts to demonstrate.

Desiree's disbelief demanded, "You've yet to sit on that man's face?"

"That's third, right?" Ava confirmed.

"Does it matter?" Leigh asked, sighing heavily. She and Quincy hadn't spent much of the holiday together. She'd gone home to St. Mary's and he'd been off doing... fancy people things involving speakeasies and more last-minute flights.

"Before I answer, I would like my Herculean restraint in this matter acknowledged. I haven't pried or asked anything untoward."

Leigh rolled her eyes. "Yes, Junior, you've been the very model of minding your own business."

"Thank you." Junior gave a small bow. "Now, if I remember correctly it goes: 1st base is over the clothes, 2nd base is under the clothes, 3rd base things go in mouths, and home run is, well... a home run!"

"That's good enough." Desiree turned her full attention on Leigh. "Using these parameters, do you maintain that you haven't even made it to 2nd base?"

"I've had so many questions." Junior added.

"Look, it's not complicated. I like him. He's a good person and we were friends. We've technically only been dating for a couple weeks. I didn't want to rush things..." Leigh looked to Ava for support, knowing she was the most likely to understand.

Ava didn't feel sexual attraction at the same rate as other people. You had to engage her mind fully before you ever got close to her body. Junior, on the other hand, would give you her body for a song without allowing you within the vicinity of her mind. The juxtaposition never failed to amuse Leigh.

"You wanted to be sure before it went someplace irreversible." Ava answered.

"Yes."

"And now you're sure?" Junior's concern crinkled the corner of her eyes.

"Yes."

"He hasn't pressured you, has he? Because you can stay right there on first base for as long as you want." Desiree added.

Leigh loved these women with her whole heart. They never made her feel awkward about herself or her celibacy. Truthfully, it rarely came up as a topic. She might be on the receiving end of some occasional flirting, but the gentle teasing only ever went as far as it took for Leigh to reject the suitor as an option. Because if there was one thing they championed, it was agency.

"He's been the perfect gentleman. Honestly we might have done it already if I weren't too scared to make a fool of myself." Leigh admitted.

"First things first," Desiree pointed at Leigh, "Even if you're both butterball naked and he's twelve inches deep—"

"Twelve!" Ava gasped.

"—stop means stop. He'd better pull out and roll over, no questions asked."

Junior nodded vigorously. "Second, use your words, mijita. Don't expect him to guess. Tell him what you want."

"Yeah, we're not doing all of that fake moaning and carrying on anymore. If he's not hitting the spot, let him know." Desiree agreed.

"But that's just it—I don't know what I want!"

"Sex isn't suddenly some unnavigable waterway. What you like will be obvious." Ava assured her.

"It's just been so long and I haven't given it any serious thought before. I mean what if I'm no good?"

"I think it's universally accepted that for men sex is like pizza." Junior shrugged.

"What?"

"Some are better than others but even bad pizza is better than no pizza at all." She clarified to Leigh's disbelieving face.

"I don't want to be bad pizza!"

"You won't be. He's so into you and he waited all this time, it's impossible for you to be bad pizza." Ava assured her. Junior and Desiree nodded their agreement.

"Besides, didn't you tell me you was a throat goat? Give him that deep-deep and he'll be hooked!" Desiree promised.

"When will you see him next?" Junior pulled her phone from her back pocket.

"I'm supposed to see him tomorrow night." Leigh wasn't sure if other couples had as much uncertainty built in as she had with Quincy. It didn't bother her, especially since his schedule was about to get worse once baseball season picked up again. She understood the vagaries of his job and with her up at four in the morning schedule, she didn't want to get in the habit of seeing each other for ten minutes after midnight.

Desiree sucked in a breath. "That's not enough time!"

"We'll make it work," Junior put her phone to her ear, "Hola, Reina! Que tal?"

"What's happening?" Leigh demanded.

Desiree was too busy scrolling through her own phone to give Leigh her full attention. "What do you think? We have to get you sex prepped."

"Assuming he's as gone as we think he is, all she has to do is show up, no?" Ava asked.

"No!"

"Amparo can fit us in for the Full Monty." Junior was still looking at her phone, "She has a two-hour block available thanks to a cancellation."

"Thank you Black baby Jesus." Desiree raised one hand to the sky.

"I don't know what the two of you are planning but I'm not even remotely interested."

"When's the last time you had a leg wax?" Junior asked sweetly.

"Never. I shave in the shower."

"Exactly." Junior indicated a table full of dishes, "Let's get moving. I ordered a car for the rest of the day; it should be here in a half hour."

"A car service, Junior?" It would never stop being weird remembering Junior behaved as though she were some entailed landowner, benevolently stimulating the village economy with gold doubloons from her coin purse. The idea of having a personal account with a car service was mind-boggling to Leigh.

"There's no time to fight with parking and whatnot in this weather and now we'll have a nice warm car at our disposal and somewhere secure to store our purchases." Junior's explanation was delivered with such nonchalance, Leigh wasn't sure they were speaking on the same subject.

"Plus, we've been drinking," Ava conceded.

"I'm still on my first," Leigh argued.

Desiree pushed the glass closer to Leigh. "Then hurry up and suck it back. We've got work to do."

In the years since she opened the doors to Peach's Books and Bakeshop, Leigh learned more about herself and her capacity to endure. She found new depths of strength and perseverance. She also discovered the well of emotion she had for these women was deeper and more abundant than she'd ever considered before. There was nothing she wouldn't do for them and knew, with everything she had, they felt the same.

Until now.

"I am a grown woman; I will not go hairless for anyone!" Leigh would say it a hundred more times if that's what it took.

She was bundled up in the very back of a Navigator with Desiree and Ava in the middle row and Junior riding shotgun, speaking animatedly with the driver.

Desiree drew in a breath and explained as patiently as possible, "I am telling you it is for your own good. The less things you have to distract you, the better your first time will go."

"I am a mother of a 27-year-old. It is hardly my first time."

"Dottie, you've had less sex than I have in the last fifteen years. Please be serious for a moment."

With an indignant huff, Leigh crossed her arms over her chest and looked out the window.

"That man is going to lick and touch and stroke you all over. Your body will be his Twister board. It'll be left hand blue, right hand green—a tongue on one spot and a finger on another, simultaneously. This isn't some repressed puritanical coupling where you keep all your clothes on and lay in the dark thinking of multiplication tables until it's over. They're eating ass in these streets, girl. Sex has evolved!" Desiree said.

Leigh's eyes went wide with shock.

Seeing her sister's panic, Ava tried a different approach. "Think of it as eliminating as many obstacles as possible. You know how your brain spirals. This way, you won't be thinking about what he may or may not find if he reaches for any part of you. You're free to focus on what you feel. Besides, it's not forever. Once you get comfortable with each other, neither of you will care about stubbly legs or hairy ball sacks."

It was closer to a scoff than snort, but the indelicate noise Leigh made conveyed her discomfort all the same. She didn't have to like Ava's words simply because they held a hint of truth.

"Jesus Cristo, you think too much!" Junior's voice sailed easily to the back of the vehicle. She heaved an annoyed sigh, irritated at having to expound on something so obvious. "The closer his parts get to your parts, the better it feels. That's why you're doing it. Because it will feel fantastic. You'll thank us when you've come multiple times on multiple parts of his body in multiple positions."

"Junior!" Ava scolded as Desiree pointed at her and said "Exactly!"

There was no more time to argue because they'd pulled in front of the wax bar.

"What, do you all plan to be in the room supervising?" Leigh snarked as she realized the three amigos were following her up the steps.

"Do you want me to come with you?" Ava's voice was filled with gentle concern.

Leigh knew any one of them would have held her hand through it if she asked, which was why it was hard to hold on to her irritation. Yes, she was being strong-armed into a grooming service she did not want, but she couldn't deny that they were trying to help. She did think too much. And having sex for the first time in almost a decade was causing her no small amount of anxiety. And she didn't want to highlight any flaws that were in her power to control. And—

"Ms. Bridger?" The soothingly bland voice broke her from her spiral. Leigh looked up to see a young, coiffed, perfectly made up curly-haired, red-headed white woman in a white cosmetology smock smiling at her with warm welcome. "If you're ready?"

Leigh inhaled deeply and held it a beat before letting it out in a slow, steady exhale. She turned to the group with a bit more steel in her spine, "See you later."

"You had a natural birth, remember? You can do this!" Desiree prompted.

"I'll be right here if you need me." Ava pledged, settling into the lobby seating with crossed legs.

"We'll be having foot massages and iced coffees." Junior corrected, tugging Ava up out of the seat. "But we'll be here when you get out."

Desiree blew her a kiss and followed Ava and Junior back outside.

Leigh returned the woman's smile, "Ready!" and followed her down the hall to her fate.

LEIGH COULD HEAR DESIREE AND Junior's muted voices—Junior oohing and ahhing while Desiree explained the latest in her line of trans-inclusive lingerie. Desiree's evolution from phone sex operator to sex toy creator to lingerie designer was slow and at times difficult. Desiree knew from personal experience how often trans people were left out of consideration in the designs and so she worked hard at filling that void.

This boutique was the sole brick-and-mortar retailer of Desiree's line of lingerie in Toronto and Leigh couldn't be prouder of her friend's hard won, entirely earned success. She'd become one of the hottest names in pleasure tools and accessories. It was only a matter of time before her lingerie line followed suit and was carried all over the country.

"Dottie?" Ava was on the other side of the curtain. "Need any help?"

She was standing in a luxuriously appointed changing room, thick velvet curtains separating her from a viewing stand in front of a tri-fold mirror, with a pile of increasingly revealing lingerie options. Still reeling from the clinical intimacy of having another human put on a headlamp and magnifying glasses to inspect her pubic area, Leigh wasn't sure she was ready for more scrutiny.

Just over an hour ago, a veritable stranger had spread her butt cheeks and murmured "Hmmm" followed closely by another perfect stranger holding her breasts and declaring "This cup is too small!" She'd never, not once in her life, been so manhandled and she'd given birth! She needed a minute to recover.

Keeping her voice pitched low, unsure of how many other customers might be in the changing area and unwilling to expose herself any more than necessary, Leigh answered, "I don't think these will work."

The curtain was pushed aside to reveal Desiree and Junior looking perplexed at Leigh's fully clothed form.

"Ma'am," Desiree scolded.

Junior, who'd rarely encountered a door closed to her and thus walked through all of them without hesitation, entered the change room and sorted through the choices. She re-ordered them on the rail and pointed to the garment closest to the back of the space. "Start with this, work your way forward until you can't anymore."

Leigh looked at Junior's extended arm and realized she'd ordered everything so Leigh would start with the most coverage and work her way to the least. That gesture of understanding, the quiet and understated acceptance of Leigh's limitations without judgement or question, was so typically Junior.

Leigh nodded. "Okay, thanks. I will."

"I have this one in rose gold. It's very comfortable." Ava said, pointing at a floral one piece.

Leigh shook herself out of her fog and started to get undressed.

Desiree reached up to pull the curtain closed and said, "Don't forget, this is for you. You're choosing the pieces that make you feel good, okay?"

Again, Leigh could only nod. The love and support she felt far outweighed the discomfort of having to face this at all. Maybe discomfort wasn't the right word. Leigh maintained the same size after Langston's birth. Her body hadn't spread so much as it had unclenched. As if the musculature of her youth was told 'at ease' and simply relaxed.

Her body was the mechanism by which she made it through each day. She took care of it with meditation, good food, routine application of exfoliants and moisturisers, and the occasional kickboxing class. What had never done, not even in her youth, was decorate it. The concept of undergarments—*lingerie*—for pleasure and not function was completely foreign to her.

After many, *many* changes, Leigh stayed fairly true to her baseline: she'd eighty-six'd any thong or crotchless numbers and gave serious consideration to the bodysuit Ava championed. In the end, she went with a gorgeous bronze lace demi-cup bra and three complementing lace cheeky boyshort panties. It was Leigh, but elevated.

She also chose a stunning embroidered chest-plate style brassiere for which she could discern no reasonable purpose other than the sheer joy of it. The group consensus helped convince her she'd made the right choices.

Leigh made her way to the cash register where her purchases were waiting. There were a few holiday decorations still out and a cute little chalkboard touting 'New Year, New You!'. Desiree put three boxes on the pile and said without preamble, "Lube and condoms. You'll feel better knowing you've got your own supply."

Leigh had barely absorbed her words before she'd strode off to the other side of the store where Junior was giving Ava her ranking of the vibrators she owned. The cashier was a lovely woman who had the type of Indigenous features that could hail anywhere from Alaska to Peru. She gave Leigh a reassuring smile and said, "This lube is our best seller."

All told, Leigh had spent an alarming amount of money. If nothing else pushed her across the finish line, maybe this would.

Chapter 23

KISSING LEIGH WAS ALWAYS a pleasure. He could, and did, spend hours just kissing her with no rush for more. It was satisfying just holding her, feeling the soft weight of her, while she sighed and sipped at his mouth.

Every time he kissed her, he felt the same mix of stunned and familiar. Whether it was in whispered awe or declarative assertion, he never doubted the *'yes, this is where my lips belong'* that thrummed through him.

There was something in the air tonight—something more than being reunited after spending the holidays apart—that told him they were about to remove the training wheels. She'd shown up at his place, skin cool from the walk through the underground parking with no coat and only a small pouch dangling from her wrist, and essentially threw herself at him.

Quincy meant what he said. He understood that she'd needed to take it slow and he honestly was enjoying himself so thoroughly that if someone had told him he'd have dated a woman for a month without so much as having a handful of flesh to show for it, he wouldn't have believed them.

Now though?

Leigh broke from the kiss and took his hand. Looking in his eyes for a moment, "Come on."

"Yeah?"

"Yeah." She tipped back up on her toes to give him a quick kiss before tugging him down the hall.

Allowing her to lead him toward his bedroom, Leigh looked over her shoulder and gave him a shy, nervous smile.

"Hey," he stopped moving, forcing her to stop as well, "we're good, Peaches. You don't have to... there's nothing to prove."

Bringing her body close to his, she put her hands on his waist and slowly ran her hands up his sides, lifting his shirt as she went. Without breaking eye contact, she continued lifting until Quincy had no choice but to raise his arms to get the shirt off, lest it strangle him.

Dropping the shirt, Leigh ran her hands back down his shoulders, along his chest, and around to his back so her chin was nuzzled against the curly hairs that ran the length of his body and disappeared below his belt loops. His muscles may have tensed from the cold of her touch, but his blood was definitely running hot.

"I don't have to," she gave him a look of heated determination, "but what if I want to?"

Quincy didn't need to hear anything else. He brought his hands to her neck and tilted her head back so he could kiss her—really kiss her—to let her know her desire was mutual.

With her hands on his skin, he lost a little of the finesse he'd relied on to keep things from spiraling. Now, they were a tangle of teeth and lips and tongue as he walked the final steps into his room. Turning her to face the room as they crossed the threshold, he placed a kiss on her temple.

"Peaches," he tried to speak, but she turned and pressed herself against him while fumbling with his belt and he momentarily lost his train of thought.

"Hmm?" Her lips were on his mouth while her hand slid into his boxers to grip his increasingly eager erection.

"What?" he gasped, unable to follow the conversation through the haze of lust.

"You said 'Peaches'. You wanted to tell me something?" Leigh's words were punctuated with hot, open-mouthed kisses while she worked his shaft.

Overwhelmed by feeling, by her sounds and taste, Quincy fought to regain a modicum of control. Giving himself a small shake, he grabbed on to the thinnest thread of composure and grabbed her hands, stilling them.

"Peaches, if at any point you need to stop or you don't like what's happening, just say the word. I want—" he felt her squeeze him under the pressure of his own hand and groaned with the sensation. "I want us to be in this together."

"If I'm not mistaken," she said with a gentle nibble of his earlobe, "you're the one currently impeding my progress."

When the lady was right, she was right.

Quincy let go of her hands and allowed his jeans to fall. Stepping out of the bundle of denim, he grabbed the backs of Leigh's thighs and hauled her up the length of his body and walked them to the bed. "You ready?"

She nodded and gave a little jostle of her hips against his hard length.

Carefully, Quincy lowered them to the mattress, kissing and touching and rubbing.

Leigh's plaintive whimper at the friction snapped him to attention. Tearing himself away from the delicacy of her mouth, Quincy raised himself on his forearms to analyze her outfit.

The soft blue jumpsuit had a draping v-neck and an elastic waistband allowing for easy access. As he worked the sleeves off her shoulder and down her arms, her breasts popped free.

Unable to maintain his objective in the face of such delicious distraction, Quincy lowered his mouth to the top of her chest and covered her flesh with worshipful kisses. Taking one of her breasts in his hands while drawing the other into his mouth, Leigh bucked underneath him, crying out her pleasure and frustration.

Encouraged, he redoubled his efforts. Alternating between caressing and devouring, Quincy ran his lips and tongue along every available patch of skin. When he ran the tip of his tongue up the valley of her bosom, up the column of her neck, and to her chin, he let his body follow the motion, grinding against her with only the thin fabric barrier between them. Leigh's whimpers were swallowed by his consuming kiss. He pulled off the bodysuit, leaving her clad in only a lacy pair of panties.

She writhed and moaned and mewled into his mouth as his hands continued their exploration and his hips dragged his erection tortuously between her legs.

"That feels good, doesn't it, Peaches?" His voice was hoarse.

"Yes!" She pulled his head back to her mouth and wrapped her legs around his waist.

Feeling Leigh wrap herself around him was pure bliss. She was hot and needy and it was all for him. He knew that it had been a long time for her. She hadn't said specifically how long but it didn't matter. He would make this good for her, gladly bringing as much pleasure as she was willing to endure.

If the dampness soaking his boxers was any indication, getting his mouth on her was going to be the sweetest torture.

"Quincy, please—I don't," Leigh gasped against her impending climax.

"Shhh." He peppered kisses along her throat, "It's okay. Let go, Peaches—I got you." She could come again and again as far as he was concerned, there was no limit to what he would manage.

"No," she shook her head while still chasing the friction. She was frantic, "Please. I want you."

She squirmed as she tried to remove the last of her clothing while he still lay atop her, pinning her to the bed.

"We got all night, Peaches, I'm not going anywhere." He tried to soothe her with calming kisses but her agitation grew.

"I don't want to be empty." She pleaded with ragged breaths.

Quincy raised himself to his knees and pulled underwear off, tossing it carelessly behind him. The crotch of her pretty lacy panties were damp as was the front panel of his boxers. He couldn't even deny that he'd made some of that moisture himself.

Just a taste, he told himself.

He bent forward and gave her thigh a quick kiss. Then a slow, lazy lick.

"Quincy!"

He looked up at Leigh and her desperate moans. He didn't think his dick had ever been harder.

Doing away with his underpants, he reached over to his nightstand for a condom. He sheathed himself with quick efficiency and returned to the cradle of Leigh's body.

He kissed her again, trying to calm himself—to regain his control—he didn't want to hurt her or, worse, nut in three strokes.

Her hunger made her mindless and she lifted her hips and maneuvered him exactly where she wanted him. "Now, Quincy," she inhaled sharply as she drove her hips up to meet his. "Please, now."

Quincy knew what he was working with. His wasn't a photo op dick, plucked and waxed to a shine, made for admiring Tumblr posts. Sure, he kept things groomed but his dick was more girth than length. And while they'd had their share of adventures together, he wasn't deluded into thinking his shit, by itself, was some insurmountable task. Still, he got stuck as Leigh tightened around the invasion.

He gave her a slow, deep, languid kiss. With her bottom lip still in his mouth, he made a small amount of progress.

"Let me in, Peaches," he plied her with kisses until he felt her soften around him, allowing Quincy to slide fully in her body.

He was certain Leigh crying out as she threw her head back in pleasure when he seated himself would stay with him for the rest of his life.

Laying fully on top of her, unmoving as she adjusted to the fit of him, Quincy cradled her head and gave her soft, gentle kisses.

"Don't leave me on my own," he whispered with a kiss behind her ear.

Slowly, with trembling breaths, Leigh met his gaze. "Hi."

"Hi."

"We're naked."

"That we are!"

Her shy giggle filled him with such affection, he was sure that the smile burning his cheeks was the goofiest one in recorded human history.

She raised her head off the mattress and kissed him, "Thank you."

This woman. What was he going to do about this woman?

He traced her features with his finger while other hand played with her hair. "Thank *you*."

It was no less consuming when his mouth fell on hers, but the frenzy had cooled, leaving behind eager exploration.

After what felt like several delicious hours of laying with her naked body wrapped around his, hands and mouths exploring, Leigh began to move.

"Fuck!" The words fought their way through his gritted teeth.

Noticing the delighted glint in her eye as she bit her bottom lip, he started to move in earnest. Long, smooth strokes in a steady rhythm.

"You like driving me out of my mind? You like that I'm so gone for you that I can barely see straight?" His mouth was right by her ear, and he felt the way the low rumble of his voice made her shiver; made her body arch beneath his.

"Is that what you like?" He rocked into her with a bit more force.

"Yes!" she cried.

Their ragged breaths mingled and the miniscule space separating them was punctuated with small nips and licks. He was so close but she was closer and he needed to feel her come undone, to cross that milestone and end her drought.

She writhed and clawed at him as her head tossed from side to side.

God, she was amazing. He pressed his cheek against hers so his voice could be heard over the sounds of moaning, panting, and slapping body parts filling the room. "I cannot wait to hear what it sounds like when you come all over my dick."

Her only reply was a whimpering sob.

Quincy stayed focused on Leigh. He followed her lead and kept his stroke at the speed and pressure she responded to best. It felt so good—*she* felt so good—he would have waited another year if this was the reward for his patience.

But a switch flipped and he lost her somehow.

"Leigh?" He slowed his movement. "Where did you go?"

"Nowhere, I'm right here." She gave him a bright, game smile. "It's okay. Keep going."

When he didn't move immediately, she ran her nails down his back until she had a handful of his ass and tugged him until he moved.

"Keep. Going." Her teeth scraped his jaw.

He kissed her, his tongue searching hers for their lost momentum, before resuming his movement. His teasing finger along her nipple brought a satisfying rise in tension. More kisses and a couple of gentle nipple tweaks put them back on track.

Relieved, he kicked things into a higher gear.

"Like this?" He asked, desperate for her satisfaction.

She moaned her approval while sliding her heels along the backs of his thighs but he was losing her again.

"Talk to me, Leigh. Tell me what you need." Quincy's hands moved down her body but she halted his progress.

She beamed at him. "I'm okay. Keep going."

Her words and expression were so at odds, Quincy couldn't be sure he wasn't hallucinating.

"What?"

"I said, I'm okay."

Quincy stopped all movement. "What does that mean?"

"You should," she squirmed, awkwardly trying to explain, "you know... *finish*."

Finish?!

Quincy immediately pulled out, hovering over her balanced on his forearms. The noisy, sloppy suction sound perfectly underscored their annihilated vibe.

***

"The fuck?"

Leigh scrambled out from beneath him, noticing how his erection bobbled at her accusingly as he sat up.

"There's no reason to get upset," she brought her knees to her chest.

"No reason—," he blurted his disbelief, "You skipped the tracks—twice—and then told me to go on without you. That's some straight bullshit, Leigh."

She winced at the force of his outburst. As if this wasn't embarrassing enough, she had to endure it stark naked.

"You're acting as though it's personal!"

"How is it not personal?"

"I was enjoying myself. Weren't you? What else matters?"

Quincy's eyes widened as he tried to comprehend the conversation they were having. With new suspicion he narrowed his eyes, "Leigh, have you ever orgasmed before? With a partner?"

"Don't be ridiculous, of course I have." She scoffed with haughty derision. Did she orgasm every single time? No, not necessarily. But she almost always enjoyed herself. They certainly didn't need to hold a referendum on the matter.

"First of all, it's not ridiculous—many women struggle with it. And second, we are supposed to be in this together—as in you nut, I nut, we all nut—that's what together means."

"This is not an indictment on your prowess, Quincy. Your reputation is safe."

"You think a give a good crackling fuck about my reputation? Get outta here with that bullshit. Look at you!" He indicated the sheer volume of moisture in the vicinity of her groin. "My reputation was never in jeopardy."

Her skin was cooling and any sense of desire had long fled, but damn if the sopping wetness wasn't all over her every fold, crease, crevice. Hell, the sheets looked as though a glass of water had toppled over.

Leigh drew in a large lungful of air and let it out silently. "I am sorry I suggested you were concerned about your reputation."

"Don't manage me, Leigh. You told me to finish like your body was just some available hole to use! You should be sorry that you closed the door on your pleasure!"

This was getting ridiculous. Wasn't he listening? "No, that was you! I was enjoying myself plenty. Instead of taking yours when I told you to, you chose to wax poetic about climaxes."

Quincy's posture deflated. He pulled off the condom, his spine not the only thing lacking in urgency, and dropped it in the waste basket beside his bed. Falling back on the headboard, he let out a humorless huff of laughter.

"The night we first met, when you and your sisters were cutting it up, I remember thinking 'damn, she's so pretty'. Then you let out a surprised little gasp when you handed me the book—your lips were parted and your eyes were wide behind your glasses—and I thought 'I want to make her do that again and again'. Your pleasure is my pleasure. How can you not know that?"

Oh.

What on Earth was she supposed to say to that? She'd wanted everything their bodies promised each other, and it had felt so good to simply feel his skin on hers, to feel the press and weight of his body on hers, she sincerely would have been satisfied had he blown his load five strokes in.

Leigh crawled to the head of the bed and sat beside him. She took the hand closest to her and clasped their fingers. Smiling up at him, she scolded "I knew you were up to no good, right from the start. Talkin' 'bout 'do you remember me?'. Too slick by half!"

Quincy laughed and brought their joined hands to his mouth to kiss her knuckles.

With some of the awful tension lifted, she nestled herself against his side. "I'm sorry."

She hated that her rambling brain had ruined this beautiful first time for them. That it would now forever be tainted.

"You don't need to apologize." His lips were pressed against her temple as though he wanted to whisper the words directly through her skull. "Tell me what happened."

"Nothing specific happened. I got in my own way and couldn't see my way through."

"Why didn't you just say that?"

She reared back to face him. "You wanted to talk about my spiraling brain during sex?"

"Of course. Maybe I could have done something to help. Maybe I still can."

"I think that ship has sailed."

"Tell me about it, anyway," he prompted, pulling her head back against his chest.

How could she articulate such a nonsensical fear? Even now, as she tried to parse the layers, it sounded foolish. It was already blown so wildly out of proportion. She needed to shut it down, not give it more room to breathe and grow.

"Talk to me, Peaches. Please."

Sighing, she forged ahead, hoping that she could give him a satisfactory explanation without dying of further embarrassment. "It's been a while since I've had sex. Of any kind."

"You mentioned." Quincy snuggled her closer.

"Yeah, no—I mean a long time."

"Okay."

"Like... a really long time. Like ten years, almost." She blurted the end of the sentence in a rush of breath.

Quincy stiffened beside her. "For real?"

"Yup." Leigh nodded to herself. "When I started to have sex, I was sneaking around with KC so it had to be quick and quiet. Then, it had to happen quickly and quietly because Langston was sleeping or otherwise distracted. After KC and I split, I only... entertained when Langston was spending the night with his dad or grandparents, but it was still quick and quiet because I didn't want anyone getting any ideas."

She'd spent so much time trying to toe the line, be responsible and not make any waves. Allowing the neighbors to think she had a stream of men in and out her home was unacceptable. No matter that it wasn't anyone's business, Leigh grew up in a small town and knew the power of being held in the community's high regard. She wasn't willing to compromise it for a roll in the hay.

"So when you said you wanted to hear me, I got distracted trying to remember what I sounded like. Then I wondered if it'd be good enough, if you'd like it. From there, I spun all the way out: should I make a lot of noise so you knew I was enjoying it? Too much noise and you'd think I was faking. But you were so attentive and responsive, surely you knew how much I was enjoying it. What if you didn't? What if I needed to say some dirty words? I'm no good at sexy talk. I don't use cuss words because I sound ridiculous when I swear. You see where I'm going with this, right?"

"You're saying I messed up your flow and took your head out the game."

He sounded so morose, it made Leigh hurt. She wouldn't allow him to think for one moment he'd held even one ounce of responsibility.

"As you pointed out, the sound of your voice has always done it for me." She gave his hand a reassuring squeeze and leaned over to kiss him. "This was about me not being able to shut my brain off long enough to enjoy myself. That's part of why I didn't want you to do the... other stuff."

He put his lips on the shell of her ear to ask with all the rumble he possessed, "Do you mean going down on you?"

"Yeah," she squirmed, "That." On a shuddering breath she continued, "I figured if I could rip the bandage off and get it over with, I could get out of my own head and everything else would fall into place."

She waved her free hand to encompass their current position as if to say 'fat lot of good that did me'.

"I'm sorry I ruined our first time together."

He leaned away from her so he could look in her eyes. "I'm not." Bending to nip at her chin, he whispered, "I had three, maybe four, strokes left. Tops. You saved me from embarrassing myself."

Giggling, she swatted his chest, "Now we'll never know!"

Leigh settled into the comfort of Quincy's embrace. Even buck naked and the mortification of their thwarted intercourse not yet dulled, talking to him was the easiest thing in the world. How he managed to say the right thing—balance the line of assertive and agreeable—was the quality she'd feared losing most when the topic of being a couple was seriously broached. And yet here he was, holding her and teasing her and making sure they got through this together.

Quincy continued to leave soft kisses along her hairline and down the side of her face, cracking more jokes to soothe her pride. He asked her something... about a glass of water? Mumbling a reply, Leigh was only vaguely aware he'd pulled the duvet up over her shoulders.

Chapter 24

LEIGH COULDN'T BREATHE. SHE was hot and there was a crick in her neck and her hip felt like someone had crazy glued the joint together. Opening her eyes was another mistake—she'd fallen asleep with her contacts in and everything was blurry. She needed to go home and sleep in her own bed.

Slowly the fragments started to come together and the hot flush of embarrassment pebbled her skin all over again.

Looking at Quincy, brought her up short. He was gone to the world and waking him to essentially complain after last night's debacle seemed cruel. More than that, it made her seem even flightier. No, Leigh had to leave him with something positive, something to assure him that she did have a good time and would again in the future. She had to prove it to herself, too.

As if sensing her intention to leave, Quincy hauled her to his side while muttering something incoherent, and settled back to sleep. She felt the rock-hard length of him against her thigh and her body clenched in anticipation. Could she bring herself to try again so soon? It'd only been a couple of hours but now that they'd discussed her hang-up, surely they could make it work.

Her gritty eyeballs and seized hip said otherwise.

"Quincy." Leigh ran her hand gently down his chest, toward his impressive erection. "Quincy, I have to go."

He muttered his response.

Taking him in hand, compelled by the need to feel him in her palm more than any discernible logic or reason, Leigh tried again. With a kiss behind his ear, she whispered, "Quincy, I'm leaving."

A short thrust joined the muttering. This time she could pick out the word 'Peaches' and 'body'. Holding him a little tighter, Leigh followed the motions of his body and fisted him with quick, shallow strokes.

"Wake up, Quincy." It might have been a while since Leigh had sex but she knew a sleeping person's erection did not equal intent or consent. "Wake up so I can say goodbye."

Leigh was squirming in her arousal. She wanted him, creaky joints be damned. She looked at the time. Could they do it quickly so she could get a couple hours of sleep at home? She didn't want to rush him but she also didn't want to hop out of his bed immediately after, either. She definitely didn't like the idea of that.

The feel of Quincy's hand around hers, halting the motion mid-stroke, startled her.

Looking up in time to see the fogginess of sleep replaced by the haze of lust, she pressed her lips to his, "Hi."

"What's going on?"

"I'm trying to say goodbye."

Quincy opened his mouth to speak but chose to pull her lips into his mouth for a long, lingering kiss.

"Is this how you say goodbye?" Her hand still encased in his, he started to move. "With a fist full of my dick?"

The low, rumbled words sent a shiver along her body and her voice quivered out a barely audible "You wouldn't wake up."

Another kiss, "I'm up now."

Leigh's other arm was trapped between their bodies. Levering herself up, she lay herself more fully atop Quincy's bare chest. The skin-to-skin friction on her nipples caused a chain reaction that ended with her squeezing him harder as she tried to regain the rhythm he'd set.

"Quincy," Leigh was aching and desperate and wasn't entirely sure what she was pleading for. Before she could say anything foolish, she slid her tongue in his mouth while their hands continued their pace and her body writhed helplessly against his thigh.

Flushed and breathless, she tried again, "Quincy, please. I—"

"Tell me." Quincy's free hand ran down her spine to her hip, pressing down to add more pressure to her grinding body. "You what, Peaches? Say it."

"I have to go home." Her entire body opposed that assertion. Even her once dissenting eyeballs were now demanding a bit of light to fully appreciate their circumstances. He didn't need light to see her for the miserable liar she was. She was a sopping tangle of need, dangling at the edge of something she was too cowardly to reach for.

"You have to go home?" Quincy repeated the words, more for Leigh's benefit than his own.

She opened her mouth but couldn't form any words. Instead, she made a helpless half shrug in response.

"Okay." Quincy immediately pulled both hands off her and clasped them under his head.

The loss of his touch, of his heat, made her feel awkward and confused. Obviously, he was respecting her wishes but his dick was a steel rod in her hand and she continued to drip obscenely against his leg. Was she supposed to stop? He didn't pressure or cajole or even so much as frown at her words. And she did want to go home... eventually. She just wanted something else first.

But that isn't what she said.

Quincy had been clear. All she'd had to do was ask him—*tell* him—about the something else and she didn't.

Couldn't.

It was last night all over again. He'd said they were in this together and she had to communicate with him so they could stay in it together. He couldn't know why this was such a difficult concept for her to grasp. Leigh's whole life had reinforced the message that she couldn't rely on anyone other than herself and saying what she wanted, expressing a need, was a waste of time. This, what he was offering? It was everything she'd ever wanted—someone to ask her what she wanted and then *do that very thing*.

And yet, she'd managed to create the exact mess she'd wanted to avoid when she first woke up. This was the complete opposite of leaving him on a positive note.

She wouldn't leave like this. Quincy didn't deserve it and neither did she.

Steeling herself, she raised herself up and said against his mouth, "I had a wonderful evening." Resuming the stroke with the speed and pressure he'd shown her, she continued "I can't wait to do it again."

"Leigh." His voice was a warning she would not heed.

"But it's late and I have to go home. So if you'd be so kind as to leave your hands right there for a moment."

His momentary confusion was all the opportunity she needed. Pushing off his chest, Leigh angled herself so she was kneeling perpendicular to his hips. With one preliminary lick up the veined underside of his dick, Leigh pushed it past her lips and slowly, directly, down her throat.

"Fuck!" Quincy's hands were on her immediately.

"Ah, ah!" Her lips were at his head like she was speaking into a microphone. Her eyes glinted with mischief as she scolded, "Hands."

"Leigh!"

Her tongue was featherlight on his skin, teasing with barely there contact.

He moved one hand to the mattress and was rewarded with a long swirling suck. Getting the message, his other hand swept her hair over her shoulder and landed at his other side.

She recalled how especially biddable men were when a blowjob was on the line. Good to see that much hadn't changed.

Returning to her task, Leigh again tried her best to relax enough to remember the ebbs and flows of doing this properly. She used to be really good at it, once upon a time. A skill born more of need than any specific desire, oftentimes oral sex was easier and faster and, as mother nature would have it, Leigh was proficient at the act because she didn't have any particular gag reflex.

She just needed to remember how to breath through the initial obstruction. Quincy's girth made it a bit of a struggle but once she relaxed, Leigh remembered what to do and, more importantly, how to enjoy herself.

And once she started to enjoy herself, she couldn't concentrate on anything else.

Not on what she looked like or sounded like. Not even on what might happen next.

Which is why Quincy's voice, deep and hoarse with his pleasure, unexpectedly pushed her over the proverbial edge.

"Is this what you wanted? You wanted me to watch you swallow my dick to the back of your throat until you feel me nut? Or do you want me to pull out of that hot mouth of yours and spill all over you?"

Oh, God—did she want that? She worked his length faster, giving extra suction at the tip.

He kept talking—making promises and offering praises—until she was out of her mind. "Maybe you want to sit on my dick while I play with your clit. I'd slide right in, nice and smooth, wouldn't I?"

This was unlike any dirty talk she'd experienced in the past. There was none of the boastful nonsense, demanding she answer what belonged who to and how. Or the silly call and response 'do you feel that?' 'Oh, yeah' 'You like that?' 'Uh huh!'. This was a platter of options being presented for her pleasure. Choices she could take or leave and all she had to do was want it.

"Do you ache, Peaches? I can fill you up. Say the word. Tell me where we should start." His voice was whispered temptation, gravelly and strained.

Her entire body clenched. If she could just loosen the valve a little then maybe she wouldn't feel like her skin was too tight. Her hand began to move toward her throbbing bundle of nerves.

"Goddamnit, Leigh, if I can't touch you..." He gripped her wrist and held it on his hip.

The sudden motion tipped her off balance and she fell forward, his hard shaft choking her as she let out a cry of frustration. Leigh's throat burned as tears spilled down her face. She squeezed her thighs together, desperate for any release.

Quincy let go of her wrist long enough to grip her below her knee and pull her legs apart. He grabbed a fistful of her hair and pulled her off him. Did she look as crazed as he did?

She felt wild and depraved. She fought a little to get her mouth back to work while simultaneously hoping he'd push her face into the mattress and thrust heedlessly into her body until she screamed. She wanted to be filled by him everywhere all at once and was frantic at the impossibility of making that desire a reality.

His chest heaved and his words came through gritted teeth. "Together or not at all."

"Please," she squirmed shamelessly. "Quincy, I want to. I will!"

What could she do to make him understand the chasm he'd unearthed. How could she articulate how far gone she was when her very essence had been reduced to an endless, throbbing need? Begging a man to let her suck his dick was outlandish. Begging *this* man was the most reasonable thing in the world.

Reaching for him, she gave the base of his erection a firm squeeze, "Please."

This time when he lowered her back to his crotch, he didn't move his hands from her hair. Instead he kept her in full view, with careful attention to her wandering fingers and slick thighs.

Leigh took him in her mouth and with every stroke she increased the suction, licking his balls with him deep in her throat. Her cheeks were practically concave and still she didn't let up.

Quincy came with a shout, holding her head still as he pumped his release into her eager mouth.

Maybe he wasn't as mindless and feverish as she was but she'd reduced him to snarled curses and blasphemous oaths which was rather satisfying, all told. The freedom of it, the power and liberation she felt, knocked something loose. Leigh's climax crashed into her by surprise. On a startled gasp, she stiffened as it took hold of her.

"You're fucking joking." Quincy's growl was lost in the pounding in her ears. He pressed her onto her back and palmed her, feeling the proof for himself. Grinding his palm against her throbbing clit, he kissed her feverishly.

Leigh couldn't get enough air into her lungs. Her eyes rolled back as her body convulsed under Quincy's brutal attention. "Quincy!"

"That was mine, Leigh." He pulled a nipple into his mouth without letting up on his palm's ministration. It was clear his intention was to draw this out for as long as her body could stand it.

Her sob did not foster any sympathy as he continued his campaign against her pulsing body. "Mine!"

Was it possible to black out from an orgasm? Leigh was sure she was on her way to finding out. Her whole body shook and still Quincy stayed with her, tormenting her, as she rode it out.

"It feels so good, doesn't it?" He kissed her tear-stained face. "You look wrecked and it's so fucking hot."

She couldn't begin to imagine what he saw. Her hair was without a doubt tangled and whatever was left of her makeup would be smeared all over her face. She was sweaty and tear-stained. Everything about her was limp and damp and she couldn't muster the wherewithal to care.

The waves of pleasure were starting to recede. Still, certain strokes caused a tiny aftershock that arched her back off the bed. He whispered into her temple, "Shhh... I've got you, Peaches."

When it seemed like she'd made it to the other side, Quincy rolled them over, draping Leigh on his chest and covering them both with the duvet. They lay together, him gently stroking her back and shoulders, while they regulated their breathing.

"I'm so pissed at you."

Leigh shifted her hips and felt his burgeoning erection thicken. "Not so pissed."

"Ignore that." He moved his groin away from hers, "I'm very pissed."

"I'll make it up to you tonight."

"Can't. Paint By Numbers tour. Tomorrow?" His kiss was wild and consuming and she cursed his job's requirement for him to be at the boxes and suites during events even in the League's off season.

Leigh moaned against his mouth, "I've got Langston's screening. Sunday? The bakery is closed on Mondays and I don't open the store until 10."

"Sunday." Quincy grabbed a hold of Leigh's head with one hand while the other caressed her face. "I'mma make you pay, Peaches. Believe that."

With one more spine melting kiss, Quincy helped Leigh to her feet.

Fumbling around in the dark, she made her way to the washroom—wincing at the racket the jet engine force of the flushing toilet made—and pulled on her discarded clothes.

If this full-body flush is the result of Quincy being indirectly involved with her orgasm, she was very much looking forward to paying whatever price he wanted.

Or so she thought.

Leigh hadn't even made it home before Quincy's first missive came through: a man eating a mango the Caribbean way—sucking the pulpy fruit through a tear in the peel, tilted slightly forward to avoid staining his clothing with any leakage.

A couple hours later, he sent her a gif of an aloe plant being peeled. A couple hours after that, it was a clip of a clear, viscous liquid being rubbed between fingers. It was likely some type of cosmetics commercial but the context was blatant.

And if it wasn't, Quincy had also found old clips of venerated British actors reading the lyrics to popular songs and sent her every suggestive one. Hearing Sir Blah-de-blah gravely orating about getting in the back seat with the windows up, the disappearance of Sprite cans, and jumping on waiting saddles all made it so Leigh remained feeling jittery and on edge.

And the worst part, worse than the constant hints and innuendo, was the fact that he never mentioned those messages directly when they spoke. Their nightly calls filled with updates about work and their day continued as though he hadn't flooded their text thread with a trail of sexual promises.

The onslaught continued the entire three days they were apart, making it impossible for Leigh to think of anything else. When Sunday finally rolled around, she was restless with anticipation.

By time she pulled into the visitor's parking, she had jittery hands and a fluttery heart.

Quincy was upstairs waiting, already alerted to her arrival by the concierge, to exact his penance for what he'd dubbed her brazen show of disrespect. He'd only brought it up once since that night but his entreaty was clear—by denying him the chance to get her off she'd stolen from him, wounded his pride, and shamed him in the eyes of his ancestors. His censure came with enough fervor, Leigh wasn't entirely sure he was joking.

Nothing for it. They both knew this day was coming and what was going to happen. It was time to pay the proverbial piper and her insides were knotted with equal parts anxiety and anticipation.

She still hadn't found the right category for what she was walking into. This could technically be considered make-up sex, though it didn't feel accurate. Obligation sex was also wrong—she wasn't being forced to sleep with him. Beholden sex? Compensatory sex, maybe? All she knew was Quincy was adamant that a debt was owed and she'd looked forward to paying it.

She smoothed down her dress in the elevator's mirror. The knee-length knit fabric garment was designed to look like a large button-down cardigan. It was warm, comfy, and appeared fancier than it was. Her hair was in a simple low ponytail and makeup was, per usual, non-existent. In her defense, she was holding a tube of dark red lipstick when she remembered the 'rainbow parties' of her youth and dropped it back in the threadbare pouch. Whether she ended up on her knees or not, she had no interest in leaving lipstick rings on Quincy's genitals.

She rapped her knuckle on the door in the incessant pattern from her youth, synonymous with the arrival of anyone from her mother's gene pool.

"Are you ready?" He asked in lieu of a greeting. He was wearing an oatmeal-coloured lounge set with wide legged drawstring pants and a loose v-neck top that was a beautiful contrast to his dark complexion.

"For?"

"You know what for."

She leaned up and kissed him as she tried to make her way past him and into the unit. Instead of letting her through, Quincy wrapped his arm around her waist and hauled her up against his body deepening the kiss. He pulled away long enough to rumble "Bedroom, Peaches. Now." against her lips.

He set her down, giving her enough time to remove her boots and set her tote on the table in the entranceway.

Quincy's room didn't look any different from the last time. His bed was impeccably made, his dresser devoid of any tchotchkes, and the night table had a pitcher of water and a lone glass on a coaster. Even the club chair in the corner was empty of clutter, save for the pink mushroom stuffie she'd gifted him. She'd have to ask him how he managed it. The chair in her room was filled with everything from purchases she needed to return to clothes she considered wearing today but hadn't put back.

She sat gingerly on the edge of the bed.

"You have two choices," he walked to the nightstand and emptied his pocket.

"What's that?"

"Electrolytes. You have two choices," he repeated, "get them clothes off yourself, or I'll do it for you."

He produced another glass and coaster from somewhere and placed it beside the tube of soluble tablets. He pulled his shirt off and placed it on the chair in the corner. Coming back to the bed by the nightstand, he put a tablet in each glass and filled them with water. Looking over at Leigh who'd only got as far as removing her glasses, he announced, "Time's up. My turn."

Leigh squeaked her surprise when he snatched the covers from beneath her and hauled her body more solidly on the bed. "Quincy!"

"I warned you."

Quincy tried to unbutton her dress from the hem.

"You can't." Leigh showed him how she couldn't slide her fingers through the spaces between buttons. "I had it sewn closed."

The short, mildly impressed sounding "Huh!" was all the notice he gave before hitching her dress up and over her head and settling between her thighs. Before she could issue any sort of order to the proceedings, he was licking her through her panties. Leigh struggled to remember which ones she'd put on, so overwhelmed was she by the onslaught. A satin-y pair with no particular gusset to speak of if the feeling of his hot, wet mouth was anything to go by. Without stopping, he slid his thumb underneath the damp fabric and stroked her.

Leigh gasped, squirming under his attention.

In a deft move, Quincy hooked his finger in the crotch of her underwear and pulled them down her legs while bending her left knee up and out the leg hole. With the scrap of fabric now dangling around her right knee, Quincy returned to his task with gusto, devouring her with large, greedy swipes of his tongue. His rumbled pleasure coaxed an echoing moan from her. He used his tongue, teeth, and lips to tease and taste her from stem to stern, making her legs quake and her core clench.

Quincy started to kiss the inside of her thigh, running his knuckle gently up and down through the mess he'd made, until his kisses reached her calf and he was kneeling. "I can not get the memory of you in my bed out of my mind. Your soft, soft body, the way you drenched my sheets, your sexy noises—I've been bricked up for days and nothing I do helps. But I have a theory." He let his knuckle stroke her clit. When she shuddered at the contact, he repeated the motion three more times before continuing, "My theory is that this is like when you fail to shut down a program correctly. It won't launch until the system resets and it has a chance to complete the process properly. What do you think?"

"I—" What did she think? She felt warm and dizzy but her skin was covered in goosebumps.

He slowly pressed his knuckle into her body. "Hmm?"

"Yes."

"Yes?"

Leigh nodded, the beginnings of her orgasm stirred to life. She didn't really know what she was agreeing to anymore, but knew she was game for whatever he had planned.

Releasing her leg, he pulled a strip of condoms from his pocket and dropped them on the bed beside her. "So we're going to reset? Let the program run its proper course."

She nodded again. How was she expected to think with his fingers roaming freely, driving her closer and closer to climax. A fleeting thought managed to break through the fog of lust clouding her mind.

Pushing herself up on her arms, she brought her face to his. "We can't reset with your pants still on."

Quincy grabbed the back of her head and pulled her in for a consuming kiss. His tongue found hers immediately and Leigh whimpered directly into his mouth when he slid two fingers into her, stroking with intention. She broke free, gasping for air, as Quincy placed wet open-mouthed kisses down her throat, his fingers never wavering in their purpose.

Leigh let her head fall back, prepared to crest the summit Quincy was dragging her to. She almost cried out when he pulled his fingers slowly out of her body and said "Good point."

She was so close, it startled her to realize how ready she was. Her attention was promptly diverted by the sight of Quincy fisting his length, his eyes on hers.

"Condom."

Giving her head a quick shake to clear the fog, she tore one from the strip and extended it to him. Before he could reach for it, Leigh pulled it back. "Let me."

He kissed her again, a slow sensual joining of their mouths. "If you insist."

It was the last clear thought she had before Quincy had her body beneath his, her right leg hitched over his waist, and his hips driving into her with firm, even strokes. Her left hand was held above her head, her right was on Quincy's arm holding on for all she was worth.

"Yes, Quincy, God—"

Her words were cut off by more deep drugging kisses while he ran his free hand up and down her side. The sound of his body meeting hers, the fine gold chain he wore occasionally bouncing off her face, the smell of their heat warmed skin—lemongrass and cocoa mingling together—was enough to bring Leigh right back to the crest of the climax she thought she'd lost.

Leigh's gasped breath sounded like a moan and a plea. Her pleasure was mined from her very core and she let him know with the guttural sound she made "Quincy, please... I—don't stop."

"I won't, Peaches—I'm not going anywhere," he vowed before leaning over and pulling one of her nipples into his mouth, teasing and licking her breast.

He let her nipple out of his mouth with a soft, wet pop and Leigh was primed for the impact of the surging orgasm.

Except... Quincy spread her right leg on the bed. So while he kept the exact same pace and pressure as promised, the growing spark had fizzled and died. She couldn't help the whimper of disappointment that escaped, squirming beneath him trying to regain the position that had brought her so close.

"Where are you going, Peaches? Isn't this what you wanted?"

Her sighed 'yes' was an incomplete answer to his question.

"And now you're running when I got all this dick to give you?" Quincy released her hand and rose up, spreading her other leg out. Keeping one hand on each thigh just above her knee, he slowed his stroke all the way down. "And I intend to give you all of it."

The slow, punishing drag of him as he pulled almost all the way out only to slide unhurriedly back in was an overwhelming kind of torture. Quincy's questing hands, running along her inner thigh, inching ever closer to where she was reduced to an exposed throbbing nerve, was a delicious cruelty.

Leigh had just given herself over to the satisfying fullness when he raised himself up on his knees and slung one leg over each shoulder, increasing his speed but not the force. Again, when she thought she'd be pulled under the tidal wave, Quincy moved her—repositioned her—nudging her orgasm just out of reach.

She couldn't manage anything more than incomprehensible sounds, moans and whimpers and mindless pleas, as Quincy strummed and stroked her body. Moving her this way and that—faster, slower, harder, quicker thrusts, or long strokes—he remained in full command of her body.

"Look at how good you're taking this dick, Peaches."

Was she actually supposed to lift her head to see? She couldn't manage such a feat at the moment. It was all she could do to string her thoughts together. She'd never known this kind of ache before. To be so pleasantly full and yet desperate to come was almost paradoxical. In truth, if she'd been asked, this type of marathon session would be exactly what she'd have wanted. His kisses and touches and glorious erection slowly building toward one mighty orgasm. But she'd been primed for days. His sexy promises and suggestive texts, his tongue proving clever in both word and deed, meant that she was a live wire of arousal ready to go off. And good Lord, how she wanted to go off!

"I—"

He murmured more words of praise that never reached her lust clouded brain.

Should she just tell him? Desiree and Junior both said it was her responsibility to say what she wanted. They said it was unfair to expect him to be a mind reader. He'd also said something similar the other night. But how mortifying was it to have to say 'Quincy, you need to rub your thumb on my clit while you grind your dick on me so I can squirt like a geyser and we can get some sleep'? She was embarrassed just thinking the words!

She'd really hoped she wouldn't have to. Especially since he'd seemed to be so in tune with her the other night. He'd been able to tell when she drifted off course and asked her what she needed.

Her lust-addled brain was trying to work something out. Something about the other night when he'd been able to tell she was close.

Wait.

He'd been able to tell.

This. *Mother*fu-

She pushed him off her body and rose to her knees facing him. "You!"

Chapter 25

"**Y**OU WERE DOING IT on purpose!" Her glare was almost lethal.

He'd hoped she'd *say* something. Tell him what she needed to tip over the edge. But this, her chest heaving and her eyes lit with furious understanding, was so much better. A fiery, provoked Leigh was the hottest thing he'd ever seen. He'd never been so turned on.

He'd been jittery with nerves and anticipation all day. It wasn't uncommon for them to go three or four days without seeing each other—their busy schedules meant these forced intervals were fairly routine. It also wasn't uncommon for them to have a visit, share some snacks, before anything physical really got started.

This time was different.

He'd been on edge waiting to repay Leigh for her disrespect the other night. Oh, he was sure some people wouldn't consider it disrespectful to be told to 'go ahead and finish' but he did. His pride did. Quincy was a lover of women. All women. And when it came to a woman's pleasure, he was like Jesus in Acts 20:35—the joy was in the giving. Which is exactly what he'd been doing for the last fifty-seven minutes.

This was a hill he was willing to die on. They would figure out how to be fully and completely intimate tonight, find a way to express themselves in pleasure, even if it sent him to the hospital for heart failure or, considering how little effect his multiple attempts at jerking off had on deflating his hard-on, priapism.

"How could you?"

"I wasn't doing anything. You were supposed to talk to me, tell me what you needed."

She was so rigid with outrage, her gasp choked any reply she might have had. He pulled her close and kissed her until she softened in his arms.

"She talks to me," he gently fingered her opening. She was so wet, he wanted back in more than he wanted anything else in that moment. "Why won't you?"

"If you weren't so busy playing games, we'd have both finished by now and there'd be nothing to say!"

Her unwillingness—or was it an inability?—to use coarse language would always tickle him. How she arrived at 'finish' instead of any other more appropriately descriptive words—come, climax, orgasm—was an endless source of delight.

"But what if you needed me to call you a 'dirty little cum slut' while I wrapped my hand around your throat and spanked your clit with my dick? What if you wanted me to finger fuck your ass after I come all over it?" She sucked her lip into her mouth and stared at him wide-eyed. The way her pupils dilated, he wondered if it was something she'd enjoy. "Maybe you wanted to hear how the memory of my dick in your mouth, your lips wrapped so perfectly around me as you swallowed me whole, was the best thing I've seen until today when you took my dick so beautifully, as though it were made specially for you. How would I know if you don't tell me?"

"Quincy, I can't... I don't..." She was a mewling, writhing mess. It seemed while his prim little bookworm might lack the words, her instincts—her desires—were pure filth. He could work with that.

"Tell me what you want," he demanded. On their knees they were almost eye to eye. Her hard nipples burrowed in his chest hair and his words were spoken almost directly on her lips. "Say you want to come."

"I want to come."

"On my dick?'"

"Yes!" She moaned enthusiastically into his kiss.

"And then?"

"And then...?" Her mouth moved, forming the words, as though testing their veracity. Finally she said, her voice hoarse with need, "And then again. With your mouth."

"Nothing would please me more."

With one hand behind her neck, he pulled Leigh in for a kiss. She tasted like deliverance. Like a cool, refreshing drink on a scorcher of a day. The relief of it, of her nimble tongue welcoming his, made him weak. When they broke, gasping for breath, Quincy tugged the condom off. "Let's start again."

Nodding, Leigh searched his dishevelled bed for the strip of condoms and tore another off. This time he took it from her, unsure he'd be able to hold out if she got her hands on his dick.

Freshly sheathed, Quincy sat back on his haunches and rubbed his thighs, "Come here."

He settled her on his lap, hands splayed on her back and held her, relishing the feel of her in his arms. With his size, this position wasn't always the most successful but he wanted—*needed*—this closeness. The sensation of her hardened nipples against his torso as he raised her up had him clenching in anticipation. Her warm, soft body sinking down on his erection, the sound of her hummed pleasure, the way her eyes fluttered, as though unsure of whether being open or closed was the best way to process his body breaching hers, all worked at hardening his dick to an almost impossible degree.

She worked herself beautifully on his length, her hips twisting and rotating, as she brought them ever closer to their peak.

When he felt her flutter around him, he claimed her mouth in a searing kiss. "You ready?"

She sighed her yes against his mouth.

"Whatever you need, Peaches. Just say the word."

Her breaths were ragged and uneven. They'd been on the razor's edge of climax for over an hour—this would not take long.

"Quincy," she panted, "I... Quincy, please—don't... don't move."

He didn't get a chance to respond. Leigh ground herself against his erection and shattered.

He held her close as her soft keening cries faded to ragged breaths. With his face buried in her neck, Quincy finally succumbed to the orgasm he'd been denying, that had been building for four days. His body shook and trembled and he couldn't be entirely sure his choked breaths weren't sobs. The rightness of feeling Leigh come apart in his arms—of her wrapped around him while he throbbed his endless release—had his sinuses burning with unshed tears.

It was all he could do to get the condom off and get back between her legs as he'd promised. He'd had to pay so much attention the first time it muted the experience. Now, without having to concentrate on keeping Leigh's bow strung tight, Quincy was free to truly indulge in the feast before him. He had little concern for the greedy, slurping noises he made—not when Leigh was lifting her hips to his face and clawing at the bedding, moaning.

He was thoroughly indelicate in his task and when Leigh cried out, he'd never felt more rewarded for such sloppiness as he did when he felt her clit pulse on the flat of his tongue.

When he pulled her up on all fours, telling her it was time to pay back the stolen orgasm she owed, the last thing he expected was the glint of mischief that flashed in her eyes. She held his gaze over her shoulder and gave her ass an enticing little wiggle. Her bottom lip caught in her teeth and her nostrils flared as he entered her. Once he was fully sheathed, she balanced herself on her elbows and threw it back on him like a god damned bronco.

It was glorious.

Leigh tried everything she could to 'win' their unspoken battle, to bring the other to a spine-tingling climax as quickly as possible. He gave her that work, though, bouncing and moaning on it as he raced her to the finish line.

Leigh tried to cheat by pressing her hand to where they were joined then gripping his balls in her slick coated palm. Well, if she wanted to play dirty...

Quincy's response was to lean over and tweak her nipple in a sharp pinch. Leigh's whole body spasmed causing her to lose her balance and fall forward on her arms. He pressed his advantage by simultaneously adding pressure to her clit and her puckered little star.

Her climax was explosive.

Her back arched at the same time her leg gave out and her gasp sounded painful even as she shuddered beneath him and the evidence of her pleasure rolled down her thigh.

Quincy legitimately worried she'd strained several muscles the way her body contorted.

It took a moment. Even the smallest movement seemed to trigger aftershocks that rocked her body and stole her breath.

"That was amazing. I can't believe how perfect you are. You did so good, Peaches. So good!"

"You're... not so bad... yourself." Leigh panted in ragged breaths.

"Think you can do it again?"

"Are you joking?"

"One more. Please, Leigh—give me one more."

"I can't!" She sobbed.

"You can." He pressed kisses up her spine until his mouth was at her ear. "I promise, you can."

She was limp and sweaty in his arms. Quincy kissed and stroked her while he waited for her to gather herself. He thought she truly had tapped out but he felt her take a deep breath in and, on a slow exhale, she said "Okay."

Kissing her behind her ear, he whispered, "I'm so fucking proud of you." Turning her, he cuddled her to his chest and raised her leg over his hip. "You ready?"

At her nod, Quincy pushed in on one smooth thrust. Their groans of pleasure filled the room as he held her close, encircled in his arms, moving together in a slow, languid pace.

Leigh was so much more than he'd ever imagined and he'd already known she was one of the most interesting and fascinating people he'd known. But after tonight, he had to reassess everything. His awe for this woman was staggering. And if he had to do it all again so he could be here with her just like this, he wouldn't hesitate.

This slow, lazy action—sharing breaths and small fluttery kisses—was no less intense for the ease of it. Maintaining eye contact, watching as each sensation passed through her, ramped everything up to an intoxicating degree.

"You're incredible."

Leigh let out a small huff of laughter, "You can let go of the hard sell, Slick—you've already got me."

Quincy pulled her close, locking their bodies tightly together and tilted her chin up. "That's not what I mean. You're fucking fearless, Leigh. Do you even see how brave you are?" He kissed her, full and lush, sucking her bottom lip into his mouth. "That shit is humbling."

He kissed her again, not knowing what else to do with the rising emotions swirling inside. Each kiss spurred the next—their tongues sucking and tasting—until he'd driven Leigh to the mattress and was plowing into her with wild abandon.

"That feels so... Oh, God, I'm—"

Leigh's orgasm stole her words. Quincy could only push himself in as deep as he could go and hold her tight as he followed her over the edge. Their soundless cries of ecstasy didn't lessen the force of their pleasure as they trembled against each other.

Quincy wasn't entirely sure he hadn't blacked out for a moment. Leigh seemed similarly trapped in between states of consciousness.

"Peaches? Peaches, look at me." Her eyes were rolled back in her head, her cheeks were tear stained, and her breathing was a shuddering rattle. He peppered her lips and jaw with soft kisses while he waited for her to come to. "Let me see those gorgeous eyes."

"Quincy..."

Her voice was barely audible. If he hadn't been nuzzling her neck, he might not have heard her. "I'm here. I'm right here, baby. I've got you."

She sighed a small, relieved sound and sunk further onto the bed.

Quincy held her close and whispered in her ear. "Thank you for sharing that with me. I'll never forget it."

He rolled them over, pulling her onto his chest and covering them both with the duvet. He let his hands wander as he brushed her hair off her face. When she seemed more stable, he gently nudged her and placed a glass in her hand, "Here. Drink this."

She was a bit shaky to start but quickly regained control of herself. "That tastes terrible."

Quincy let out a low, rumbling laugh as he replaced her empty glass with the other full one. "It does. Drink more anyway."

They lay in silence, the city's lights providing ambiance, as Leigh slowly sipped her water and Quincy tried to calm his rioting emotions in the setting sun.

He briefly considered telling her how crazy he was about her before acknowledging bringing something like that up after such an intense sexual encounter would rightly be seen as unhinged behaviour. So instead, he took her almost empty glass, swallowed the contents and placed it back on the nightstand.

A pleasant warmth bloomed in his chest when Leigh let out a contented sigh and snuggled closer to him.

"You good?"

"Yeah," she yawned into her fist, "Please say that the system has properly reset itself. I don't think I can do that too many more times."

He stroked her skin with an aimless indulgence, tracing the shell of her ear and outlining the jut of her jaw, while he nuzzled the top of her head. "Don't get too comfortable, Peaches. You need to eat something."

Leigh burrowed herself further into the covers in response. He tried to pull them down but she had a surprisingly firm grip for someone whose muscles very recently quivered under the strain of putting a glass to her lips.

"I'm too tired."

"It's been a minute since you got here." It'd been exactly three hours and twenty-one minutes since she'd crossed the threshold of his apartment. He really needed to feed her, no matter how adorably she pouted to the contrary. "Let's get you a quick snack, then you can grab your phone to set an alarm so you don't over-sleep. How's that sound?"

"Like a lot of work."

He may never know how he managed to keep his laughter inside at Leigh's adorable pout of exhaustion but he was damn impressed with himself. "Use this bathroom. I'll use the one in the hall and meet you in the kitchen."

"Fine." She grumped.

Quincy watched as she stumbled across to his ensuite. She'd made a half-hearted attempt at closing the door behind her and he shook his head in disbelief when it became clear she had no intention of turning the light on. Quincy clicked on one of the lamps before heading down the hall to see to his own bathroom needs.

He'd done it. *They'd* done it. He was crazy about Dorothy Leigh Bridger and knowing they could work through something as fraught as sexual communication gave him hope. If they could get through this, they could get through anything. Couldn't they?

Chapter 26

L EIGH STEPPED OUT OF the shower on firmer legs than she'd had stepping into it. She kept the temperature cool to both refresh her cloudy mind and keep the steam from further destroying her hair. There had been enough sweat and fisting and writhing in cotton pillowcases, she didn't need to add humidity to the mix.

There weren't many choices as to what to wear, though. She was certain her underpants were destroyed. She'd been so turned on she was almost embarrassed by the feel of the flimsy fabric being peeled off her skin. Poking her head around the door to find the room empty, Leigh picked her way to the pile of discarded clothes. Deciding his t-shirt was better than the towel currently wrapped around her frame, she pulled it on, grabbed her glasses from the nightstand, and went to find Mr. Temple.

She was both impressed and self-conscious when she stumbled down to his kitchen to see just how much effort Quincy had put into his 'Operation: Denied Orgasm Retribution'. Beside the electrolytes, which she admitted made a lot of difference, he'd had a small plate of fruit, peanut butter and honey sandwiches cut into triangles, a mini egg cup, and a few slices of cheese, all waiting for her beside a small glass of orange juice and an intimidatingly large jug of ice water. His matching plate was larger in portion, though he'd traded her OJ for apple juice.

"You need protein and sugars." He explained, giving the hem of his shirt at her thighs a heated look. "You also need to hydrate."

"Well!" She couldn't think of anything else to say. Taking a careful seat at the counter, Leigh popped a few blueberries in her mouth. "This is something else."

"Too much?"

"No…" she hesitated with a chunk of pineapple at her lips, "Not too much. Unexpected."

He leaned over and planted a kiss on her face that landed somewhere close to her nose, smudging her glasses. "Please eat something other than fruit."

She picked up a triangle of sandwich and nibbled delicately while ordering her thoughts. Taking a sip of juice she cleared her throat. "Outline the plan for me. I show up and you, what, keep at it indefinitely? What if my mind wandered again? Or you three pump chumped? Then what?"

"First, I didn't think we'd have to go at it all night. You were pretty close before you got in your own way last time. So that was the whole plan, really—keep you out of your head so you could nut. Second, I have never been a three-pump chump but if I was ever so afflicted my hands and mouth would happily report for duty. Not that it was an issue today. I meant what I said—the memory of you gobbling my shit? Look!" He stepped back to show his thickening length in his pyjama bottoms, "I've been hard for *days.*"

"At ease, soldier." She said around a mouthful of cheese. "We're in recovery mode now."

Quincy laughed and bit into a large strawberry. He poured her a glass of water and pushed another piece of sandwich forward on her plate. His expression sobered. "About that. Are you... I mean, I wasn't... too rough? You're okay?"

Her heart gave a little pang of affection at his thoughtfulness. Not that it was a surprise. She'd known Quincy to be a considerate and decent person. How many men did she know who would have taken her kiss as the line crossing it was? Only someone truly honourable would insist on upholding the rules of consent when disregarding it was working in their favour.

"I'm a bit tired and I'll definitely pay for some of my more acrobatic attempts tomorrow, but I feel fantastic. Thank you for asking." There weren't any more pieces of sandwich on her plate. Did she have three or four pieces? Chalking it up to exhaustion, she picked at some melon and asked, "Are you okay? You put a lot of work in today."

"I have never been better." The certainty in his words made her blush.

Quincy pulled a dish out of his fridge and laid it on the counter between them. He reached a box of pita chips out the cupboard and made a small serving of chicken salad and pita chips on her plate. Leigh looked down and was startled to realize she'd eaten all the food he'd laid out.

"Eat. Please." He made a slightly larger serving on his plate and packed all the components away before tucking in. "We can go lay down after this."

Apparently hungrier than she even realized, Leigh happily tucked into the second course of her post-sex meal. They ate in companionable silence and Leigh pulled her lips into her mouth to keep from cooing at Quincy's diligent and methodical loading of his dishwasher. Taking his outstretched hand, she followed him around the apartment as he prepared for their nap.

She'd been so close to sleep when she'd been tucked into Quincy's side. But now, with a bit of movement and something to eat, she felt wide awake. Taking his suggestion, she set her phone alarm and plugged it in, leaving it on the nightstand to charge.

Quincy exited the washroom, turned off the lights, and climbed into bed beside her. She liked how the city's light pollution provided enough ambient light for them to see each other without it being disruptive. Once he was settled, he too had phone related tasks to complete, she snuggled right up under him enjoying the heat of his skin and the firm but soft comfort of his wide chest.

"Quincy?"

His answer was a rumble that she felt more than heard.

How to broach the subject? As much as her senses had been overloaded with sensation, she didn't forget the litany of options he offered as ways to bring her pleasure. He'd also done it when she'd had a throat full of his erection the other day. It wasn't even that she wanted him to elaborate but she couldn't stop thinking about the ease with which the provocative words spilled from his mouth.

His lips brushed the side of her face. His voice was thick with sleep but he still managed a small laugh when he said, "You're doing an awful lot of thinking, Peaches. What's up?"

Letting the shiver caused by his touch and the sound of his voice so close to her ear wash over her, Leigh looked up and asked, "Did you mean it?"

"Mean what?"

"Those things you said to me. Before? Would you have done that?"

Leigh was too curious to be embarrassed. Well, that wasn't entirely true. She was plenty embarrassed but it wasn't by his words. It was the possibility, the implication, of them.

"I thought I'd put in some solid work and here you are thinking about what more I could have done?" His scoff was as playful as the nudge he gave her shoulder. "Unbelievable!"

"Quincy, I'm being serious!"

"So am I!"

Leigh flopped on her back with a huffy eye-roll in a bit of rarely employed melodrama, "All that 'tell me what you want' talk was just that, I see."

Quincy rolled to his side, his body making a ninety-degree angle out of hers. Lowering his mouth to her ear, he rumbled, "You want to hear about what it felt like when I came deep inside your tight little body the first time? How I almost blacked out from the force of it?"

She couldn't help but writhe in response.

"Maybe you want to know what I thought seeing you barefoot in nothing but my t-shirt." Leigh felt her arousal as it raised its sleepy head and snuck a curious glance around. He noticed and continued, relentless, "Or do you want to know if I'd be willing to see if you can orgasm solely from me playing with your nipples." Leigh's breath hitched in her throat and he continued in an almost whisper, "The answer is yes. I think you can and I am extremely willing to try."

"How can you—" Leigh swallowed and tried to regain her composure. "How do you just *say* things like that?!"

"I'm gonna be honest with you, there isn't much I wouldn't do for your pleasure."

Leigh let the comment roll around her brain for a moment. His answer was easy enough to believe based on tonight's performance alone. Still...

"Okay, but... you couldn't have been saying that stuff for my benefit alone, right?" She certainly hadn't given any indication that she needed anyone to do anything with her ass at any point. "So is it just how you are? In bed?"

Quincy seemed to be thinking about how to answer her and she appreciated the consideration even if his idly wandering hands were making it hard for her to concentrate.

"I don't know how to answer your question. I was saying it for your benefit in the sense that I wanted you to know I'm open minded enough that you could ask me for whatever you need to get you there." His wandering hands stilled on her hip and he pulled her closer to his body. "The words in that case were just words. They weren't specific to you, if that's what you're worried about."

Was that what she was worried about? Leigh was honest enough with herself to admit it was more than a morbid curiosity. She wasn't sure if she wanted to hear him say that there was something about her that inspired such lurid thoughts or if she wanted it to be something every woman who'd shared his bed received. Both were equally thrilling and terrifying.

"I..."

Quincy cut her off with a quick kiss before she could complete her sentence. "But I'd be lying if I said I wouldn't be interested in going as far as you wanted in any direction. I'd never want my woman to feel like I didn't have her back in all things."

There it was. Leigh's biggest fear was knowing Quincy had participated in such things, that he enjoyed them—*preferred* them—and would find her relatively vanilla offerings lacking.

Instead of addressing it, she chose a bit of deflection. "Is that what I am? Your woman?"

"Aren't you?"

Leigh didn't need to hesitate. The time for that type of uncertainty was before they'd gone on their first date. Before she'd had her pubic hairs unceremoniously ripped from her body. Before she'd been trussed in lace and underwire. Before their genitals had been in each other's mouths.

"I am."

"You're goddamned right." Quincy pulled her close as he grumbled his reply.

They laughed into the darkness of his room. When Leigh's jaw almost cracked from a yawn, Quincy pulled her back onto his chest and settled the covers over them. "Get some sleep, Peaches."

LEIGH SPENT THE FOLLOWING WEEKS categorizing the orgasms she shared with Quincy. For ease of reference and universality, she decided to equate them to various firecrackers.

Sparklers, for example, were a fairly tame bit of crowd-pleasing dazzle that flared hot and ended just as quickly. Roman candles were intense but unpredictable in that there was no guarantee of the frequency or quantity of bursts and the potential for damage was high if not operated responsibly. Bombshells were the largest single shot bursts in the sky. They both agreed there was a fourth type—the slow gentle rolling orgasm—but disagreed on its corresponding firecracker, so they simply called them rollers.

It was a satisfying bit of foolishness she indulged in for his amusement.

Sometimes he took his sweet time, coaxing a roman candle from her body. Other times he took her hard and fast against the door and caused a bombshell. Sometimes it felt like a bombshell was building only to land like a sparkler. Each time, they giggled together as she categorised her pleasure.

Quincy gamely played along, daring her to try for a roman candle within a finite window of opportunity. Or he would proudly stride down the hall crowing about the bang-for-your-buck value of a sparkler. No matter what they were doing, she found joy in going through it together.

After Quincy broke through her reservations about talking during sex, after he'd broken more than just her reservations, he'd dared her to attempt what he called gentle recklessness. Her strict adherence to all rules needed a bit of loosening, he'd claimed, and she was to engage in petty acts of disobedience as often as possible. Nothing law-breaking, they'd agreed. Just enough to shake her out of her comfort zone.

And so here she stood, at a photography exhibit in an art gallery in Parkdale, trying to keep it together while perusing a collection called "Uncommon Sensuality." Leigh considered the outing her big step outside the familiar. She liked and appreciated art, enough to be able to recognise a Chagall or a Matisse, for example, or to hold her own when discussing Modernism vs Surrealism, but she wasn't well versed in photography as a discipline. She didn't have a critical enough eye to do more than like a picture for its subject matter.

When Quincy told her about the exhibit, she thought she would be walking into a room of half nude forms *in flagrante* which absolutely qualified as outside the norm as far as Leigh was concerned. Quincy, she guessed, thought the same because when faced with the very large, very chaste photos—a woman's skirt hiked up exposing her calf as she sat on the grass, a close up of a throat beaded with sweat, a barefoot in the sand—he'd proceeded to engage her in a game of chicken, the dirty talk edition.

It wasn't at all fair. Leigh was outmatched in every way. She sounded ridiculous when she used curse words and Quincy's voice was already set at a register that made her insides quiver. But it had been almost an hour of escalating stories whispered in full view of the general public and Leigh was doing her best to hang on.

In front of a black and white photo of a man's back muscles, possibly doing a pull-up or push-up based on his shoulder position, Quincy whispered, "Can you imagine being restrained, unable to move or touch, while pleasure was inflicted upon you?"

Leigh rallied with, "She's just brought herself to a shuddering climax thinking about her lover, missing her, and she's taking a moment to recover," when they were in front of an Asian woman's upper body in profile, head tilted back on the chair, one hand on her throat and the other out of the frame.

Quincy's volley didn't register because his lips caressed her ear as he spoke, the cheater. She decided two could play that game and discreetly ran her nose up the column of his throat when next she spoke.

Looking at an image of a young, white man with a low fade wearing grey sweatpants, flip flops, and a sleeveless shirt that was more holes than not crossing a small residential street in the pale morning light with a small carton of milk in his hand, Quincy pressed his front to her back and whispered, "He woke her up on his dick. He threw her leg over his hip and fucked her long and slow until she shook in his arms, watching as she fell back asleep. Tucking the sheets up under her chin and placing a kiss on her forehead, he slipped out to the kitchen to make her a cup of tea like she likes. Realizing he doesn't have the right milk, he throws on the first thing he can find to run to the corner store. He's heading back to her now and seriously considering waking her up with his tongue this time."

Leigh was agitated. All she could do was focus on her breathing. What he'd described was so close to what happened between them two nights ago—the way he'd woken her with his erection nudging her back, then stayed with her, praising and cajoling, until he'd essentially orgasmed her back to sleep—her whole body flushed with the memory.

Standing there, in a room full of people casually milling about taking in the artwork, Leigh was the physical embodiment of the word clench. Her skin felt hot, her throat was tight, and she was gripped by need so powerful she feared for her composure. An hour of Quincy's sexy voice and dirty talk whispered directly into her bloodstream and she was a puddle of wanton desire.

This wasn't gentle recklessness. This was violence. It was all out madness.

She couldn't win this illicit game, she never stood a chance. But she could make sure she went out swinging, leaving it all on the field as they say.

Leigh looked around the room at the remaining images and found one that was closest to the exit. It was a woman's hand grasping a man's wrist. Standing by themselves in the small corner, she faced Quincy and said, "She's forced him face down on the bed. He keeps squirming as she uses the lube to prep him for the dildo she's strapped on so she's decided to tie both hands together at the small of his back since he can't follow instructions."

Leigh held his stare. She would use everything she had to lay this particular gauntlet down. She was the owner and operator of a romance only bookstore for chrissakes. She'd read everything from shifters, cyborgs, and aliens to mafia, yakuza, and bratva. From fated mates to alpha knots, Leigh had the means to make herself understood even if she did sound ridiculous saying the word 'cock'.

She continued, "She's warned him, repeatedly, that he doesn't get to come if he can't behave. He knows that she'll keep his hands bound while she sits on his face until he either passes out from lack of oxygen or until his jaws lock, whichever happens first, and then she'll punish him for that, too. The chastity cage sits in full view on the nightstand as a reminder of what happens to naughty men who ejaculate without permission."

Leigh had never spoken words like this with the intention to stimulate. Normally, she approached the subject matter with an almost academic detachment. *'Why, yes, this one does feature pegging.' 'No, the gargoyle only has one penis but also, conveniently, a prehensile tail.' 'Motorcycle gang shifters who share one mate? Right this way.'* She'd even remained conversational when a reader told her *'The pivotal moment of this book is deeply emotional anal sex'* while discussing a football romance. But this, Quincy looking at her, chest heaving, while everything between her legs felt... slippery—this was all new territory.

Quincy wrapped his hand around the back of her neck and pulled her in for a kiss that was fairly quick for all its hungry indecency. "Panties. Go get 'em."

Leigh was all overtaxed synapses and cloudy headed arousal. Where was she supposed to find undergarments? Maybe she'd missed part of the installation? Or perhaps there were some for sale in the gift shop? The incessant throb in her core was unbearably distracting. "Panties?"

He stepped closer to her so that he could speak directly in her ear. "Go to the washroom," he looked pointedly at the sign above the makeshift wall that separated them from the lobby area, "take off your panties and bring them to me."

"Wha? I... I can't. I—"

Quincy's expression lost some of its intensity. He cupped her face, running his thumb in a soothing motion behind her ears. "Is that too far for you, Peaches?" He asked with genuine concern. "Worried about getting in trouble? Being too irresponsible?"

Well, yes, actually—she was always worried about those things. But today, she had a more pressing concern. She took a quick peek around Quincy's frame to be sure they still had relative privacy. There was an older couple taking in the frame on the adjacent wall but they were basically out of sight. "I *can't*."

"It's okay, I—"

"No, Quincy," she interrupted, pulling his one hand down into the pleats of her coat and between her thighs, "I can't because I'm not wearing any."

She'd felt so brave when she'd decided to forgo underwear with the tweed romper. She'd paired it with a merino mock neck, wool thigh-high socks, and her vintage swing coat.

He raised his eyes over her head to take a similar stock of their surroundings and then, imperceptibly, so smoothly she mightn't have noticed if it wasn't happening to her, he swiped his fingers through the mess his words had made. She quaked at the touch.

"Quincy!" she whined.

"Outside. Right now."

All she could do was nod vigorously as he took her hand and led her out to the car.

The quick three blocks to the above ground parking garage helped her gain some semblance of control. The fresh air, bright sun, and all the people on the sidewalk going about their merry business helped clear her head and snap her back to reality. The four flights of stairs and all the slick friction they created, however, stole some of the ground she'd gained.

Quincy led her to the railing behind his car and swung open the tailgate of his Suburban. She turned to look out onto the street where they'd just been and marveled at how little of the city sounds made it through the concrete structure and how warm it managed to be when standing directly in a patch of sun.

"What else do you need?"

Leigh blinked at him. Why was he offering her a face cloth? Following his gaze, she noticed the moisture on her thighs and was horrified. Taking the rag, she muttered, "Oh, my God—how embarrassing!"

"Hey." He tugged at her arm when she didn't look at him, "Hey, there's nothing to be embarrassed about. That shit is so fucking sexy."

"I guess it's what I get for leaving the house without any drawers on."

"I'm gonna be honest, Peaches, that is also incredibly sexy." Quincy pulled her close and let his lips rest on her forehead to murmur, "What else do you need? Can you make it to my place?"

What kind of question was that? Of course she could make it to his house. It was barely a twenty-minute drive in traffic! Did he think she was some kind of brainwashed husk being led around by her vaginal canal? She'd gone ten *years* without sex. She could last ten minutes, the fool! She was about to open her mouth and tell him as much when he kissed her.

His tongue licked into her mouth and she moaned at the sensation. His gentle hold was at odds with his determined kiss. When she broke, gasping for breath, he said, "You're getting all worked up for nothing, Peaches. Don't get it twisted. I'm so turned on; I could probably steer with my dick. I need a minute and I'm asking if you do, too."

Oh. Well. That made sense, she supposed.

Except his attempt to calm her down with kisses failed and instead, fanned the flames of her desire making her a complete liar. She needed... something. Something she couldn't have in an open air above ground parking structure.

"There's nothing we can do about it."

"Of course we can. Are we supposed to? Probably not. Are we allowed to? No. But we most certainly *can*."

Her breath caught at his words. "You're not suggesting what I think you are... right?"

"I'm not suggesting anything at all. I'm saying if you want something, we can find a way to make it happen."

She looked around trying to puzzle it out. There were way less cars on this level than when they'd arrived but they certainly weren't the only ones. Quincy's truck was parked beside the wall with no cars immediately in front or to the left of him and his tailgate shielded them from any casual bystanders walking by. If someone were to take a closer look, they might be able to figure it out but they'd have to really be looking. And the beauty of Toronto was that no one had time to ever be really looking.

Good Lord, was she actually considering this? Where did pre-kiss Leigh and all her fiery indignation go? Had she simply been a mindless sex fiend beholden only to her wanton desires in sheep's clothing all this time? This horniness he'd awoken in her was like a chronic illness that flared in her system without enough warning to brace for its effects.

"You're doing an awful lot of thinking for something fairly uncomplicated."

Quincy's tone wasn't mean or mocking or impatient, which she appreciated. What she wasn't a huge fan of was the casual indifference with which he offered to fornicate in public. This would be the first time in forty-four years she'd even contemplated doing something illegal. Unless you counted her childhood rum cake consumption, which she categorically did not, Leigh was an unimpeachable law abider.

He kissed her again. A lingering press of lips that scattered her thoughts.

"It's all good, Peaches. Come on. Let's go."

Go? But...

"Wait."

Quincy turned back to face her, his features soft with affection. "Yeah?"

Wasn't this the cold war they'd been battling this whole time? They'd been on opposite sides of this from the beginning. He believed she should ask for what she wanted. Not only ask for it, but expect that she would get it. She, on the other hand, had long since been conditioned to self-reliance because, whether explicitly stated or not, her needs had never been the priority and so it was pointless to vocalise them.

And here was Quincy, offering again and again, to fulfill those requests if only she'd be brave enough to speak them into existence.

She took a deep breath. "I want to come. Now. But I don't think I can actually, you know..." She raised her eyebrows for emphasis, "*do it* here."

Quincy licked his lips, "Aight, bet."

He reached into his gym bag and pulled out an impeccably folded towel and laid on the ledge of his trunk. Then he lifted Leigh off her feet and sat her gingerly atop it. He took the face cloth she'd been clutching and lay it on the duffle bag before spreading her legs wide enough for him to stand between.

"When you say 'do it', I take it you mean balls deep penetration and not a little fooling around?"

She nodded. That is exactly what she meant. Sure, she knew you didn't have to get completely naked to have sex—there were quite a few times in her youth when her and KC's clothing had barely shifted much less been removed. But as far as acts of gentle recklessness went, public fornication was way out of her comfort range. This proposed level of touches was already making her head spin.

"Are you gonna do it yourself or do you want me to?"

"You do it."

Leigh's experience with self pleasure wasn't extensive, but historically she'd never been able to perform the task with any kind of haste. This was not the time or place for a drawn out session. Though, at this point, she was so over-stimulated with nerves and arousal she might go off like a bottle rocket at the first brush of fingers.

Quincy ran his hands up and down her wool covered thighs a couple of times before letting one rest on her hip while the other one made its way under the opening in her shorts. She let out a harsh gasp when she felt the cold of his touch. The pleasure was a sharp sting that made her recoil.

"Shhh... I've got you, Peaches."

She settled back into position, going so far as to tilt her hips a bit forward to give him even more access.

There was so little resistance to Quincy's two fingers sliding into her yet she felt it *everywhere*. Her arched back, rolled eyes, parted lips, creased brow, tightened nipples, and clenched muscles were all working in concert in the expression of her pleasure.

Quincy's low rumble landed in the center of her body, like a heat seeking missile always finding its target. She felt him spread his thumb through the moisture before rubbing it on her clit. "Mmm. Is this all for me?"

"Yes," her voice was more breath than sound.

"Thank you." He kissed behind her ear. "I'm flattered."

His cheeky response inspired some cheekiness of her own. "And do I have any reason to be flattered?"

"You have to ask?" He thrust his very visible arousal at her.

Leigh tried to focus but it was so hard to concentrate when her body was trembling with sensation. With some effort, she got his zipper down and her hands on his boxer-covered erection. Oh, she was plenty flattered.

She was amazed he was even upright for all the blood required to power such a protrusion.

Quincy's fingers and thumb continued apace, working diligently on the fire he was stoking within her. She slipped her hand in his fly to stroke him flesh to flesh and his moan of pleasure rattled through her. This angle, this position, feeling the hot, hard length of him in such a confined space, didn't afford her much range of motion which was somehow perfect for their little illicit sex cocoon.

"You sure you should be doing that, Peaches?"

She squeezed harder and spoke in ragged breaths as her hips moved in time with his stroking fingers. "Together. Or not at all."

Their kiss was a clash of teeth and tongues, their rapid breaths and fevered noises, filling the small space.

The distant echo of voices in the stairwell made Leigh's body still in panic.

"They're coming up the stairs. You've got a minute, maybe two, tops."

Her eyes were wide with horror. "No! I can't!"

"What did I tell you about that? You can but you have to do it quietly. This ain't for them, Peaches, just us."

She shook her head wildly but no sound came from her throat. "Ready?"

She opened her mouth to try refusing again at the same moment Quincy slid a third finger in and sucked her tongue into his mouth.

The overwhelming fullness, the delicious drag in and out that bordered on painful yet caressed her everywhere, coupled with his mouth on hers, was too much. Like an overloaded transformer exceeding its designated voltage, Leigh's body erupted in a shower of sparks.

It came on too fast and she couldn't contain it. She let out a broken sob and fell forward on Quincy's chest filling her mouth with flesh and fabric as she tried to stifle the sound of her spine-tingling orgasm. Her whole body shook and she was helpless to do anything else but hold on to Quincy's arm as he drew wave after wave of pleasure from her spasming body. Her ragged breaths sawed through her nostrils like a furious, charging bull. And maybe that's what she was, furious he had the ability to make her feel this way.

"Bombshell," she panted, still succumbing to the tremors wracking her body.

"Didn't I say you could do it?" His voice sounded like it was coming from somewhere distant, though she could feel the press of his lips on her temple. "You were spectacular! The way you squeezed me so tight, I thought you were going to rip my shit off and honestly, to experience what I just did? I was cool with it."

The last bit startled Leigh back to awareness. She realized she was, in fact, still holding on to his now softening erection. Leigh let out a small yelp of apology. Pulling her hand from his fly, the sticky evidence of his enjoyment coated her hand.

Quincy took her hand in his and wiped it clean with the face cloth he'd given her earlier. He placed a gentle kiss on the side of her face and murmured, "Feeling you squeezing my fingers and my dick like that at the same time? You don't ever have to apologise to me for that."

She felt herself fall forward, allowing Quincy's broad chest to hold her weight. It felt so good to relinquish control in this moment. To let go and trust Quincy to take care of her. She wasn't sure how long this freedom would last but she made herself a promise right then—legs dangling off the back of his truck, limp and sated—she was going to embrace this asking for things business and see where it took her.

Chapter 27

"THE MANDEM ARE THROWING a party for my Jesus year." They were relaxing on Leigh's couch, enjoying the small moment of quiet between the inevitable flurries of activity in their schedules. He'd insisted on making her breakfast to celebrate their six-week anniversary—a milestone he claimed was more like their one-month anniversary since they lost a week to both the winter league meetings and to the black hole of Christmas and New Years.

He only had a couple of real showstopper recipes in his repertoire and only two of those were breakfast. Making Leigh his father's famous breakfast skillet had filled him with equal parts nerves and pride. That she'd enjoyed it, complimented him on his chopping and prep skills, was the icing on his heart bursting cake.

Now, with the confirmation that the party was in fact going forward, he wanted her at his side.

Leigh pushed herself up onto her elbow to look at him. "Your what?"

"You know, thirty-three, the age Jesus was when he died? It's supposed to be a year of change and rebirth."

"Do you mean your vinyl year? Which is thirty-three and a third, not that you youngins would know anything about that."

"No," Quincy stole a quick kiss instead of allowing his irritation at yet another age comment take hold. "I meant what I said."

"I think you're making that up."

Quincy ran his hand along the side of her face until he was holding her head. He pulled her down for a kiss and smiled at the contented sound she made. "Well I'm not. Will you be my plus one?"

"Your plus one? How can I refuse such an offer?" She mockingly fanned herself with her other hand.

He tugged her hand, causing her to lose her balance and topple onto his chest. Stealing another kiss, he murmured, "I'm hoping the lure of me in a suit will entice you."

"A suit? What kind of party is this?"

"I have no idea."

"You… is it a surprise party?" She levered on his shoulders to free herself but he pulled her back down. Relenting, she settled herself, fidgeting slightly like an indulged house cat until she found a position she liked. "Travis seems like he'd be the loose set of lips on that sinking ship."

Quincy's whole body shook with laughter. Everyone figured Travis for a gossip when in reality it was Yemi who couldn't keep a secret even if he was paid to do it. "It's not a surprise party, I'm just not involved in the planning. I show up at the appointed time for merriment. So? Will you be my date?"

"Will Miles be there?"

"Probably."

Leigh gnawed on her bottom lip. Quincy's hand lazily sweeping up and down her spine didn't distract her from her apprehension. This was taking a declarative step. Yes, they were dating, and yes they were having sex. But they hadn't been attending functions together.

"When is it?"

Quincy gave her a playful smack on the ass. "Are you worried about being double booked?"

"No! I'm trying to figure out how long I'll be stressing about the event."

"Party starts on the 13th so we can ring in my Valentine's birthday." Quincy brought his lips to hers in a soft, lingering kiss. "But you don't need to stress. It's just you and me; nothing else matters."

He tried to moderate his tone. The truth of the words, the bone deep certainty he felt, overwhelmed him. He couldn't imagine how she might react if she knew.

"What should I wear?"

"Wear whatever you like, Peaches." He gave her lips a quick swipe with his tongue. "You'll be the finest woman there."

Leigh drew in a quick breath, "That's not helpful."

"You wanna see how helpful I can be?" Quincy pulled her over his body, arranging her legs so she straddled him. He ran his hands up her thighs until he had two healthy handfuls of her bottom. With a gentle squeeze, he pulled her tighter against his burgeoning erection.

Squirming a little, Leigh grumbled. "This isn't helpful, either."

Quincy wasn't sure what could and couldn't be considered helpful at this juncture. All he knew was Leigh was in his arms, her soft curves pressed against his, and her kisses tasted like the peach lip balm he'd bought her for their Secret Santa gift exchange.

"Explain it to me. The mandem," she stressed the word with something Quincy felt was too close to derision for his liking, "are going to tell you when to show up and that's all you know? How is this the process?"

He told her about the evolution of birthday parties. How, with ethnic parents of varying degrees of strict, the landmark birthdays were something they did together regardless of what their families managed.

The year they turned sixteen, they arranged a trip to Mr. Greenjeans at the Eaton Centre for Yemi because his academic, African, Muslim parents did not consider sixteen a landmark of any kind.

The year they turned nineteen, they waited in the parking lot while William went into the LCBO to buy a bottle—some sweet, cheap thing he couldn't remember the name of—for them to all toast with because the drinking age wasn't note-worthy in a household that had permitted underage drinking.

The year they turned twenty-one, two of Paviter's sisters got married and totally hogged the family's attention. The mandem got together at Travis and Carter's cottage and pro-jected his favorite movies on the side of the building while high on mushrooms.

They'd been celebrating milestones together for decades. Whether anyone thought thirty-three counted as a milestone was irrelevant. Quincy's birthday would be feted the way they decided.

How could this be news to her?

"So it could be anything from a foam party to a bonfire?"

He gave her a narrowed glance, not sure where she was getting this from. "... sure, I guess?"

"We'll get dressed up for a rousing game of beer pong with a side order of keg stands? Or bottle service at a noisy exposed brick 'gastro pub'? That's more on brand for your social media obsessed generation, right?"

What the fuck? The laughter in her voice in no way mitigated the sheer condescension of her words. "It's my birthday, Leigh. I'm asking you to spend it with me. What does it matter what we do?"

"It doesn't matter, Quincy. I just—"

"You just what? Suddenly forgot we're in a relationship? That I'm your man?"

Her brow furrowed in genuine confusion.

Maybe he was overreacting but this obsession about their ages was exhausting. Smiling through her jabs and dismissals was starting to feel like Chinese water torture and his control was weakening.

"No, of course I haven't forgot Quincy. I was joking."

"But you weren't, though."

She opened her mouth to argue but he didn't wait to hear what she had to say. Quincy lifted Leigh off his lap and stood. Pulling his shoulders down and away from his ears, he curled his hands into tight fists at his side.

"You keep acting like there's some insurmountable gulf between us when there isn't. I'm not a child, Leigh. I'm thirty-two fucking years old. I have a demanding, full-time job that doesn't offer a ton of opportunity for growth, a mortgage I will never pay off, and aging parents I'll have to fight to convince to move out of the house they've lived in for fifty goddamned years!" He paused to get a hold of himself. He kept opening and closing his fists in an attempt to regulate the emotion roiling in him but it wasn't working. "You're not in some wildly different place in life than I am."

"Quincy, I—"

"I'm crazy about you. I like you so much, it's scary. But I don't run. I stand here, scared out of my fucking mind, to be with you. And for what? So you can talk to me, about me, like I'm a child? Nah. I'm not having that." He shook his head as if it would underscore his words. With his mouth turned downward and his body jittery with nerves, Quincy stepped around Leigh toward the door.

"Quincy," she called after him. She grabbed his forearm with both hands. "Quincy, I'm sorry."

He looked at his arm, both praising and cursing the cashmere barrier between them. "When can we get past it? What can I do to prove it to you?"

"I..." Leigh trailed off, not knowing what to say.

With a resigned sigh, he pulled his arm free and ran his hands over his face. He'd wanted her to say she was crazy about him, too. He'd wanted to hear her admit their ages didn't need to stay the obstacle she'd believed it to be. He'd wanted her to pull him close and kiss him, tell him everything would be alright.

What he didn't want was this doomed silence.

"I gotta go." He placed a firm, closed mouth kiss on her lips. "I'll call you later."

All she could do was nod.

That was it, then.

Quincy turned and made his way down the stairs and out the door. He needed to get out of there before things got any worse.

Chapter 28

A T THE SOUND OF his truck starting, Leigh wilted, landing in an inelegant slump on her couch. Had anyone else in recorded history made such an unforced error in as little time? In her desperation to cope, she'd made light of his feelings and ruined their morning.

How long had she been pressing on that bruise without realizing it? How long had he gritted his teeth, bearing her slights?

It wasn't even something she could justify. Being dismissive of how he and his friends chose to celebrate his birthday was inexcusable and she was ashamed of her behavior.

She couldn't even lie to herself and pretend it wasn't as bad as she knew it to be. His clenched jaw and stiffened spine told her exactly how annoyed he was. It was how he'd looked at her when she'd kissed him before they'd agreed to start dating—the same cocktail of irritation and disappointment.

The realization rendered her speechless which only made him clench his jaw harder. It only got worse when he'd said he was scared of how big his feelings for her were and she floundered to come up with a response. His defeated gesture twisted her already tangled nerves.

The truth was she'd felt insecure about the prospect of spending an evening planned by his friends and she'd made her insensitive joke to deflect. What did she know about moving in the world Quincy inhabited? She was a middle-aged woman from a no-horse town whose biggest accomplishment in the field of glamor was not breaking her ankle when walking in three-inch heels. A feat, it should be said, she'd only accomplished by keeping those instances to a bare, quantifiable minimum.

He was right. They needed to get past it. *She* needed to get past it. The proof would have to be in her actions—words wouldn't cut it this time.

Besides, it wasn't as though she had the combination of words needed to make this right. Leigh needed to step out of her comfort zone and show Quincy he wasn't the only one willing to pull their weight, to acknowledge their terror and stare it in the face.

Her phone buzzed against her hip. The feeling of it registered in her awareness like a skinned knee. There was enough sensation to get her attention but not enough to distract from her immediate predicament.

She hoped it wasn't more about the custom order Luc left her a note about. Apparently the customer had come in while Junior had been in the store, giving them a whole sob story about 'grand gestures' and 'declarations of the heart' the two of them undoubtedly devoured. She couldn't deal with someone else's love dramas whilst in the midst of her own.

Fumbling for her phone in her pocket, Leigh answered without looking to see who was on the line.

"Hey, you girl. Mind if I swing by a bit early so we can stop at the studio before the movie? I need to put eyes on a shipment. UPS texted me about a delivery but I don't trust their bitch asses."

Leigh heard Desiree's voice but couldn't concentrate enough to make sense of the words. All she could see was Quincy's face, soured with disappointment, as he walked out.

"Desiree? I messed up."

Desiree let loose a knowing chuckle. "You get distracted and lose track of time? We don't have to go to the movie. I don't even know what it's about. I only said I'd go with you because I like seeing historical Black folks giving white people the business."

Leigh felt her mouth open and close but wasn't sure any words came out. She cleared her throat and tried again, lacking the strength to disguise the hollowness she felt. "I messed up and I need to make it right. I don't know what to do."

"I'll be there in a half hour. If you don't want me to come in there hollerin' be ready to jump in my car when I come to a rolling stop outside." All of the humor left Desiree's voice.

At that, Desiree hung up and Leigh got moving. She wasn't any less cloudy headed or distracted, as evidenced by the different Chucks on her feet—though, honestly, one low top floral and one high top pink didn't look so bad together—but she was ready and waiting as instructed.

She was barely settled in with her seatbelt buckled when Desiree handed her an Iced Capp. "Here. Drink this. The sugar and caffeine will spin you out but I don't want to be tipped into vehicular homicide because I lose control of my car listening to whatever it is you are going to spill every word of. So drink this and don't say a word until I can concentrate."

Leigh opened her mouth to question, to argue, but Desiree made a silencing motion with her hand. "Aht! Drink."

So that's what she did. She sipped her sugary, frozen, coffee milkshake and stared out the window while Desiree navigated them the short drive to her studio.

Leigh didn't say a word as Desiree cut around a streetcar, stuck her head out the window to curse out a bike courier, and parallel parked her car inches away from being too close to a hydrant. She followed silently, mind still replaying the morning's events, while Desiree unlocked the door, turned on the lights, and guided her bodily to the couch by the window.

While Desiree checked the delivery, Leigh took in the familiar space. Dubbed the Studio because it was, in essence, a studio apartment converted for commercial use, it boasted an 800 square foot open layout, concrete walls that had been painted white, and the kind of beautifully designed stucco ceilings no longer found in newer builds. There were work tables overflowing with fabric samples and prototypes and drawings tacked all over the walls. The dress forms Jermaine and Julissa, so named because Desiree rebuked the industry standard James and Judy, were lacking their usual bit of razzle dazzle.

Desiree opened the mini fridge that doubled as a side table and pulled out a glass dish of fruit salad and two bottles of water. Passing a bottle to Leigh, she said "Start at the beginning."

"God, which one?" Leigh complained.

"Girl!"

Leigh flinched a little, knowing Desiree wouldn't put up with any dithering when she waited almost an hour to know what happened. "Quincy's friends are throwing him a party for his Jesus year."

"His what?"

"Right? That's what I said! It's for thirty-three, apparently." Leigh's head shake was a mix of vindicated righteousness and eye-rolling annoyance. "Anyway, he invited me as his date and, in the process of asking for more details, I was mean and dismissive and he told me off—which I fully deserved but did not enjoy."

"*Girl.*"

"I know." Leigh covered her face with her hands. "I know!"

"Okay, now tell me what happened."

Leigh looked at her friend as though she'd sprouted wings and a tail. "I just told you!"

"No, you told me what you did. I'm asking what happened," Desiree tapped Leigh's forehead with her stiletto nail, "In here."

For all of Desiree's noise and bluster, her Scotian joie de vivre as she called it, Leigh always forgot she was a keen observer of the human condition. Until moments like this, when Desiree forced her to go beyond the surface to solve her problems, when she used the skills she'd honed to cope in a world that tried to tell Desiree she didn't belong.

So Leigh gave the question the respect it deserved and really considered what happened.

Then she let all her insecurities and frustrations and reservations pour out.

She told Desiree about how much she worried about opening herself up to Quincy only for him to wake up one fine morning and leave because something better came along.

She admitted how she had panicked during sex that first time and, as a result, still secretly wondered if she was enough for Quincy or if she was, in fact, bad pizza.

She confessed how Quincy's unrelenting demand that she speak the words, express herself sexually, forced her to confront the bleak reality that she'd never really engaged with the concept of her desires and had essentially let sex simply happen to her.

She agonized aloud why someone as exceptional as Quincy, with his fast life and lofty goals, would have anything to do with someone as plain and regular as Leigh.

"Excuse you?" Until that moment, Desiree had nodded along, nibbling on chunks of fruit and sipping her water, murmuring her support without interruption. Now she was one curled lip and lewd gesture away from starting a street brawl like a voluptuous, bewigged Tybalt.

Leigh jumped a little, startled by Desiree's vehemence.

"You know how poor I was growing up? Sometimes, not only did the ends not meet, they didn't even recognize each other in the street. My mama used to borrow rolls of toilet paper from her sister. She moved us to my grandmama's tiny house, all of us living in the den, because she couldn't afford another place to live. That's the kind of poor we were." Her bangles chimed frantically with every wild gesture Desiree made.

"Des, I—"

"And here my Black trans ass sits, a businesswoman, in my studio where I work on my very successful line of lingerie. *I* am exceptional!" Desiree slammed her hand onto her chest. "Do you also wonder why I have anything to do with you?"

"No! I—"

"Because you don't think I'm exceptional?" She challenged, barely allowing Leigh to get a word in.

"Of course I think you're exceptional. More than!"

Desiree wasn't finished. "You don't think you're exceptional? After everything you've accomplished, everything you've done? You think befriending a literal heiress is something regular degular people do? How often does one even meet a millionaire much less earn their trust and loyalty?" That last was said more to herself than Leigh but before any comment could be made, Desiree kept going. "You're a hot piece of ass who is smart and kind and everyone who meets you falls a little in love with you. You don't think Quincy is lucky to have you?"

"I hear what you're saying, Des. I do."

"Then?" When Leigh didn't answer, when she couldn't manage more than a gaping jaw, Desiree pointed a menacing finger in her face. "Talk about my friend like that again and I *will* put my hands on you. You have some goddamn nerve!"

Leigh's eyes were wide in her head. She'd never considered... In over twenty years of friendship, Desiree hadn't ever let a slight against Leigh go unchallenged. Even when Leigh didn't feel particularly slighted, Desiree made sure to call out the transgression.

Desiree Walker had made an art form out of making a person's life miserable. It never once occurred to Leigh she would also get called out for doing the same thing. Whether it was the stutter step her brain took as she processed this information or the sheer force of her frazzled emotions, Leigh barely registered the welling tears before Desiree swooped her into a firm, glasses smushing embrace.

"I love you."

"I love you, too." Leigh sniffled into the cavern of Desiree's cleavage. A cleavage, Desiree took pride in pointing out, that was one hundred percent natural.

She felt foolish for even having such a reaction. She wasn't crying. No tears fell, yet she was weeping all the same. Desiree held her, rubbing her arms and back in soothing circles, while Leigh waded through the tumult of her emotions.

"You know what your problem is, don't you? You've never had to work for anything."

The soft, hazy feelings Leigh was wallowing in burnt away by an outrage so profound it seized her muscles.

"Listen to what I'm saying before you get all bent out of shape," Desiree held her tighter, "you've always worked *toward* something. You set a goal and make a plan and chip away at it relentlessly until you've accomplished it. Working *for* something is different."

The tightness in Leigh's limbs loosened a fraction as she tried to make sense of her friend's words. She sat up, hoping to gather her frayed nerves in a less vulnerable position.

"Working for something means you might not get it and you don't have enough experience with failure to act right. You've never failed at anything and in this you might. Instead of figuring yourself out, you're busy making your built-in excuses, so when it doesn't work it won't be because of anything you did. But guess what?"

Leigh gave her friend a look that could be considered engagement, but only just.

"This hang-up about his age is all on you."

That was a lot of insight and Leigh wasn't entirely sure she'd absorbed enough of it to have a real conversation. But what she did know was Desiree was an unrepentant truth teller and if Leigh wanted to push back against her words, she'd have to do a lot more introspection than she was currently capable of processing.

"Twelve years isn't nothing." It wasn't obstinance, exactly, but Leigh still sounded petulant.

"If it were *your* Jesus year, I'd agree. A twenty-year-old man is essentially a child who can get drunk and vote. But he's in his thirties. It's a different conversation."

"Is it?"

Desiree levelled her with a look that told her she needed to stop playing and start figuring things out.

The heart of the matter, the part Leigh couldn't reconcile, was the difference in their *caliber* of life. Leigh dreamed as big as she could and came up with a bakery bookshop. She'd spent her entire adult life planning and learning and manifesting until it was hers. And she'd been proud of her accomplishment. Proud of the community she'd built and the readers she'd grown to know. Then Quincy walked through the door.

Quincy whose dreams couldn't be contained by something as insubstantial as Earth's atmosphere.

"So I just stop thinking about the fact we live our lives at different speeds? That his age is a big factor in why that is?"

Desiree rolled her eyes so magnificently, Leigh almost wanted to ask her to do it again so it could be captured on camera. When her irises finally settled, they bore into her with unbridled mockery.

Leigh held her gaze and waited.

The standoff broke with Desiree's raised brow. The arch of which seemed to ask Leigh if she was sure she wanted to hear what Desiree had to say before the words themselves came forth.

"Kingston Calvin Coffield is only four months older than you and lives his life at an entirely different speed than you do."

"That's different!" Leigh reflexively let the rebuttal fly.

Desiree crossed her arms over her ample bosom and gave Leigh a disgusted head shake. "No, it isn't!"

Allowing the censure to sink in, the truth of Desiree's words took shape. KC had always lived a life in the fast lane. He was the youngest of four equally handsome and athletic brothers who smiled big and laughed easily. He was a popular jock in a small town where everyone accepted his place in the majors as a forgone conclusion. He was a schmoozer and a charmer and had been the entire time she'd known him. It was part of the reason they'd decided to split three years after he got called up.

"No." Leigh finally admitted. "It isn't."

"It's one thing to be afraid to go after something. It's entirely another to be afraid to even want it at all."

Giving her shoulder a squeeze, Desiree pushed herself up from the couch and left Leigh to make peace with the revelation.

She was grateful for the break. She didn't know what to do about any of it, but she appreciated it all the same.

Leigh knew this wasn't a normal 'one month anniversary' problem, for all that they'd been officially dating for almost seven weeks. They'd fallen quite far rather fast and none of this would matter, she realized, if they didn't care so much about each other.

Leigh told herself it wasn't happening. After the way things played out at Christmas, she figured she'd been granted a reprieve of sorts. A bit of space to prove things weren't as intense as they felt. But the truth was she already cared deeply for him, the same gut churning fear he admitted to feeling for her, on account of the twisting, winding road they took to get from friends to lovers.

But how was she supposed to make this right?

How was she supposed to move herself from this weird, jittery panic to serene acceptance. Because from where Leigh was sitting, there was no solution. Even if she could get over his age, and there was a significant part of her that had already, she had never been the kind of person who thrived in the limelight.

KC—her oldest friend, her first love, the father of her child, the man who would always and forever hold a special place in her heart—hadn't found a way to get her to enjoy life in the fast lane. How could Quincy?

Furthermore, wasn't it disingenuous to expect him to change when it was exactly who he'd been from the start? It would be like complaining about the smell of cigarettes when choosing to date a smoker.

And, since she was telling herself the hard truths, she didn't want him to change. She liked that Quincy was always willing to try something different. Always looking for new experiences. Always striving for more.

No, what had to happen was all on her. She needed to make the move. She needed to accept this reality. She needed to face her hangups. Quincy had already proven he was happy to meet her where she lived. Their 'takeout on the couch while the game was on' routine was the same easy comfort they'd built together, only now with the added benefit of orgasms.

If Quincy was worth the effort, and Leigh already knew he was, then the minor discomfort she'd feel—*anticipated* she'd feel, because at this point it was all in her head, wasn't it?—would be a small price to pay.

Looking up to find Desiree to tell her about this revelation, Leigh watched as her friend unpacked the box she'd received and hung the prototypes on an empty clothes rack when an idea struck.

She didn't need Ava's effortless style or Junior's infinite connections. For this grand gesture, what Leigh needed was Desiree's full assortment of sex trappings.

"Des? I've got an idea."

Chapter 29

QUINCY HUSTLED UP THE stairs, wondering what Leigh needed.

When her text came in earlier apologizing for her thoughtlessness, he'd hoped there'd be a little more to the conversation. Yes, she said they'd speak later and they both were busy all day but when she called, he wasn't expecting her to ask if he could swing by because she was in a bit of a bind.

"Peaches?"

"In the dressing room!"

Quincy laughed to himself, despite his mood. He would never not think it funny that her spare room wasn't called a guest room or an office like everyone else. Leigh insisted on living in her entire space and keeping Langston's basically unused room was as far as she was willing to go.

Kicking off his boots and shrugging out of his coat, Quincy made his way down the hall and almost swallowed his tongue when he stepped in the doorway. His shock had him collapsing against the wall, his brain no longer capable of powering his muscles enough to keep him upright of his own power.

Leigh was standing on a wooden cube in front of her full-length mirror, twisting and turning, trying to see herself from the back. She must have heard him connect with the wall as he struggled to pull in a full breath because she turned to him and smiled brightly.

"What do you think?" She spread her arms wide and gave a slow turn. Before Quincy could form any words, she continued, "Versatile, right? I'll stay dry at a foam party and it's surprisingly breathable so I won't melt at a bonfire. It allows for full range of motion for beer pong or keg stands," Leigh brought her knee up to her chest to demonstrate. "Full disclosure, I've never actually done a keg stand but I'm sure there's some modified version for beginners I could try."

"I—" Quincy was gobsmacked. Leigh was wearing a black leather-looking bodysuit with a zipper that climbed up her left leg and crossed her body diagonally to her neck. With her glasses and her hair twisted in the clip she always wore, she looked like a librarian who moonlighted as a burglar of sex dungeons. He wouldn't be surprised if she said she'd had to have it poured on, it was so fitted to her body.

"It also came in patent leather which I have a fondness for from a phase in the 90s I never really grew out of. But I figured if we end up playing paintball or laser tag, the reflective surface would work against us and we don't want that."

He was rooted to the spot by the door, unable to process her words with his raging hard-on demanding his frontal lobe's full attention. The small percentage of his brain not working on maintaining his erection was busy running a slideshow of every filthy fantasy he'd ever had, starring Leigh in her catsuit.

Seizing a modicum of control from his lust-addled mind, Quincy cleared his throat. "You said you were 'in a bind'?"

If his voice was a bit high and uneven, it was still better than he could hope for all things considered.

"Oh, yes!" Leigh hopped off her little podium and stood next to some shoes that were piled up behind her. She gestured to black platform heels and a pair of sequined hightops. "These are very gastropub, feature wall, IG glam but *these* are more comfortable. Left to my own devices we both know what I'd choose but I wanted to be sure I was striking the right tone. Which do you prefer? There's no wrong answer."

"Leigh."

"Yeah?"

He saw it then, the way she ran her hand down her torso smoothing the already taut fabric. Finally, something other than how tempting she looked broke through and he could *see* her standing there, nibbling on the corner of her bottom lip, the nervous vulnerability broadcasting like a klaxon. It gave him the clarity needed to stop leaning against the wall.

"Come here, Peaches." She made her way to him, wringing her hands together and still chewing on her bottom lip. When she got within touching distance, he pulled her close and wrapped her in his arms.

The soft hum she made was so sweet and so welcoming, he almost forgot that she was cosplaying Catwoman.

Pressing a kiss to her forehead he asked, "What are you doing?"

"Apologizing?" Her eyebrows were somehow both furrowed and raised as she continued to gnaw on her lip.

Quincy didn't know how she managed to swing from sexy to adorable so seamlessly but he suspected it was a large part of what drew him to her again and again.

"This," he repeated, giving her outfit a blatant once over, "Is your apology?"

"Well, yes. I mean, no! Kinda?"

Her nails caught in the knit of his fisherman's sweater as her hands flapped in the same flustered manner as her voice. He pulled her into his arms and indulged himself in a deep inhale of her herb-y, lemon-y scent.

"It doesn't matter how you and your friends celebrate your birthday. I'll be there with bells on." Leigh's wool muffled voice was a bit shaky.

"This outfit doesn't leave a lot of room for accessories, much less any bells." He teased, giving the tab of her zipper a gentle tug.

"I'm not usually the center of attention. When you asked me this morning, I panicked. The thought of standing there, surrounded by you and all your people gathered together... I'm sorry for being mean and dismissive."

Oh, Quincy was in trouble.

He felt it in the kneejerk way he wanted to reassure her she hadn't been mean, hadn't hurt his feelings. Diminishing his own pain to protect her? It was a dangerous place to be. And yet, he wasn't frantically scanning the room for emergency exits. Instead, he was shifting his proverbial weight and engaging his core to make himself as sturdy and immovable as possible. It took everything he had to simply say, "I accept your apology."

That, and steal a kiss.

When he finally released her lips, she gave a soft contented sigh as her eyes fluttered open. She rubbed her eyes behind her glasses and asked, "So, sneakers or heels?"

Quincy blinked his confusion. He didn't know why it hadn't registered in his brain that she seriously intended to wear this to his party. Well, it wasn't entirely true. He knew why. His brain was too overloaded with illicit thoughts, there wasn't any bandwidth left for processing implications.

"Peaches..."

"I wasn't lying, it is surprisingly comfortable. Plus, it has the added symbolic benefit."

"Symbolic benefit?" Quincy ran his hands down her sides, feeling the supple fabric under his palm. The only thing this outfit symbolized was sin.

Leigh raised on to her tiptoes and wrapped her arms around his neck. "Yeah, like I'm letting go of my hangups and reservations to stand at your side with nothing between us. Just you and me, nothing else matters."

She parroted his words back to him with such proud conviction. If Quincy thought he was in a dangerous place before, it was downright hazardous now. This brave, courageous, magnificent woman would be his ruin and rather than engage in some safety protocols, some method by which he could protect himself, his fool heart beat out a steady rhythm.

Leigh. Mine. *Leigh*. Mine.

He wrapped his arms around her and lowered his mouth to meet her kiss.

Her soft lips opened immediately, letting him taste and suck and savor. As their kiss continued, Leigh pressed herself more firmly against him and he felt every twitch and flex of her muscles through the thin barrier separating them. Tempted to see what more he could feel, Quincy ran his hand down her spine and palmed her ass. Gasping into his mouth, Leigh wrapped her legs around his waist, blindly trusting the wall to support their combined weight, as she rubbed herself against him.

Breaking the kiss, Quincy looked down to see the outline of her hardened nipples. Using one hand to hold her more securely, his other teased her with his thumb.

"Quincy..." Leigh's voice was high and breathy.

He lay a trail of kisses up the column of her throat until he got to her ear. With her lobe caught between his teeth, he rumbled in her ear, "Look at you, your nipples hard as shit for anyone to see."

Leigh's hips gave his length an exploratory press.

"You think that's what I want? For everyone to see how crazy you make me? Have me walking around bricked up knowing you're soaked in here?" He palmed her seat, bringing their groins together in a long, slow grind. "That's what I'll find when I unzip this, isn't it? You, all slippery for me."

Leigh was panting inarticulate sounds of pleasure as her body moved, chasing the sensations his hands and lips and words offered.

"But I'm not going to unzip this. Not yet."

"Please, I—"

"Let's see something first." Leigh was too far gone to participate in conversation. He tweaked one nipple and hummed his approval at her hitched breath. He loved how responsive she was. Feeling her body thrumming with need, knowing that he managed to drive her out of her own head with desire, was one of his life's crowning achievements.

Raising them both from his position leaning against the wall, Quincy moved the few steps into the room and settled himself, with Leigh on his lap, on the armchair in the corner. He sincerely hoped there wasn't anything fragile or delicate buried in the pile of clothes they now sat on. He'd happily replace anything damaged. It was a small price to pay when Leigh was mewling into his mouth and writhing on his rock-hard dick.

"If you think I'd be able to keep my hands off you while you're in this," Quincy said while taking small sips of her mouth, "you're mad."

Leigh pushed her glasses up onto her head and rubbed her eyes in exasperation. "We're going to be at a party, Quincy. You can't—"

"Can't what, Peaches?" He demanded while flicking both nipples with his thumbs. "What can't I do?"

She shivered from the pleasure, causing him to redouble his efforts—both thumbs teasing and stroking while palming her breasts.

"You can't... fondle me... in the middle of... a crowd." Leigh struggled to get the words out in the face of her body's response to his attentions.

Her fluttery pulse under his tongue while her body arched and contorted was making him dizzy with lust. Sucking on her neck, he blew a cool stream of air on her moistened skin. "And I'm supposed to what, just walk on by when I see you like this?" He pinched her nipples to underscore his point.

Leigh cried out as her orgasm took her. She fell forward, limp and boneless, while her ragged sobs filled the room.

Quincy kissed her face without removing his hands from her breasts. Tracing her nipples in tight circles, he praised her, "Fuck, Peaches. You come so beautifully. I love feeling your clit throb. My favorite is when you pulse on my tongue. Do you think I can feel your clit pulsing right now?"

Quincy cupped her even as the tremors of her climax made her twitch uncontrollably.

"I know what you're thinking, but you're wrong." He said, low in her ear.

Leigh's laugh sounded more like a wheezing huff, "About what?"

"We still haven't figured out if you can come from nipple play alone. My dick was heavily involved in that..." He trailed off, one eyebrow raised, waiting for Leigh to fill in the blank.

"Roller," she sighed dreamily into his neck.

"My dick was crucial in the acquisition of that roller."

"You're a ridiculous man."

Her scold lost its impact when he began running his hand between their bodies. He brought his lips back to her ear and whispered, "I can feel how swollen you are. I bet this catsuit is positively flooded."

Before she could answer, Quincy brought his other hand to her nape and pulled her in for a wet, possessive kiss. His tongue tasting and teasing hers, daring her to take a breath from anywhere but his lungs. He swallowed her moans and sighs, all while maintaining his glorious purpose between her legs.

Finally breaking for air in large, noisy, gulps Quincy kept his lips on hers. "You ready?"

She nodded while her chest heaved.

"Then let me feel it throb, Peaches."

"Yes," she breathed. Her hips chased his fingers. Grinding on his hand, she pleaded, "Faster."

Quincy didn't need to be told twice. Moving his two fingers in a firm, steady rhythm against her core, he braced his forearm along her spine still clasping her neck.

"Now, Quincy," she sobbed, "Now, now, now."

He pulled her body down on his hand, applying even more pressure to her clit, as she came apart in his arms.

Leigh's eyes rolled in her head, her mouth open in a silent cry, before she collapsed on his chest in a panting, shuddering heap.

Try as he might, Quincy couldn't discern with any certainty whether he actually felt her clit throbbing on his fingers, if it was the tremble of Leigh's limbs, or his own body's reaction to the sheer ecstasy of bringing this woman pleasure. What he did know was he'd given Leigh one hell of a wedgie. Or was it a camel toe?

Smoothing the material down her thighs, he brought his hands to rest on the globes of her ass and basked in the afterglow. Leigh's contented breathing, her arms wrapped around his body as she snuggled closer to him, very nearly distracted him from the pain of his monumental erection.

His dick had maintained a constant state of ready alertness from the moment he walked in the room and bringing Leigh to orgasm twice in quick succession did nothing to ease its vigilance.

Pressing a kiss to the top of her head, Quincy murmured, "While I won't argue about it moving well, there is no way this is breathable."

Leigh raised herself up to a seating position. "What? Why not?"

Quincy placed his nose to her navel and pulled in a big, showy sniff.

Leigh giggled, "Stop that!" while pushing his head away from her body.

"Can't smell anything. I don't think air is getting in or out of this getup." He nuzzled her neck while she laughed at his antics. "I bet it's steamier than a pot of boiling rice in there."

She threw her head back laughing, launching her glasses off her head somewhere across the room. "Quin-cy!"

"I'm sorry, Leigh but this outfit won't do. It's... inappropriate." He said, peppering her jawline with kisses. "Your lewd, obscene nipples poking through the fabric will have people wondering if you're so needy for it the only solution is for me to drag you to the coat check, stuff my leather gloves in your mouth, and take you hard and fast just so you can make it through the evening." Leigh's shock-widened eyes didn't stop him from giving her lips an indecent swipe of his tongue and lowering his voice to continue, "And while that may be true, and I would certainly be more than happy to oblige, it's not what I want people thinking about when they look at you."

She squirmed in his lap. Her familiar response to being equal parts aroused and scandalized, her turmoil of not knowing what to do about the contradiction, drove him to find more and more ways to push those buttons. It wasn't difficult. Everything about Leigh inspired this brand of depravity in him. Knowing he was tapping into the similar vein of filth she had coursing through her was simply the maraschino cherry on top.

"From now on, any time you wear this, your nipples will get hard and make a vulgar show of themselves as you remember how I unzipped it without bothering to take it completely off so I could bend you over this chair and fuck you hoarse."

Leigh shivered in his lap, "That's not what happened."

"Not yet, it hasn't," Quincy said darkly. "Stand up, Peaches. We've got memories to make."

Chapter 30

No MATTER HOW MANY different ways she tried to angle herself, Leigh couldn't wrap her arms around Quincy's body when he was flat on his back. The result was she always ended up sprawled atop him like a house cat. She didn't mind it in the least, especially not when cuddling his soft hard body was the reward.

His soft hard body was recovering from a particularly vigorous round of sex. He'd bent her over the chair without fully removing her catsuit as promised and the sensory dissonance of having both arms and her right leg covered but one breast, her entire torso, and whole left leg bare did something to both of them.

He'd thrust so hard the chair shifted across the floor, her feet barely grazing the surface, placing them directly in front of her mirror. He'd thrown things into a whole other gear as they locked eyes with their reflections. Quincy was like a man possessed, bringing her to three climaxes so intense and devastating—playing with her nipples, her clit, and her ass — she had to tap out and beg him to find his own release.

If he'd wanted to make sure Leigh couldn't so much as look at the outfit without shivering with the memory of the pleasure he'd foisted on her, his mission had been accomplished. Just thinking about dropping it off at the cleaners was making her blush.

"What are you thinking about, Peaches?" His deep voice rumbled through her chest.

"You." She said simply.

"Yeah?" He kissed her, his lips landing at the side of her head closest to his mouth.

"I'm sorry about earlier. I was disrespectful and out of line and I'm horrified I let my own insecurities run loose like that."

Quincy sat up a little, shifting them both. "As much as I enjoyed your apology outfit, I don't want this to keep being a thing between us."

"No, I know." Leigh kissed his chest right above his heart.

And she meant it, too. Talking it through with Desiree helped her realize her idea of thirty was skewed.

When Leigh was thirty, she was seeing Langston off to high school and helping KC come to terms with the end of his career. That wasn't a reasonable benchmark.

Junior was only two years older than Quincy but had always seemed older than her actual age. And even if her seeming maturity were all an act, Leigh wasn't often with her and her peers to see when she did 'act her age'. The only other thirty-year-old she was close to was her brother Julian, who might have had his shit together professionally but was a living, breathing timebomb of anxiety their father could set off at any moment.

Holding Quincy to those standards wasn't fair.

He was his own person, with his own flaws and fears. He deserved to be seen for his individual accomplishments, the way he lived and acted and strived, without her weird hangups clouding the proceedings.

"I've always been old." She felt his chest expand on his inhale, no doubt to level her with a hearty rebuttal. "No, I mean even as a child I was steadfast. My dad would always say things like 'What would I do without my special helper?' and then scoop me up to swing me around. I loved it. Loved being a part of the solution, his reliable assistant. Somehow, without really thinking about it, I went about anticipating needs to gain his attention."

Leigh could usually speak about her dad without getting too choked up. But having to face some of her deeper-seated traumas, the ones that were so tied to her sense of self and her current success as a functioning member of society, brought too many conflicting emotions to the fore.

Was she responsible or had she grown into self-reliance in response to neglect? Had she always had a penchant for rule following or was it the only way she knew to gain positive acknowledgement? Did she truly prefer to do things on her own or was she petrified to face the possibility no one cared enough about her to help her when she needed it?

Her throat was tight and her voice was thick, but she forced herself to continue. "I have a terrible relationship to age and expectation. I wasn't encouraged to be a child when I should have been, then I was unceremoniously tossed into responsibility I didn't know I shouldn't've had. I have no idea what 'thirty' means anymore. Maybe I never did. Yet I still cast it as young in a way that was synonymous with immature in my mind and that was terrible of me."

"Peaches," Quincy's voice was hoarse with emotion. He wrapped her in his arms and shifted them to their sides so they were face to face on her pillow. "You aren't terrible, you're human."

"Oh, is that all?" She felt raw and vulnerable. Exposed.

"You're a sore loser. An even worse winner." Quincy punctuated each assertion with a kiss. "You're clever. You're talented.

You're judgemental. You're ambitious. You're kind. You're the most capable woman I've ever had the pleasure of making scream." This last was said with a quick up-down flick of her nipple that made her breath hitch. "I'm here for all of it. I can't get enough."

Leigh didn't know what else to do with the emotional upheaval, didn't know what to say to this man who'd so deftly carried her through the minefield of her feelings, so she tipped her face forward and kissed him.

She kissed him to say sorry. To say thank you. She kissed him because she couldn't remember the last time she felt as supported, as valued, as she did right then.

And of course, this beautiful unstoppable man understood. "I already told you, Peaches, I'm crazy about you. You can't scare me off so easily."

"I'm going to be better," she vowed against his lips.

"Yeah?" He ran a finger along the curve of her breast. "How much better?"

"So much!"

"You won't comment on the cut of my suit when we go pick it up next week?"

Leigh wiggled away a little so he could see her put her hand on her heart. "I won't say a solitary word about your Dapper Dan style, I'll simply gush about how handsome you look."

Quincy smiled, rolling his eyes fondly, at her solemnity. "You really mean business, huh?"

"I'm so serious." She insisted. "And to prove it to you, if someone says 'Energy' uses a Mariah Carey sample I promise to not even mention Tom Tom Club."

That made him laugh. The sound sent her insides quivering as it rumbled through her chest.

"Besides." She reclaimed the distance she'd put between their bodies, sliding her top leg between his. "It's the least I can do since you've saddled yourself with an old lady."

She watched his frown develop, slow and uneven, like a polaroid image, obviously confused and unhappy she was making disparaging age comments so soon after promising they were passed it. She bent her knee, raising her thigh until it was nestled under his crotch, Leigh smiled crookedly and said, "It's a big responsibility keeping me limber. I spend all day on my feet and it's hell on my back. I need it cracked all the time."

Finally catching on, Quincy's frown deepened into something truly sinister. "Peaches, I'll crack your back day and night. You don't have to worry nothing about that."

Leigh felt lighter and freer than she had in years. Opening herself up this way didn't come naturally to her, but she'd forced herself to make the effort knowing, *trusting*, Quincy would be there to stand with her through it. Being proven right so spectacularly was a heady feeling. She had no idea what came next, but allowing herself to believe in the future, in a relationship with Quincy, was getting easier and easier.

She complained dramatically, "I am starting to feel a bit stiff, lying here like I have –"

She didn't even finish her sentence before Quincy rolled them over, hooked her knee over the crook of his elbow and pressed his body flush against hers. "Then I'd better get to work."

Leigh didn't have any complaints.

Chapter 31

L EIGH PULLED UP TO the venue and looked around. In the bright February sun and bustling street traffic, it didn't seem like much from the outside but this section of the city was notorious for trendy spaces in deceptively ordinary buildings.

Tapping a 30 minute block on the parking app, Leigh ran through her mental checklist.

She'd prepped the fruit, pastry, and sauces needed for tomorrow, she'd packed and labeled all the pickup orders, her overnight bag was ready to go with an added birthday surprise from the lingerie shop, and her outfit for tonight was hanging in the closet. Ava had come over earlier in the week to help her and they'd settled on a navy jumpsuit with orange heels and a braided Crown for her hair. It was the exact amount of sexy she felt she could pull off which is why she had left Desiree and Junior out of the exercise.

This delivery was the final thing before she was off the clock for the night. Quincy was picking her up at 8 so they could have a quiet dinner together before the revelry which, if all went well, she'd have just over 2 hours to herself before her home was overrun with the chaos demons known as Desiree Walker and Junior Sano.

A young man in catering whites exited the front door.

Perfect. Leigh could slip in and figure out where she was meant to set up before lugging the heavy boxes of cake tiers.

"Is this the Freeman party?" She engaged the car alarm as she approached.

"Yeah, we're setting up now." He had the gangly limbs of one recently welcomed by puberty.

"Great. I'm delivering the birthday cake—can I go check it out?"

He'd already lost interest in Leigh and her intentions and nodded with a vague gesture to the door.

Smiling to herself, Leigh remembered when Langston was that age, all teeth and limbs and sullen moodiness. Growing up was such a chaotic experience and Langston had a father who was so athletic, he continuously suggested Langston turn all that undirected energy to sport. Unfortunately for KC's dreams of legacy, Langston showed zero aptitude.

Up a small flight of stairs the venue opened to a wide, high-ceilinged room with an exposed brick wall and a dramatic crystal chandelier.

As expected, the nondescript building housed a stunning interior space.

The decorations were tasteful and the wrought iron staircase led to a smaller area overlooking the main floor. There was a long bar along the length of the brick wall on the main floor and a shorter matching bar upstairs. Based on the lack of activity and decoration in the darkened area, Leigh figured the party did not have access to that section.

The air carried the mismatched aroma of plastic, cooked food, and sweat typical of banquet hall setups. People buzzed around unpacking serving wear, linens, and centerpieces. A large round gala table sat in the corner. Was that for the cake? Leigh looked for someone in charge—if she had to put the cake together now, she needed to get started.

"Excuse me? This is a private event?" Her sentences came out like questions.

Leigh turned into the perfectly coiffed face of Alice. She wasn't in her party clothes but her hair was flawlessly straight and her poreless skin shimmered.

"Oh, it's you." Alice's posture stiffened. "What are you doing here? Please don't tell me you're delivering the cake. Don't people usually have staff for that?"

Leigh pasted on her pleasant for-customers smile, "I'm sure they do. But since I'm here anyway... shall I bring it in?"

Leigh's heart raced. What were the odds that Alice was throwing an unrelated birthday party on the same night as Quincy's not surprise party? Unlikely. But her brain irrationally held on to the possibility.

"God, you're pathetic." Alice sneered. The words dribbled from her lips, as though they'd been numbed at the dentist and couldn't hold a sip of water.

Leigh was so shocked by the comment she convinced herself she'd misheard the woman. "I beg your pardon?"

Alice shook her head with mild disgust. "You and your ridiculous store and your big woodland fairy princess eyes really think you're a match for a man like Quincy?"

Leigh was too startled to respond. Where would she even begin? Not that it mattered. Alice kept on talking.

"Tonight is for people of influence? For people who make an actual impact? Not used up divorcées." Tossing her hair back over her shoulder, Alice gave Leigh a withering look before rolling her eyes. "Quincy needs someone who can move in his world, someone who can elevate him."

What was happening?

Leigh could hear the rush of her blood in her ears and her vision went a bit woozy at the edges. This woman was staking a claim on Quincy and expected Leigh to, what?

"I'm not…" Leigh couldn't believe she was about to utter these words. Her voice was thick with mortified bewilderment. "I'm not going to fight you for him."

Arm crossed, Alice's head tilted to the side and scrutinized her like a livestock inspector searching for the presence of disease. "I don't need to fight you. All I need to do is wait until he's done with you. He'll find his way to me in the end. He always does."

Leigh could only blink. She had no frame of reference for what to do when being so summarily insulted by someone she'd never given more than a passing thought.

"Well," Leigh said with a professionalism she was grateful to have accessed in her current state, "I'll let you sort that out for yourselves. Where do you want the cake?"

Some secret sense of self preservation took over moving her limbs and giving instructions. On autopilot when Alice motioned to the back, she stumbled into the kitchen to ask for help without noticing who followed as she made her way outside.

Gulping fresh air into her lungs didn't help the pounding in her ears. Nor did the thrumming white noise of traffic. She smiled, she nodded, she said yes and no and please and thank you and when the giant banner unfurled gold letters—a gold that was noticeably close to orange—loudly announcing Happy Birthday Quincy she didn't react at all.

Her mind raced the entire drive home. Was Alice acting alone or had his friends been laughing at her behind her back? Had they said something to Quincy? Did he know how they saw her and… agreed? Laughed along with them?

Surely if he knew, he would have said something – done something – to defend her, right? Did that mean they hadn't said anything yet? Was that what she had to look forward to tonight?

What would happen if Quincy were forced to choose? It wouldn't be a choice at all, would it? Obviously, the friends he'd had for more than a decade, some closer to two decades, would win that face off. And even in the unlikely scenario that he did choose her, how would that work?

And when *her* friends found out? Leigh couldn't imagine so much as dining with someone her friends actively disliked. How could a relationship function?

Parked behind her home where she no longer required higher brain function, the force that animated her body left and the embarrassment flooded her system. She was an exposed nerve, tender like the blistered skin of a burnt marshmallow.

That was the order was placed by a woman who wanted to make a play for her guy to remind him of the choice still available to him. What was the plan? Did Alice expect some hair pulling confrontation? A concession and graceful exit? This shot across the bow only made Leigh feel tired and sad.

Drawing from the last reserves of her will, Leigh got out of the car and made her way inside.

Leigh heard them before she saw them. Too distracted to think it through, Leigh entered the front door. She tried to conjure a pleasant facade but hadn't the energy to pull it off. Instead, her face caused a veritable record scratch halting all merriment.

"What happened?" Desiree demanded.

Ava hurried to her side. "Dottie, what's wrong?"

Junior finished ringing up the remaining customer. Walking him to the door, she flipped the closed sign, engaged the lock, and turned off the main lights. "Upstairs. Now."

An hour later Leigh still felt numb. None of Junior's swearing, Desiree's plotting, or Ava's quiet murmuring helped her understand.

"It doesn't make any sense," Leigh muttered. "She had to know he'd invite me. Why make me deliver the cake?"

"She probably didn't expect you to be the one delivering it," Junior mused.

"What? Why?" Ava kept rubbing Leigh's back.

"I think you're right," Desiree added.

"Of course I'm right. I have a PhD in white girl antics."

Ava frowned her disagreement, "Isn't she, like, Brazilian or something?"

"The difference between race and nationality won't let you breathe, will it?" Ignoring Ava's flummoxed pout, Junior sat beside Leigh and explained her theory. "I'm sure she thought the order would be delivered by someone else. Then, the 'oh we were meant to be he just needs to see it' act would have landed even harder when you showed up to see your cake there."

"That's a stretch. And too many moving parts," Leigh reasoned.

"No, Junior is right. Think about it: you show up and recognise the cake you made for 'the one that got away'. What do you do? Either way it ruins your night." Desiree started to warm to Junior's premise.

"One hundred gold doubloons says she had some cake emergency planned that you'd have to fix," Junior stood up and paced in front of the couch.

"And just like that, she's re-framed you as staff." Desiree added.

They continued feeding their wild conspiracy theory until even Ava was on board. "Oh and your teen pregnancy undoubtedly comes up."

"Yes, but in the guise of bravery. After overcoming the odds she's finally attempting to achieve her dreams isn't that amazing?" Junior affected a saccharine vocal fry that was remarkably accurate.

"So the plan is to discredit me?" Leigh didn't buy it.

"It's to paint your relationship in an untenable light. Seeds of discord and so on," Desiree clarified

Junior's 'scheming furrow' deepened between her brow as she mused in a low voice, almost to herself, "Quincy must have mentioned how reluctant you were about getting involved. If it wasn't said directly to her, it definitely got back to her. She figured she didn't have to push too hard to send you running...since she couldn't make Quincy leave, she banked on you pulling up stakes."

"Classic strategy. Find and exploit your enemy's weakness. In your case it's your age gap insecurity," Ava added.

"This whole thing is childish and pathetic and all I feel is sad." Leigh heaved a forlorn sigh and sunk into her couch. It didn't matter if they were right or if their theory made sense. It didn't matter if they ever learned the truth of Alice's plan. All that mattered was the sting of irritation she felt to even be in this situation.

Of course, that was the exact moment Quincy showed up. All eyes turned to Leigh at the sound of his knuckles on the door. Leigh shrunk impossibly further into herself. She allowed herself a solitary moment to hide before straightening her spine and getting up to answer the door.

"What are you doing?" Desiree followed her down the hall with Ava and junior hot on her heels.

"Please. I just want to send him away and forget about this whole day." Leigh's voice was cracked and dry. The last thing she needed right now was to face Quincy as she explained what his friends—the friends that meant so much to him—did. Her imagination came up with all manner of reactions and few of them were in her favor.

"Allow me." Junior undoubtedly had grand intentions toward fiery retribution. She made eye contact with Leigh and, seeing her exhaustion, gave her arm a squeeze and headed to the door.

Leigh didn't want the ensuing explosion she knew would come from sending Junior's flame into that particular powder keg but she was still too shell-shocked to step in. But if there was a time when she could divest herself of the responsibility—to act in her own self interest without concern for the consequences—surely it was this?

She'd have to talk to him about it, eventually. She'd explain all the jumbled thoughts in her mind but she didn't have the wherewithal to accomplish it just then.

She couldn't face him now. She couldn't bear his reaction to this ridiculous situation. To hear it was okay, it didn't matter, it did matter—no answer was the one she needed and Leigh didn't want Quincy to see how upset she was.

Instead, she listened as Junior's voice floated up the stairwell.

"Well, if it isn't the birthday boy."

"How's my girl? Almost ready?" Leigh could hear the smile in Quincy's voice. She could picture the silly face he made asking her friend if he should get comfortable waiting for her.

"Your girl is running a little behind." The emphasis Junior put on 'your girl' should have been a warning. Her tone was tight and unyielding

"Does she need a real five minutes or, like, like five minutes left in the 4th quarter and both teams have all their timeouts?"

Desiree shared a knowing look with Leigh that, if she had to put it in words, said 'Junior's allowing him to get a lot of words in—I would have cussed him out in the parking lot before he got his seatbelt off'.

"She had a delivery."

Quincy's voice was still light and jovial "Yeah, she mentioned. Was it bad?"

"You tell me. The delivery was for *your* party." Junior stressed.

Whatever his reaction, Junior continued as though she were discussing nothing more than the unseasonably warm February temperatures, "She sent someone here to place the order, you know. It wasn't particularly complicated. She could have done it online but then we wouldn't have heard her sad tale of woe. You see, tonight she's laying her cards on the table and this party is her last stand. She's finally going to get him to see how perfectly they belong together."

Leigh knew what Junior was doing. Quincy was about to walk boldly into her trap. Ordinarily she would have intervened. Right now, she wasn't so inclined.

Still in that blasé manner, Junior pivoted, "I heard it was Alice that dubbed your ragtag little group The Byrons. A little esoteric, sure, but admittedly better than something like Pussy Posse."

"Look, Junior, let me talk to Leigh."

Leigh flinched. Quincy's voice told her he was losing his grip on his irritation.

"Lo siento amigo, she's unavailable. Why don't you go ahead and get started on your celebration?" If Leigh didn't know better, she could believe that Junior was truly disappointed to not be able to fulfill Quincy's request.

"My celebration is with Leigh. Nothing else matters."

Junior's steely delivery was unyielding. "Those plans have changed."

"Leigh!" Quincy's voice rose up the stairwell in desperate frustration, "Leigh! Please. I know you can hear me!"

Leigh felt Ava's hand in hers. Some of her resolve crumbled at his pleading.

Desiree raised an inquiring eyebrow. She'd tell Junior to stand down if Leigh gave the word.

Leigh drew in a fortifying breath and shook her head. Alice set them on this path and now they were going to walk it.

"You're not helping," she heard Junior say.

"Respectfully, this is between me and Leigh. I'm gonna need you to mind the business that pays you." Quincy was doing his level best to keep his cool and Leigh wondered how much longer he could endure.

"The business that pays me? Funny you should mention it."

Leigh's breath caught in her throat.

Quincy would have fared better provoking a venomous snake. Few things in life were certain—among them were death, taxes, and her friend's pathological inability to turn the other cheek.

The fact that Junior helped Leigh get the money to open Peach's was known exactly by two people in this building. Desiree, with her considerable experience applying for loans and grants, had worked with her for months on the small business application process. They honed the pitch until it gleamed and still Leigh couldn't get approved. Junior stepped in and arranged for the institution that held her assets to meet with Leigh. Junior had essentially underwritten the loan, granting Leigh a similar rate as the banks that had rejected her, and the rest was history.

They never spoke of it, never alluded to it, both understanding that it was a favor to be kept between the two of them. It wouldn't be beyond the realm of possibility for that number to climb to five if Junior's temper got away from her.

"Word on the street is you're close to securing a five-year suite lease from Morenal, Smith & Sano. It would be a real coup. They generally prefer to remain behind the scenes and don't do a lot of public wining and dining. They prefer to let their stellar track record do the impressing." Leigh heard Quincy's acknowledging grunt before Junior carried on conversationally. "Did you know their first big client was JRR Freight & Shipping and I, Jamie Guillermo Sano Rosales, am the majority shareholder of that empire? That's the business that pays me, Quincy. Which means *I* am the one who is mad, bad, and dangerous to know and *you* should not come back here until Leigh sends for you."

Leigh didn't hear anything else from the stairwell. Either they were engaged in a face off or the pressure of holding her breath had blown out her ear drums. Two things could be true at once, right?

"Leigh," Quincy called up the stairs.

Oh. So it was option A and the standoff was now broken.

"Leigh, I'm leaving because that's what you want but this isn't over!"

She rushed to the window in the kitchen to reassure herself he was actually leaving. The demand in his voice made her wonder if he would.

Leigh knew Junior's brand of spite wouldn't allow Quincy to have the last word so she wasn't surprised to hear her call out to his retreating form, "Enjoy your party, Slick—Alice put a lot of time and energy into planning it!"

Collapsing on the couch Leigh was overcome by an uncontrollable giggle fit. "This is ridiculous. I'm forty-four years old! I don't court drama. I don't break rules. How has this become my life?"

"Not that it was a question, but Quincy had no idea what Alice was about. He is wrecked." Junior admitted, returning to the group, fingers flying on her phone's screen.

"Then why didn't you take your foot off his neck?" Ava's face was flush with disbelief.

Junior's eyebrows and shoulders rose, "He needed sufficient motivation."

"For what?" Ava tucked herself behind Leigh, the big spoon to Leigh's tiny, exhausted one.

Junior tilted toward Ava, hands on her hips. "To gather that cabrona. Quincy already chose Leigh. His people need to fall in line."

"I'd say the message was received." Desiree wriggled on to the edge of the couch to make a Leigh sandwich, "Now we wait."

"Like fuck!" Junior blurted. "We're going to that party and we're going to make a scene, no jodas."

"Prancing around, mutton dressed as lamb," Leigh balked, "make a fool of myself, more like."

"This is not jealous-making. This is turf-claiming. You're going to walk in there with 100% conquistadora vibes and show them what grown and sexy looks like." Junior insisted. "She wanted to know what you bring to the table? Let's show her!"

Ava's eyes narrowed in confusion "…. Conquistadora?"

"Latina for thug shit," Desiree explained.

"What do you think?" Ava sounded on the verge of sleep as she posed the question to her sister.

Desiree rolled over to face Leigh, "She has a point. If you fall off a horse, you're supposed to get right back on."

"People should not be atop horses in the first place," Leigh grumbled obstinately.

Junior knelt in front of the couch so Leigh was surrounded by faces at close range. In a gentle, soothing voice she said, "I ordered a car to pick you up in three hours. Take a bath or a disco nap or scream along to some angsty teenager playlists. At 11 o'clock you will be downstairs looking for all the world like the stunner you are. I want your hair big and your glorious bosom freed from the shackles of your sports bras." She ran a finger on a delicate path along Leigh's hairline and said softly, "I love you."

Then Junior pushed herself to standing, made eye contact with each of them and nodded, once, decisively. "Do not disappoint me."

Desiree sat up, pulling Leigh and Ava with her. "We'll be ready," she vowed.

"Call in reinforcements if you need to. We'll meet at Reposado at 11:30 and move at midnight."

"He'll still be there at midnight," Leigh murmured.

Ava wrapped her arms around her sister's shoulders and nuzzled her neck. "It's not about him, remember?"

Nodding, Leigh shared a look with Junior before she stormed off like an avenging angel.

"You heard the woman," Desiree said. She reached for Leigh and pulled her to her feet. "Let's get to it."

Chapter 32

After haggling wardrobe choices with Desiree, Leigh had taken Junior's advice and spent the remainder of the time taking both a warm bath and a disco nap. She'd earned it.

The plan, as much as Leigh was able to follow it, was for them to show up at midnight, party for an hour, and then go back to Reposado after they'd made their scene. Which is how Leigh found herself flanked by five women entering the birthday party with military precision at exactly midnight.

Junior was out in front and wore only a man's white dress shirt, designer knee high combat boots, and dozens of gold chains layered around her neck. Desiree donned a halter tube dress that looked made of rubber and matched her skin tone perfectly, giving the illusion of nudity. Ava managed sexy androgyny with black cigarette pants, white tank top, and black suspenders. Rounding out their little posse was Ava's roommate Erica in a backless animal print catsuit, and Desiree's other best friend and semi famous porn star Rio, who wore skin tight jeans and a flouncy black lace blouse that left no question as to the state of her undergarments.

Leigh didn't want to think about what Ava and Desiree told their friends but whatever it was, they came ready to play.

Surrounded by these women, Leigh's outfit was tame in comparison. She'd decided against the outfit she'd planned for tonight and went for something a little bolder. Her royal blue dress—a skin tight sleeveless turtleneck style that fell just below her knees with a daring slit up the back—and orange heels was plenty scandalous for her.

They were greeted by the owner or manager or someone who had the power to turn the balcony at the top of the wrought iron staircase into a VIP section. He'd given Leigh air kisses and apologized for not having enough time to stock the bar but promised two dedicated bartenders to handle their drinks orders. Junior had also managed to finagle a bouncer to keep the newly created VIP section exclusive.

As they made their way through the venue, Leigh noted while the music was pumping through the speakers, it was low enough that various whispers and gasps made their way to her. There was a low whistle and some interested commentary on their outfit choices and a particularly keen, "Who are *they*?" She made a point of not turning to look when she heard "Damn! Is that Peaches?!"

There was a large bucket of champagne on ice, a tray of champagne flutes, and ice-cold bottles of water sweating all over the table. Rio made a show of opening the first bottle and pouring them each a glass just as the lights dimmed and the cake was rolled out with sparklers dazzling in its path. This is why Junior was adamant they show up exactly at midnight.

With the sheer force of her will, aided by the depths of her pockets, Junior had forcibly wrenched the spotlight from Alice and placed it squarely on Leigh, causing the scene she'd wanted and amping up the tension tenfold.

Alice's smile was brittle at the edges as she wheeled the cake towards where Quincy stood. Her plans so monumentally derailed, she could only go through the motions to save any modicum of her dignity.

Leigh took a small amount of satisfaction in noticing Alice didn't even have the attention of the man she'd gone to all this effort for as Quincy's eyes were locked on hers above the crowd. He had on the suit she'd chosen and looked impossibly more handsome despite the weariness she could see even from this distance.

If she thought people were staring before, Quincy's intense unbroken eye contact added fuel to that fire. Lifting her glass, she toasted him. Leigh waited for him to return the gesture before she drained her champagne and turned her back on the revelry. She knew he wasn't part of Alice's plan, knew this wasn't the birthday he wanted, but seeing her there with the cake Leigh made, singing and posturing, was too much.

They'd made their point—they disrupted the event. Now all Leigh had to do was sit in a corner out of sight until it was time to go. So of course, that would be the moment her favorite song came on. She wouldn't be surprised if the next hour was marked with songs she categorically could not sit through.

Leigh knew Desiree and Junior were conniving and ruthless, but this was the work of her sister Ava. As if she'd had any doubts, as soon as Janet demanded a beat, Ava started the choreography they'd practiced as girls until it was muscle memory.

That's all it took for Leigh to put her woes aside for a moment and let loose.

This was the reality of her life. She didn't have to be one or the other—she could be methodical and spontaneous, responsible and carefree—because her choices were hers alone. No one else had a say and worrying about the future could only do so much good if her present was slipping through her fingers.

And she had Quincy to thank for helping her recognize her duality. He showed her the power of wanting. The strength of expectation. His ability to be uniquely himself at all times, taking up as much space as possible without apology, while he took what he wanted for himself was intoxicating. That he gave her the courage to attempt it in her own way was nothing short of miraculous.

Maybe Quincy wasn't the destination but he'd made the journey worthwhile. It was why it was so easy to love him. And she did. She loved him and she hoped she'd get a chance to tell him. She was willing to admit she might not. The realization hurt like a bruised muscle, deep and tender. But like a bruised muscle, Leigh knew she would get through it.

He'd given her that, too.

She held onto that truth, letting it warm her, and let herself enjoy the night without reservation.

Leigh was having so much fun laughing and being silly she had no idea how much time had passed until Desiree made her way over, singing along at the top of her tone-deaf lungs, with Junior in tow. Ava threw her arms around them both and joined in swaying drunkenly.

Leigh laughed at her sister. "Someone's turning into a pumpkin."

"No, I'm not," Ava sang.

"Desiree!"

They all turned to see who was hollering. It was Travis. He was wearing a kilt in a grey, brown and red tartan, with a soft grey dress shirt and a black leather harness. His light brown curls were braided off his face into a topknot.

"Is that one of yours?" Ava asked wide-eyed.

Desiree, equally stunned, nodded. "I think it might be."

Before any of them could process the information, could reconcile that Travis knew Desiree had a line of fetish wear and had managed to purchase some, he opened his hand and Carter, standing sentinel in matching kilt sans harness, placed something in his palm. Dangling it from his fingers, he called up "Slut me out. Any time, any place."

"Is that the matching collar? Jesus Cristo, I told that payaso you liked slutty and he skipped straight to fetish!"

Leigh could only laugh. "I think that's our cue."

"Yes, agreed." Junior looked down at the remnants of Alice's party. Those who hadn't fled for greener pastures were now upstairs partying with them. "I'll have the car pull up front."

As they made their way through the city members of their entourage peeled off until only Desiree and Junior remained in the chauffeured car with Leigh.

Driving down her street Desiree asked, "Did that help?"

"I'm going to pay for all that champagne but yes, this was way better than wallowing in my pajamas." Leigh admitted.

"But?" Desiree prompted.

The car stopped in the back of her building.

"No 'but'. I just... I guess I thought he'd try to talk to me. After all his 'it's not over', I thought..." Leigh trailed off, exhaustion working in tandem with the alcohol to slur her words and thoughts.

Maybe he'd already heard what his friends had to say and made his decision. They probably took him somewhere exclusive and exciting to find someone better.

More befitting, she thought miserably.

"I wouldn't worry about that," Junior said, looking out the passenger side window. Leigh leaned over to see Quincy waiting on the stoop.

"Oh."

"You can say that again." Desiree smirked.

"Indeed." Junior agreed.

Stepping out of the car, Leigh gingerly made her way to the door. "You're here."

"It's my birthday. We were supposed to have dinner, go to the party, and then go to my place so I could open my present." His words were quietly admonishing.

The headlights momentarily blinded them as the Navigator made its way back to the main road. Before making the turn, Junior stuck her head out the window. "Are you good?"

"Yeah, I'm good," Leigh answered.

"I see you, Junior," Quincy called out. "That was some real impressive dick swinging."

She cackled into the night sky. "Good luck, Slick—we're rooting for you!"

The SUV pulled away and finally, for the first time since she woke up this morning, she was alone with Quincy.

Leigh punched in the code to unlock the door. She didn't know what to say to him so she fell back on her home training. "Have you been out here long? Are you thirsty?"

"I would have waited all night. We need to talk about what happened."

"Please." She heaved a drunk and weary sigh. Leigh was so tired of talking about it. "Not now."

"I'm sure after showing up like a prize fighter to crash the party and then disappearing into the night you might not have the energy." Quincy didn't sound angry but he certainly wasn't happy about it, either. "But this can't wait."

"I fell off the horse so I had to get back on the bicycle," she muttered.

"Sounds like you're the one who needs some water," he looked in her eyes with a gentle fondness that belied the severity of the moment.

She didn't want his care and concern. She did not want to face Quincy and all her stupid feelings. She wanted to peel herself out of her dress, have a couple of clementines, then head to bed buoyed by the champagne bubble she'd floated home on.

Leigh needed to get away from him before he completely harshed her mellow.

"No. I'm just one glass past buzzed. I'm too old to get polluted." Leigh demurred, breaking eye contact and heading up the stairs. They'd barely rounded the corner before Quincy took hold of her arm and spun her to face him.

"You're not too old, Leigh." He grit his teeth as though his patience was attempting to escape through his clenched jaw. "You're not too old for drinking, you're not too old to party, and you're not too old for me."

"But I am, apparently, too old for your friends." Before he could say another word, she pulled free of his hold, and moved further into the house. "Quincy, please, can we talk about this later?"

He gave her a hard look, "Fine."

Quincy pulled off his jacket and laid it on the back of the dining room chair. Unbuttoning his shirt, he headed to the bedroom.

"What are you doing?"

"Getting ready for bed. You want to talk later, we'll talk later."

"You're sleeping here?"

"I'm not?"

Leigh was flustered "I... when I said talk later—"

"I'm not going to pay for a crime I didn't commit so either we deal with it now or in the morning but I'm not leaving until we figure this out."

"You're not leaving?" She said with no small amount of derision, "You get to decide that?"

"I didn't get to decide anything! I spent dinner alone, arrived at my party alone and left alone, when all I wanted was to spend time with you! Now, because of some shit I didn't even do, I should go home and sleep alone? Nah, fuck that."

He didn't get to decide? Wasn't that rich!

She'd dreamed as big as she could and this, 'Peach's Books and Bakeshop', is what she came up with. Achieving this goal had driven her, kept her focused for many long, tired years. Maybe she was alone but at least she'd had this. This stunt had made it seem small. It embarrassed her. Then she was ashamed that she'd been embarrassed. Which enraged her.

"All of this drama because you don't have the sense to quit while you're ahead. There's no future here, Quincy! This is a road to *nowhere*, don't you get that? Kids, globe trotting, you get none of it here. This right here is my world—these books and this bakery."

She was so angry. This was the very thing she'd been trying to avoid. It seemed obvious to her all roads were eventually leading here, to this place where the clashing of their worlds would leave her standing alone in the rubble. Each and every time she pointed to one of the signposts, calling attention to the trouble ahead, she was told she was wrong, that she was overreacting.

But she wasn't wrong, was she? Not when they were faced off over actions taken by those in his circle who claimed to care about him but had a problem with her.

There was a reason why she didn't rely on other people. There was a reason why she kept her own counsel and chose life in the commuter lane. The simple fact of the matter was she'd seen this coming, no one believed her–went so far as to tell her to ignore her instincts–and like a fool, she left her safe life in the wading pool for the deep end.

"You don't even like cake!" She yelled, entering the arbitrary grievance phase of this fight.

"What?"

"The whole thing is already stupid and ridiculous but on top of it all, she spent all that money and the exorbitant delivery fee Junior levied and you don't like cake!"

Leigh was the wrong mix of drunk and exhausted.

"You're definitely dangerous to know, I'll give you that much. I bought a strappy orange corset thing. Orange!" She was muttering to herself and pacing through the living room.

"I'm... sorry?"

"You should be!" She threw her hands in the air, causing her furniture to woosh furiously around. Or maybe it was her head that sloshed messily. It was hard to tell.

"Maybe you should sit down."

"No, I don't want to!" She yelled. Yelling felt amazing! Why hadn't she spent more of her time yelling at people? "What I *want* is for you to admit I was right!"

Quincy remained annoyingly calm. "Right about what, Leigh?"

"About this!" The room gave another lurch and Leigh looked at the floor with suspicion. Why wouldn't it stay flat? Noticing she still had her heels on, she accurately surmised they were the source of her unsteadiness.

"Leigh. Please." Quincy pleaded, dodging the shoe she'd kicked off.

"Don't 'Leigh Please' me! I was fine!" Leigh kicked off the other shoe, heedless of its trajectory. "I had a plan!"

Her life was full. She had a business to run and three agents of chaos who loved her fiercely. Her son was grown and off living his life. She had family and customers and sales reps to fill in the rest of the spaces. She wasn't looking for a relationship. She hadn't had the time! But did anybody listen? No!

Instead she'd convinced herself to enter this ill-advised union and forced herself out of her comfort zone. She put herself out there, worn that revealing catsuit, so she could prove she was willing to work for something. Willing to fail.

Leigh had scoured every dark corner of herself, she'd shone a light on her deepest fears and cracked her ribcage open to dig her own heart out of her chest. And for what?

Now standing barefoot in her living room, Leigh heaved a lungful of air and released it noisily.

"What was your plan, Leigh?"

She hated, *hated*, that he sounded so calm. Like she was being unreasonable and over-emotional. As if they weren't in this situation because of him! "It doesn't matter anymore, does it, because you ruined it!"

Her voice cracked on the last word which she felt lessened the impact of delivery somewhat but she couldn't fully deal with it because something spilled on her clenched fists. Confused, she looked around until she noticed the anguish on Quincy's face.

What was he so upset about? Nothing spilled on him, did it?

When it happened again, she'd realized with no small amount of mortification that she was crying.

<h1 style="text-align:center">Chapter 33</h1>

HE WAS GOING TO kill them. Alice and whoever helped her were going to feel the full force of his rage.

Two days ago he woke up in Leigh's bed, her sleepy smile wishing him a good morning. He'd almost told her then and there that he loved her but she'd leaned over and whispered that her alarm would go off in six minutes, challenging him to do his worst.

Now? She was drunk and questioning everything as angry tears spilled down her face.

He was going to fucking end them.

"Life isn't a series of scheduled events written on your whiteboard in black marker. I have no idea what comes next." He'd been trying for calm, striving to keep things as rational as possible when they were both so obviously in their feelings. But the softer he spoke, the angrier she seemed to get.

"That is exactly my point, Quincy! I don't want five years to go by and have you resent all the things you gave up to be with me!"

"God damnit, Leigh!"

She changed tracks. "Haven't you ever thought about whether you'd have kids?"

"Not really, no," he admitted. Some of his friends had kids but he honestly hadn't put too much thought into it. Partly because he hadn't met anyone to make him consider jumpstarting the conversation, partly because he wasn't in a real rush for that level of responsibility.

The other part, the part people kept forgetting, was his parents were older. He was thirty-three with eighty-year-old parents. As much as he loved them, and knew they loved him, he didn't think he wanted to do that to a child of his own. Every year that went by, was another year closer to Quincy simply saying no to the entire prospect. "Like, sure, in the abstract but kids were always something I figured would just happen to me."

"Yeah, well, a kid *just happened* to me twenty-seven years ago and there is no scenario where I do it again."

"What do you want me to say, Leigh? You don't think I know that? That I haven't fucking wrestled with it? I am where I want to be right now."

It was the truest thing he had to offer her. She was everything he wanted right now.

"So I should bide my time until you decide you want to be somewhere else?"

"Yes!"

She recoiled in horror. "No!"

"That's how it works! We choose to be here until the day we don't." Quincy wouldn't pretend he had some vast well of knowledge when it came to relationships but surely this was the central tenet, no?

Leigh flinched, clearly finding the picture he painted cavalier and unstable. "I can't exist with that level of uncertainty."

"I do!" The words burst from him, stored under extreme pressure until this moment. What was the point of holding it in, pretending it didn't plague him – pretending he wasn't as furious as she was? If they were laying shit on the line, then so be it. "You're a full fucking flight risk! Every day I wake up wondering if it's the last time you'll be mine." Quincy's breath hitched as he spoke, "You think I don't know the only reason you don't date is because you haven't bothered to try? What if I'm the training wheels? Now you've broken the seal, been back out there, maybe you'll aim higher. What happens to me when you find a silver fox who's settled in his career and doesn't have to hustle? You can sit around with his friends drinking fancy wine reminiscing about where you were and how it felt to hear 'Touch em all Joe!'? What happens then? This shit goes both ways, Leigh!"

He couldn't pinpoint exactly when this particular fear manifested itself. It was likely a sequence of events starting with Leigh telling him he was too young and ending with every single viable man who entered her orbit. All he knew was his current life's happiness ebbed and flowed with Leigh's favor.

Her eyes glistened with hot, miserable tears, the fight and booze seemed to have fizzled out of her system leaving her listless. "Why didn't you take no for an answer?"

"Because having this time with you, for however long it happens to be, is worth it. Getting to love you is worth it."

That seemed to release the final hold to her tether. She collapsed on the armchair and buried her face in her hands.

Quincy wasted no time going to her. He kneeled at her feet, his hands on either side of her hips, as he bent his forehead to hers. "I love you. I love you, Dorothy Leigh Bridger, and I don't care how long I get to do it because the idea of not loving you is inconceivable to me. So whether you let me love you for a year, for a week, or until the sun rises in the morning, it will have been worth it."

Her hands dropped to her lap in clenched fists but she didn't pull away from him. That was good, wasn't it?

"Who would have known my specific kink was 'aggressively hetero bookish rule-following women from St. Mary's who spent their high school lunch hours at the sub shop and their afternoons at Teddy's field'? I certainly had no idea."

"I'm not *aggressively* hetero," she sulked quietly, almost to herself. He hoped her sniffling signaled the end of her tears.

"What about... audaciously hetero? Energetically? Vigorously?" He kept his voice low and gentle as he teased her, careful to not disturb this temporary break in hostilities.

Her tiny huff of laughter was felt more than heard. When her warm champagne scented breath landed on his mouth, he couldn't resist the urge to kiss her. A quick, gentle press of lips.

The taste of her tears rekindled his anger. "I'm sorry you were hurt today. I promise I will deal with everyone involved."

She pulled away from him to shake her head, "And then what? You lose your friends, the people who've been with you all this time? I don't want that responsibility."

Quincy was reasonably certain none of the mandem had anything to do with what happened tonight. They'd been integral parts of each other's lives for more than two decades. He trusted them blindly with everything he had. He couldn't imagine them hurting Leigh, even without knowing exactly what she meant to him, and thinking he'd be cool with it.

And he planned to be really rather *un*cool about it, actually.

Besides Domenic, and maybe Morgan and Ruby who were kind of a package deal, he couldn't honestly say he'd notice any one member of the greater group's absence in any appreciable way. Not in the face of this kind of disrespect. There would be no stopping him from handing out burn notices.

So if it turned out he was wrong, and one of the mandem did this? It would break his heart, sure, but they wouldn't be safe from the consequences he was going to dole out either.

Quincy's hands itched. Rubbing them on the fabric of the armchair hadn't worked and neither had digging his nails into his palms. He needed to find the perfect combination of words to make Leigh understand. That he was coming up blank, a man who had to weave words into results every day for a living, was as concerning as it was frustrating.

Taking her tiny fists in each hand, he took a deep breath and explained, "It might not feel like it, but what happened tonight wasn't about you. What Vargas did, why she did it, is exactly why she and I would never work. The fact she could even believe this would somehow clear a path for us to be together is fucking wild. I don't knowingly associate with delusional individuals."

"I love you." It felt fucking amazing to say. "I love you and I choose you."

He held her gaze, her eyes wide and shimmering, willing her to understand. He watched as a series of emotions flickered across her face.

"You love me? Even with all this?"

"All what, Peaches? It's just you and me."

The smallest smile curved her lips. Some of the tension left her shoulders and he felt her fists loosen under his palms.

Leigh sighed heavily and fell back on the chair. Her hands still in his, she spoke her words to the ceiling, "I was embarrassed. Mostly for her but also for me. I did all that work to make peace with my age thing, to prove to you that I could, and was almost immediately slapped down in the most immature way possible. It made me feel like I'd wasted my time, like I was right to have told you no."

She pulled her hands free to rub her eyes. "I wasn't going to show up tonight. But Junior insisted." Leigh gave a wry shake of her head, "She was right, of course. I had fun and came to some necessary realizations."

"Like what?"

She took so long to answer he wasn't sure if she'd fallen asleep or was refusing to answer. Quincy didn't know how to interpret her silence and it made him unreasonably nervous.

"Lots of little things, really. But mainly, I realized it was okay if you didn't end up being the destination." Her voice was thin and she sounded miles away.

No, the nerves were not unreasonable at all. His body was obviously trying to brace him for devastation. His gut instincts rarely steered him wrong. At least he still had that, if nothing else.

"It's okay if you're not the destination," she repeated, finally facing him. Her voice louder and more assured, "because you made the journey worthwhile."

As goodbyes went, it was the kindest and most generous he'd experienced.

The most Leigh.

He moved himself to a seated position, both because his knees were starting to complain and also, he supposed, because he needed to get his body used to not being able to touch her anymore. Lowering his head so he could breathe through the tightness in his chest, he jumped a little when he felt Leigh slide off the chair and into his lap.

"Make."

He blinked his confusion, "What?"

"When I was at your party, I thought to myself, 'Maybe Quincy wasn't the destination but he'd made the journey worthwhile'. But now that I'm trying to tell you I love you, too, I should have said 'make'. Present tense."

He didn't bother trying to get words out this time. He simply gaped uncomprehendingly.

"I love you, Quincy Temple. I'm sorry your birthday was ruined."

She... wait, what?

"It's not ruined anymore." He held her face and kissed her, a slow, lingering exploration of her champagne flavoured mouth. "Now it's perfect."

She wrapped arms around his body and snuggled close to his chest. "I'm also sorry I yelled at you."

He kissed the side of her head and smiled, "You seemed like you were really enjoying yourself!"

"It did feel good in the moment."

"A well-placed f-bomb might have also helped." He ran his hands up and down her back in a soothing motion. "A hearty, robust, perfectly timed '*fuck*' can be cathartic."

Her laughter rang out in the room and all the tension that had been gathering in his shoulders melted away.

"I'll keep that in mind for next time."

He held her as her laughter died and morphed into a jaw cracking yawn. With another quick kiss he said against her lips, "Come on, Peaches. Let's go to sleep."

He stood, scooped an almost sleeping Leigh off the floor, and took them to bed.

THE SUN CAME THROUGH THE window directly on his face.

In the turmoil of the evening, they'd curled up together in her bed without turning off the lights in the living room or shutting the blinds and pulling the curtains down. He was just so desperate to hold her–no provocative words or feats of stamina–he didn't allow responsibility to interfere with having Leigh in his arms.

Now, with a beam of light slashing across Leigh's pale blue sheets making them seem almost white, he was slightly less sure of his decision.

She gave an adorably affronted grunt, turning away from the sun and burrowing her face in his chest.

God, she was pretty. Her hair was tousled and spread out on the pillow and her makeup was still relatively intact–more things they'd forsaken–if a little faded. She looked like a dream and watching her sleep, as creepy as it sounded, was very relaxing.

His phone buzzed on the nightstand beside him, and he reached over to silence it before it disturbed Leigh.

Paviter had posted a picture of the two of them as kids, maybe eleven or twelve years old, on his front steps with the caption, 'Celebrating this icon #jesusyear' and Yemi, the golden doodle of his friend group, tagged him in the comments, 'counting candles and blessings @QPidTemple'.

Rolling his eyes, he liked both messages. Being able to look down at Leigh's perfect face as she slept in his arms was the only blessing he needed.

Without giving it too much thought, he snapped a picture of him gazing fondly at her as the sun bathed them in golden light, and posted it with the caption, 'waking up with my Valentine is the best birthday present I could ask for'. His phone now on Do Not Disturb, he put it on the nightstand and settled himself, allowing his eyes to drift close and carry him gently back to sleep.

Later, it could have been minutes or hours, he woke up disoriented with a stiff neck. He had no idea where Leigh went, but since the original plan was for her to sleep at his place, and he knew she'd made all the arrangements for the shop to open without her, she couldn't be far. Sitting up and giving his shoulder a couple of rolls, Quincy took a second to get his bearings. He needed to get dressed and find Leigh, and not necessarily in that order.

Noticing some clothes neatly folded on her dresser, Quincy went over and found his t-shirt–the oatmeal colored one she'd worn home the night they'd 'reset the system'–with a note in

Leigh's neat, scholarly script telling him she was downstairs. Well, that solved both his problems, didn't it? Taking a moment to freshen up, Quincy used a small amount of Leigh's lotion and made his way to the shop.

If he wondered why she went and stayed downstairs, the sight of the mandem mingling with Leigh's people answered his question.

Paviter saw him first. "Don't be shy, we call it a stride of pride now. Nothing to be ashamed of!"

"Happy Birthday, Slick!" Desiree and Junior chimed from the counter while Ava gave him a friendly wave.

"Here's to many more, man." KC gave him a knowing smile and threw up a peace sign.

He shook his head at his friends' presence in this place that had come to mean so much to him and clasped Paviter's fist, bringing their shoulders together. "What are you all doing here?"

"Nǐ shǎ ya? Yemi activated the phone tree." William said, using one of the Mandarin expressions they all used when someone was being dumb, before pulling him in for the same greeting he gave Pav. "What do you think?"

Yemi defended himself from across the room, "No one knew if we were still on for breakfast!"

"My phone is on Do Not Disturb," he said, in a bit of a daze. It wasn't that he'd forgot about their plans, but in light of what happened last night he had allowed it to fall to the wayside. Making things right with Leigh had been his only focus and he was prepared to push everything else to the background.

He should have known Yemi wouldn't go for it. If he was in town for a birthday, and he somehow managed to mostly be, then they upheld their birthday breakfast tradition. Even if, with their hectic schedules and demanding jobs, it sometimes amounted to little more than a coffee on the fly.

Apparently, coffee on the fly was taking place at Peach's Books and Bakeshop.

"Well re-disturb it, Bro. Yemi was blowing us up all morning." Travis complained, tearing himself from Desiree's orbit. Wrapping Quincy in a bear hug, Travis said, "Congratulations on another trip around the sun."

He laughed to himself. In recent years, they'd taken to finding increasingly more obnoxious ways to wish each other happy birthday. 'Trip around the sun' was fairly tame compared to the year William wished Paviter 'more presents unboxed and more potential unlocked' or when Carter wished Yemi 'eight thousand seven hundred and sixty more hours of life well lived'. Having them here keeping these long-held traditions alive almost made up for waking up without Leigh beside him.

Almost.

"You smell like Pledge." Carter announced while giving Quincy's back a manly thump. "When I hug her, she smells like summertime, yet you manage to smell like my mom's playing Anita Baker on Saturday morning. How'd you fuck up *fragrance*, Negro?"

Ignoring Carter's dig, and the fact that he'd hugged Leigh enough to recognise her scent, Quincy turned to find the her in question. She was holding a platter with a large quiche and a fancy '33' candle lit in the middle.

"Happy birthday, Quincy." She looked equal parts shy and mischievous. "I figured since you don't like cake..."

"You did all this?"

She smirked a little, "I didn't do all of it. William wasn't joking. Yemi was determined to locate you. I figured... I wanted you to have a better party than you did last night."

He wrapped his arm around her waist and kissed her full on the mouth. She let out a surprised little squeak and shifted herself in his hold to keep the platter balanced. Ava was at her side in an instant, relieving her of the quiche, and Quincy wasted no time hauling her up his body and devouring her.

His heart was so full, he couldn't think of another way to express it to her but to pour all of his feelings into this kiss. Nothing distracted him from his purpose. Not the hooting shouts and applause of their friends, not the way her glasses skewed between them, and not the bell over the door signalling a new arrival.

"In the store, Mom?" Langston cried, holding a large bag of mixed greens. "Is this what you think it means to be Instagram official?"

Still wrapped around him, Leigh straightened her glasses and asked, "Instagram what, now?"

"This should be good," Luc said, taking the bag from Langston and passing it to Mo.

The room erupted into more rowdiness, but Quincy blocked it all out and focused his full attention on Leigh.

Setting her down on her feet he explained, "I posted a picture of us this morning. I should have checked with you first. I'm sorry." He handed her his phone so she could see for herself. He hoped she saw what he did, the sun caressing her skin, her pretty, peaceful face resting on his shoulder, and Quincy's expression full of love and wonder.

She didn't say anything for a long time, just looked at the image. Then her eyes lit with the look of devious competition he'd come to know so well.

"Well," she said airily, "That's one way to set her straight." She handed him his phone, popped up on her toes to place a quick kiss on his lips and said, "I love you. Let's go cut your 'cake'."

And that was all she had to say about the matter.

And, really, what else was there to say?

He followed Leigh to the counter where she and Mo plated quiche and salad, and Luc filled and refilled drink orders. Everyone pulled up a seat at one of the bistro tables and, like that, their three worlds became one. He couldn't ask for a better 'do over'.

Quincy sat enjoying the chatter around him, joining in different conversations here and there, while always keeping an eye on Leigh as she puttered around the counter. When she finally sat beside him with her own plate, her look of studied innocence made him suspicious.

Before he could interrogate, his phone buzzed on the table. It was a picture of Leigh holding the platter of quiche, her face turned up to him while he looked intently down at her, captioned 'wishing our favorite Valentine @QPidTemple a Happy Birthday #SavoryNotSweet'.

"You post that on Peach's official account?" He asked, a little stunned by the gesture.

"Isn't that what Instagram official means?"

Quincy nuzzled nose behind her ear, feeling the tiny hairs at her nape as he inhaled her summertime scent. "It is."

"Well then?" She turned her head so his mouth was right in front of hers and said, against his lips, "Together. Or not at all. Right?"

He kissed her. A tender declaration, just for them, in the midst of chaos. He was going to enjoy loving this woman for a long, long time.

"Together or not at all."

THE END

Thank you, gorgeous reader, for making it to the end of my *second* novel. I don't really have an explanation for it other than to say once the voices started talking to me – once they realised I'd listen – they simply refused to stop! And, I guess I *did* say at the end of my debut that I'd see you on the next one so wasn't a whole lot of choice in the matter.

(This doesn't bode well for my overall sanity but, if we're being completely honest, it was always at risk.)

Again, I would be nowhere without my early readers and champions. Thank you to AC, D, Hockey-Name, and The Boss – your notes and enthusiasm for this story made all the difference.

Quincy's job, handsomeness, charm, and dick-forward energy are all directly inspired by my cousin's husband, Sam. He has forgot more about sports than you or I will ever know and he was an invaluable resource in the crafting of Quincy Temple. I have since learned that Directors of Premium Sale at the venue I allude to do not operate the in same way because Canada has different rules/policies and procedures than the US. This in no way invalidates the information he provided nor does it account for the way I applied it. All it means is I made up a bunch more stuff and we all agree to be cool about it.

I also need to thank Jordan who acted as my prototypical "33-year-old Toronto Man" even though he is not 33 anymore (a fact he reminded me of to my eternal delight). He gamely answered random questions without a second thought and the gap between myself and Quincy/the mandem was made much smaller thanks to him!

I have the immense privilege of knowing Jenny C, who has changed my life in ways big and small. Leigh Bridger being from her hometown of St. Mary's, Ontario is my small way of saying *thanks... for everything*!

While I didn't have to resort to the same level of thievery I did on Dickface when crafting these characters, there was still a light bit of pilfering involved. Big love to Amy, Candice, Francine, Gurjeet, Jennifer (yes, another one), Jordana, Karla, Kyle, Loffieann, Marr, Michelle, Nicole, Sade, Sam (yes, another one), and Stinder for the inspiration.

I remain in awe of boundless kindness of the collective known as Romancelandia. I am still the happy and eager recipient of their generously shared knowledge and proud beneficiary of their fundraising efforts. This time for: aid for the people of Palestine, the children of Sudan and Congo, and combating voter suppression in the US. Thank you to Meg Opalescent, Elizabeth Kilcoyne, and Yuvashri Harish, for donating your time and expertise. You make it easy to continuously celebrate Happily Ever After in all its forms.

This part is a word-for-word rehash from my debut because it remains as true now as it was then: I want to thank my family. Specifically my father, who has waited a long time for this moment; my mother, who doesn't think there's a thing I can't accomplish once I set my mind to it; my brother, who has always been my biggest fan; and to my big, loud, supportive, Latino-Caribbean family for filling my life with love, inspiration, and endless laughter.

And, finally, to my husband. The swiftness with which he has adjusted to this new reality – 'yeah, my wife is a Romance author' – is a large part of why I'm still happily married twenty years later. Thank you for your endless acceptance, love, and enthusiasm.

Claudia's book is up next, y'all. Get ready!

xx

About the Author

L INDO FORBES IS A first gen Canadian who lives in Toronto where you can find her at her day job or procrastinating on social media – sometimes both, simultaneously. She speaks enough French to not disgrace herself when she visits Montreal but not enough Spanish to please her abuela. She's also been known to spend her free time working on her works-in-progress, battling with the Libby App, thinking of varied ways to corrupt her nieces and nephews, holding grudges against fictional characters and celebrities she's never met, and/or searching for the world's best street food with her husband.

Join her mailing list to get updates on these very noble endeavors.